The Ice Shelf

An Eco-Comedy

Anne Kennedy

Victoria University Press

VICTORIA UNIVERSITY PRESS
Victoria University of Wellington
PO Box 600 Wellington
vup.victoria.ac.nz

A catalogue record is available at the National Library of New Zealand

ISBN 9781776562015

Published with the assistance of a grant from

Printed by Printlink, Wellington

Gratitude is not only the greatest of virtues, but the parent of all the others.

—Cicero

Here then I retreated, and lay down happy to have found a shelter, however miserable, from the inclemency of the season, and still more from the barbarity of man.

—Mary Shelley, *Frankenstein*

Acknowledgements

First and foremost, I would like to thank the person who made all this possible, my ex-partner. This book would never have been written without his warm, witty and intellectually stimulating influence. So thanks to Miles from the very bottom of my heart. There are not many real thinkers in this world, but I had the good fortune to spend nearly three years of my life with one and continue to this day, despite our differences, to have a stellar friendship with a true Ideas Man. I will be forever in his debt. In all honesty, I can lay claim to little of what sparked *The Ice Shelf*.

My next debt is of course to Arts New Zealand who so generously sponsor the marvellous Antarctica Residency. I am humbled to have been offered the once-in-a-lifetime (even less for some people) opportunity to respond creatively to the ice. I hope the story that follows goes some way towards expressing my gratitude, as I share my contemplations about the cold expanse that lies not too far away from our islands and perhaps even closer to the New Zealand psyche. Thank you, Arts New Zealand.

I would also like to extend my deepest and most grateful thanks to the other recipients of the Antarctica Residency—for friendship, encouragement and the odd good-humoured jibe, not to mention sharing a quaff or two of vodka. We made a vibrant group as we flew the flag for our various artistic media—dancer Beatrice Grant, visual artist Tom Atutola and composer Clement de Saint-Antoine-Smith, all of whom need longer introductions than I have space for here; and, of course, yours truly. I want to particularly thank the artists for their actions on the night of the Antarctica Awards ceremony when we made plans to go for a drink afterwards so we could get to know each other even better before being thrown together willy-nilly at Scott Base. I am very lucky; I don't know many writers who have had as many encouraging spurs. When a group of fellow artists with whom you will go to Antarctica abandons you in a bar while you are visiting the bathroom, you grasp that moment by the horns and turn it to your greatest advantage.

Before I continue with my Acknowledgements (and there are a lot of them—I have many friends, and I know for certain that I couldn't have done this without each and every one of you), I would like to take a moment to reflect briefly on the notion of thankfulness. It resides, I have no doubt now, at the very heart of creativity. Our appreciation of the bounty of Earth and the fragile gift of existence is precisely what moves us to invent in the first place. Furthermore, in the process of writing *The Ice Shelf*, I have come to believe that the reverse is true, that *in*gratitude is not merely a neutral state but a destructive force. Take the sorry state of the planet as a case in point. The wholesale lack of regard for our majestic forests and mountains, our sublime rivers and lakes, our vast oceans and continents, and not least our marbly mysterious ice, has led us to the position we now find ourselves in, teetering on the brink of ecological disaster. I suggest that instead of continuing on the well-worn path of heedless destruction, a path fast-tracking us to catastrophe, we all literally thank our lucky stars and create rather than destroy.

I for one will be taking stock of my personal good fortune in these next few pages. I have much to be thankful for—the extraordinary good luck of having my first little book *Utter and Terrible Destruction* published, even though it doesn't have a spine; the humbling honour of being accepted into ENG 209: Theory of Creative Writing as part of my BA (which I'm in the process of finishing) although initially I was waitlisted (someone apparently more talented than me was perhaps run over by a bus, not that I'm pleased about that I hasten to add); the amazing course in creative writing I took at the Global School under the tutelage of Clancy McKinney. I am also thankful for the vibrant community of literary bloggers, tweeters and Facebookers that I am privileged to count myself part of.

But bear with me while I unpack in a little more detail the connection between gratitude and creativity. To do that, I need to first consider creativity in general and writing in particular—without sounding too pompous, I hope. I invite you, Reader, into the Theory of Creative Writing classroom of 2011 (my first year, I might add, with the spectacular Miles).

Why write? This was something we asked ourselves in the class (which consisted of the anointed, and, having submitted a writing sample, I was lucky enough to find myself with an oily patch on my forehead). I have a big thank you to make vis-à-vis that happy experience and will do so in due course. But for the moment—*why write?* The variety of answers from the students, including me, indicated that creativity's birth is unknowable, much like the curious fecundity of our planet. In search of answers, the class researched widely. We read Aristotle and Plato, we read Sartre and Nietzsche, Lorca and Gardiner, Pound and Stern, Lodge and Doctorow, even Stephen King. No texts by women, but what can you expect when the lecturer is a male chauvinist pig? Excuse my little joke, my retro rhetoric! In fact, I am sincerely grateful that I was able to get to know one of the last still oinking. Thank you, Professor Julian 'Big Julie' Major. But seriously, what *is* it that catapults a person into, let's face it, a crazy state of make-believe? Why *do* some people jettison the real world for a world of pretend, of verisimilitude? I still don't know all the answers to the questions we posed in the class, but I do know now that circumstance has something to do with it, and for that I return to thankfulness, to these Acknowledgements, and to Miles. Without Miles, I would not be the creative person I am today, and I certainly would never have written this book.

It was Miles's idea that we should finally go our separate ways. That radical and profound change was undoubtedly responsible for the freeing state in which I found myself in early 2014 and from where, I discovered happily, I was fully able to embrace writing. Calling it quits was not something I would've thought of myself, but how thankful I am that Miles, always in the vanguard, had the foresight to imagine a new way of being. Miles was the first to recognise that he and I had fallen out of love. Ah well, it happens! It's all so much easier when both parties are in agreement on the issue, and thankfully we were.

Looking back, things had been unravelling slowly for a while, but we'd naïvely ignored the signs, at least I had.

I blame my trusting nature. It's true that I had called off the relationship three or four times over the previous few months, but none of that was serious. We trundled along, Miles and me. As for our eventual demise, with the wisdom of hindsight, one evening in particular stands out as being portentous.

It was a mild night weather-wise, which was unusual in itself; indeed, the still days, the balmy nights that had been going on for some weeks, made Wellingtonians nervous. I didn't even have clothes for the high-twenties temperatures but instead steamed gently in my leggings and big shirt. Perhaps we were already primed then, Miles and me, for something strange to happen.

We were having dinner at home in the apartment, but I don't even think about that anymore because I'm not a materialist. I bear absolutely no malice towards Miles that he ended up in full ownership of the 1950s fourth-storey apartment with gleaming wood floors, smooth stuccoed walls and a panoramic view over the harbour, while I live in an unstable series of cheap rentals and am even sometimes reduced to couch-surfing. In short, I have a life. Visitors to the apartment these days—friends of Miles's, who are no doubt in ignorance of the true legal history of the estate or they wouldn't be speaking to him, and some of you reading this might fall into that category—might notice the teal paintwork in the kitchen, rather nicely executed in my humble opinion, and the living-room curtains with their surreal blue leaves. No prizes for guessing who inserted 234 plastic hooks in the rufflette tape, hauled the enormous weight of lined linen up a ladder and beached last every juddery hook.

But I digress. This night, we were to eat well in the lovely apartment. Miles was cooking, which I was pleased about because I was enrolled at the Global School at the time and working on a particularly tricky section of the novel you will read later in these pages. I was perched at the dining room table, fingers riverdancing over my laptop. (Miles had the study. But aren't *you* the writer, I can hear you ask? Sweet of you to notice, Reader, but honestly, I never minded not having an iota of personal space in the apartment. I think it made me a stronger person and of course writer.) Anyway, despite having moved into my fiction (as you do), a primal part of me antennaed the delicious smells coming from the kitchen and looked forward to dinner. Among his many other attributes, Miles is a superlative cook, not that he put his skills into practice very often during our time together. To be honest, cooking was an issue between us. Miles had indicated, in his endearing way, and I quote, that he would 'put effort in when I did', which was pretty unfair, because his attitude to food was quite bourgeois, and I was actually really reliable. The odd pie from the dairy never killed anyone. We never starved on my watch. Plus, I was trying to juggle everything, like when Emily Brontë was kneading bread while reading poetry, not that I'm comparing my modest talent with her genius, I hasten to add. But this night, Miles had decided to pull out all the stops.

What I realised over time was, a Miles cooking spree generally coincided with peculiar or momentous events, like his return after I'd kicked him out once or twice. The night after the big thing happened, for instance, he cooked a chicken dish, but I couldn't swallow it. So if I'd had my wits about me on this particular night, which turned out to be our last night together, if I'd not been so distracted by writing this novel, I would've known that *Miles cooking* meant something was up. Instead, from my pozzy at the dining table, I noticed his shadow sailing from bench to stove only in my peripheral vision. I might've glanced briefly into the teal shine of the kitchen and taken in the top-heavy frame rounded in concentration, the black-wired fingers performing a delicate task in the light from the window.

Miles served the food with panache, his black clothes adding to the sense of theatre. He always dressed in black button-down shirts which he slightly burst out of, and black pants, like a stagehand who flits on half-invisibly between acts. On this evening (it was seven-ish, late summer), his permanent five o'clock shadow looked polished-on in the sunlit living room, and I noticed his hair was freshly washed, fluffy and Einsteiny. We dined, looking into the middle distance, on the melt-in-your-mouth white flesh of one of the last extant twenty-five-year-old orange roughies. The fish was lightly rolled in chopped pecans from America, fried in olive oil from Greece and served with sautéed autumn vegetables, at least autumn in the northern hemisphere. Some people might think this kind of dish pretentious, wasteful and ecologically unfriendly, but I didn't. I ate it appreciatively.

I was vacuuming up the last slivers of pecan when Miles plinked his knife and fork together and disappeared in a Dementor-like blur around the corner into the bedroom. In retrospect, the hollow clunks that echoed through the wall as I chewed (it's always a little weird to be left at the table on your own), the distant racing-car squeal of a zip, should've raised my suspicions, but because I'm quite trusting I thought nothing of it. I set up my laptop to face me like a fellow diner and started clicking on arts articles on the *Pantograph Punch*. When I got up to pour myself a vodka at the sideboard (art reviews can make one very depressed), I noticed a gap, like lost teeth, where Miles's CDs and retro tapes were customarily stacked in their yellowing cases beside the stereo. Miles is an obscure-jazz buff, so the absence of the twin plastic towers was puzzling. I allowed myself a splash more vodka while I contemplated the loss.

A moment later I gashed my head painfully backing out of the sideboard cupboard; Miles had had a wowserish objection to alcohol since he'd cut down, and I'd felt his disapproving shadow like a barometer dropping. I stood and squeaked the cupboard closed behind me, fingering the tender egg on the back of my head. Miles indeed filled the room. He stooped slightly over the handle of a wheelie suitcase, serif to his inky bulk. His jaw was purplish in a gash of sunlight. The notion that I'd once considered him good-looking never ceases to amaze me. Such is love. I feel a little sorry for my spin-off in this regard—more on her later.

'Janice,' said Miles, in the flat tone he always used.

'Yes,' I said, my own inflection horizontal as Morse code. I tended to parrot Miles's deadpan, perhaps in my desire to be a real Kiwi; I don't know.

Miles continued levelly. 'I think I'm probably going to leave you to eat the sago pudding on your own.'

'There's pudding?' I marvelled. Miles had excelled himself.

'The, you know.' He gestured roundness, I filled in the blanks; he'd made sago pudding once before, a cold gluey thing, stylishly down-home. 'I think you'll probably find it in the fridge.'

To prevent myself jumping to conclusions—I'm the first to admit I have that tendency—I performed a technique in stress management I learned a few years back when I went through a tricky patch: I counted to twenty and poured myself a vodka and orange (just one, because I wouldn't want a repeat of certain events). As I reached back into the sideboard for the bottle, I could sense Miles looking on censoriously, but I didn't care. Calmed by my relaxation routine, I pushed past him, went through to the kitchen and opened the fridge to get the orange juice. We had a lovely green fifties-style fridge which I'd bought with my payout for unlawful dismissal (long story I won't bother you with, but I *was* unlawfully dismissed no matter what the Glass Menagerie maintained about the broken stock. And I won, ha ha. Not that I wanted that job back, the bitch). No juice, dammit. But sure enough, the pudding sat on the middle shelf swathed in the fridge's over-zealous dry ice. When I put the crystal bowl on the table, its mealy contents wobbled like an old Pākehā woman's arm. I photographed it with my phone. I don't usually tweet pictures of food, but something told me this pudding was going to be auspicious, that one day some interested person might trawl back through my online presence and pinpoint the sago pudding eaten on that particular night as having import, especially as my accompanying tweet was The last supper ☺. The pic appeared simultaneously on Facebook, such is my set-up. Immediately, Mandy liked it. Mandy is my best friend and an absolutely fab poet in her own endearing way, and we have many invigorating exchanges on Twitter, where she has an excellent presence, with 176 followers. I have 900 followers at last count, which is 23 more than I follow. Sure enough, Mandy retweeted the photo of the sago pudding and replied, Looks delish @Janiceawriter xxx. I replied, Thanks muchly @mandycoot <3 <3 <3. I have much to thank her for in these pages. But I digress. Pocketing my phone, I turned to Miles, who stood watching, contained as ever, and I told him I hated sago pudding. His jaw went spade-like. He said quietly that that was strange because I'd wolfed down most of it last time he'd made it. Absolute lies of course, but I stayed centred, having practised my technique. I told him I'd only pretended to like the sago pudding.

'You pretended, all this time?' Then he mumbled something incomprehensible about my photograph.

'All this *time?*' I said.

Two long years had elapsed between sago puddings; the last rendition had occurred during our honeymoon period. Those two years, however, didn't count for much according to the New Zealand statutes book; legally, we were barely acquainted, so I was to find out later to my cost. Anyway, I told Miles I'd eaten his sago pudding to please him. This wasn't quite true, because I did actually like the pudding. I guess I said I didn't like it to make a point. What else could I do? I'm unburdening my soul with my flaws in full view, but I believe in honesty.

'To please me!' spluttered Miles. He was getting quite verbose. He almost looked at me, his slightly prominent brown gaze just missing on its way out to the sky. 'When've you ever done that, in two years and seven months?'

I told him it sounded like he'd been counting the days.

'I have been counting the days.' He swung his head away like a dentist's lamp. 'I've been counting the days since—' He mopped his brow again.

'Go on, say it,' I said, but he wouldn't continue.

At the window I looked out over the harbour, sipping my drink. A plane laboured up over the hills leaving a wobbly smudge of exhaust across the sepia-coloured sky. 'Say it,' I said to the view. I knew he wouldn't. He was a coward. I turned. Miles was braced against the couch. Under the upholstery the wood creaked secretly.

'You know what?' I said. 'I'm tired of silence. I'm tired of tiredness. Do you understand that?'

He shook himself free of the couch and stood. He was of average height, but bulky, and he threw a big shadow. 'I can't stand another day of this,' he said, so low I could hardly hear it. I guessed the last bit. He would move back into the apartment after I'd moved out.

I felt a deep pity for Miles. His passive-aggressive personality wasn't his fault. He'd had an incredibly uptight white Protestant middle-class upbringing in the outer suburbs. We're talking Noa Valley. You can't imagine more of a cultural wasteland. I don't blame poor Miles for anything; in fact I am full of admiration for the way he's coped.

All the same, at this juncture—especially because Miles's parents had outright given him the deposit for the apartment, and he always emitted an unspoken and quite frankly disgusting sense of entitlement over it—I had no intention of going anywhere.

I made a bit of a joke of it. 'Woo, going too fast!' I said, backing away for emphasis. I realised I was just the littlest bit wobbly on my pins. I must say, I'd always thought that if there was any leaving to be done, I would be the leaver and Miles would be the leavee. The CDs, the bag, the pudding thing, all seemed like empty gestures. I wasn't too perturbed, even when Miles wheeled his suitcase over to the doorway and stood there with it cocked while he looked at the carpet and said he didn't know if he loved me anymore, he probably didn't, and perhaps—here his voice double-clutched for a second—perhaps he never had.

'Even before,' he added and looked up, finally.

'Before what?' I asked, and I stared out his brown eyes.

'Janice.'

'Before *what?*'

With his big, slightly greenish teeth gritted, and as if

something were being twisted out of him like water out of a wet cloth, he said loudly: 'Before the murder.'

I felt a section of my face fall away, yes, like an avalanche, but I didn't care. It was madness. He was mad. I searched back out the window, the harbour, the wind visible in the quivering waves, trees, sails, like a Van Gogh. I checked Twitter. Linda Dent had retweeted my pudding. Linda was a trouper, and a frequent profile-picture updater. I saw she was sporting giant black nerd glasses which seemed to stay on her tiny white face only by some miracle. I replied, Thanks for the RT @heartwriter xxxx <3.

I'd like to break off here and spend a moment, if I may, analysing Miles's manner when he said the words 'I don't think I love you anymore, perhaps I never did'. We New Zealanders have a reputation for being low-key; diffident, flat as a pancake, if you like, in our verbal delivery. We're dark and brooding and we're always second-guessing ourselves, at least that's how we behave in our novels and films. Just watch Sam Neill's *Cinema of Unease* and you'll see what a complicated bunch we are. The trouble is—and this used to bother me a lot, made me feel a sense of un-belonging in my own country—I'd never actually met anyone who behaved as if they'd just stepped out of *Vigil*. Perhaps that's a bad example, since the characters in *Vigil* are relatively loquacious, especially the wiry guy who carries the dead father back to the farmhouse on his back like a sheep. *In My Father's Den* is a better case in point. The protagonists in that novel (and in the film) stand around with their shoulders hiked, looking sideways at the other characters as if they (the other characters) might run them through with a meat cleaver. They don't say much, as you wouldn't;

the odd monosyllable, sometimes with a qualifier attached like a shaky lean-to. My point is, most people I knew in real life yammered on, full of their own opinions, and having no trouble expressing their feelings verbally at any pitch. In fact, sometimes you'd wish they were more like the characters in *In My Father's Den* so you could get some peace and quiet. For years I felt stranded—an alienating mismatch between me and the characters I met in New Zealand literature. That was until: enter Miles.

When I first met Miles, at Meow Café, a very cool bar that has slam nights, book launches and indie bands, I recognised like a lightning bolt the New Zealand character. There he was, leaning against the bar or, rather, hovering nervously next to it. He was perfect, from his Munster shoulders to his brooding frown to his startled yeah-nah—an endearing New Zealand bet-each-way mannerism. I went over and said hello. He was big and blocky, the upper part of his body dominant in a way I found sexy. He smiled at me, his square teeth little photo-reversals of his square head, and I felt a charge like an electric current, only pleasant. Later I invited him out as part of a dating phase I was on (long story) and things went on from there. As I got to know Miles, I discovered I was not mistaken in my assessment. He *is* the thinking person I first introduced in these Acknowledgements— smart, funny, sensitive, and somehow he holds down a job as a curator at an art gallery in town. But he also maintains a glorious diffidence; he is never quite sure, he is a master of the modifier. How excited I was, that night at Meow, that I had finally met a true New Zealander. Of course, now I understand that my slightly unorthodox upbringing (for which I am supremely grateful, I hasten to add, and I will show just how grateful later in these Acknowledgements) was responsible for this process taking so long. There weren't many true Kiwis at the commune, for instance. The upshot is, I have another profound debt to Miles. Not only do I understand the quintessential New Zealand *élan vital* as Sam Neill explains it, I also know how to write characters like Maurice Gee writes them, which is of course a gift for any writer.

Let me return to the night in question—Sago Pudding Night, as I fondly dubbed it. I could look at Miles, zipped up in his black thinking-urban-person's jacket (despite the weather) and telling me in a voice as flat as road-kill (a possum, if you could still tell) that he thought perhaps he didn't love me anymore, and I could say, 'Hallelujah, I hear you, I get it.' I laughed. Then I cried. I suppose I was feeling a jumble of emotions as I tried to interpret the qualifiers—and I was probably still under the misapprehension that the Miles-and-me equation was more-or-less mathematically correct. Of course now— *now*—I can see I was sorely mistaken, but that night, as it dawned on me that Miles really was leaving, I have to admit, I did get a bit hysterical. I would probably not have got a role in a film adaptation of a Maurice Gee novel. It's true that I did plead with Miles. I did dispose of a few breakables. I did unpack Miles's wheelie suitcase out the window. I remember the vibrant shape of a pair of pants caught momentarily against the pulsing harbour lights. Despite the jangle, I still noticed concrete significant details. I remember Miles's hairy ankles like tussock between my fingers as I crawled along the hall floor. How silly I was. But it was just one of those bittersweet argy-bargies that happen between lovers, or at least 'lovers'. I want to add here that if anyone happens to hear Miles's version of events, visitors to the apartment for instance, I can assure you that none of it is true.

And, of course, as it turned out, by leaving that night Miles was doing me a huge favour, and the proof of the pudding (which on Sago Pudding Night was a pertinent saying indeed), is the very book you are reading. I don't know how I can ever repay him, but hopefully these Acknowledgements will go some way towards doing so.

A few minutes after Miles had wrested his ankles from my grasp, I found myself at the living-room window while he bobbed about in the courtyard with a flashlight, dodging cars and gathering his clothes. As I stood watching, it occurred to me all of a rush that I didn't have a clue what I was going to do next. Where would I go if—just suppose, on some future occasion—I had to leave the apartment? And what would I do after my course at the Global School finished in a few weeks? For the first time in quite a while—two years at least—I felt a great nothingness yawning ahead, and to tell the truth it frightened me. In my chest, where my heartbeat should've been the biggest show in town, a trembling had taken over. Hearing Miles clattering back inside, I ran to the study and locked the door. It was warm in there from the heat of the day. I sat down at the big brown desk. Presently I could hear Miles knocking politely (his lovely low-key New Zealandness) and bleating, 'Janice, Janice.' He knocked and knocked, but I wouldn't let him in. We had a pathetic Janice / Go away / But Janice / Fuck off kind of conversation. I sat in the dark red den-ish room with nothingness stretching ahead of me, and I had an idea.

I did what any sane person would do under the circumstances: I applied for an Arts New Zealand grant. My tutor at the Global School, Clancy McKinney (whom I will thank later in these pages), had been telling me for months I should apply for something—if you're not in you can't

21

win, sort of thing—but I'm actually a modest person and I'd brushed off her advice. Now, the throes of relationship crisis appeared to have made me reckless. Maybe Clancy was right; maybe it *was* my turn for a serving of gravy after all. Because nek minnit I found myself ambling through the Arts New Zealand site, and, I have to say, I was pleasantly surprised by what I saw. While not on the scale of Sweden and Denmark and countries with well-educated children and stylish blond furniture, little New Zealand, for all its isolation, rural economy, neoliberal ways and second-hand recession, wasn't doing too badly where arts funding was concerned. There was a certain gamut: you could get a quick injection of cash to fund a slim volume of poetry while you continued with your little life in your scungy flat; you could score enough to live almost like a middle-class person for a year, burning fossil fuels while you wrote, say, a novel; you could jet to Menton and write in the very room where Katherine Mansfield worked, plus swan around Paris in the summer; and the biggest grant of all was the one you got when you were nearly dead and they'd better give it to you now or they'd be sorry.

I trawled through the list, feeling like Goldilocks trying things on for size: the big gruff Papa Bear grant, the medium-sized Mama Bear grant, the squeaky little Baby Bear grant. I soon realised, though, being realistic, that the first two categories were out of my league; to get them you needed to have been an arse-licker for years. Hopefully there would be something for me, but, as I scrolled down, despite the abundance, nothing seemed quite right.

I'll pause at this juncture to note—and I think this is important—that I've never been the kind of writer who busily and immodestly applies for every hand-out going. I believe one should be restrained in applying for tax-funded dollops, and when I see the line-up of B-team writers of chick-lit and chick-with-dick-lit and microscopic collections of poetry who get mountains of dosh for their little enterprises, I think to myself, there is no justice in the world. But I keep my equilibrium in the knowledge that posterity will sort it out, and I continue on my self-funded, self-starter, starter-pack approach to my writing.

In the den, feeling a rash of prickly heat engulf me, I noticed that the atmosphere in the room was, in fact, quite suffocating. I turned from the computer and did something rare for a Wellingtonian: I opened the window. A welcome gust of cool air floated in, plus the merry sound of the traffic grunting and tooting in the streets below. The harbour shimmered like a stage lit for Swan Lake, while the sun slipped behind the black cardboard hills in the distance. As I shaded my eyes I felt strangely enveloped by the evening, as if the apartment, the outdoors—harbour, hills, air— and myself, were all on a continuum, our cells somehow intermingled. I shivered, inhaled some exhaust and blew it out again. There was another knock from Miles, a last muffled message; goodbye, he couldn't live with a murderer. (He seriously said that.) I was about to close the Arts New Zealand site forever when, taking one last scroll through the list of grants and residencies, something caught my eye. The award that seemed just right leapt out at me like a beacon— none other than the Antarctica Residency.

I imagined myself a lone figure in a vast white landscape, made small by the steppe and the distant white horizon, so frozen I couldn't feel my hands or my nose. I wanted to make the little space inside me which had once been warm but was now cold, *was* a coldness—I wanted to make it normal, and in a white-out it would be acclimatised. It hit me that that was what I'd wanted for some time. Now I imagined myself a snow angel beating my wings slowly, a fuzzy dot having a tiny, whispery impact on the vast whiteness, and at the point where thought meets feeling, everything would fade and go numb including the coldness inside me, and I wouldn't need to bother about it anymore.

Coming to from my reverie in the study, I realised two things. One, the knocking on the door had stopped; two, I should abso-fucking-lutely apply for some dollars!

I considered my chances fair to medium. My CV was looking pretty damn healthy, though I say it myself. I'd already published a little book, the aforementioned *Utter and Terrible Destruction*, my *roman à clef*, with publisher Tree Murphy of Chook Books (whom I will thank later in these Acknowledgements), even though it didn't have a spine; I'd almost completed my course at the Global School; I'd once been the featured writer at Meow Café's Poetry Live; I blog at janonice.com and keep a buoyant writer's profile on Facebook and Twitter and also post quite a bit of political stuff. Just recently, a fellow blogger wrote a review of *Utter and Terrible* and said it was 'like fine wine'.

So with all this good luck and good circumstance going on in my life, I thought, Why Not? Why Fucking Not, Janice? I had a brainstorm of inspiration and found myself furiously typing up a story about a young woman who's had quite a tough life for various reasons and who has this crazy idea to go down to the ice and lie in it like a snow angel and warm up a little patch just the size of herself (imagine if we all did that), and that piece breaks off and floats away and gradually melts but in the process warms up a little neighbourhood in the ocean and that causes an island to be engulfed. Though

I say it myself, my concept was quite allegorical. The rest, as they said, is history.

At one point, as I filled in the online form, I looked up from my pool of light and heard a roller door shudder closed in the courtyard below and the throaty rev of Miles's ancient Peugeot accelerating into the night. I was beginning to think this little sojourn on my own in the apartment wouldn't be so bad after all. Miles would be back and in the meantime I would get on with things in an extremely productive way. I tweeted a screenshot of my application. On Facebook my post got three likes within five minutes, from Mandy, Linda Dent and Nick Hall. Back on Twitter, Mandy had retweeted it, and I'd also been faved by @fringefestdweller in the UK who wished me luck. I replied, Thanks muchly for the RT @fringefestdweller, fingers crossed! I did a few favs and retweets, tweeted a link about this massive, disgusting whirlpool of plastic that's in the middle of the Pacific Ocean, considered following a new follower but decided not to and followed someone I'd been thinking for some time now should've been following me. And then who should fav my tweet but Clancy McKinney, who only goes online once in a blue moon. I replied, Thanks so so much for the <3 @fancyclancy. Hope you're having a nice evening :-)). No reply, but that was okay; I retweeted it. My application had created a bit of a flurry, which I saw as a good sign.

Although things avalanched somewhat alarmingly after the formative Sago Pudding Night, I soon realised that Miles was right—we had fallen utterly and completely out of love. Erotic love, I hasten to add. I still hold Miles in high regard, and we remain the best of platonic friends to this day. I did experience a certain amount of heartache though, and I'd like to return for a moment to the question 'What sparks creativity?' I do believe now—older and wiser, if only by a year—that pain may be partially at the root of it. If that's the case, I'm forever in Miles's debt, because without the fast-turnaround fuck-fest he embarked upon immediately following Sago Pudding Night, which really was quite a tawdry laundry list, I don't think I would've had the benefit of going through the emotional agony necessary to be a writer. I especially can't thank Miles enough for the final vulgar leg of the slut-gala, which turned out to be the one that stuck (and I suppose became, by definition, not-tawdry, not-vulgar, but I will leave you, Reader, to make up your own mind about that). It was this last affair (the reader might also ponder the term 'last' in context of a man who has a history of unfaithfulness) that led to the total and, as it turned out, silver-lined destruction of our relationship. I am delighted to report that Miles and Dorothy—of the fifties outfits and Femme De Rochas perfume—are now a devoted (sic) husband and wife.

The result of Sago Pudding Night, then, was that I suddenly found myself with my life restored to me. With Miles out of the apartment, I took over his study as my preferred place of writing, feeling some relish that this russet, mannish space was now mine, at least for now. Before this, I'd written at the dining table, as described earlier, or on the couch or in bed. The apartment was reasonably spacious, but still, it was a city pad. I didn't mind, honestly; in fact I found it wonderfully ironic. This might be vital information for anyone researching certain things in the future: that most of *The Ice Shelf* was written in makeshift liminal spaces. Nevertheless, on moving into Miles's study, I felt a surge of expansiveness amongst the solid furniture, the wall-to-wall carpet, the purring dehumidifier. I had a room of my own, albeit temporary. When Miles came back, I would no doubt be called upon to relinquish the study because Miles happened to have been born into a family with their mitts on cash. The truth is, no one ever really has a room of one's own; everything is temporary, all things must pass. Nevertheless, I spread my books and papers around the leathery surfaces and got stuck into finishing the first draft of *The Ice Shelf*.

Those last couple of months alone in the apartment were magical. This was a writer's retreat with yours truly blissfully ensconced. The weather remained eerily sub-tropical, but I wasn't complaining. I fell into a routine of working late into the warm night, cocooned in the plush burgundies of the study, swivelling on the old wooden chairman-of-the-board chair, shifting sometimes to unstick my thighs. Through the open window, traffic noise and the smell of exhaust— which in Wellington usually blew away before they could be clocked—hung on the air, and that was somehow exciting. Occasionally I would look away from my work, down at the harbour which, with its little moonlit scallops, spread like a petticoat out from Oriental Bay. I would watch planes trembling up from behind the craggy silhouette of the eastern hills.

Eleven o'clock in the morning would find me sitting at the same study window with coffee, looking out at the same view in its daytime garb of dappled green and khaki, of military camouflage. This was the life! In the afternoon (which, come to think of it, was only an hour later, but days spent alone are strangely long) I'd find myself wandering from room to room. I'd never been so alone, and I was absolutely loving it. I would reward myself for my morning's work with a little finger of vodka and orange, then get back to my manuscript.

In the late afternoons I'd pop down the hill to pick up some supplies for dinner from the superette on the corner. It turned out that the liquor store man next door, an alt-rock type with a long stringy hair, liked films, especially French New Wave cinema, and we'd have a really excellent rave about Truffaut, Rivette et al., and once he even forgot to charge me for a bottle of vodka, so engrossed was he in our conversation on *Céline and Julie Go Boating*.

The evenings were long, and I found I had oodles of time to watch the harbour lights twinkling and plunging. I'd mull a bit. I'd check Facebook, do a few tweets, see if anyone famous had died or if anyone I knew had published a book with a spine, but was usually relieved to find not—I mean that no one had died, of course—and I'd post a link about rising sea levels because I know this really good site that most people don't know and also about the Syrian refugee crisis urging people to sign up to take a family (I definitely would if I had a house). Perhaps smoke a bit of weed to pass the time, truth be told. Out the front windows and obliquely to the north, ant-like people promenaded along Oriental Parade. On occasion I experienced a slight pang of loneliness watching tiny couples enfolded romantically as they trimmed the shoreline, but when I got out the binoculars, they seemed to be propping each other up in their drunken stupors. What a fitting metaphor for my new state of freedom, I thought; I didn't need to hold anyone else upright, and I certainly did not need to cling to another person to move forward on life's upmarket foreshore.

Then I'd do some more writing—nobody to please, nobody to worry with the light, nobody to disturb with the creaky floorboard near the sideboard. The city would quieten, the promenaders would battle home, and I'd have the night to myself.

Before I turned in, I'd check Facebook and post about how many words I'd written that day, and Mandy, Linda Dent and Nick Hall would like it, and there might be a comment like Keep on keeping on Janice!, or, Woohoo!, which I'd like. I'd check the *Guardian* to see if anyone who'd won the Nobel Prize for Literature in 1970 or something had died, and maybe get a quote that was worth tweeting. I've always been polite about thanking people for their RTs. That's just me. Plus I'd usually post a link about the environment, because actually that's the most important thing. We've reached CO_2 levels of 400ppm and when we get to 450 the polar ice caps will melt, sea levels will rise—wiping out cities and huge tracts of farmland, causing widespread famine—the ocean will become more acidic, threatening fish and coral reefs, and all around the world there'll be extreme weather—hurricanes, blizzards, tornadoes, droughts—and because it's warmer there'll be more mosquitoes carrying disease. And so to bed. It would feel like about a year since I got up. A day that feels like a year is an immeasurable gift for any writer.

After a couple of weeks of this, I felt like I was a character in one of those John Wyndham novels in which everyone else has died but I've been spared because I've been having some kind of operation. I peered down at the windswept shrubs in front of the building, half expecting them to walk. I tweeted, I feel like a character in a John Wyndham novel #whereiseverybody? and waited for the RTs to roll in, but only Mandy obliged with, Watch out for the Triffids @Janiceawriter!!! It's probably a bit perverse, if I'm being perfectly honest, and I do value honesty above everything, but somehow Mandy's RT annoyed me. I replied all the same, Thanks muchly for the RT @mandycoot!

*

In the middle of all this, I went along to the last class (sadly) of my Global School course. Clancy lived in a Newtown council flat complex that looked like a slum on the outside—the seventies rustic timber cladding was black with mould—but she'd made it nice inside. Clancy teaches creative writing from her kitchen table and is absolutely awesome. Because I'd been a latecomer to sign up (I'd just got my payout for unlawful dismissal from the Glass Menagerie), and she could only fit six students in her kitchen, after one class of trying to squeeze me in Clancy decided she would open up a second class just for me, which suited me fine because, to tell the truth, there were a couple of really annoying people in the other class. The one drawback was that Clancy's three boys, who were with their dad on the other class night, were there and Clancy had get up periodically to go and break up fights in the bedroom. I am never having children. Anyway, Clancy really knows her stuff. We'd been working on *The Ice Shelf* since July. I was looking forward to getting any final pearls of wisdom Clancy could offer me.

She ushered me in with a big-gauge beckoning arm. Clancy has a get-on-with-it manner and always dresses in a Lycra top and sweatpants, as if she's about to go for a run. We settled at the kitchen table with tea and gingernuts, and Clancy folded herself on her chair. She was lean and intent, and her waka-blond afro was squeezed into a topknot like Māui's mother, with her red supermarket glasses perched there. I opened up my draft and pushed my laptop towards her, a bit bashfully actually, and Clancy pulled her glasses down onto her nose and frowned at my latest crots, jotting down the odd comment and going 'Mm, mm', but that was just her. (Crots are the short prose pieces that make up a discontinuous narrative, according to my dictionary of literary terms, but not many people know that.) Yelling and thumping could be heard in the bedroom. From her folded position, Clancy looked at me over her glasses.

'You know what I'm going to say, right?'

I wriggled about, because I had a fair idea.

'Edit it down, Suga. It's too . . .'

Too what? I could feel my lips going like the wah-wah emoji.

'Too *too*,' we said together, and laughed, and Clancy went into a paroxysm of coughing. When she'd recovered she said, 'Don't be offended, okay? You have to be thick-skinned.'

I assured her my skin was really thick. Then Clancy had to go into the bedroom to deal with the yelling and thumping. She could make her voice sound surprisingly like a foghorn when she wanted to. Tears sprang into my eyes, but I brushed them away. The thing is, being too *too* is also my strong point. It's actually what Clancy, awesome as she is, will never get. And what no one ever seems to get, but they will, one day, although probably when I'm dead. The noise in the bedroom ceased suddenly, as if a switch had been flicked. I am never having children. Clancy reappeared and took up her position.

'Don't be offended,' she said.

I wasn't in the least offended.

'You know what I'm going to say next, right?'

I sort of did.

'Kill your darlings, darling.' Clancy laughed, and coughed. She always said that. 'Kill 'em dead,' she added for emphasis, but I got it.

I promised I would.

'Don't be offended, okay?'

'Okay,' I said.

Clancy clucked all the way through the rest of my pages, laughing sometimes, sighing, jotting, mm-mm-ing—the whole Shakespearean gamut. She had to go back into the bedroom to sort out the yelling a couple of times. When she came back the second or third time, she sat down at the table and sighed. I sighed. We laughed. 'Life, eh?' 'Yeah, life,' said Clancy. 'More tea?' she offered, but I happened to have half a bottle of vodka in my bag because I'd been to see a friend earlier and this was what was left and she hadn't wanted me to leave it at her house because she might drink it, so that's why it was in my bag.

Clancy seemed quite pleased at this and grabbed two glasses.

'The ice shelf,' I said idly.

'To *The Ice Shelf*!' said Clancy, and we drank. After a while she said, 'Saw you applied for that thing.'

'The Antarctica thing,' I said.

'Yup. Yay. Good for you, you go girl!' said Clancy.

'Thanks,' I said. Because Clancy is awesome.

She went to the bedroom to break up a fight, and when she came back she said, 'Suga, what I want to know is, how're you actually going to *get* this fucking residency? Like, in your hot little hand.' She closed my laptop, which I tried not to take personally.

I explained that I'd slaved over my application, that my CV was healthy; I even started to describe how the whole impetus for it had been Sago Pudding Night. Clancy interrupted.

'Your application? Your CV? Are you kidding me? Girl, it won't cut the mustard.' I suppose Clancy realised she'd made a dent in my ego—I'm usually thick-skinned—because she added, 'Don't go all offended on me.'

I said I wouldn't. I poured more vodka.

'Are you sure? Because I know you.' Clancy got up and lit a fag out the open window, and talked back into the kitchen on the inhale. 'Tell me, did you get straight into Theory of Creative Writing or whatever the fuck they call it?'

She knew I hadn't.

'Or were you waitlisted?'

She knew I had been.

'Were you in the main part of the Borich Festival?'

'Clancy,' I said.

'Or were you in the fringe?'

I sighed.

'Did you grow up in fucking Noa Valley?'

Clancy ducked into the bedroom, and I sat listening to the distant rumpus, feeling a bit hopeless, if truth be told. I looked around the kitchen, at the worn orange bench, the wire dishrack stacked neatly, the blue dishcloth hung on a little rail beside the bottle of dishwash, green as a duckpond. When the yelling from afar suddenly cut out, I heard instead the soft hum of the white fridge. I took a breath. It was true, I didn't grow up in fucking Noa Valley. Thank Christ for that.

Clancy came back to the table and looked at me curiously.

'What?' I said.

'No, you what?' she said.

'Nothing,' I said.

'Good,' said Clancy. 'Let's get to work.' She opened her ancient laptop and drummed her fingers on the cracked Formica table while it came back from the dead. 'Come on, you crock of shit.' It whirred and clicked, and finally coloured up. 'Okay,' said Clancy, reattaching her glasses. She perused the site like an abseiler. 'The usual suspects. Dean Cuntface, Roderick the Dick, and Dame fucking Carol.'

'Phew,' I said. 'Thought you were going to say Dame Bev.'

Clancy looked at me over her glasses. 'Would that be some kind of problemo?'

I assured Clancy it wouldn't be, it was just I'd had a run-in with Dame Bev once, but actually I admire her hugely and will thank her later in these Acknowledgements. We laughed, and I emptied the last drops of the vodka, being careful not to give Clancy too much because she's a cheap drunk.

Clancy busily wrote the names of the committee on an envelope, and on the back she scrawled a to-do list, getting quite excited. 'You're gonna slay 'em, Suga.' She handed me the list but grabbed it back to add a last item, shuddering a bit and mouthing silently, 'So-cial media.'

We laughed and I filed the list in my laptop bag.

On the doorstep we hugged for a long time. I heard myself whimpering a bit, and Clancy said, 'Do it, Suga,' and I murmured, 'I will, for sure.' Clancy is the bomb. I walked away from the mouldy housing complex, the sound of the boys' yells and thumps receding, and I felt a jumble of emotions—yes, I was sad that it was my last class at the Global School, but on the other hand I was all fired up. I knew what I had to do. I would kill 'em dead.

To return to the aftermath of Sago Pudding Night: my writer's retreat progressed. I wrote my novel and things were generally magical, although the apartment started getting the teensiest bit messy. Being tied up with my *roman*, I hadn't been as zealous as usual in picking up bottles and plates or putting out the rubbish, plus the soprano of the washing machine on spin was distracting, so I was waiting until I'd worn all my clothes before running it. Occasionally, it's true, I did look across the room and remember the life

Miles and I had planned in the lovely fifties apartment, our little family, calmly living each day, portioning them out, this day, that day, under one roof while everything moved subtly around us, while the universe cooled. But mostly, I was so engrossed in my work I didn't even know what day it *was*.

With my Global School course finished, I had nothing to disturb me apart from the odd phone call from Miles. He seemed regretful about how things were going, but I wasn't going to let him come back just yet. I was having too much of a good time alone, getting on with my writing, which is the main thing. When he called, I'd say sorry but I wanted to keep the experiment going a little longer. Miles would make noises—I'd pick up the odd 'possibly', 'maybe', 'might'—and then he'd hang up.

I also read the scrawl on the back of the envelope Clancy had given me, which went thus:

1) Review *Punch and Judy at New Brighton* (Roderick the Dick's new book) on blog favourably!!! even tho it's a crock of colonial shit!!!
2) Go to Dean Cuntface's book launch, Blondini's, Feb 12 at six, buy the book, get it signed even tho you'll have to talk to the wanker.
3) Retweet all their tweets, including anything!!! to do with Dame Carol.

Love Clancy xxxxx

I started busily retweeting Dean Cuntface, @hattencoat, who tweets funny little things people said in the LRB, and Roderick Lane, @gimmeshelflife, who's the most shameless

35

humblebraggart you've ever come across. Dame Carol isn't on Twitter, thank God, at least there's one pie she doesn't have a finger in, but she is on Facebook. I researched all of them on the internet and just about threw up over pics of their blond grandchildren at their holiday baches and close-ups of the medals they got for their Queen's Birthday honours. Roderick the Dick also blogs (probably at selfaggrandisement.com). I started writing a review of his new book which I couldn't afford to buy, and it wasn't in the library yet, so I read it quickly crouched down in Unity Books. Clancy was right, it was a shocker. I noticed it was published by my publisher, but everyone makes mistakes. Here is a greatly abridged version of my review:

***Punch and Judy at New Brighton*, by Roderick Lane (Chook Books, 50pp, $24.99). Reviewed by Janice Redmond.**
Roderick Lane is a household name in poetry in this country with two collections of lyric verse published to acclaim, so it will be music to the ears of his readers that he has turned his attention to the long narrative poem form. *Punch and Judy at New Brighton* is a finely tuned, lovingly crafted poetic reimagining of his childhood. It is a gorgeous, sensuous poem of sea, sand and sky, of roast lamb and warm tomatoes, and of the eponymous Punch and Judy shows that were staged on the very seashore of his youth.

Lane takes us on a magical journey through 1950s New Brighton. He engages with a love for the land that has been in his family since the 1860s acquisitions, contends with the burden of a colonial heritage which he reworks finely into an appreciation of what it was/is to Be Pākehā and distills into poetic form the idiosyncrasies of a certain New Zealand hesitation. This text could arguably be aligned with the seminal film *Cinema of Unease*. Throughout, Lane's voice is spare, new and utterly beautiful:

> Mum pegs
> washing
> on the line.
> Dad fixes
> the car.
> (From, 'The Backyard')

Punch and Judy at New Brighton tantalises, shocks and surprises. I wholeheartedly recommend this book to all who enjoy the very best of New Zealand poetry. Roderick Lane is a national treasure.

I followed Roderick the Dick on Twitter then tweeted my review and bingo, a few hours later Rod faved it and retweeted it. Yuss! I ticked off the first item on Clancy's list and allowed myself a small vodka and orange to celebrate.

One evening while I was punching away at my keyboard in the subdued velvetiness of the study, I made a discovery that I *don't* think was meant for my eyes. I'd paused in my typing, casting around for the right word, how you do, when something made me reach down and try to open one of the dark polished desk drawers. I don't know why I hadn't thought of this before, perhaps my trusting nature, but the drawer mysteriously would not open, which of course piqued my interest. I wrestled with the bone handle. Surely it was just stuck; but no, it was locked.

How to proceed? First, I poured myself a vodka (sans orange—run out). Then it occurred to me there might be a key to the desk drawer somewhere in the apartment. I flew from room to room, kicking rubbish and clothes out of the way as I went, ferreting through other drawers and cupboards. I did find some keys, several in fact, and each time, I rushed back to the desk in excitement, but when I tried them they didn't work, and I slumped over in disappointment. Finally kneeling in front of the drawer like a religious nutter, I tried, in succession, a hairpin, a nail file, a wire coathanger, a box-cutter, a piece of floppy blue nylon strip from a package. Janice 'Fingers' Redmond! Nothing worked. I gave up.

Nek afternoon when I went into the study and saw again the drawer barred to me, even though the room was currently my own, I was seized with new determination. I fetched a screwdriver and proceeded to prise off the front of the drawer. This took some doing. The desk was none of your flimsy custom-wood; it was solid mahogany, had belonged to Miles's father before the parents downsized. (Miles's father even looked like the Chairman of the Board on the 'Chance' card in Monopoly—small feet, big 'corporation'.) I found I had to plunge the screwdriver into the join in several places and in each one to wrestle and wrench, and finally the front of drawer came free, leaving a bright rawness. Gazing at the splintery mess, I realised something hilarious about this episode, and I don't know why it hadn't occurred to me before: when Miles had used the room with his father's swivel chair, in the flat he'd been given the deposit for, he'd been *in his father's den*. And now I occupied it! I sat back on my heels and rocked with laughter.

Although the desk wasn't in the greatest shape now, I thought I could glue the front of the drawer back on later without leaving too much trace. But, Reader, my break-in was all in a good cause, and I'll tell you why. Lying in the tray of the drawer was a slim sheaf of densely lettered papers.

We knew it was going to be papers, didn't we? I picked them up gingerly, snared off the single silver paperclip which left a barbed hole in the corner and settled cross-legged on the floor to read. Boxy, inhuman typeface downloaded from the internet bled to the edges of the sheet; this text had no respect for the A4 page. It was, as they say, an education, and I think it's safe to say my jaw dropped as, sitting on the dusky carpet, I read information from the Ministry of Justice about what would kick in once the dissolution of our de facto relationship was complete. The first realisation, of course, was that I knew Miles and I were curtains. I'd perhaps imagined a reunification at some point, like one of those Russian states returning to the Soviet bloc. A bittersweet reunion. It would never be. But after my weeks alone in the apartment, I was not so sorry. I'd come around to the idea that Miles and I were better off apart, that we'd fallen out of love and should go full steam ahead separately into the rest of our lives. However, there was more.

I read that if a couple were together for three years, whether married or de facto (it made no difference), their worldly goods would be split down the middle; read, Miles's modernist apartment and my green fridge, 50–50.

I thought hard. It was comforting to know I'd be in ownership of half the apartment; that was as it should be. But surely when settling-up time came, Miles would not be so petty as to deny me the whole of the fridge which I loved, and which he did not. I hoped I wouldn't have to pay him twenty-five dollars for the privilege of keeping it when I'd bought it with my payout from the Glass Menagerie, a place where I had suffered. My mind raced ahead. Half the apartment would be very nice, enough for a deposit on a lesser flat somewhere, not Mount Victoria, but perhaps tumbledown, Bohemian Newtown or Berhampore, and that would be absolutely fine with me because I'm not a materialist.

As I scanned the busily formatted pages, I saw that there was a very serious proviso which could affect us if things went awry, though I hoped they wouldn't: if a couple were together for fewer than three years, each would have no claim on the others' assets. Miles would not be entitled to half my fridge, and I would have no claim on the apartment.

This state of affairs simply must not be allowed to manifest. I quickly totted up in my head that I needed to stay in residence in the apartment until the 1st of March, which was three years to the day after I'd first moved in. Then all would be well. I could hold out in the apartment until the 1st of March—under siege, it's true, but all for a good cause. So that there'd be no chance of me forgetting the date—as if I would, but just to be sure—I photographed the docs with my phone.

As the steamy months of my writer's retreat passed, Miles called a few times to ask me, in the nicest possible way, to move out of the apartment. He would string together a bejewelled necklace of qualifiers, each more uselessly decorative than the last—'thinking perhaps', 'probably going to have to', 'hopefully in the end'. The calls were excruciating, but I wasn't budging, not even with 'the best will in the world'. I came to regard Miles's polite, hedged phrases as standover tactics. I was being asked to do my own dirty work, to reassure Miles that there was nothing unpleasant and move out at the same time. But knowing what I did about New Zealand law and the official length of a relationship, I wasn't going anywhere in a hurry, at least not until after the 1st of March.

In the middle of this I got an email from Arts New Zealand informing me I'd been waitlisted for Antarctica, which felt like a visceral blow—I nearly toppled backwards off my chair with disappointment. But I recovered my spirits quickly and strode around the study telling myself things could be worse; it was okay, I was okay. I was waitlisted, not rejected outright. I decided to call Arts New Zealand to see exactly what was going on. It was just before five o'clock, so I dialled quickly. In a few seconds, unbelievably, I was talking to an Arts New Zealand human being. Having already thanked that esteemed institution for its generosity with taxpayer money, I would like to especially thank one person within its hallowed halls, Didi Musgrove, the junior assistant administrator who proved to be really excellent at her job as zealous gatekeeper. When I asked in a perfectly reasonable tone of voice why I'd been waitlisted, Didi's officious telephone manner, her verbal attack when asked for an explanation, did her proud. The phone call ended, I have to say, in an extremely unprofessional slamming down of the phone and not on my part. I don't think I would've summoned the determination to continue waiting if it hadn't been for that spur. So thanks *very* much, Didi 'You'll never get an Arts New Zealand grant as long as I'm working here' Musgrove, love from—although I may not be as smarmy and as sold-out as some Arts New Zealand applicants—an Award Winner, a successful recipient of the Antarctica Residency. I filed my waitlisting under the 'Give me the grace to accept what I cannot change' category and allowed myself a vodka and orange to celebrate my mindfulness.

One afternoon in the middle of my halcyon (apart from the waitlisting) period in the apartment, Miles turned up at the door. It seemed he'd given up the phone calls as a dead loss; round one to me! I got out of bed and let him in, and he waltzed through kitchen and living room, not so much as a by-your-leave, and continued to the bedroom. This was extremely decisive behaviour by Miles's standards—his only mumble was about the state of the place—and I thought for a moment he wanted sex and was prepared to dilly-dally, for dignity's sake. But, instead, he sank to his knees and rooted around in the bottom of the wardrobe.

'Lost something?' I inquired from the doorway. He looked up from grovelling among the shoes, and it seemed he'd had his teeth whitened; they were so ultraviolet he could've used them as a torch. The new him, no doubt—which I found a bit creepy, to tell the truth.

'No,' he said, holding up a pair of black leather dress shoes.

'Going somewhere fancy?' I asked.

'Yeah-nah,' he said and started on his jackets.

I had a brief fantasy about asking him archly whether he wanted his paperwork back, but of course that would've been cutting off the proverbial nose. Then it occurred to me that *he* might rummage in his desk. Leaving him flipping through clothes as if through A2 posters in a record store, I sidled out and quietly shut the door to the study. By the time he came into the living room I was watching boats idling on the harbour. Out of the corner of my eye, I saw him drape some clothes over the couch and head for the study. With a Usain Bolt-style rush, I intercepted him in the doorway. Our hands met on the polished wooden knob. Miles looked at me coldly and seemed about to say something, but *Cinema of Unease* set in.

I smiled. It's funny how you can be coy with someone you've fucked madly. 'I've been working in here,' I said. 'It might be a teensy bit of a mess.'

'I can sort of probably imagine,' he said.

'Can I fetch something for you?'

Miles looked quizzical. 'It is, you know, after all is said and done, my study.'

Hearing this line-up of qualifiers, the big guns of passive-aggression, I realised there was no way I was going to keep Miles out. I thought quickly. Flinging open the door, I darted ahead of him into the room and flopped into the swivel chair, and as I did so I remarked on how hot it was, wriggled out of my dressing gown and draped it over the severed drawer.

Miles went beady-eyed. In one giant arc, he was over at the desk and swiping away the dressing gown, which landed softly on the carpet like a gull on sand. He looked at the hole, which if I'm completely honest was rather rough. He spluttered, did a top-heavy dance, then ravaged through the drawer and came up clench-mouthed with the papers in his fist like a trophy. Then he had, on a scale of *Cinema of Unease*, a major climax, the big one in which the main character loses it at the end of Act II. Except that this was only Act I, and I was the main character.

On my wheelie chair I pushed myself out into the middle of the room, the way one does from the side of a pool, and twirled back and forth, treading the carpet, just watching. I already knew the contents of the drawer, and I wasn't going to leave the apartment until the 1st of March.

Miles cradled the papers protectively. His big shoulders were wilted, and I thought for a strange moment that he might cry. Miles doesn't cry. I don't think Miles has cried since he was a baby. I briefly imagined him as an eight-year-old at school, holding back the tears while being bullied by a purple-faced bruiser. Still cuddling the sheaf to his chest, he turned to me.

'You probably shouldn't have done it.' His voice was weak and groany.

'I had to,' I said. 'It was locked.'

He was suddenly as wild-eyed as a Kaimanawa horse. 'No! I mean you shouldn't have done, you know, what you did.'

My lungs went tight, and everything suddenly seemed bad—the study, the apartment, the harbour, Miles, they were all intolerable, and I couldn't stand any of them. Things, people, they were all on the same horrible spectrum.

'If it weren't for you—' began Miles, but he got no further. He turned and left the apartment briskly, as if none of this had happened, as if everything were perfectly normal and he had a train to catch.

Alone again, I sat swivelling in the hateful chair which itself had now joined the hateful litany of objects and people, the material world. I wanted it gone. I was not thankful for it.

I woke very late next afternoon and wondered, as I lay in the lather and tangle of my bed, if I could go on with *The Ice Shelf*. This was the terrible stage things had come to. As you know, I did go on with it, because you are reading the result right here in this very volume. Somehow on that poisonous afternoon, I dragged myself out of bed and went back into the hated study, sat at the hated desk with the abominable drawer beside me where Miles had dropped it on the carpet, and I started typing. And *The Ice Shelf* got me out of my personal climate change; it closed up the hole in the ozone layer that had come to hover over my head and give me a stress headache, just the way it does over New Zealand.

I'd set myself back on my path, or rather *The Ice Shelf* had.

The letter from the lawyer changed things somewhat, but a legal document is always going to skim over the emotion of the situation. In the interim Miles and I had shared a few emails back and forth about moving-out dates and about my novel, which was at a crucial stage. Tree Murphy was waiting for the final draft, and I couldn't let her down or my name would be mud and no publisher, not even Tree, would touch me with a barge pole. My career would go down the gurgler. But Miles wasn't buying it. I skim-read the letter from Medlyn Limpert and Associates and saw mention of a date in late February by which I should have vacated the property. As I had no intention of going anywhere before March the 1st, I did not open any subsequent letters from Medlyn Limpert.

One afternoon there was a knock at the door. I thought it must be Miles, although he had a key, so I wondered to what I owed such coyness. I put on my dressing gown, and as I approached the door and saw the figure silhouetted there, the hair stood up on the back of my neck. The visitor wasn't Miles but a beast of prey. If there's one thing I learned as a child, it's how to tell a summons deliverer at a hundred paces, and I certainly had no trouble detecting same through the bobbly glass door of a modernist apartment. Yes, papers were being served, and I had an inkling they were to do with my tenure in the apartment. The other thing I learned as a child was how to be *not at home* when the summons deliverer calls. I crouched beneath the kitchen window, poked my head up lightning fast like a lemur and withdrew again. Lying flat on the floor, jammed right up against the wall, I digested the image I'd glimpsed—a man, jockey-like with a shiny bomber jacket, a shaved head and worried expression; the epitome of the legal lackey. I remembered my great days at the commune Hoki Aroha, which is where I learned the delicate art of summons avoidance, I will be thanking the good people associated with that experience later in these Acknowledgements.

Over the next several weeks, the light brothel-creeper squelch of the summons deliverer became a frequent sound on the balcony; also his sharp, practised knock, his heavy breathing after the climb up the jagged edge of the building (I dubbed the eight flights 'the Southeast Ridge', after Sir Edmund Hillary's ascent of Everest). I even got quite fond of the summons deliverer's routine and felt sorry for his trouble, his tender rasping on the doormat, the dejected squeak of his footsteps as he sloped off a failure; it all wrenched at my heart just a little. I'd like to take the opportunity to thank the summons deliverer for reminding me to have compassion for the plight of mercenaries everywhere. What a terrible thing to spend your days carrying out the unethical wishes of financial thugs. I will be raising awareness in the community on this issue as soon as I am in a position to do so. All the same, I wasn't ever going to open the door to a summons deliverer. I took to living with the kitchen blinds shut permanently and to going out to shop only at night.

My intensely creative period, however, was not to last. Things came to a dramatic head one late summer night when I'd popped out for half an hour, had had an interesting conversation about *4 aventures de Reinette et Mirabelle* with the grunge-styled assistant in the liquor store, and had returned home to an interesting development. The first indicator was when I stood in the doorway of the apartment and took a giant, diagnostic sniff: Femme de Rochas. Dorothy was in the house, which meant that Miles was almost certainly in here too. Also I was the wee-est bit stoned.

Here I have something very important to relate. This was the very day on which my de facto relationship with Miles had hit the three-year mark. And so, no matter what Miles did, no matter what Miles and Dorothy did—they could throw me out, they could toss me in the air, they could chop me up into little bits and put me in a black plastic rubbish bag—legally, half of the apartment was mine. And half of the green fridge was Miles's (but I hoped he would not try to claim it). Armed with such knowledge, I took this little home invasion in my stride. It was neither here nor there to me. In fact, deep down, I suppose I'd been expecting this all along. At the very least, I'd anticipated that at some point I would receive another social call from Miles, and I was only surprised that it had not happened earlier. I'd thought Miles was either being kind to me, or a little stupid.

'Happy anniversary!' I called from the front door.

Some clunks reverberated from deep in the apartment. No verbal reply, but I didn't expect one. How could Miles put his feelings into words, having grown up in the Noa Valley, his father the Chairman of the Board, the family muffled by a certain cinematic unease? It was impossible, and I understood and forgave him. I still do. Miles, I forgive you.

Looking back, I'm thankful for the way the events of this night unfolded. Later, I fondly dubbed it the Tortuous Sex Night, especially when regaling Mandy with the details. Before this, even with Miles's phone calls, his unpleasant visit, his emails, the lawyer's letter and the summons, I had not come around to the view that he and I were better apart. I am so, *so* grateful to Miles and of course to Dorothy, because without that reality check, without that reminder, I would not have known, and we might have suffered on in the relationship for years. But as I walked through the apartment, the situation unfolded before me like crystal left to grow overnight in a science lab, like certain experiments I remember from school when we'd set two elements together and on entering the salt- and meth-smelling lab in the morning would see that the two materials had acted on each other forming the most surprising, the most shocking shapes and colours—spindly and blue, or bulky and pink, or finely gossamered like spun sugar. That was how I experienced my progress through the apartment on this night.

I had no idea what I'd discover as the rooms opened before me. In the sepia hall, where I stopped to clink my keys on the small table, I saw, lying on the floor, a delicate silk chiffon scarf, umber-coloured and so fine it would be see-through if you held it up to the light. From the careless manner in which it had been dropped, the way it twisted kanji-like across the carpet, it emanated a sense of occupation. The scarf said, 'I live here now.'

I'd met Dorothy before, of course, when she'd come for drinks once or twice. She was a lovely person—a diminutive elf with a black wavy bob, pixie ears and a reserved manner. I'd warmed to her immediately. She wore 1950s dresses with full skirts and big polkadots or stripes which filled doorways despite her birdlike frame; her red high-heeled Mary Janes seemed to tango on the parquet floors, and of course the scent of Femme de Rochas disseminated through the apartment. (I'd be reminded of the famous Coco Chanel quote, 'A woman who doesn't wear perfume has no future', and I'd make a mental note to give myself a squirt from my ancient bottle of Fendi next time I wanted to do anything important, but I always forget.) Miles, Dorothy and I, with the harbour lights as a backdrop, would engage in vibrant conversations about art—Dorothy was an artist, and with Miles being a curator it was natural they should have a lot in common. I didn't actually have much to say, but I was just grateful to soak up the high-minded and knowledgeable discourse while serving the drinks and tidying up afterwards. I learned a lot about how bitchy people in the art scene can be, especially towards poor Dorothy, and that's actually really useful stuff for a novelist, vis-à-vis human nature.

I hesitated, then stepped over the chiffon character and continued on. Perhaps in the living room, but no, perhaps in the study, but no—and then to glimpse Dorothy in a compromising position which lasted no more than a second before one of them, I think Miles, kicked the bedroom door shut with a bang. It was still long enough for me to register tortuous sex, an extremely skinny bum, in fact none to speak of, doing calisthenics on top of Miles's rectangular torso as if he were a yoga mat, a vision which cast me in a peculiar ontological situation regarding where Dorothy rates on the attractiveness scale compared to me; that is, she doesn't, so I was left wondering why Miles would trade in someone like me for someone considerably less commercial, let's be honest, and the conclusion I came to was that he had gone completely insane. That knowledge lifted some weight from my shoulders, and as I stood in the hall, rather frozen, I realised that I had actually, deep down, been taking some blame for the break-up, but when I had the opportunity to gaze into the abyss of Miles's madness, I understood. Without Miles and Dorothy pointing this out to me, I am certain that I would not be where I am today.

After a thud-filled minute, Miles and Dorothy erupted from the bedroom, and I had an immediate impression of Miles—wild-eyed, untucked and muss-haired—and of Dorothy's 1950s polkadots gone all out of shape like in *Put*

Me in the Zoo ('I will go into the zoo. I want to see it. Yes I do'). I thought I heard her say, 'Oh no, it's the murderer.' That was all I had time to take in, because after Miles asked, 'Ah, Janice, you wouldn't have the keys to the apartment by any chance, would you?' there was a tumult.

I hadn't thought about the keys. I rushed back to the hall and snatched them up from the little side table, but as I did, I felt Dorothy's hand close over mine. She'd scooted right up to my elbow in a nanosecond, even in her ruffly skirt. I must say I applaud her sense of involvement. Half an hour in the house and she was shouldering responsibilities that, frankly, no one would expect of her. Go, Dorothy! However, I wasn't giving up the keys.

Dorothy lunged at the hand in which I clutched the keys. She yelled 'Miles!' over her shoulder, as if she might need him to take a pass in a game of basketball. I was only dimly aware of Miles hovering in the background. With Dorothy gripping my hand, we wrestled, at first in a jokey way, then getting a bit more serious. She was surprisingly strong for such a tiny person. Staring up into my face, she squeezed my hand like a vice. The keys dug into my palm and I struggled like crazy—this was getting much less friendly—as she bent my fingers back one by one, starting with the index finger and arriving eventually at the pinkie, and as she wrenched that finger back I yelped in pain and felt her small hand dive like the teeth of a fish into my palm and swallow the keys. She stared at me in triumph. Miles coughed lightly.

I guess my being a bit stoned turned out to be an unfortunate handicap, otherwise I might've put up a better fight. But it doesn't matter, it's actually fine. I have no problem whatsoever with Dorothy, then or now. As I stemmed the flow of blood from my hand (keys are surprisingly sharp), I realised that she was an innocent bystander in all this. When people are on the rebound they will flick out randomly like a snake's tongue at any passing thing, just to see, and that thing happened to be Dorothy. In fact, Dorothy is very nice. I would go so far as to say, Dorothy is spectacular. As I ruminated on this, Dorothy abruptly left the apartment, and I thought that might be the last I saw of her and felt wistful and worried on her behalf. I hoped she wouldn't be too heartbroken. But read on. I was not to be lumbered with Miles for very much longer.

With Dorothy off the premises, I was alone with Miles, just like the old days. We stood about silently scuffing our heels for a bit. 'I think,' Miles began, 'no, I know, I know for sure, I've probably, no, not probably, really, certainly . . .'

Then Miles looked at me, and he was no longer the quintessential Kiwi man described in *Cinema of Unease*. And I was no longer the woman who wanted an uneasy man.

'I've never loved you,' he said levelly.

Immediately I got out my phone and opened Facebook to change my relationship status. Single. I also posted a status update: Relationship over, don't ask ☹ ☹ ☹ and got three likes straight away from Mandy, Linda Dent and Nick Hall; Mandy replied, succinctly, xxxx, and Linda commented, Oh no! Big hugs! <3 <3 <3 xxxxxx. I replied, It's fine! Really!!! Thanks anyway! Xxxx And to show just how fine, I tweeted a link about taking your own utensils to Chinese restaurants rather than using the plastic ones, and this was already causing a stir before I'd pocketed my phone. So, more or less immediately, I could see that Miles leaving me was the best thing that had ever happened, and perhaps ever *would* happen in my life.

I told him I was taking the fridge.

He tossed his head in a wild, leonine way, and I prepared

for battle, but instead he wailed, 'Take it, take the fucking fridge, I don't care!'

I'd never heard Miles so impassioned, and it shocked me. But I wasn't going to wait for a second invitation, because I *was* going to take the fridge. I admit I was tremulous as I yanked its heavy black reconditioned plug from the spidery zone and started ferrying food from wire shelves to table. I would've uplifted it right then if at that moment there hadn't been an urgent grinding of keys and a gust of Femme de Rochas. Strangely, at that point it occurred to me for the first time, as Dorothy filled the doorway in her poodle skirt, that she matched the fifties apartment.

'What's she doing?' asked Dorothy, referring to yours truly in a rather impolite third person, even though I was only a metre or two away. Plus I was technically still the lady of the house. I continued to unpack the fridge systematically, knowing that Miles wouldn't stop me. He's actually a nice person. He stood with his shoulders buckled at odd angles, saying nothing.

Dorothy pawed at his arm. 'Don't let her take the fridge, Miles!'

Miles had a new wild look in his eye; he seemed stretched like a drying pelt.

I watched these antics from under my brow in the course of my travels between fridge and table. I also noticed a bulging bag at Dorothy's feet. She'd obviously gone home for the proverbial carpet bag, plus the scent; perhaps she'd had a quick shower after the evening's kinky antics. Good for her. I didn't mind. Miles replied *sotto voce* to Dorothy re the fridge: yes, he thought it was probably half his.

'Well,' said Dorothy, whose forthright manner would've made her most unwelcome in *In My Father's Den*, 'it's settled.

Don't let the murderer take the fridge.'

'Don't say that,' hissed Miles to Dorothy.

'*You* said it,' Dorothy hissed back.

Miles shook his head over and over. I ferried chutneys, jams, butter.

Of course, none of this had any veracity. First of all, I bought the fridge with my payout for unlawful dismissal from the Glass Menagerie in 2011. And secondly, I'd been stuffing my face from this fridge for almost three years. I think you'll agree, Reader, that this establishes a primal kind of ownership, or at least part-ownership. Since mid 2011 I'd eaten just as much food from this fridge as Miles had— in fact, more, because I snacked and lunched at home on account of my temporary unemployed status, while Miles frequented various cafés around town in his lunch hour, no doubt hoofing down quiche and roquette salad in the company of an assortment of other people on a payroll. The truth is, if I were to finish a degree in something random like archeology or psychology, I could have one of those jobs too and would have enough money to buy something in a ramekin for lunch. Good thing I haven't. Good thing I stuck to my creative guns and kept writing and eating lunch on the wing, otherwise there'd be no *Utter and Terrible Destruction* (which you might remember is my first little effort, the autobiographical novella/*roman à clef*, which appeared from Chook Books in 2010, and for which I am hugely grateful, even though it didn't have a spine) and there'd be no *The Ice Shelf*. My time would be gobbled up in a frenzy of meetings and sit-down soup-and-crouton lunches. Clearly I was and am more entitled to the fridge than Miles.

However, I didn't want to make a scene. How can we be defined, except by how we behave? So, on that Night of the

Tortuous Sex, I left the apartment without a single fridge. In the fridge department I possessed at that moment none, zero, zilch milch. I am, then, deeply indebted to the scrawny Dorothy over the transactions of the evening on several counts. Firstly, because the fridge that was rightfully mine had been wrested from me so callously, I was in the fortunate position of being able to exit the apartment, where I'd resided for exactly three years, quickly and cleanly with no trappings. My decamp would've been much trickier encumbered with a fridge, let alone any of the other possessions I'd accumulated over those three years, especially on account of the Southeast Ridge. It is all thanks to Dorothy that I got to experience the graceful sensation of freefall that comes with having, at least temporarily, almost nothing. But more importantly, if not for Dorothy's bull-headedness and Miles's lily-livered demurring, I would not have been offered the opportunity to assess the fridge's importance to me and to make arrangements for my future uplifting of it. I wasn't going to make the same mistake as Sorrell and be left high and dry, at room temperature, without the fridge. My most heartfelt gratitude to Miles and Dorothy.

It's true that I did experience a certain amount of trauma over being evicted from the glorious fifties space that was half mine. It might sound fanciful, but I had the impression of ice melting in the palm of my hand and dripping onto the carpet.

I am pleased to report that even though feelings were high, I found it within myself to vacate the premises in a dignified manner. Far be it from me to comment on the dignity of Miles and Dorothy, but in the hall, Miles pushed my coat at me and Dorothy even wound my scarf several times around my neck. They frog-marched me down the Southeast Ridge, which was something of a mission due to the narrowness of the staircase; we jostled for room and almost lost our collective footing on more than one occasion, like some ungainly six-legged creature tumbling sideways. Down in the courtyard, which is desolate at the best of times, we all paused. Perhaps it was exhaustion, or realisation; I don't know, but it seemed that time and space stood still, that we were suspended in a heterotopia where everything was equal, neutral, balanced, and that anything could happen, things could go forward in a different way if we so desired. I felt a surge of hope. Miles and I were kaput, but perhaps I could wish him well. I didn't really mind about Dorothy in her fifties clothes in the fifties apartment. Perhaps Miles would wish *me* well.

But the moment passed and we were back in the unruly night. Miles held out my overstuffed hold-all which he'd apparently thought to pack and which I supposed contained most of my worldly possessions except for half the fridge and half the apartment, while Dorothy leered from the sidelines. I snatched the hold-all, turned out of the courtyard onto Majoribanks Street and headed up the hill to Mandy's.

If it weren't for the seemingly cut-throat actions of the happy (sic) couple, I would not be where I am today. I would not have divested myself of the bourgeois shackles of the modernist apartment, would not have moved in with my friend Mandy and had a whale of a time doing Book Club 24/7, would not have assumed rightful ownership of my fridge, nor generally branched out in every area of my life. The most crucial thing of course was receiving the Antarctica Residency, which led to the writing of the text which follows these tributes.

*

Roar ahead really fast and come to a shuddering stop nine months after the Tortuous Sex Night, and here I am in front of Mandy's bathroom mirror (she's at her job as an assistant at Kilbirnie Library), inching up the zip on a floaty red chiffon dress in anticipation of attending the awards ceremony, which is happening at the National Library at six o'clock this evening. Having posed in various angles in front of the mirror, I've decided none of my regular clothes apply. I tend to hang out in big tops, short skirts, leggings and pixie boots, retro eighties-wear, and while I'm fond of my style, it's not quite right for the Antarctica Awards. So now I'm not looking like me anymore, a strange feeling that I find I actually quite like! Plus, I'm the wee-est bit nervous because I don't relish being the centre of attention at the awards ceremony. For Dutch courage I've allowed myself a small vodka and orange, which is teetering on the bathroom shelf. I'm also punching my thank yous into a doc on my phone as they occur to me; there are going to be a lot, and I want to get a head start before the book is accepted for publication, and at the same time I'm tweeting about the night to come (feeling humble), *plus* posting a link to a great article I half read earlier and I don't think anyone else will have seen about Environmental Gratitude and the middle class, basically the ethics of trashing the planet when you take it for granted. So, definitely multi-tasking. Through the French doors, I see there's a furious summer thunderstorm in action over the harbour; lightning walks on water like some supernatural being. I hope the inclement weather will have passed by the time I need to leave.

Having succeeded with the dress, which was a bit of struggle (Mandy is way too thin, but thank you anyway, Mandy), I'm finding it hard to breathe but it's just temporary.

I slap on some warpaint (ditto to Mandy) to counteract my pale cheeks. In the living room I stuff into my hold-all the clumpy, mouse-smelling down jacket they gave us at training plus the snowboots for Antarctica; my hold-all is cylindrical and over-the-shoulder, as I anticipate wheels will be almost useless when walking up the permafrost path to Scott Base. We Antarctica Residency recipients fly out to Christchurch in the morning from whence we will board a New Zealand Army Hercules aircraft bound for the Polar Ice Cap. After a little *contretemps* earlier, nothing serious, Mandy has kicked me out of her abode, so I need to find somewhere to stay tonight. But it's only a heartbeat in the scheme of things, and it's not like I wanted to stay on in her poxy flat post-Antarctica. But on top of that, she has refused to look after my fridge—an ungenerous gesture that has me doubting myself as a judge of character. Because of my trusting nature, I've always regarded Mandy as a nice person. And in fact I have a lot to thank her for, despite everything, and will do so in a little while.

In the bathroom something rather unfortunate happens. I am a little overenthusiastic about my last slug of vodka and orange and in reaching for the glass on the shelf I knock my smartphone into the toilet. It lands with a Tiffany kind of splash, high-pitched and beaded. All I need! I dash to the kitchen to get tongs. Back in the bathroom, I fish in the toilet bowl for the phone, and as I do I think about what an amazing coincidence this is—the little phone, swallowed by the great white telephone. Despite this surprising truth hidden in the language, the reality is not so good. My Android is sodden. Once I've beached it on the basin counter, I perform an operation with a nail file. I read somewhere that smartphones can recover from a dunking as long as you don't turn them on and you dry then out quickly, so I prise open the wafer-like back of the phone. Exposed, the fine metal plate patterned with an intricate grid is strangely beautiful; the fact it is boggy with bog-water makes it appear like a tiny cemetery on a wet day, and I picture a funeral happening and almost shed a tear. Under normal circumstances, I could've dried out the phone in the sun on the windowsill or in the hot-water cupboard, but I'm an itinerant artist, so I trot back to the kitchen and get a plastic bag from the bottom drawer (Mandy is nothing if not well organised). I have no choice but to discard quite a few items on the floor (sorry, Mandy), but in the end I find the perfect small, sturdy bag, fill it with rice, and in the bathroom I drop the smartphone bits into their new short-stay, entertaining briefly an analogy about me and my temporary homes. I stow the bag in my hold-all and finish off by returning to the bathroom to mop the toilet seat and floor with scads of toilet paper. Leaving a mess for Mandy is the last thing I want to do.

Now, of course, I can't tweet or make status updates from my phone, not to mention save my draft Acknowledgements. I happen to know that Mandy keeps her camera in the hall cupboard, so I rummage through, find the old Sanyo brick and take a quick shot of Me-with-Manuscript, which I load onto my laptop. So far so good. But do you think I can make a simple post or tweet? Oh no. I discover, in a rather agonising, slo-mo kind of way as I attempt multiple, *multiple* times to log on, that I no longer have access to Mandy's WiFi. I suppose this is a follow-up to our little disagreement of the morning. I wouldn't have picked that Mandy even knew how to change the password. She's not the sharpest pencil in the box. I try to hack into Mandy's account, knowing her birthday of course and the street she grew up in. Can't. Never mind, onward. Thank goodness I'd been scribbling down these Acknowledgements with biro in a good old-fashioned notebook, otherwise they'd have gone west as well. I continue in this manner. This is what you are reading!

I'm aware that while I'm fussing with appliances both dry and wet, with cameras and selfies and internet connections or lack of, valuable time is ticking away. I'm due at the Antarctica Awards in under an hour. And there is still a rather large problem to solve.

My fridge is wedged between the dining table and the living-room door, where it has been for only a little over a year, no trouble to anyone. We've simply eaten dinner on the couch and been careful going in and out of the room. In fact, the fridge has provided a handy surface—though high in altitude—for my in-tray, not to mention its capacious shelves for my early drafts. The shelves are now empty, as I've packed the drafts in a carton marked 'The Ice Shelf drafts 1–7' and left them in the attic. Yes, they're a loss to me and undoubtedly to my future estate, but I chuckle to myself at the thought of a tenant in, say, two hundred years, if Earth is still habitable then, coming across a very lucky find and then making a breathless phone call—or perhaps apparating, because we're talking 2212—to my literary executor. The truth is, although like Gertrude Stein I 'never throw away a piece of paper upon which I have written', I can't carry my papers around with me and have nowhere of my own to store them. (Same with my clothes, which I've left in a chest of drawers in the sun-porch; I'm sure Mandy will keep them for me.) Such is the itinerant life of the artist. Perhaps that was the situation for Bach when he left a trunkful of compositions in an attic in Leipzig. I've planted other such troves around various Wellington flats I've lived in. Early drafts of *Utter and Terrible Destruction* are in a shed out back of 14B Rintoul Street, Newtown, and of course many of my papers reside in the cubbyhole at the apartment in Mount Victoria with the view over the harbour.

Even as I prepare to leave Mandy's, I have no idea what I am going to do with my fridge while I'm away in Antarctica, not to mention after I get back and am scanning the Flatmates Wanted. This scenario makes me the teensiest bit downhearted. I stand in front of the fridge, surveying its cool green flank and racking my brains, and I take a big breath (the snug dress is making me light-headed). It occurs to me that Miles might store the fridge at the apartment on a temporary basis seeing as we're still good friends, and especially seeing as I should by rights be part-owner of said apartment. Surely I should be due the space of a fridge for a few weeks? I wonder also if Mandy might relent and let me leave the fridge in her living room where it has been no trouble at all, but, given what happened when I plugged it in the day before, I don't really think so. I'm certain there's something wrong with the power box. Well, there is now, but I absolutely refute that it had anything to do with my fridge. It doesn't even use that much electricity. While I'm mulling over my dilemma, I suction open the fridge door. The shelves are empty save for one lone document, and in that moment the sway of the fridge rocking on its unstable feet causes the wodge that is *The Ice Shelf* to slide out and onto the floor in a soft flurry, like snow.

The sight of the pretty fan of pages on Mandy's dusky pink rug pulls at my heartstrings. We've been through a lot, my manuscript and me, over the last rather tumultuous year. I know what you're thinking, Reader—why do I even have a manuscript at this point? Surely *The Ice Shelf* will be the product of my trip to Antarctica? The truth is, my imagination has been running overtime even before I set foot on the icy football fields. I haven't been able to stop the sentences from pouring out of me like a renewable resource—make that a non-renewable resource, because *The Ice Shelf* is obviously a one-off. I can hear a few bleats of surprise from those of you who don't know much about the nature of creativity. You're asking, What about research? Wasn't I meant to go down to Antarctica first? Wasn't that the whole point? That I would be like the past recipients of the Antarctica Residency, the Bill Manhires, the Anne Nobles, the Gareth Farrs? Hurtle down to Antarctica, check out the whiteness and the yellow-eyed penguins, take notes in shorthand (or a few photos, in Anne's case; some noises in Gareth's), come back to EnZed, and *then* make a work of art? Which would happen to be a book in my case because I am the writer. But you're forgetting one thing, quite an important thing with a capital I. The Imagination. The sheer power of *What If?* Those words, those little guys signifying the big idea, made me surge ahead with my novel.

Rest assured, at this point I'm not under any illusions about the completeness or otherwise of *The Ice Shelf*. Far from the manuscript being finished, far from my trip being redundant, I'm going to Antarctica to do something crucial: to chase concrete significant detail. Once I've seen the way light jumps off the ice with the sun low on the horizon, tasted matchlessly cold air, felt the numbness of frozen hands, and heard the crack of a huge ice shelf falling into the sea and the whimper of a baby polar bear separated from its mother— make that the 'arp' of a seal pup, because yes, I know there are no polar bears on the Southern Polar Cap—*The Ice Shelf* will leap off the page.

Doubtless I will come back with a whole lot more thank yous to add to these Acknowledgements. For instance, the people who are there with me—the artists with whom I will go to Antarctica, the staff, the scientists; I will even, perhaps, without sounding too pompous I hope, want to thank the landscape, the ice. I'm open to the possibility that something profound could confront me down there, as I look out into white nothingness, as I perhaps lie down on a vast frozen white sheet and the little cold space inside me becomes accustomed to the cold. Is that possible? I don't know, but I do know the ice will be momentous. The frozen landscape may do—or appear to do—something transformative with time. Time will be frozen. Everything will be stopped. To be honest, I am a little afraid.

As I stand on Mandy's rug looking down at the pages scattered at my feet, I pause. Although it's getting on for twenty past five and high time I left for the awards ceremony where I will be honoured with my prize and people will applaud, I find that I am literally incapable of putting the baubles of success before art. I kneel and tenderly scoop the leaves of *The Ice Shelf* into my lap. I begin to flip fondly though the elegant, double-spaced pages I know so well.

But at this point something else distracts me. In the process of my scooping I notice a small hole in the pink rug. I am a little abashed because it looks like a cigarette hole and I'm hoping that I'm not responsible. Just the night before, there'd been a bit of a to-do about some minor scorching, and I'm anxious not to be the perpetrator of any outstanding burn issues. Tentatively, I insert my finger in the hole. The perimeter is singed black and feels crisp to the touch. I push through to the carpet underneath but it has gone, and the underlay has gone. My heart flutters while my finger continues on into nothingness—through the place where floorboards should be and into the ceiling of the flat below. I push on and on, and soon my whole hand is swallowed. It feels hot, very hot. I pull my hand out quickly and crouch down to peer into the hole. It seems that where the downstairs flat should be is fiery chaos and I think I hear a soundbite of a great multitude of people wailing.

I sit up and shake myself. My mind is leading me a merry dance, no doubt because I've had much going in my life over the past several months. But things are distinctly looking up. To summarise:

1. My settlement with Miles, although not pretty, is at least resolved.

2. My ten months at Mandy's are coming to a natural end.

3. The night of the awards ceremony stretches excitingly ahead.

4. It is the eve of my prestigious journey to Antarctica.

5. I have stopped thinking about the little warmth that is now cold.

I'm poised at a junction, some paths ending, others beginning. My heart literally leaps. I feel cleansed and joyful and I also remember my digital community of fellow writers. Is it this charged state I am in that compels me to see with new eyes the manuscript that has been my intimate friend all year? I don't know, but I do know that creativity is fickle. It turns corners, does somersaults, goes its own way, and it certainly doesn't sit around waiting for the right moment to do so. Then and there on the rug, with the fanned pages of *The Ice Shelf*, brilliant white in the glowing post-storm light, I remember Clancy's advice to me, that the manuscript was too *too*. I decide she meant it is flabby, but

I may have unwittingly soaked up a self-deprecating manner from Miles over the last almost-three years. Maybe I could rate a mention in *Cinema of Unease* after all. Rather than flabby, my novel is a bit discursive around the edges. But truth be told, I'm also slightly worried I may be unleashing something. Without further ado—all dressed up in a posh frock and finishing the last dregs of my vodka and orange which I'd forgotten about during the smartphone fiasco—I decide to carry out some judicious edits on *The Ice Shelf* to make room for the concrete significant details that I will acquire in Antarctica like extra luggage. I suppose this process is not especially new to me. I've always been the kind of writer who lets her work see the light of day only when it has been rigorously drafted. I'm probably too much of a perfectionist for my own good, and that's why I don't have the publication record of some people I could mention who fling things into the world half baked. And although it may seem a shame—a tragedy even—to cut bits out of *The Ice Shelf,* the artist in me knows it will be towards a greater good. As a writer, one needs to be a Libertarian of the page, lopping words that do not earn their keep, like so many homeless and disabled people. Not that I am like that politically, I hasten to add!

I whip out the pages that concern the protagonist finding that she has outgrown her boyfriend because she's been developing as a person whereas he has stayed still, even slid backwards, and she has embraced a new life of freedom and creativity. Pages 1–12, gone. I stuff them into the foot-operated rubbish bin in the kitchen, pushing them well down underneath polystyrene meat trays and plastic yoghurt cartons because actually, I'm a bit shy about my writing and I wouldn't want Mandy to discover my rejects.

While I'm in the kitchen, I remember that the previous night I'd put Mandy's one pair of heels (she doesn't get out much) in the freezer. Like the dress, they were a little on the small side, so I'd employed a stretching technique I found on the internet, namely to fill a Ziploc bag with water, feed it into the shoe and leave it to expand overnight in the freezer. I retrieve the shoes from the freezer and wriggle my feet into them like Cinderella #2. They're not too bad.

I still haven't solved the problem of where to stay tonight, or what to do with the fridge for that matter. As things stand, I have no choice but to take it with me, odd as it may seem to wheel a fridge through town, but I've no doubt a solution will present itself shortly; I have friends dotted about the place, and I'm confident that in the course of the evening— best scenario, on the way to the Antarctica Awards—one of them, most likely Francie in Aro Valley, will agree to house my fridge temporarily. As a last resort there's always Linda Dent, a really excellent friend who'd do anything for me. She lives in Island Bay so quite a trek tugging my handcart, and I hope it won't come to that, but at least the journey out there is reasonably flat, nothing compared with the cantilevering that's gone on vis-à-vis Mandy's fire escape and the Southeast Ridge of the fifties apartment. Suffice to say, I know I won't have too much trouble finding a short-stay for my beloved green appliance. I wheel my handcart out from where it's been propped against the fridge and announce to the room that I'm going to hell in a handcart, even though I'm going to the cold, but Antarctica is getting less cold all the time, and perhaps in the future there *will* be a little man with a pitchfork down there, in a hot, muddy Inferno, and my metaphor will resound prophetically. Manoeuvring the fridge onto the handcart takes some effort, but finally

I manage to tip the big green chunk to a 35-degree angle and reverse it from its ten-month tenure in front of the TV (there were never any good programmes on anyway). I award myself a little rest, my arms crossed over the cart handle like a roadworker on their shovel. From this position I notice the copy of *Frankenstein* that I hurled across the room back in about April is facedown where the fridge was. I recoil, reliving in a rush the horror of the monster and monstress, or at least the *idea* of her—it's a long story. But after a moment my heart calms down and my palms dry off, and I realise I don't need these feelings anymore, and actually, over the last few months, I've moved on from all that. I pick up the paperback, blow away some dust-bunnies and a couple of dead daddy longlegs and put it on the coffee table.

The lightning has stopped, the rain has cleared, and all that's left of the storm is grey clouds shredding over the western hills. I decide to stuff my regular khaki jacket into the sunroom drawers—it doesn't look good with the red dress, and I'll only be out and about for a couple of hours. By mid-evening I'll be snug as a bug at a friend's house for the night. And tomorrow—Antarctica-wear! I shoulder my hold-all (the dress makes a farting sound somewhere under the sleeve where something separates, but it's not too bad), and grasp my cart. Complete with my laptop bag containing my laptop and my slimmed-down manuscript, I manoeuvre out of Mandy's door for the last time. I spend the next twenty minutes bumping my fridge very cautiously down the fire escape, having one or two teetering close calls (especially in the heels) when steps give way, but I make it.

As I journey down, I can't help but recall the reverse trip I made, ten months earlier, coming up the hill with the fridge.

But more importantly, it reminds me that I have deep and heartfelt thanks to make to Mandy vis-à-vis the Tortuous Sex Night and beyond, as you will see.

As things turned out, I am of course deeply, *deeply* indebted to Miles and Dorothy for all that ensued following the evening of docudrama described above because once I'd escaped the shackles of the relationship, once I was *fancy free* (to quote Janet Frame's little friend), I embarked on what became a truly halcyon period of my life. In the short-term, however, being unceremoniously ejected from the apartment, I stood on the pavement that night ten months ago and considered my options.

To provide some setting: the weather conditions were not just windy but gale-force. (Wellington.) My scarf remained horizontal, like that of the Petit Prince; conversely, my spirits sank. I have to admit that on being newly single, I was flummoxed. Some people finding themselves in such a situation would simply trot off home to Mummy and Daddy where a childhood bedroom would be waiting, a frilly bed made up with an electric blanket turned on excitedly by Mummy after the phone call in anticipation of arrival, and with stuffed toys from long ago, Bimpy and Eeyore among them, still lining the pelmet. If, however, you happen to have parents who are more interested in art and substances, they may not have provided stability and continuity for you in that way. You probably do not have a twee childhood bedroom to return to every time things go awry. You are exceedingly grateful for this state of affairs because otherwise you would be a smug, self-satisfied prat. But you can't suppress the pang of despair that rises up when you realise that, having been dispatched from the apartment, you have nowhere to go but up Majoribanks Street to Mandy's flat.

I turned on my heel and began my toiling ascent of Majoribanks Street, stopping for breath several times. If anyone had cared to look out their window they would've seen a person apparently devolving—yours truly, loping up the gradient between the wooden villas, bowed down by my hold-all and my troubles, which I can tell you on that night seemed very great. But it was one o'clock in the morning, and I doubt if anyone was watching me in the throes of my devolution. In the liminal space between the fifties apartment and Mandy's flat, I was perhaps more alone than I'd ever been in my life, and that's saying something. The journey seemed to take hours and to suck me into an abyss in which anything was possible. But in fact, within ten minutes I was standing in Mandy's cracked concrete yard, exhausted but beginning to recover my good humour which had not, I'm pleased to report, strayed very far. Mandy rents the top floor of a villa, a rickety specimen, makeshift, carved up into flats, so not quite as luxurious as the fifties apartment. But did I care? Not a bit. As I stood there, breathing hard, I noticed a handcart tucked along the side of the villa, cocked outside another flat, and I filed that information for future reference. Gathering the last watts of my energy, I scaled the steps of the glorified wooden fire escape, hanging on tight in the wind, and was soon knocking on the glass door.

Eventually Mandy appeared, blinking in her mousy polar-fleece dressing gown. 'Oh, it's you,' she said—as if there could be any doubt. She opened up, and I limped through into the living room and dumped my hold-all with relief. Mandy was looking at me as if I'd stepped out of *The Woman in White* (which springs to mind), and I had to beg her for a drink, which I wouldn't normally do to *anyone*, but these were extraordinary circumstances. I mean, I'd just a few minutes ago broken up with the love of my life. I guess, to give her her due, Mandy wouldn't understand that because she is not exactly relationship material. A certain frumpiness, that's all.

Mandy didn't have much of a drinks cabinet, but I remembered a wine-dark trifle she'd made for her Book Club Christmas party, which I was invited to even though I didn't belong to Book Club (long story), so I knew there must be something in the house, a fact proven by a recce to the kitchen. Drinking a rather sticky sherry while sitting cross-legged on the pink rug, I poured out the sorry tale of the evening—the turgid sex scene, the defamatory name-calling and my eventual stately exit. Mandy was so shocked by all this (she really is a sweetie, sheltered and naïve) that I had to literally ask if I could stay. She agreed of course, and I mentioned how it would be preferable for me to have her bedroom rather than the porch because of my allergies. I should add that Mandy had been advertising her porch on Trade Me for weeks but hadn't managed to rent it despite a succession of deadpan (I imagine) interviews. I suppose Mandy isn't cool enough to attract a big awesome houseful of interesting flatmates. Lucky for me! Right now, fresh from a broken relationship, I couldn't have cared less that it was just Mandy and me; despite everything, I've always held her in the highest esteem. As I snuggled into bed, listening to the cyclone rattling the windows of the porch but feeling cosy in the bedroom, I thanked her from the bottom of my heart, and I do so again in these pages. Thank you, Mandy! I can almost hear her desultory, 'You're welcome.'

On my second night at Mandy's, a Saturday, I suggested something to her as we ate our vegetarian stir-fry in front of the TV. Mandy liked to watch the news, and then reruns of BBC mini-series about self-satisfied middle-class white

English couples and their tragic but humorous existential travails. They were up to episode something, but I had a better plan for the late-late show. Mandy wasn't too keen, but after my pointing out the ethical rightness of it, she agreed to help. One of the things I love about Mandy is that she's open to anything. At around eleven, while Mandy crashed around doing the dishes, I dialled the fifties apartment on her smartphone (she had more minutes than me). There was no answer.

'Bingo!' I called to Mandy.

'Really?' said Mandy meekly from the doorway, her hands like two starfish in red rubber gloves.

'Are you joking!' I said. I informed Mandy that this was an incredible stroke of luck. We might've gone on night after night waiting for Miles and Dorothy to be out. I had a routine all practised in the eventuality of either of them answering the phone, to do with wrong numbers, thick accents and random security checks, but none of it was necessary; we'd scored a hole in one. It also probably meant they weren't having sex, unless they were going at it in the back of a car or in the bathroom at some party, but that was unlikely given Miles's endearing sense of propriety and Dorothy's staidness. I did briefly entertain the idea that they were so busy porking in the apartment they couldn't come to the phone, but that also seemed off the radar. The more likely scenario was that sex had worn off for them licketty split, as I'd predicted. I didn't mention this analysis to Mandy, as she doesn't really get the whole sex thing. A certain purse-lipped prudishness.

I was the first to emerge from the glass doors of Mandy's flat and to drop like a spider, down, down the fire escape in the dark. I could hear Mandy clambering after me, feel her vibrations on the slats. Once on terra firma, I fetched the handcart from the side of the villa. It was good and robust with a sturdy red frame in tubular steel and firm tyres. I decided the neighbours wouldn't mind if we borrowed it for an hour.

We set off jauntily down the deserted street, our journey resounding with the downward thwack of our footsteps and the bouncy rumble of the cart. We passed the odd house with a minor party going on, music thumping, and this added to the sense of excitement. I have to say, on that trip down the hill in the dark with Mandy and cart in tow, I felt more revved up than I'd ever been. I began to hurtle faster and faster down Majoribanks Street until I was running, almost out of control, as if I might surge with momentum through Courtenay Place and out into the harbour. But I managed to come to a screeching halt in the eerie shadow of the apartment building.

As I stood catching my breath, with cart and Mandy piled up behind me, I remembered something very unfortunate and experienced a plummet in mood: I no longer had the keys to the former chez nous because of course Dorothy had weasled them from me. When I informed Mandy, I must say I expected a show of solidarity. I thought Mandy and I, partners in crime, would stomp around on the corner blowing off steam then hunker down on the curb, chins cupped, thinking caps on, and we'd have a no-holds-barred brainstorm about how to go forward. I suppose I'm idealistic in nature, and I expect other people to be the same, mistakenly as it turned out. Because what I saw on Mandy's face, caught as it was in an octagon of unaccustomed light, was not solidarity, not resolve, but relief. Clearly, for Mandy, the project stopped here. If I'd thought for even a second of giving up because of one teensy obstacle, the sight of Mandy's lineny, ironed-out features were all the encouragement I needed *not* to be swayed from my mission. I suppose being brought up in a creative environment among artists and thinkers has an effect. 'Risk, risk anything!' Katherine Mansfield wrote. Without further ado I took off across the courtyard clattering the cart behind me, past the row of garages, towards the entrance to the building. Glancing back I saw Mandy step cautiously onto the concrete tiles.

I pulled the cart up the Southeast Ridge. In the daytime the steps were a dull pink, but in this light everything was dead grey, plus it was a little chilly, but I was full of beans, twisting up and up with Mandy following a couple of flights below. When I reached the narrow landing that ran along the back of the building linking all the apartments on the fourth floor, I gripped the cart and waited for Mandy to join me. On the way along the balcony, we did make a bit of a racket with Mandy's blundering footsteps, and I suppose me banging the cart into a couple of clothes racks and peg baskets didn't help, but then trust Mandy to trip on a flowerpot and go kersplat. I shushed her wail and groaned inwardly. We were goners. But you know what? Nothing. Not a peep. I guess all the Radio New Zealand and art gallery types who lived in the building were down in the trendy bars of Courtenay Place swilling martinis and dissing Capitalism—it being Saturday night. The few oldies who'd been resident since before the apartments were fashionable would've turned off their hearing aids hours before. A warm, pleased feeling expanded inside me, and I continued on. When I knew we'd reached the very apartment that would've been, should've been, half mine but for a technicality involving spurious matrimonial laws and a leap year, I stopped and whispered to Mandy that this was it.

Mandy flailed, tangling with a doormat or something. 'What?' she said loudly. Then, at my pūkana: 'Oh.' I put my finger to my lips in an exaggerated manner.

Through the kitchen window I could see, deep inside the apartment, the glow of the hall lamp which Miles always left on to deter burglars. I mouthed this ironic information to Mandy, but instead of seeing the funny side she starting wittering on about being arrested and complaining about her bleeding shin needing stitches. I hissed at her to pipe down or someone *would* call the fuzz. Dropping to one knee, I patted around near the doorstep. I suppressed a yelp as I encountered one of the more ferocious specimens of Miles's OCD collection of miniature cacti, which he had growing in tiny terracotta pots. Other pots rolled around on the balcony. When I had one tiny terracotta receptacle grasped securely in my fist, I took aim and walloped a small pane of glass in the back door. At the tinkling noise, Mandy and I froze— but, once again, nothing. Three cheers for old deaf people, for meandering conversations about dialectical materialism in the clubs of Courtenay Place. Feeling a renewed sense of thrill, I reached through the window—gingerly, to avoid shards of glass—and rotated the key in the lock. It opened like a charm.

As I stepped into the familiar tiled kitchen, a chill ran up my spine and I hesitated. The flat was quiet as the grave; the high-gloss cupboards gleamed like stainless steel in the moonlight. I felt as if a net had dropped over me—a heaviness, a tightness. I know it's ridiculous, but a sob fought its way up from my chest like a balloon. I must've made some kind of noise because I could hear Mandy way off in the distance, it seemed, bleating, 'What? What?' Part of me wanted to turn around and run back along the balcony, not looking back, and to never set foot in the apartment again. But I'm made of sterner stuff. I had business to do. I shook myself—literally—and said (inwardly), Janice, don't be such a sook. I beckoned Mandy. Her baleful face trembled across the doorstep like a Thunderbird.

'And bring the cart!' I hissed.

Honestly.

Mandy hurried back out. I opened the fridge and phosphorescence poured out, illuminating the kitchen I knew so well, but I was no longer deterred by sentimental thoughts. I went hell for leather transferring waxed paper packages and pickle jars to the table. Mandy manoeuvered the cart wheels through the doorway and began to help in lacklustre fashion. At one point I rescued a quarter-full bottle of vermouth, of which I knew not the origin, from anonymity among the forest of bottles and quaffed a few mouthfuls, just to keep warm really. Mandy is traditionally a wowser about these things, but, lo and behold, she put out her hand for the bottle. We polished it off standing in the moony atmosphere. She wasn't so bad, Mandy—*isn't* so bad. If I've depicted her in any way whatsoever in these pages as wet, cautious and generally lacking in spark, that's not what I intend. Mandy is actually kick-ass, in her own way. As we passed the vermouth bottle back and forth in the kitchen in preparation for our descent with the fridge, we started to giggle. Mandy's face went pink. The sob that had been lurking in my windpipe since we came in was escorted off the premises.

Mandy and I ping-ponged between fridge and table with what must have been Dorothy's special cheeses and her jars of sundried tomatoes until the shelves were empty. I yanked on the power cord and the fridge motor grumbled to a stop like a tired animal. With a bit of oofing and huffing, we hefted the fridge onto the cart, then Mandy, still giggling, held the back door open while I made a few attempts at wheeling the fridge through. Unfortunately I took a chunk of doorframe with me on the way out. In the weeks to come, I began to think of the gash on the side of my fridge and the corresponding bite in the green paintwork as symbolic of, well, a lot of things. Suffice to say at this point, I needed to make the most of that gash because it was all I was ever going to get out of the apartment.

We had a pretty clear run whizzing back along the balcony, as most of the neighbours' paraphernalia had been knocked over on the way in, but the Southeast Ridge was a bit of a challenge. I lowered the fridge, bump, bump, bump, down the first flight. Mandy was positioned just underneath in case it toppled, but I was glad that didn't happen because, to be honest, I don't know if she would've had much of a chance if a five-foot fridge had come chonking down on top of her. I had a letter to Mandy's mother composed in my head—'a truer friend there never was, it was mercifully quick, she didn't suffer'. Luckily I never needed to write that letter. Another flight of steps and we were across the courtyard then bouncing back up Majoribanks Street, staunching our laughter because of the late hour.

Near the top of the hill where it's steepest, the going got tough and the cart and fridge, having no purchase, felt as if they were in danger of hurtling back down the slope like a runaway train. We needed a new plan of action; while I wedged the cart still with my back, Mandy galumphed the fridge onto the footpath and together we walked it, like a well-rounded character in a novel, up the remainder of the incline. Mandy went back down for the cart. Outside her villa, as we caught our breath, Mandy came up with the ludicrous suggestion that we store the fridge in the shed around the back. Mandy's innocence is actually what I love about her. I pointed out, hello, thieves, and it sort of came out that Mandy didn't want the fridge in her flat. I got a little bit upset, which I'm not proud of.

We managed to lollop it onto the first step of the fire escape and thereafter to ease it up step by step. The fire escape is rather rickety, and a couple of planks gave out under the fridge's weight; in fact we almost lost it once or twice. There was much giggling and shooshing and pausing for breath, I can tell you. What a hoot. At one point, when we were trying to turn one of the bends in the steps, we got stuck for so long it seemed as though we would need to spend the night on the fire escape. But then we had a final surge and hey presto, the fridge was on the upper landing.

Once inside the flat we collapsed on the living-room rug in gales of laughter. I went to the kitchen for the last of the sherry to celebrate. When I came back Mandy was trying to wedge the fridge between door and table. I lay back down on the rug, gazing at its olivey flank and musing on how it was green, but not *Green*. But hey, I didn't have a car and still don't. I don't fly back and forth to Menton and Berlin on literary jaunts. I think I can allow myself a few fluorocarbons.

And anyway, it wasn't even plugged in. And Mandy's living room was where it stayed for several months until, as you know, the night of the Antarctica Awards.

Reader, before I thank the people involved in the rather complicated night of the awards, I would like to go back to the beginning. As I write these Acknowledgements, I'm realising more and more just how much I've been blessed, and how this good luck, this good fortune, the workings of fate, serendipity, however you want to look at it, has shaped me as a writer and as a person. Perhaps I will discover the source of my good fortune if I start at the year dot.

I thank of course, profoundly, my parents, Sorrell and Harry, for a lifetime of unstinting love and support. I've been incredibly fortunate. Sorrell and Harry are characters, both of them, tell-it-how-it-is hard cases. Phew, Sorrell and Harry never ceased to provide fertile ground in which a child's imagination could grow strong and free. I have no doubt whatsoever that I would not be where I am today without them. As teachers, as role models, they've been the best parents a writer could possibly have. I don't think I'm giving anything away when I say that in the tight-knit community of my childhood—which got slightly looser as time went on, like knitting done on those big wooden needles they used in the seventies, indeed could perhaps best be described in the end as finger-knitting—these two big personalities were well known for their colourful antics. Never a dull moment. They were both artists: Harry a sculptor, and Sorrell a painter, I think. To grow up in such a stimulating atmosphere is truly extending to the creative mind. At times, the excitement was so great that all I could do was cower in my room and write my lisping early prose.

I would like to thank my mother, Sorrell, for up and leaving my father, Harry, on Christmas Eve 1987, and for taking me, aged seven, with her. Without this melodramatic move, which occasioned me to embark on a rollercoaster ride of hippy schools, scungy flats and hairy stepfathers, plus a stepmother, I wouldn't have learned key lessons about narrative. My knowledge of subplot was further extended when, five years later, Sorrell dumped me back with Harry and his new wife, Nico.

The night Sorrell packed her bags was the end of a very long, warm Christmas Eve. Remember, this is the Southern Hemisphere, so Christmas comes in summer, when hay is dried and tethered, as they say, although not in the middle of Wellington where the fake snow shone brilliantly on the trees. I remember I was excited about the presents I might get from Santa, which would appear under said tree that night. My natural optimism was apparent even at that age. The tree had been leaning against the back door for three days. There'd been some discussion, if I remember rightly, about who should put the tree in a pot with bricks to make it stand upright. Sorrell said she did enough around this fucking place without starting on the tree, and Harry said it wasn't his idea to have a tree in the first place and if Sorrell wanted a tree she should do the fucking tree. But I just knew that the tree would be up by Christmas.

I went next door to my friend Mandy's place—yes, we go way back, Mandy and me. Their tree smelt evocatively of a European forest of the kind we don't have in temperate New Zealand. It smelt of Christmas, and each branch sparkled with a decoration that could tell a story. Sometimes Mandy would pore over the tree, saying, 'And this glass angel was from Aunty Petty, and this silver reindeer was from Grandma Rose,' in what some people might think a sickening manner, but I never did. I filled my asthmatic lungs (not diagnosed, but my attacks have proved useful in writing near-death scenes) with the scent of the tree and envisaged how when I got back home our own tree would be standing tall in its pot all ready to decorate with the as-yet-unopened box of Woolworths baubles. But I soon forgot about it, as Mandy and her mother and I, having finished the tree, began to decorate their family Christmas cake with glass figurines—a tiny orchestra of angels playing flutes and trumpets and violins led by a tiny glass conductor. There was a fat glass Santa, and the glass Christmas tree had pride of place in the middle of the cake. We went delicately, handling the fragile ornaments with our fat little fingers, laughing and listening to carols on the radio. When we'd finished the cake, Mandy's mother made us chocolate milk and we knelt under the tree and shook the presents and speculated as to what each one was.

Then Mandy's mother said maybe I should go home, seeing I didn't actually live at their house. She must've known how it was at our place, with my parents being artistic— sound reverberated through the walls of those wooden houses—and I am ever-grateful to her for her tactful non-intervention. I would've been so embarrassed if she'd alerted social services to my predicament, which likely would have meant a predictable, safe, secure childhood for me with loving foster parents. I would certainly not be the writer I am today if a concerned bystander had intervened. These Acknowledgements are the perfect opportunity to thank Mandy's mother for her kindness all those years ago, but she is now ten years into a continuous game of bowls on the lawn of a brick-and-tile retirement village in Tauranga (if Mandy's accounts are anything to go by, reading between the lines), a game which goes on till death, and I'm not sure she will get around to reading *The Ice Shelf.* Who cares? I certainly don't. I don't expect everybody to read my oeuvre; that would be a very conceited ideal. But if you're out there, Mandy's mother, moving from section to section of the water-guzzling leisure lawn and contributing to humanity with the subtle bias of your delivery, thank you from the bottom of my heart, for telling me, on that Christmas Eve when I was seven years old, to Go Home. I went home, through your dinky white picket gate, over our gate which had always lain flat on the ground and through the front door because the back door was unavailable on account of the tree.

I paused in the dark passage. There was an argument going on, but it would soon be Christmas and the tree would be up and Santa would come. It's true that the tree itself wasn't up yet, but Sorrell's familiar cigar-shape was planted in the middle of the kitchen/living room (a wall had been knocked out once for one of Harry's art projects and you could see its interesting history), her hair mussed up, face all blotchy. She was saying something like, 'Trust me to choose a miserable fucking dopehead loser who doesn't even like Christmas.' I couldn't quite catch it. But I did hear Harry, loud and clear, bellowing, 'I like Christmas well enough, I just don't like it your way you fucking cunt.' He was sprawled in his chair in front of the TV news. Sorrell and Harry kept themselves well informed about the world. I had reasonable general knowledge (not to blow my own trumpet) and always did well in general knowledge quizzes at school, well, at several of the schools I went to. Sorrell, from the middle of the kitchen, told Harry that she knew how he liked Christmas: 'You like it off your fucking face.' Harry snorted and parried wittily with, 'You like it out of your tree, yes, out of your motherfucking tree!' The exchange went back and forth some more. I'm very lucky that Sorrell and Harry were walking lexicons of colourful expressions; it is to them that I attribute my love of language.

Sorrell went over to Harry's chair and stood touching it with her pale-jeaned knees wishing to any kind of god you could think of that she'd never met him. Harry peered up at her with the blinking innocence he always wore and told her she'd taken the words right out of his mouth. Sorrell turned to me and I watched through the doorway her brown eyes go misty in their kidney-dark sockets, her T-shirt twist tighter over her pouchy stomach.

'Just look at him,' she said, spitting a bit, 'the artist! Promise me one thing.' Sorrell looked at me from under her brow and waited for the reply.

'What?' I murmured, fearful of what I was signing up for.

'Promise me you'll never marry a piss-artist like him.' She whirled back to Harry, bent down and pushed him on the chest pathetically.

Harry rumbled from deep in his chair. Sorrell pushed him again and he laughed louder. 'Fuck you fuck you fuck you,' or something similar was coming from under Sorrell's breath, I couldn't quite catch it. I just hoped we'd do the tree soon. Suddenly Harry rose from his chair like a phoenix from the ashes. I've always had an interest in Classics, which has informed my writing on a really deep level. I'm a fan of Anne Carson and James Joyce. Harry swatted Sorrell across the face. She screamed and staggered backwards but recovered against the dining table. He took a step forward and punched her hard in the mouth, and this time she fell, hitting her head on the table on the way down. Blood trickled from her lip onto the rag rug. Sorrell told me in an urgent but muffled voice to call the police. I stood frozen in the doorway. The phone was in the kitchen and I'd have to tiptoe over her to get to it. Harry said not to be a freaking drama queen, which meant not to call the cops. I knew their number. I looked at Sorrell. 'Call the cops,' she said into the rug. I looked at Harry. He had his arms folded and was watching a news item. Sorrell unwound off the floor and stumped into the bathroom. Water tinkled, a lovely sound. I thought one or other of them might be going to put the tree in its bucket now that peace was restored, but unfortunately, no; the tree was forgotten.

I can't remember how I moved from the doorway, but I must've eventually gone into my room and done some writing, just childish stuff, you know, juvenilia, my little poems which are now stored in a blue foolscap filing box marked JUVENILIA with my papers in the basement at 5 McKinley Cres, Brooklyn. Later that evening I ate a bag of liquorice allsorts. I thought someone might put the tree in a bucket, especially after wine had been poured (I'd heard the pissing squirt from the box) and everyone seemed to have cheered up, and Sorrell had told Harry he'd never loved her. She was in a foetal position on the beanbag. He'd never loved her, she said, not for one fucking second. Harry, who was watching a documentary about people with strange sexual fetishes, said at least she'd got one thing right. Sorrell craned her head up from the beanbag, which was reddish and corduroy and smelt like vomit. I never sat in it, but I could describe to you using concrete significant details and a metaphor that a rust-coloured vomity corduroy beanbag is like a pub, it's like an afternoon in a pub. Harry repeated what he'd said. Sorrell struggled up, all limbs, and sidled up to Harry. I would never have guessed she was such a good spitter. Her spit flew right into his face, bullseye. She said she was leaving. Harry wiped his face on his sleeve.

'Can't wait,' he said, looking mild and inoffensive. He always had that baby-faced look, no matter what.

Sorrell burst into wild tears and ran about the room scooping things up and stuffing them into a plastic bag. Over her shoulder she told me to pack. When I just stood there, she yelled, 'Go on, pack a fucking bag!'

I went into my bedroom and stuffed my other pair of jeans, my three T-shirts and some underpants and socks into my schoolbag. A flare of holiday excitement burned in my chest. We were going away. From various parts of the house, I could hear Sorrell's sobs rushing up the scale. When I went back into the kitchen Harry was snoring peacefully in his chair. Sorrell appeared in the doorway. She looked at Harry and went over to him. She seemed on the verge of doing something to him but didn't.

Sorrell backed the Holden off the front lawn in a puff of acrid smoke, and we drove somewhat erratically (but exhilaratingly) to her friend Poppy's place, an old villa jammed up against the side of a damp, ferny hill in Newtown. Poppy greeted Sorrell in a tattered pink silk evening gown through which a few bones protruded.

'*Finally*,' she said, wincing through her cigarette, 'finally. You're too good for him, darling, an educated woman like yourself.'

The passage smelt of mould and was wide as a motorway. Rooms opened off either side with acres of floorboard and heavy brocade curtains bunched on the floor like the trousers of someone sitting on a toilet. I followed Sorrell clomping in her cowboy boots, who followed Poppy swaying in her stiletto sandals, and even at my tender age I knew Poppy had some kind of *je ne sais quoi*. Sorrell had once told me that Poppy inherited style from her mother, along with the villa; her mother had been an actress. Poppy was telling Sorrell over her shoulder that this visit was amazingly serendipitous because she, Poppy, had just that moment been wondering what to do with the evening. In the big bay-windowed living room, she turned and flicked her opalescent nails over her gown by way of evidence and mouthed soulfully, 'And then you turn up.' Poppy never acknowledged my existence, but I knew I was lucky to know her. With her cigarette holder, her vintage clothes (her dead mother's apparently), her wobbling walk, and her clinking gin and tonics which she clutched passionately in a surprisingly old-looking hand until they ran out, she exuded sophistication. When the gin and tonics did run out, there was the most inventive stream of curses you've ever heard, and Poppy resigned herself to the wine-box.

That evening I crouched on the floor and ate fish and chips while Sorrell and Poppy rearranged themselves restlessly on one of the big moquette couches in front of the ornately tiled fireplace (empty because it was summer) and drank the wine-box flat. Sorrell talked on and on about what a nightmare Harry was, and Poppy said, 'I know, I know, oh I know. Live here, darling, live here with me, I've always told you that.' Actually there was a little fire at one point—Poppy's cigarette dangling on a polyester cushion—which Sorrell put out briskly with my glass of water. When the wine-box innard had gone like a collapsed lung, we all went to bed. I slept in a big room with a red bedspread and pillows and red brocade curtains through which a streetlight glowed. I was reminded of the Red Room in *Jane Eyre* and I was, like Jane, terrified of the red, shifting, coal-like shadows, and also of the strange creaks that resounded along the floorboards in the passage and some strange, cat-like moaning and yowling that went on and on into the night. I sat cuddling my knees because I had nothing else to cuddle. But I'm grateful for the experience because I think it was where I further developed my sense of the Gothic, so useful when writing New Zealand literature.

On Christmas morning, or it might've been the afternoon, I was wandering up and down the long, hollow passage listening to my stomach grumbling and running my fingers along the textured wallpaper when the door to one of the bedrooms opened onto the perpetual night of black-out curtains, and Poppy peered out. She seemed shocked to see me, as if she'd forgotten I was in the house, and we stared at each other for a few seconds until Sorrell, wearing the pink satin robe Poppy had been in the night before but incongruously filling it out, pushed past. She pecked the top of my head on the way to the kitchen.

'Happy Christmas, Monster.' This was Sorrell's pet name for me, a term of endearment I look back on fondly. When Sorrell called me Monster, I knew things were looking up.

Midway through Sorrell and Poppy drinking their wake-me-up tea a bit morosely on the couch, Sorrell clapped her hand to her forehead. 'Stupid me, I've left your presents at the house!'

I looked up from the etching I'd been making in the carpet. Presents, plural? That's what she'd said. I never got to find out if it was true—although I'm sure it was as Sorrell always had the drinker's scrupulous honesty—because after a debate with Poppy, during which I carried on making indentations in the carpet, Sorrell decided not to go back and get the presents because she might encounter *him*. How glad I am that she didn't. It's not like Sorrell was blowing Santa's cover; I already knew he didn't exist. I'd worked that out as I'd sat in the bay window all morning on my own, tracing with my feet the sun's journey across the room. If Santa were real, I reasoned, he would've known somehow that I was spending Christmas Eve at Poppy's and not at our own little house. He would've known there was a girl waiting for her presents in a big bed in a strange red room in a creaking villa with a chimney in Newtown. So there was no problem whatsoever with the Barthian death of Santa, he had to go sometime. What I'm so grateful for is the lesson in non-materialism that I learned that Christmas, a lesson so essential for a writer. I don't think I ever could've produced *The Ice Shelf* if I'd been one of those children who gets everything, who is given, you know, one or two presents on Christmas morning and is allowed the indulgence of pretending to believe in Santa past the age of seven, who leaves a bottle of ginger-beer out for the jolly man and carrots for his reindeer, who looks up at the Christmas tree (in its pot, with its baubles) with shining eyes and a heart full to bursting with excitement. I have Sorrell to thank for the fact that I was never one of those children. Being such a child would just ruin you. You'd be one of those people with a sense of entitlement the size of Belgium. Thank you, Sorrell! I'd go so far as to say that experience was the best Christmas present I ever had.

From that Christmas on, Sorrell and I lived in a succession of flats around Wellington. All our possessions could fit in the Holden—a couple of squab mattresses, a vinyl-smelling suitcase of clothes and towels, a box of kitchen stuff, and a little cube of a TV. It was fine, really. We didn't have a fridge, but aside from that, it was freeing to be so portable. Sorrell wasn't great at keeping up with the rent, so we'd pack up and leave in the middle of the night, giggling sometimes— it just depended. I'd have a few days' holiday then turn up as the new girl at some foreign-seeming primary school. Sometimes there was no money to fill the tank (the Holden was a gas guzzler) and we'd wait it out, not answering the door, poised to do a runner as soon as the money came through. Sorrell was on a sickness benefit. Over the next few years, moving from place to place, each more unsuitable than the last, I was like the protagonist in *Annie and Moon*, without the cat. I could've written *Annie and Moon* if I'd ever had a cat. As it was, I could only have written *Annie and*. That title, its incomplete sentence, reflects poignantly (isn't language wonderful?) my loneliness, my poverty, my disrupted education. I went to Ridgeway School, Newtown School, Island Bay School, Clyde Quay School, and so on. I think this is why I write crots—discontinuous narratives— and so, in the end I'm grateful for being dragged from pillar to post. I also had the advantage of getting to know a spectacular stepfather, Michael, whom I will call Michael the First (there was another Michael later) and will thank for his input in due course.

After what seemed like a year at Poppy's, but it can't have been more than a few weeks because it was the end of the long summer holidays, things came to a head over a wine bladder. It was one of those long summer twilights when the air is pink and the flowers glow like lanterns in the last of the sun, when Poppy and Sorrell began a raging fight. I listened from my red room. I was reading *Valley of the Dolls*, which constituted Poppy's book collection. That was the excellent thing about living there that summer, actually. There was nothing to do and no one to talk to, so I read *Valley of the Dolls* five times. Eleanor Catton has said that one of the best things for a writer is to read books over and over, so in terms of credentials, I was doing the reqs—not that I'm claiming any great Booker-winning abilities for myself, I hasten to add. I was up to the part in *Valley* where Neely comes to Jennifer's funeral after Jennifer has committed suicide rather than have a double mastectomy and Neely stays with Anne and loses the ability to sing for psychological reasons when I heard, 'Are you sure that's the last of the wine, Poppy?'

And this was to prove portentous, given we were on the cusp of our own trip.

The fight that ensued laid down the template for most if not all the major scenes of conflict in my fiction, and, as I'm sure you know, conflict is at the heart of any story. It's true that I'd been exposed to a rich trove of conflict up to this point, but the evening of the Fight Between Sorrell and Poppy was different. Sorrell and Harry's fights had been haphazard in structure—not that that was necessarily a negative; I developed a deep understanding of and love for stream-of-consciousness—but Sorrell and Poppy fought with a formal elegance that was breathtaking. From that early age, I understood about escalation. A line of dialogue such as, 'Are you sure that's the last of the wine, Poppy?', uttered in a reasonable and modulated voice, gets rather louder on the second iteration. The third try is becoming tetchy. Soon after, there is shouting, screeching and name-calling. I abandoned Neely and came out into the living room. Sorrell and Poppy were facing each other, each crimson with rage. With perfectly judged timing, they erupted into scratching, swatting and hair-pulling. They toppled in a dramatic two-body crash onto the carpet, where the action continued with an almighty tussle involving throttling and punching. At this climactic juncture, one might truly fear for the participants' safety.

Of course from the point in time at which I am writing, I know the outcome of the fight, but as things developed that night, I did not know. I watched events unfold before me, certain there would be a death. I hoped it would not be Sorrell. I loved Sorrell desperately. I certainly loved Sorrell more than Poppy, and if one of them had to die, I prayed to some god or other—knowing even at that young age that this wasn't a very ethical prayer—that Poppy would be the one to croak. Even though I'd at times fantasised about being adopted by, for instance, Mandy's family next door, or some lovely family with an orderly house, dinnertimes, and a dog, as I watched Sorrell lying on the carpet with Poppy's hands fastened around her throat I wanted passionately for Sorrell to remain my mother. But Sorrell's face was going the colour of pomegranates while her fingers, embedded in Poppy's dark hair, were knotted like root ginger.

From the sidelines I wrung my hands.

Suddenly the two of them went slack and lay on the carpet, lifeless and lumpy, and I thought they were both dead. I froze quickly from neck to toe the way ice progresses in a disaster movie. However, my panic was short-lived because in a moment it became apparent that they weren't dead; rather, by silent agreement they had called a truce. Sorrell struggled to her feet and brushed herself off. Poppy looked up at me from the floor, her face bloody, her collar ripped. 'What do you think you're looking at?' she snarled. At the time, I thought the question a trifle unfair, and also that Sorrell didn't defend me, standing there with her hair askew, her ear bleeding— something like 'give the kid a break' or 'shut the fuck up you nasty cow'. But in retrospect, I see the wisdom of it. If she had stuck up for me, I don't think I would have developed my affinity with the abject, so I am grateful to both Sorrell and Poppy because the plight of the basest creature has become a strong element in my fiction. Keri Hulme has done this too, not that I'm equating myself with the brilliant Keri, I hasten to add. There's an excellent essay by Janet Wilson on 'the abject' in *the bone people* that could just as well be about *Utter and Terrible Destruction* and probably would've been, only I hadn't written it then.

Sorrell stomped barefoot along the passage and into the bedroom, hurling the door shut behind her. I followed timidly—not wanting to be left alone with the fabulous but slightly intimidating Poppy—in time to see the door bounce open a little on impact and for one of the panels to crack. Through the sliver of the ajar door I watched Sorrell pack her bag with athletic fury. I was a fast learner; I went to the red room and packed my own bag.

Ten minutes later, I found myself being flung against the passenger door of the Holden as Sorrell reversed at speed from the parking pad outside the villa. We drove through the dark suburban streets, desolate at this time of night, and ended up sleeping in the car under some pine trees on a lonely road.

Bruise-like red-mauve clouds part raggedly as I loop my way—a bit tremulous in Mandy's heels, and negotiating the fridge on its cart—through the grounds of Parliament to the National Library and the Antarctica Awards. Against the bashed-up backdrop, trees and shrubs gather blackly and the grey buildings of the old Parliament are stern and upright like Edwardian gentlemen. Halfway across the manicured gardens, I rest on the steps of the Beehive but am moved on by a security guard with a big moustache and a chip on his shoulder the size of Belgium. I amble down the slope and find a bench to sit on at the edge of a fine lawn. The buoyancy I felt at Mandy's has deserted me and my mood takes a sudden, gull-like descent—perhaps because my friend Francie in Aro Valley who I was sure would look after my fridge while I was transitional voted *No* on the doorstep of her downstairs flat—but more likely it's simply that I've had a lot on my plate recently. I look out from my bench. The grounds of Parliament have taken on an abysmal

Gothicism in the dirty ambience. Not being one to wallow, I open my laptop bag and pull *The Ice Shelf* unceremoniously from it.

Even at the time, I find it ironic to be shunted along by a lackey of the state on my way to the very library where no doubt the manuscript I have in my hands will be housed in future along with other national literary treasures. If I crane my neck I can glimpse, nestled in the background between Parliament buildings and the Beehive, the old Turnbull Library, the cute brick English-looking two-storey house on Bowen Street that belonged to Alexander Turnbull, book collector and instigator of the archive. The Turnbull collection is now housed in the National Library building, the venue of tonight's ceremony, having outgrown the original Turnbull House. Plus the building would be an earthquake risk, whereas the new National Library sits on a slab of state-of-the-art earthquake-proof rubber. But safeguards for posterity are none of my concern. I just get on with it and let future generations deal with all that. As I perch on the bench in Parliament grounds, the pages of *The Ice Shelf* flutter in the ubiquitous wind. I lick my finger and scamper humidly through the text and after a few moments of flurry I find what I am looking for. Like a gardener coming upon Oxalis, I subtract a melodramatic subplot about a crazy, self-centred baby boomer called S who thinks the world owes her a living, and her high-octane relationship with an anorexic viper called P. Gone, just like that.

From force of habit, I am about to slide my recent *Ice Shelf* offcut into one of the concertina-like pockets of my laptop bag when I stop. Things need to change.

Let me describe here one of my favourite sites in the world: my laptop bag. Black vinyl, labyrinthine, well-worn, this bag alone would be of great interest to the Turnbull Library. For several years I've been in the practice of stuffing all and sundry—drafts, notes, tickets, letters—into its wasteland. My laptop bag is my personal Limbo; like unbaptised babies and philosophers, some papers get stuck there forever. It occurs to me that if I continue with the process of editing *The Ice Shelf*, I am going to accumulate a substantial bundle, that is to say a shit-load of discarded text. I'm also going to be *on the road*. While I could continue to harbour these off-cuts and at some future date store them in an attic, *à la* J.S. Bach, I am already quite burdened with possessions—my Antarctica hold-all, my fridge, my laptop, not to mention the extant pages of my manuscript. There on the bench in the diffuse post-storm light, I experience another shift in consciousness apropos *The Ice Shelf*, and this one really is profound. As outlined above, I've always been a meticulous archivist of my work, but now, in an incredible reversal, I decide that I will *not* keep past drafts of *The Ice Shelf*. With this novel, I'll be ruthless. I will dispose of all my edits completely. Though this might seem shocking, even violent, I am seized with a sense of rightness about this decision. True, the Turnbull Library will never take delivery of my rejects, but the draft that remains will have—without sounding too pompous, I hope—purity on a scale I've never achieved before. At the end of the process, I will transfer the edits to the complete file which I have, of course, on my laptop. *The Ice Shelf* will be the novel with one, single, pristine final draft. *The Ice Shelf* will be like the life we are striving for.

Looking up from the bench after this revelation, I see that I am right next to the statue of King Dick, Premier Richard Seddon, who around the turn of the century (the previous century) solidified the colonial state. He is big and brassy and holds his hand aloft as if to say, 'We're over here!' in case no one had noticed the little nation at the bottom of the world. A few metres from him, beside a bed of bright red cannas, a drain makes a phlegmatic gurgle as if clearing its throat shyly to get my attention. No doubt the downpour earlier has made a river of the city waterways.

Without further ado, I hobble over to the drain (I'm somewhat hog-tied by my heels sinking into the soggy lawn) and file my edits about S and P between its russet bars. The pages funnel down into the oily rainbow-water where, despite the swift current, they lurk greasily. I hope they won't cause a blockage; I'd hate to think of sewage backing up in the grounds of Parliament on my account, even if it is for a good cause.

The really excellent thing about writing discontinuous narrative is that bits come away cleanly from the text, for the most part. There might be a stray reference left behind in another crot, the odd snippet of cause and effect caused by S getting back together with P multiple times, but those will be picked up by the blue pencil of Tree Murphy (who will be thanked later).

Feeling an incredible sense of lightness now that S and P's combined weight is gone from the text (not that P's scrawny frame contributed much heft), I pick myself up and skip, as much as I am able while shouldering a hold-all and a laptop bag and pushing a fridge over the lawn in three-inch heels, towards the National Library.

Of course I wouldn't have been within cooee of an awards ceremony if it had not been for the next phase of my childhood. I was summarily shipped off to live with Harry because Sorrell appeared to have got sick of me, judging by the drunken evenings, the missed meals and the general neglect to the point of my head becoming a nit farm. (For evidence see a note home from my teacher Miss McEntee, c.1988, housed in the green filebox, hall cupboard, 15 Stafford Street, Mount Victoria.) Not that I have any recriminations or bitterness whatsoever towards Sorrell. On the contrary, I count myself lucky to have had a mother who valued herself. How glad I am that I wasn't cursed with one of those sad-sack mothers with low self-esteem who make themselves a slave to their children's every whim— you know, driving them to Brownies and sports games, encouraging them with their homework, giving them lunch money, taking them on holiday or to one lousy movie during winter break. Luckily, I got to see at close range how it is to really Be Yourself: to sleep—heck!—all day if you feel like it; dispatch your current lover after a screaming fight; pour yourself a stiff gin and tonic mid-afternoon and gaze moodily out the window while creating brilliant rhetorical diatribes about how life has mistreated you. I am absolutely certain that I would not be the creative person I am today if Sorrell hadn't insisted on not just the odd evening to herself, not just the occasional weekend, but a year—yes, a solid year—of freedom. Hence me being pushed, at the age of twelve, onto a train at Wellington Railway Station with all my worldly possessions, not that they amounted to much, thank goodness, or I would've ended up a materialist, and being told by Sorrell to get off at Taihape, while Poppy, with whom she was *giving it another go*, smoked and turned away on the platform. As I was kissed on the cheek and told, 'Chin up, Monster,' I must've looked a bit like one of those interesting children being evacuated during World War II, with my hand-me-down coat, my battered suitcase and my anxious frown.

That was how I came to the commune Hoki Aroha.

Harry would be waiting on the station platform to meet me. At least, that was what Sorrell had said, but to be fair she did add as an aside to the giggling Poppy, 'But don't be surprised if the dweeb isn't on time.' He wasn't. I perched on a bench in the elegant waiting room which only slightly smelt of pee and clutched my suitcase. They really are perfections of design, those provincial New Zealand railways stations, and I had time to analyse in detail the cream colonial weatherboards, the red facings, the glorious curve of the veranda struts and their decorative iron filigree. I also observed the station cat—I imagine in the same way Ted Hughes watched animals as a child. I watched closely as it strutted many times up and down the platform. Like Ted Hughes, I could write an animal poem, a poem about the lanky shoulder joints of a cat, its plush one-piece, its urbane air.

When the light was beginning to fade, a man dressed in navy blue who was noisily locking doors frowned at me and disappeared into an office. I could hear him making a phone call and before long I found myself in the back of a police car. Talk about exciting; I'd always wanted to ride with Mr Plod. Beside me was a kindly female officer dressed a little like Miss Trunchbull from *Matilda*. We were on our way to the lock-up. But I didn't spend the night in the cells, and I wasn't the least bit traumatised to arrive at a brick shithouse in the middle of nowhere with a couple of sour-faced uniforms. I simply sat on the bench in the foyer of the little drunk-tank, staring balefully into the middle distance while evening came on. A dorky constable in a varnished cubicle eyed me worriedly. And in any case, it wasn't long, well, under two hours, before I heard the explosions of an engine backfiring outside, and I peered out to see a rusty ute shut down suddenly in a puff of smoke and none other than Harry clamber out. He was thinner and greyer than I remembered as he loped, wild-eyed, across the forecourt to the cop shop.

He paused in the doorway and I prepared a huge smile in anticipation of him looking around to see me perching on my bench with my suitcase. But instead, there in the doorway, Harry did something strange (then again, strangeness is the stuff of fiction). He pulled the neck of his jersey up over his mouth and nose and huffed all of his breath into it, right down to the last gritty wheeze, and then, revealing his face again, he drew in an enormous, fresh gulp of oxygen. Thus fortified, he descended on the cop behind the desk with whom he conducted a brief, strangely squeaky conversation. Before long, Harry was signing a form and shoving it in the cop's face, then turning to me. Ah, finally, the moment of our reunion! I want to thank Harry for not running towards me, picking me up and whirling me about with tears of joy in his eyes; I'd like to thank him for not kneeling down and enveloping me in a warm, fatherly bear-hug; for not raising a smile, for not raising his eyebrow in the most cursory of greetings. As I've pondered the nature of writing, one thing I've learned is that feeling safe, wanted and loved is the worst possible condition for a writer. A writer needs to have nothing to fall back on apart from her writing. And so, on that occasion in the cop shop, Harry's frown as he approached my bench, his furious grab at my suitcase and his stride as he exited the nick followed by the trotting yours truly, were all just the ticket for a writer. How grateful I am that Harry didn't seem in the least pleased to see me, only anxious to be shot of the pigs. A moment later we were we roaring off in a cloud of exhaust and speeding into the countryside.

It was a wonderful reunion, that journey in the ute. I hadn't seen Harry since the Christmas Eve five years earlier when he had socked Sorrell in the jaw, so we had a lot of catching up to do. As I said, he was a bit older, a bit more wizened, a bit hairier. His knees twitched and his fingers drummed on the steering wheel as we drove through the dilapidated outskirts of town.

'How's tricks?' he asked presently.

I said tricks were fine, and he thought this was hilarious. More minutes passed and Harry seemed to have forgotten that he'd already asked me how tricks were, because he asked again, 'How's tricks?' This time I paused to consider. Nothing had changed, there'd been no development in the status of tricks since a few minutes earlier, so I reported that tricks were still fine. Harry laughed again. While the countryside flashed by on the long journey out to Hoki Aroha, Harry asked me how tricks were seven or eight times. There seemed not to be a whole lot of other questions up his sleeve, but he did have an interesting repertoire of laughs.

Now that I have many years of serious reading behind me (I could go so far as to say I am well-read, not to blow my own trumpet), I can recall the playwright Bruce Mason's famous character, Firpo, meeting the alter-ego of the young Mason on Takapuna Beach and asking 'How's tricks?' on a regular basis. I am filled with excitement to think that someone asked me that resoundingly literary question, perhaps the most famous question in all of New Zealand letters—'How's tricks?' I don't know many other New Zealand writers who had an episode in their youth when they were asked repeatedly, 'How's tricks?'

But each time Harry asked me this question—even though I was a budding writer *and* I was racking my brains—I couldn't think of an answer apropos tricks, at least not one that I thought Harry would find interesting. I considered filling him in on Ridgeway School, on Newtown School, Island Bay School, Clyde Quay School, and how hard it was to make friends when you moved so often; and also that I didn't have a cat. I considered telling him about the suave and sophisticated Poppy whom I was privileged to know, about her big house and vintage clothes, but somehow I needed to keep it all inside. I am reminded of how James Joyce said that if he had stayed in Ireland he would've told all his writings over a few afternoons in the pub. How lucky I am. If I'd felt even slightly that I could confide in Harry, I am certain I would've squandered my talent orally—probably most of it in the car on that single evening as rolling fields, grey in the dusk, gave way to dense bush and tarseal gave way to gravel and then to dirt. I would certainly not be the writer I am today. I would like to thank Harry from the bottom of my heart for being the sort of person who asks repeatedly 'How's tricks?' but does not want to know the answer.

It was dark when we got to the commune, although a partial moon had come out from behind the clouds, so I had a hazy impression of about ten charmingly ramshackle dwellings and a few car-bodies dotted about a dirt compound. In a corner of the yard, a goat munched peacefully on a clump of weeds. As the ute bumped over the rubble, Harry cleared his throat, and I had the feeling some kind of announcement was coming. I wasn't wrong. After a few false starts, Harry told me that it wasn't going to be just me and him in the house. I swivelled my head and watched Harry's fingers dancing on the steering wheel. This new information certainly spiked my interest.

'Who else will be in the, um, house?' I asked as we pulled up in front of one of the sweet, rustic dwellings.

Harry got out of the car, walked around it, and spoke inaudibly through the passenger window. I wound the window down. Turned out there was a girlfriend, which I suppose wasn't such a surprise. 'And three kids,' said Harry.

I peered through the car window at the moonlit clearing. A long clothesline off to one side jostled with desultory rags. Pine trees waved in the distance. I had an instant new stepmother and three half-siblings whom I'd be meeting in half a minute. This is why I'm so good at certain techniques in narrative structure, namely the New Development, the Spanner in the Works, the Surprise but Not a Shock. Even though I was gobsmacked by these new developments, they weren't outside the realm of possibility. All the writing manuals in the world can't replace the experience of real life. I almost feel I have an unfair advantage over writers who had peaceful, stable, predictable childhoods, writers who knew what the next day would bring, who had a solid knowledge of who their family members were. Where do they get their sense of drama from? I feel sorry for them.

Buzzing with the anticipation of meeting my new family, or half-family, or step-family, I tumbled out of the car and felt my shoes sink into viscous mud. (I was to learn that drainage was an ongoing saga at Hoki Aroha and the subject of lively debate at community meetings.) As Harry and I squelched up to the doorstep, neighbours' curtains, in the form of tea towels and bits of sacking, twitched. Fighting off a giddy feeling, I gripped my suitcase and made my grand entrance to the whare at Hoki Aroha. The shock of seeing and smelling my new home that night is undoubtedly where I get my skill at world-building, so I'd particularly like to thank Harry for that. I don't know where I'd be if I couldn't summon sensuously a strange and confronting space.

First of all, there was a bit of a pong which I identified gradually as baby poo, old vegetable and cat's pee. As my eyes became accustomed to the light I saw that the little wooden room was pleasantly jam-packed in an arty intellectual way—books, guitars, trailing pot plants. The table was covered in a crimson lava-lava and lightly sprinkled with pastel artworks torn from the spiral edge of a sketching block. The same Pasifika material screened shelves under a worn wooden sink bench. I noticed there wasn't a fridge, but I was used to that. To one side of the kitchen, an open wood fire shifted, sending a chug of ashy smoke out into the atmosphere. On the other side of the room angled in the corner were two tiny beds with little mounds sleeping in them. Then I saw, on a saggy maroon couch in the furthest corner, a round woman flipping through a magazine with one hand and breastfeeding a baby from the other arm. The sucking little blob was clearly the youngest of my half-somethings, brother or sister, at this point I didn't know. The woman—my new step-mum, I realised with a fresh jolt—blinked at me and said hello in an incredibly calm voice. She went back to browsing the magazine. No doubt she was trying to put me at my ease by not overwhelming me with gooey smiles and attention.

I stood there wondering what to do, stranded somewhat but slowly acquainting myself with my surroundings and my new life. Harry had gone outside. I found myself taking an instant liking to Nico who, it seemed, was the opposite of Sorrell—comfortably roly-poly, dressed in swishy dark-pink clothes, and with this amazing serenity. I admire people like that. It was as if she was meditating all the time and I was a train going past on her distant horizon. Nothing could ruffle her composure, not even the arrival of her new step-daughter, the sister to her babies. I lurked around awkwardly among the books, bumping a guitar on a stand, and probably resonating like a stringed instrument myself because I kept saying, 'Um, um.' By this time Harry had come back inside, much happier and saying, 'Um what?' And we all laughed. Well, except Nico and the baby.

Harry continued: 'Um, do you want a, you know, meal or something? There's some soup, I think.' Nico said calmly that the soup was gone, and Harry said, 'Oh well, some bread then,' and Nico said the bread was gone. I murmured that I wasn't hungry anyway, and Harry said, 'Okay, that's good,' and everyone agreed it was a good thing. Nico maintained her inscrutable Siamese cat demeanour, but I could tell she agreed.

After a while, Nico heaved up from the couch, cast the magazine aside (the *New Yorker*: I guess you never knew when you might be flying from Hoki Aroha to the Big Apple to see a play off-Broadway), and with baby crooked in her arm, clacked through a fiery beaded curtain into a back room. I was still sort of wondering what to do. Harry was sloshing red wine into a jam jar at the kitchen table. He offered me some, then laughed. 'Only joking.' He really was quite hilarious. I began to feel at my ease as I sidled uninvited onto the bench behind the table. We both sniggered. I thought Harry was going to ask me how tricks were again, but instead he said, 'Isn't she great?'

I blinked. 'Who?'

'*Who!*' Harry dissolved with laughter into his wine-jar.

'The baby?' I ventured.

'The baby's a boy,' said Harry. 'Sascha.'

'Oh,' I said. 'Sascha.'

'Isn't she great though?' said Harry.

I nodded. 'She's great.'

'She's the real thing,' said Harry, looking at me very intently. 'I'm a lucky guy. Oh and those two, by the way'—Harry indicated the two little mounds snoozing against the wall—'they're from before me, but that's cool. And I mean, she's the real thing.' After a while, Harry added thoughtfully, 'Unlike a certain other person.'

It was a little hard to breathe, jammed up so tightly between the wall and the table, but I managed to collect some oxygen. Something quite profound began to occur to me as I digested Harry's words—my first brush with the existential. It went like this: Sorrell was my mother (obviously). To hear from arguably the only person qualified to have an opinion about her corporeality, her thingness, that she *wasn't* the real thing blew my mind. The table graunched away a centimetre as I nodded, and I was able to breathe easier. The next logical step was—because I was/am my mother's daughter—to ask the question 'Am I, therefore, the real thing?' The self-doubt involved in that ontological question, especially in the lisping first-rationalising of a twelve-year-old, set the imagination soaring. I want to thank Harry most sincerely for planting a great big seed of second-guessing in my young breast which I lug about with me to this day. It has long, twisting, ropy tendrils now. I know I never could've produced *The Ice Shelf*—or any work of literature—without it.

That first night at Hoki Aroha, since there wasn't a bedroom for me, I slept on the self-same couch Nico had been sitting on. That was okay; we have too much regard for space in the West. The couch sagged like an S in the middle, so I had a slightly agonising back in the morning, but nothing major. As it was, during my time at Hoki Aroha I slept in a liminal space, a gift for any writer. I was like Tony Warren, the creator of *Coronation Street*, who spent his childhood sitting under the table listening to his grandmother, his mother, his aunts gossiping. *I* now had extended family. *I* could listen to some gossip. This would be of the utmost use to a fiction writer, and I think even then, twelve-year-old that I was, I knew that I was going to pack down some gems at Hoki Aroha. At least I would if Nico ever came to from her trance and said something.

I woke to two little cannonballs, who turned out to be my step-siblings, Zack and Zoë, jumping up and down on my stomach. Nico was bashing about in the kitchen, a few centimetres from my head. From under the army blanket I could see she wore her Mona Lisa smile, a red muslin dress, and Sascha, attached like a limpet. I pushed off Thing One and Thing Two to ricochet around the room, and sat up. After a while I inquired politely where the bathroom was. Nico seemed not to register me on her radar, but when I headed towards the beaded curtain, she gave an earthy chuckle.

Hearing the laugh, Thing One paused mid-boing and gestured outside with a wide arm. 'Stinky poos!'

'And wees!' piped Thing Two, and they screamed madly.

I ventured out into the muddy yard. As I picked my way past the ten huts whose quaint crooked chimneys were all pumping out thick smoke and making the air choky with ash, I saw some of the residents, men with beards like Harry and women who looked quite a lot like Nico, and kids, lots of kids, all Pākehā, with greyish faces and snot running into their mouths. Honestly, they were so cute. A few of them stared at me vacantly as I passed. I think if they'd waved to me, or if I'd felt even the teensiest bit welcome by anyone at Hoki Aroha, I wouldn't be the writer I am today. That sense of being an outsider has been one of the most important things in shaping my creativity, so I'm grateful, despite the fact that I felt like a hopeless piece of shit as I waded—eventually—through long wet grass to the bog that morning. I looked out for Harry, but he was nowhere to be seen.

The long-drop, inside its little chalet, is, I'm sorry to say, outside my powers of description. I concede to the superior literary talent of Irvine Welsh in *Trainspotting*.

Back at the hut, I spied a bowl of porridge on the table. My stomach was yowling like a cat, so I slid onto the wooden bench (this time in a shuddering manner because it was covered with something sticky) and asked Nico rather hopefully if it was for me. Nico maintained her characteristic silence which by this time was getting rather endearing. By way of answer, she sat at the table with Sascha on her lap and began to feed him tenderly from the bowl. He opened his mouth like a baby bird. As he masticated, his big blue eyes stared at me with an expression of smug entitlement. So adorable. I knew we'd have a lifelong attachment.

There is something incredibly powerful about ignoring someone while maintaining a fixed smile. A smile can mean so much more than it is. My heartfelt thanks go out to Nico for teaching me a valuable lesson about subtext which I've used to great effect for several of my most beloved characters. People (Clancy, for instance) have commented that my portrayal of N is a brilliant example of subtext—she remains silent but her insults, conveyed through body language, speak volumes. I am hugely indebted to Nico for ignoring me for the entire year I was at Hoki Aroha. Thank you, Nico. Even though things between Nico and Harry didn't work out in the end, I enjoy the regular updates I hear on the family grapevine. Nico lives on Waiheke Island and sells home-baked bread under the table at the farmers market to supplement her benefit. The adorable Sascha of the big blue eyes, who once scoffed porridge, brews meth in west Auckland, but that's just a temporary thing while he saves up to take a course in glass-blowing. Things One and Two moved to Brisbane.

But I'm getting ahead of myself. I have more tributes connected to my fruitful stay at Hoki Aroha. After breakfast on that first day (I learned to make my own porridge), Harry breezed in, incredibly happy, and announced that I was going to school. My heart leapt. Not that I'd ever had much truck with school, or rather the eight schools I'd already been to, but at least it would be something to do. Harry told me to go out into the yard and join in. I poked my face outside the hut, feeling a bit timid, and saw in the smoky haze a raggle-taggle troop of the most adorable children you've ever seen. They were around my age and upwards, older than the ones I'd seen earlier on my way to the bog, and they stared at me as if they'd never seen another human being.

Soon I was trudging after them through the compound behind a bearded man in bright red jeans who looked like Harry. All the men at Hoki Aroha looked pretty much the same, with their skinny frames, bushy beards and red trousers. We wended our way through some scrub until we were getting into tree country. As we traipsed along single file, we must've looked like the bedraggled actors on the set of another *Hobbit* film, plunging deeper and deeper into the forest. Eventually we halted at a small field cultivated with knee-high plants with almond-shaped leaves. For some reason, the growing had to take place way out here.

The bearded man summoned everyone. We gathered around and he announced that we had a new person. Me!

He called me Janet. I mentioned, smiling a bit with shyness, that actually I was Janice.

'And Janet,' said the bearded man, 'you can call me Valour.'

'Valour,' I repeated.

'Janet, here,' Valour told the assembled crew, 'is going to be joining our community, so I want you all to make her welcome.'

I found myself the recipient of a row of hostile blue stares. In fact, I'm grateful for that, and I think by now you'll be able to understand why: a comfortable life, some security, a sense of inclusion, is all anathema to the life of a writer. Those kids at Hoki Aroha who didn't speak to me the whole year I was there, honestly—respect.

Valour said he was going to show me a really important skill today. He came close and cupped his hand, which smelt strongly of mulch, under my chin. I stood stock still, not sure if squirming out from under his hand would be allowed, seeing he was the teacher. Finally, Valour stepped back and put his head on one side, considering me.

'I suppose you've been at a school dedicated to the principles of dialectical materialism?'

Perhaps I had been at a school like that. I wasn't sure. But from Valour's certain tone, I understood that he knew for a fact I'd been to one of these schools—he'd likely been talking to Harry and had prior knowledge of Ridgeway School, Brooklyn School, Clyde Quay School. I nodded.

Valour leapt on this concession. 'Ah, I thought so. Well, I'm pretty sure you'll find that things are very different here. We're a cool school, aren't we, whānau?'

Valour looked piercingly round the class and the whānau didn't disagree.

'We're a cool school and we learn useful things. For

instance.' Valour, getting into his stride, pointed to a gangly boy of about fourteen. 'Willow here wanted to learn how to balance the books so he'd know how to make a living wage from a crop. Can't argue with that, can you? Willow asked, Show me how? So I showed him how. Didn't I, Willow?'

Willow nodded, trying not to smile.

'And Zac here'—Valour pointed to another gangly boy— 'Zac wanted to learn how to build a drying shed. He asked, Show me how?' Valour opened his eyes wide in an apparent rendition of Zac pleading to be shown how. 'So I showed him how, didn't I, Zac?' Zac blushed with pride.

Then there was another boy, Kai, who'd wanted to learn how to make clay pipes to sell and he'd said, Show me how, and Valour had shown him how, and there was quite an art to it, it wasn't easy. Valour worked his way around the class, making the boys smile coyly one by one with stories of how they'd asked to be shown how, but he stopped when he came to the girls, who were looking at the ground anyway. It was a bit of shame, but they seemed not to want to learn.

Valour turned back to me. 'So, Janet, tell me, have you ever asked, Show me how?'

I shook my head. Unfortunately, I'd never asked to be shown how.

'Perhaps you could start right now, Janet,' said Valour. 'Why don't you ask me, right now, here, "Valour, show me how." What do you want to learn, Janet? What?'

I opened my mouth, but nothing came out. I felt my face flush with shame.

'What do you want to *know*?' insisted Valour. He was right up in my face and I got a whiff of gum disease.

I racked my brains but came up with nothing. Just beyond my concentration, I could hear the other kids snickering.

This was the teensiest bit unfair, as I hadn't had the advantage of being at a cool school. In all my years at various State Primaries I'd never been invited to ask, 'Show me how.'

'Okay,' said Valour finally, releasing me from a kind of spiritual vice. He paced around in a professorial way. 'See, Janet, I'm not surprised you don't have a clue what you want to know, because I bet you've been at a school where they shut you down. Did you go to a school where they shut you down, Janet?'

I had to admit that I had. In my defence, though, I think I'd moved enough times to avoid being hermetically sealed by the policies of any school in particular.

'I suppose they taught you reading and writing, did they?' asked Valour. He was smiling at his joke while distributing gardening implements to the class.

'A bit,' I conceded.

The other kids tittered and brandished their hoes.

'Maths?' asked Valour, playing to the crowd.

I humbly nodded.

'What about science?' called Valour to all and sundry.

I could not tell a lie. I'd learned general science.

The kids doubled up laughing. By the time they'd subsided, Valour seemed to soften a little and was stroking his beard, looking at me kindly, no doubt concerned at the terrible turn my education had taken.

'It's not your fault, Janet.'

'No,' I chimed in quickly, 'it's not my fault.'

'I think you'll find it very different here, Janet. I think you'll find that here we *don't* shut people down. It's the opposite, isn't it, whānau?' He enlisted the kids' mumbles. 'We open people up.'

Now Valour and the children plunged into their tasks:

weeding the rows, checking the plants for some disease I couldn't catch the name of, and spraying a white chemical onto them for which Valour wore a mask but there didn't seem to be enough for the kids to wear. There, under the blue sky, on the tilled field, in the beautiful clean air, we toiled, and I tried to keep up although I was hampered by my limited past access to the epistemology of the dope crop.

I want to break off from this idyllic scene for a moment to express my huge thanks to Valour. If it hadn't been for him, I might've gone for my entire schooling without asking, 'Show me how.' If I'm honest, I didn't want to be shown how to grow hectares of weed, but that seemed to be pathetically beside the main pedagogical principle that Valour was trying to get across. And here I only mention it as tiny aside to the main gist of this, which is my enormous gratitude to Valour, who is serving time in Mt Eden Prison now. That was nothing to do with the crop. It was the girls.

In the afternoon, a bearded man named Hector, who had just arrived from Germany and had a nice new pair of Birkenstocks, taught us how to make a clay wall with beer bottles embedded prettily in it. Hector also greeted me with a caress of the chin and face which extended to opening my mouth a little. This seemed to be the conventional way to say hello at Hoki Aroha.

At midday we all sat around eating the packed lunch the women had prepared earlier. I noticed that Hector disappeared into the bush with one of the girls. I wondered if she needed special tuition because she had not asked, 'Show me how.' Perhaps Hector was giving her special instruction in what it was important to be shown. Somehow I hoped I would not need remedial help with Show Me How.

I started going every day to help grow and harvest the rows

of the semi-tropical plants and to learn skills like building shithouses with beer bottles in them, fashioning clay pipes which got baked in a kiln, and making two columns of figures, one for debit, one for credit. But that first night I was initiated into the evening rituals that marked the end of each day at Hoki Aroha.

At six o'clock, everyone assembled in the Big Kitchen for supper. The community, which I now saw numbered about fifty, sat at long tables while several women in bright purple and orange muslin brought out the food, and everyone bowed their heads over their rough earthen plates. I did the same, while peeking up at the bearded man at the head of the table who seemed to be in charge and who said grace in Māori.

I tucked into my food, which that first night was a big stew from a communal pot with everything in it, a bit on the sloppy side and truth be told not much taste to it, but I could see I was going to have a more nutritious diet while I was Hoki-side than I'd had with Sorrell, where fridgelessness reduced us pretty much to pies from the dairy. At the commune there was no fridge, but you know what? It didn't matter. The produce was gathered fresh every day from the land (a fact I'd picked up from the karakia). I was to learn that something new was added to the pot every day. Sometimes it got a little repetitive, such as when the bean, broccoli and cabbage crops failed and there was just carrots for a few months. Over the week, the flavour of the stew would get better and better, until it didn't, and that was not a very good night, but the next day one of the women, maybe Nico, would decide it was time to start a new pot, and this was quite a festive occasion and a bottle of undisclosed liquor in a dark green dirty-looking bottle might be passed around among the men and some of the teenage boys. They would get drunk in a very short time, and sometimes a fight would erupt later.

After dinner—in summer as the sun sank and threw long dark arteries over the weedy compound, in winter with the coal range glowing in the Big Kitchen—the little kids would scatter underfoot, the teenage boys retreat to lurk darkly in the shadows, and the women and sentient girls including yours truly would do the dishes. The dishes were not done lightly, for a start, on account of there being no running water. Earlier in the day, buckets had been carried up from the stream one hundred metres away. I learned that water is heavy and that as you walk with it, a tide gets established in the bucket which gathers momentum, growing bigger and bigger until it's a neap tide and half the water is slopping out of the bucket and disappearing (pardon my ings) into the parched yard which doesn't need water because only weeds grow there, and this can be annoying because it means you've lost so much water on the journey that it's going to take even more journeys to fill the wetback. The wetback situated on the side of the coal range is in turn fuelled by wood gathered from the forest. Carrying an armload of wood from the forest half a kilometre away is a poky, spine-wrenching exercise and once you've done this several times in a day, your arms and your back are quite sore and your chest and forearms are scratched to pieces. However, once the hand-carried water was bubbling away merrily in the wood-fuelled wetback, the dishes proper could begin.

Twenty women and girls were involved in the dishes, and on that first night as I picked up what was once a tea towel only to have it snatched out of my hands by an outraged older woman, I learned that doing the dishes was a privilege, and convened by the established matrons of the commune.

Chastened, my fingers stinging after the flick of the rag, I stood politely to one side and waited to be given a job. One doyenne in particular, a grey-maned woman called Barb, officiated this evening at the big stone tub. I watched as she rolled up her muslin sleeves seriously, plunged her fleshy hands into the murky water, and got to work. This was no child's play. Making a lather by swishing yellow soap in a little cage on a stick—a task I could only just glimpse if I stood on tiptoes—took some expertise. Once Barb had produced a thin film of fat on the surface of the water, the scrubbing began. She went at it like a cattle-wrangler, head down, all elbows and sweat and grunt, getting through fifty plates, an array of cutlery like a huge catch of fish, plus random pots (but not the Pot). Simultaneously, a chain of older girls brought more water from the creek and topped up the wetback and set extra cauldrons brimming on the range. About half a tree went into doing the dishes. A fleet of established matrons swooped in and out, plucking washed dishes from the draining bench and giving each one a good polishing with a rag. They polished as if their life depended on it and stacked them on the nearest table. Lastly, and this is where I came in, and felt lucky to do so, the younger girls ferried the dried earthenware, extremely carefully, from the table to the big rough-hewn cabinet on the other side of the kitchen and stowed them away, coming back for more like sparrows.

All in all, doing the dishes at Hoki Aroha was a lot of donkeywork, but it didn't feel like that in the least; it felt like an honour.

While the dishes were being done, a meeting was taking place at one of the big tables on the other side of the dining hall. If The Meeting was populated only by men, that wasn't

112

the result of any kind of prejudice, it was just because the women hadn't finished the washing up yet. I have to add here that everyone at Hoki knew that the women's jobs were valued very highly by the men, probably more so than their own jobs. At the beginning of each meeting, as I ferried clean dishes, I would hear from the edges that the first item on the agenda was to thank and honour the women of Hoki Aroha, who were wāhine toa, strong women, the backbone of the community. Roger would raise a hand: 'All respect to the wāhine of Hoki Aroha.' And the other men, including Harry of course who was at the table jiggling his knees, would chime in raggedly, 'Respect, sisters.' The women wouldn't notice this tribute, as they were too busy scrubbing fat off pans with pig-bristles and trying to stop the sweat running into their eyes, but the sentiment was there.

That first night, Roger opened up a discussion on drainage. 'Let's talk to drainage,' he said. Listening, carrying plates, I learned quickly that there was no drainage at Hoki Aroha, and that unless the community could come up with $20,000 to get connected to the town sewerage and wastewater system, things on the land were going to go from a bit smelly to cholerically toxic, and the commune would be shut down.

Harry was all for digging a new channel down to the river. Valour said that that would be disadvantageous to the community, because the route went too close to the crop. 'If the plot's contaminated, what are we going to sell? Our own shit?' There was a ripple round the table and the tenor of the discussion ramped up a notch. Hector, who had a manner like the social worker in *That Sinking Feeling*, thought that the community should take out a loan and pay to have the drains built by professional drainlayers.

'That would serve ze community for ze next generation, yes?' he said. He cited the example of how they cleaned up the Rhine.

At this, Harry, Valour and a few of the other men got a bit heated, yelling and threatening and so forth, until Roger half rose from his chair and told them to settle down, that everyone's voice was important, and everyone would be treated with respect because this was Hoki Aroha was about. He sank back down, and peace reigned. 'So, what have we resolved?'

'To dig a new channel down to the river,' said Harry.

Valour looked daggers at Harry. 'You already said that, and I'm forced to repeat—' and he launched into a tirade about Harry's idea being the dumbest of all the dumb things they could possibly do. Not only would all the crap run near to the crop, it would go into the river and the fucking Māoris would complain about their fucking shellfish and there'd be some kind of fucking ritual down there and the fucking media would arrive followed by the fucking fuzz. He added, 'You dumb fuck,' which seemed necessary, given the seriousness of the allegations.

Hector intervened here, the voice of reason. 'Gentlemen, having a proper drain laid would serve ze community well in ze years to come, yes? And that would mean—'

I was halfway across the kitchen with some cutlery when I saw Valour rush over to Hector, who just had time to say, 'Yes?' before he was punched in the mouth. He fell against the pile of wood in the corner. A couple of the other men ran over and joined in, Harry included, and soon they were like a cluster of peasants harvesting turnips in *Tess of the d'Urbervilles*. I looked at the women to see what they would do about the fight, but they didn't seem to turn a hair. Eventually someone hauled the men off Hector, they all collapsed back into their hand-hewn chairs, and the meeting was adjourned. As the dishes were also done, everyone bid each other goodnight and dispersed to their respective dwellings. Nico, carrying the baby, helped the bleeding Harry to limp over the uneven yard back to our hut. Things One and Two followed, crying a bit and sniffing and eating the snot that ran down into their mouths. I brought up the rear.

I relate this event to show how, even though the philosophy of the commune was to foster mindfulness, it was at the same time a stimulating place intellectually and physically, full of talk and action, and for that I am grateful. It certainly wasn't an environment where your mind would go to mush, despite the permanent fug of dope smoke. I'm happy to report that the culture described in *Cinema of Unease* was nowhere to be found.

The next morning—only my second morning at Hoki Aroha, but it felt like I'd been there for months—I was in the hut when I heard loud yahooing in the yard and went out see what was going on. Several of the men including Harry were prancing about, slapping their knees and chanting. When Harry sashayed by and saw my puzzlement, he spluttered, 'The blue meanie just, the blue meanie just . . . !' but it was apparently so funny he couldn't get the words out. Zac, one of the teenage boys who'd asked 'Show me how', was lolling against the fence, and he filled me in. The blue meanies were the inspectors who regularly visited the commune. There was the Council man who came about the drains, the Health Department man who came about the Dirt, and the Treaty man who had an envelope to deliver about some claim on the property under the Treaty of Waitangi, which was crap because the people at Hoki loved the land. Why do you think it had a Māori name? Zac told me that the Council man had just driven into the compound and gone away again at the sight of the empty yard, hence the celebration. I watched while Harry et al. did funny walks up to the doors of the huts and pretended to knock on them, to general hilarity. It was the beginning of a new day.

During the course of my year at Hoki Aroha, I saw a lot of blue meanies try unsuccessfully to storm the commune. At first sighting of a neat white car bumping up the road in a cloud of dust, the cry would go up, 'The blue meanies, the blue meanies!' and within seconds the compound would clear and hut doors slam. I'd crouch under the window with Things One and Two, peeking out to see the bureaucratic vehicle reversing back down the chunky road. Then everyone would emerge and a party atmosphere would reign for a few hours. To tell the truth, I don't know what the commune would've done for entertainment without visits from the blue meanies; it was the most fun anyone ever had. No one bothered to explain to me what would happen if a Blue Meanie ever did gain access. This discrepancy is something I will come to in the course of my Acknowledgements.

For the present, my grateful thanks to all who were in residence at Hoki Aroha in 1992 would not be complete without describing the Dirt. Indeed, my *story* would not be complete without conveying the integral position of filth at the commune. The Dirt was a member of the community. Cleaning had not been high on my list of priorities at the age of twelve, especially while living with Sorrell, but part of my re-education at Hoki Aroha was to learn that cleaning is what OCD people and capitalists do in the *weekends* (in the commune, every day was the same, as nature intended it). Everything in the compound was filthy, from black, sticky floors to surfaces layered with years of grease to windows clouded like cataracts. The bathrooms were spectacular: the basins were a fuzzy grey, the walls pink with mould and the toddlers' piss pots a rusty earwax colour and streaked darker inside. The smell was at first like a punch in the face, but it was something you got used to.

As a reference, may I point the reader in the direction of the chapter entitled 'The Scum' in *On Chesil Beach* by Ian McEwan. In that novel, the mother has a head injury from being hit by a carriage door while getting out of a train. The members of Hoki Aroha had sustained no such trauma, but they did smoke a lot of weed. I could've written 'The Scum', not that I'm comparing myself with Ian McEwan, I hasten to add.

The Dirt prompted many a visit from the Health Department man, but each time disaster was neatly sidestepped by everyone performing blue meanie drill until he went away.

However, one morning it was different. I saw the events unfold from the smoky hut window. A little car, white as a dentist's surgery, came chugging up the road as usual, and as usual the commune broke from its morning duties (the women hanging washing, men rolling joints on their doorsteps) and fled towards their huts. But instead of driving away, the white car stopped in the compound, the door opened, and a court shoe on the end of a stockinged leg emerged. The windows of Hoki flickered like old-fashioned videos on pause as the owner of the stockinged leg stood in the yard in her grey skirt and white blouse. She made her way, managing her heels in the clay rubble, and knocked on the first door. Amazingly, it was answered.

Looking back, I think the commune allowed this health

inspector in because she was a woman, and they thought she would be nice. At Hoki, women were lovely people, they were feminine and benign. The worst you could expect from a Hoki woman was the silent treatment, and although this could feel unpleasant, and perhaps even fuck one up for life, in the immediate present it posed no threat. It's my humble opinion that living in this sheltered environment for years had made everyone at the commune forget what a woman from the outside could be like. This proved a fatal mistake; once she had breached the huts, the health inspector revealed herself to be, although definitely a woman, not lovely, feminine or benign, but hard-arsed and horrible. One could not imagine this woman doing the dishes with any integrity whatsoever.

To make matters more complicated, on the morning the health inspector arrived I was having a little setback. Of course, this wasn't uncommon at Hoki. Most of the children had setbacks from time to time, of the stomach cramps and upchucking variety. When the knock came, I was lying on my couch curled like a nautilus. Nico looked up from the other end of the couch where she sat nursing the baby and reading *The New Yorker*. Without waiting to be invited, the health inspector pushed open the door, barked 'Inspection!' and stepped inside. She was skinny and white with a dark, gamine haircut like Donna Tartt and a clipboard hugged to her chest. I felt Nico rearrange herself with the utmost passive aggression.

The health inspector clacked around the hut in her heels, going over everything with a fine-toothed comb. She turned the taps (a hopeful gesture, because of course there was no running water), lifted the lava-lava under the sink and poked around, and—this last performed with a wince—nudged the chamber pot by the bench with her pointy shoe. Frequently she shook her head and scribbled on her clipboard and wiped her fingers on a wet wipe plucked from her shoulder bag. All through, she maintained an expression of extreme disgust. Finally I came under her gaze. She put her head on one side. 'What's the story with you?' she asked matter-of-factly.

I was about to explain how I had excruciating pains in my intestines and felt sick to the pit of my stomach, but Nico eyeballed me in a terrifying way from the other end of the couch.

I blinked up at the inspector. 'Nothing,' I squeaked.

The inspector leaned down and put her cool palm on my forehead. For a split second I was plunged into a little reverie whereby a concerned adult was offering me sympathy and support; this concerned adult held a cold cloth to my brow, brought me chicken soup on a tray, and worriedly called the doctor. Such were the workings of my fevered imagination. In reality, the health inspector sprang back as if burned. 'Good gracious!' She turned to Nico. 'This child has a high fever. She needs to see a doctor.'

Nico looked at the inspector as if she were a train on her distant horizon. Kudos to Nico, she maintained this impressive mindfulness while the inspector demanded to know if there was any Panadol in the house, dug some tablets out of her own bag, expressed disgust at the smeary glass on the bench and cleaned it with one of her special wet wipes, expressed more and greater disgust at the pitcher of water, then sniffed it and apparently decided it was drinkable.

While the inspector scribbled busily on her clipboard, I felt another retch coming on, but Nico's gimlet gaze was clear: *Do not on any account throw up.* This was the most attention Nico had ever paid me, so part of me felt special. I did my best to oblige and everything oozed painfully downwards in my body. This is how I know about translation.

The health inspector thumbed through her list and spoke to no one in particular. There were a couple of things, she said, that might need some attention, which turned out to be a New Zealand way of saying there were twenty-five shockingly bad areas of concern. From the haze of my sickbed, I didn't understand why she was bothering to tell us all this. It's not as if we didn't know the chamber pot lived next to the bench, the cupboards were infested with cockroaches, and there was a dead rat under the table. Across the room, Nico was half smiling and rocking the baby in a way that said to this woman, 'Uptight bitch.' If Nico had been looking at me like that, I would've understood perfectly that I wasn't behaving in a cool way and would've taken immediate steps to remedy the situation by being quiet and still. But the Nico treatment wasn't working on the health inspector, not one bit. Instead, she made more notes on her clipboard and looked at Nico with a loathing gaze.

As soon as she'd gone, briefly blocking the light in the doorway, I leaned over and vomited into the red plastic bucket. Nico lit a joint and listed verbally the health inspector's attributes, which were strangely feminine. I felt a warmth fill the space where my breakfast had been to have Nico take me into her confidence so.

I lay back on the couch and listened to the health inspector's heels and taut voice roving from hut to hut. A while later, I was woken from a feverish doze to hear a commotion in the Big Kitchen—a lot of shouting and banging of pot lids and smashing of crockery—and someone shouting, 'Harry, Harry, smashing things won't do any good!' This was followed by an almighty crash that sounded as if the cabinet that held the crockery for the whole commune—the very cabinet I stocked with clean dishes in my job as a girl—had been pushed over.

I looked at Nico and said, kind of nervously, 'Do you think that was Harry?'

Nico nodded benignly as if the crash was a train on her distant horizon.

All things must pass, and eventually the health inspector's car whined out of the compound. A rousing cheer followed her exit, and a bit of a shindig ensued. No doubt several green bottles of indeterminate liquor were passed about. At one point I sat up groggily and peered through the grimy pane. The health inspector's list was being bandied about and quoted from, to much hilarity. 'Rat droppings in food storage area. Handwashing facilities covered in toxic mould. Food in the safe unsafe for human consumption.' Each item on the List was recited in a posh, declamatory, Sam Hunt kind of way.

A day or so later, when I was starting to get better, I crawled over to the Big Kitchen in search of food and saw that the dishes cabinet indeed lay face down as if it had got very drunk on indeterminate liquor. No one had bothered to put it upright. Nor was there a single plate intact and the meal had been eaten off big leaves (the traditional Māori way, fitting the bicultural principles of Hoki Aroha, I might add). I sat at one of the long tables trying to sup a thin gruel from a leaf (difficult) while the women and girls cleaned up around me, not that there was much to do. I was excused from my duties owing to my setback. A Meeting began, with the usual chime, 'Respect, sisters!' Roger said they were there to discuss the visit of the health inspector, the breached trust between Hoki Aroha and social services and the collective and personal trauma suffered by the community. The other men nodded and ahhed in agreement.

At this point, Harry held up the List as if it were the used snotrag of someone with one of the respiratory ailments the residents of Hoki Aroha tended to come down with. There was general disgust at the sight.

'So,' said Harry, scanning the room with a wide-eyed stare, 'how to proceed?'

'We ignore it of course,' said Valour. 'We ignore the state.'

Roger spoke: 'All those in favour of ignoring the state?'

The Ayes rushed in.

One voice, however, could be heard thrusting up from the chorus with a dissenting 'No.' Everyone swivelled suspiciously towards Hector.

'I merely suggest,' said Hector in a reasonable tone, 'that we consider fixing one or two items from ze List, yes?'

There followed a few seconds of silence, then general hubbub. In the midst of the clamour, Harry stood up and spoke in a voice that began strained but grew in fruitiness. 'Fix a few things? Fix a few *things*? Fix a *few things*?'

Valour joined in. 'Fix a few things from *the List*?'

Hector, remaining seated, spread his palms. 'It seems ze sensible thing, yes? The harassment from ze Council would cease, and who knows, maybe ze children would stop getting sick, yes?'

I glanced at Harry. He would undoubtedly throw a small, sympathetic look in my direction as I sat shivering at the table slurping gruel from my rubber leaf. But Harry didn't have time to consider the welfare of his first-born because, at that moment, the List was tweaked from his hands by Hector, who perused its contents, his brow like a *fleur-de-lis*. Harry blinked and snatched the List back. Then Valour grabbed it, and then the teenage boys joined in, ripping the List from each other as they spilled out into the twilit yard bellowing like young bulls. There ensued a giant game of tag which criss-crossed all over the compound, involving everyone expect me who was too sick and the women who were too meek. Everything in the path of the game was sent flying, bottles and buckets and stray cats. In and out of the huts it raged, and into the bush and back again and finally, when it seemed the players were exhausted, a stick was poked through the List and it was held high. Someone found another stick and lit it on fire and reached up and set alight the document and everyone went quiet and it was an awe-inspiring sight to see the List burning, burning against the darkening sky, a cape of fine ash falling.

I cannot underestimate what I learned witnessing the members of Hoki Aroha rise up against the Kafkaesque figures of authority who visited in their neat little cars, the subversive way they thumbed their communal nose at the List and in the end claimed back power from the state. In the end, all I can say is—to Harry, Roger, Hector, Valour—I am so grateful for the lesson in activism. Without it, I would not be a fraction of the writer I am today.

Over the months I got used to the rhythm of life at Hoki Aroha. Because the commune's kaupapa was to be self-sustaining, everything ticked over simply in a clean and green way. Living so far out in the country meant the air was fresh, apart from the smoke from the chimneys which could be dense at times. Plus a couple of times a day a convoy of six or seven badly tuned utes revved out of the yard bound for town, for beer and cigarettes and fun, leaving a thick fug of exhaust hanging in the air for an hour or so. The old pickups weren't in the best condition, but the community wasn't materialistic, so there was no choice but to use gas like there was no tomorrow. Really, it was an idyll.

It was probably due to having learned maths at schools, which shuts you down, that I thought of this equation:

like there's no tomorrow

$\therefore$ there will be no tomorrow

The reason I've described the Dirt and its ramifications in such detail is that in the end it was responsible for hurrying Hoki Aroha to its demise. It's a long story, but bear with me because I have some very important thank yous to make in the process.

One day, while the whānau was out at the crop and had broken for lunch, Valour came up to me and I felt my hand swallowed by his big dirty sweaty one. I knew that finally it was my turn to for instruction in Show Me How. We tromped through some undergrowth, Valour pulling me and smiling back at me. His teeth weren't in very good nick, but this wasn't the concern of someone who had rejected dialectical materialism, so I put the thought of it aside. Finally we came to a secluded copse lined with fern leaves. Valour gazed at me.

'Are you ready to become a woman, Janet?'

I didn't know what to say, but the right answer seemed to be, 'Yes.'

'Yes?' said Valour. He looked serious but gleeful.

'Yes.'

'Good,' said Valour. He was salivating a bit. 'That's good. Because I think you are. I think you're very ready to become a woman, and you're going to be a beautiful woman.'

He smiled and I smiled back.

'In fact, I think you're already a beautiful woman, and do you know what beautiful women like?'

I shook my head. I didn't know. I hoped this didn't mean that I wasn't beautiful.

'Pleasure,' said Valour. 'They like pleasure.'

He reached down and fumbled my hand. It seemed unbelievably quick, but he had already unzipped his pants. He put his cock in my hand. I gasped because it was such a new thing. I hadn't ever thought much about what a man's cock would be like. Now I found it was big and veiny and hard like a Banksia flower and I have to say, at this point I thought it rather disgusting, but I tried not to show it because that would be rude.

'Do you like my cock?' asked Valour. He was breathing in a strange, hard way.

I nodded.

'Tell me,' he said, 'in words.'

'Pardon?' I asked politely.

'Say, "I like your cock",' said Valour.

'I like your cock,' I said.

'Say it louder.'

'I like your cock!' I said as loudly as I could.

'Not that loud,' Valour hissed angrily. He craned back through the bush towards where the whānau were having lunch. I could hear their subdued talk.

Valour pushed his face very close to mine and smiled. I saw the interesting teeth up close and tried not gag on the fetid smell of his breath because that would be, you know, rude.

'That's great,' he said. 'I'm glad you like my cock. You're sure you do?'

'I do.'

'Say all of it.'

'I like your cock.'

'Do you love my cock?'

I paused for a second. Love is a strong emotion. Truth be told, I wasn't sure if I even liked Valour's cock; I'd just agreed on that to be friendly, but I was pretty certain I didn't love his cock. But apparently I'd upset Valour by not rushing to express my affection for his cock, because now he wrestled me to the ground angrily. He insisted that I say I loved his cock, so I said it. By this time I couldn't help crying; it was involuntary. Valour put his hand over my mouth, saying, 'Shh, shh.' He yanked down my jeans and tipped me over on the ground. I felt an enormous pain explode into something down there. It seemed that the cock which I'd been asked to love was now doing something in my body which I supposed was sex. I knew about sex. I didn't know it would be like this. I'd thought it would be gentle. I'd thought there would be some nice feelings, some pleasure attached to it. Valour kept ramming his cock into this part of me that didn't really take to it kindly, I guess because I was uptight. In truth, I wasn't into it, and I felt bad about that because Hoki Aroha was a cool place full of cool people with a cool school where people didn't get shut down, they learned instead, Show Me How. And I did really want to be a woman, a beautiful woman. I wished I weren't so uptight. I wished I didn't have what seemed to be a door over the part of me down there that stopped the cock, which I was meant to love, from going any further. For a long time, during a lot of pushing, I wished it were not so painful. Because it was very painful; in fact, I'd never felt anything so excruciating. That this was meant to be in the pursuit of pleasure seemed to be the most unfair thing; it was meant to be nice, but it was not. The pain kept going for so long, on and on, that at one point I thought I would die from it and that that would be a good thing. I didn't care if I never came back to this planet because I was done with it. I was done with pain and the, well, the disgusting feeling of it. I felt unbearably disgusting, like I'd turned into a person who was revolting from head to foot. I was in the midst of this feeling when, all of a sudden, something gave way and Valour, with a groan, graduated to further inside me. Now it was less painful but still somewhat painful. When they ask you at the doctors, what would this pain be on a scale of one to ten, I would say, eight. The first pain, before the door gave way, was nine, but this long-term ramming pain was an eight. It kept going for a long long time, and I thought *this* bit would never end, but suddenly, Valour collapsed on me in a huge shudder and a blinding pain, up to ten, ripped thought me, and I thought *he* had died, not me, and I hoped it were true.

But after a few minutes he came back from the dead and lay on top of me, squashing me with his weight so I couldn't breathe and I thought I might die again, this time of asphyxiation.

'Did you like that?' Valour whispered in my ear, but I couldn't answer.

He rolled partially off me and repeated the question.

I said yes quickly so he would turn his face away. His breath was like a sewer.

'Pardon?'

'Yes.'

Then he got up and out of the corner of my eye I could see him doing up his pants, then he left.

I came back to join the whānau a different person. Before I'd been a child, now I was a woman. It felt like shit. For the rest of the day, I was dazed and cold, trembling. I could feel myself vulnerable and shaky with a pain between my legs and another pain somewhere deep in my chest.

And here I want to thank Valour profoundly and from the bottom of my heart. Because where would a woman writer be without having been at the very least sexually abused as a child? For a start, he gave me the means to draw upon personal experience when writing rape scenes—I had all the concrete significant detail right there at my fingertips—but, more importantly, he showed me that I had the ability to carry with me forever the kind of self-loathing and base sense of the abject that are invaluable gifts to any writer.

I think because I already had an underlying health problem (which turned out to be hepatitis, but I didn't know it then), and because I'd found the whole sex thing, to be honest, stupefying, the next day I woke once again in a cold sweat and with a cramp gripping my stomach. I lay huddled until it passed, but soon I was feeling queasy and bile was rising in my mouth. Eventually, I had to rush outside and pitch everything I'd eaten the night before into the weeds. I crawled back inside and lay on my couch, groaning and waiting for the sun to come up.

When Nico clattered through the bead curtain, the baby crooked in her arm, she paused and looked blankly down at me like I was a train going down that feat of engineering, the Raurimu Spiral. I mentioned that I was sick again. She nodded and for a moment a flicker of something crossed her face—compassion? She fetched the red bucket, which was fast becoming my closest friend. Then she went to the bench to start the breakfast with one hand. When Harry got up half an hour later she intercepted him with a murmured, 'She's sick again.' Harry came and put his hand on my burning forehead. He looked at me with tenderness. 'Janice,' he said.

'Yes,' I said thickly, gazing up at him.

'How's tricks?'

I started to tell him that tricks were not so good, but he was already having a conversation with Nico about the doctor, and Nico said it cost thirty dollars ($\therefore$). I stayed retching and sweating on the couch. I'm actually grateful to Nico for that. I have an intimate knowledge of what it feels like to be very sick when no one gives a fuck. I could write a book like *The Collector* by John Fowles, in which the girl is 'collected' by the creepy man and then gets sick. I could write a book the equivalent of that and one day I will.

If they'd driven me to the doctor that morning, Hoki Aroha might still be a going concern today, but they did not. Harry went to do stuff and Nico, with the baby on her hip and Things One and Two trailing behind, went off to a really important music class in the bush with the other mothers. I lay listening to the quiet of the deserted compound and eventually fell into a restless doze.

I was woken by what I at first thought were the dregs of a dream—I'd been dreaming I was running across a frozen steppe and with each footfall the ice cracked with a loud knocking sound. But the knocking was real and in my delirious state I got up, wove over to the door and opened it. A man in a grey suit filled the doorway, surrounded by light.

'Does Harry Redmond live here?' he asked.

'Yes,' I said.

He held out an envelope to me.

'Would you give him this, please.' He smiled kindly.

I accepted the envelope.

The man in the grey suit slumped as if a weight had been lifted off his shoulders. He walked back to his car, whistling, and that was the end of Hoki Aroha.

But first of all it was the end of me at Hoki Aroha.

I would like to thank Harry in particular for not telling me about the summons. There is nothing like public humiliation for shaping a writer. The shame I felt at the manner in which the commune turned on me after I'd accepted the summons was something that I am convinced every writer should experience.

When Harry got home, it seemed he already knew what was awaiting him. He stood in the doorway and like a sharpshooter his gaze lined up the envelope on the table immediately. In a couple of strides he'd snatched it from the knotty surface and stood judging its weight in the palm of his hand as if the contents might be explosive. His face bleached whiter and whiter. Meanwhile Nico had erupted from the couch and was at his elbow, fully out of her trance for the first time since I'd been at Hoki Aroha.

Later I thought back on the usefulness of this detail, the foreshadowing, that Nico needed always to be in a trance for her *not* to be in a trance to have meaning. Events seemed to unfold in slow motion. When Harry wobbled the summons at Nico, his words to her were indecipherable, like an audiotape gone slow and monstrous, and when Nico replied her vocals were distorted beyond recognition. This was all diametrically opposed to what I'd come to expect of Hoki Aroha. Right now, I felt the gaze of Harry and Nico upon me: his stoned blue stare, her scorching brown bullets. I lay on my couch helplessly. What could I do? Things One and Two watched silently, seemingly scared by the vibe. Then Harry rushed out of the hut.

I heard the news making its way around the commune, the yells and shrieks, the cursing and thumping on walls. A few times the members of the community, briefly abandoning the spirit of aroha, came to scream obscenities at me from outside the hut.

And so, on the very day I accepted the summons, I was summarily excommunicated from Hoki Aroha. I was bundled with my suitcase, a little shaky on my pins, into Harry's ute. As we roared out of the gates, I looked back to see commune members running after the car shaking their fists until they couldn't stand the exhaust anymore. Harry planted his foot and we sped to town, and soon I was disgorged onto the railway platform, where I had more opportunity to observe the elegance of the architecture as I waited for the train back to the city, and to Sorrell.

An update on the commune, in case you were wondering: after it was shut down under a section of the Public Health Act, Harry and Nico decided to give up their Bohemian lifestyle. They moved with Sascha, Thing One and Thing Two to Tītahi Bay and took out a mortgage on a little fibro house, and Harry remembered that he had a degree in Sociology and got a job teaching maths at a high school (there was a teacher shortage). They had a couple more kids and then split up. I spent a Christmas with them once, watching Harry smoke and pace around the little lawn as if it were an exercise yard. One time as I hovered in the kitchen doorway, not sure what to do with myself, Christmas tree lights flickering in the corner of my eye, he turned from where he stood enveloped in the clothesline and told me how he would've been an artist rather than teaching simultaneous equations to thirteen-year-olds if it hadn't been for Sorrell and me. He could've been someone, he said, as he ground his cigarette butt into the grass.

Harry's second family got to (mostly) grow up in a cosy house with walls and a tree at Christmas time, but they're not *writers*. There is some justice in the world. I am very grateful to Harry for everything he gave me.

*

Reader, this has been a rather long telling of my stint at Hoki Aroha but thank you for bearing with me. My Acknowledgements would have in no way been complete without a full and frank account of the events that transpired at the commune and the chance to express my deep gratitude to those concerned.

To return to my progress on the night of the Antarctica Awards—because I'm brimming with gratitude about being an award-winner and have more thank yous to make in that regard—I have to say that despite the enormous honour, I'm *not* looking forward to the moment when I will step up to the podium to be handed my award, and everyone will clap and cheer. (My modesty actually is a curse, and no doubt is the reason I'm not as successful as some people I could mention. A certain arrogance on their part, that's all.) So, on this night, I stoically cantilever my fridge up the steps of the National Library. I had no intention of bringing it this far and hope to be relieved of any encumbrance before the evening gets much older, but in the meantime, I've become expert at manoeuvring the appliance around on its sturdy cart—like a rather stocky extra limb. To be honest, Mandy's shoes pose more of a problem, as the stretching technique hasn't worked as well as I'd hoped and I'm blistering something dreadful. Plus the wind has got up (Wellington), which impedes my progress. But I heave my fridge up the last few steps to the patio and there, feeling like the giantess in a certain verse novel I read once (on account of the heels), I have an urgent need to perform another edit on my text. Other Awards participants file past, looking on curiously, perhaps even enviously, but I don't mind because one of the things about being a writer is to seize the moment and not care a hoot for what anyone thinks. I snap crisply through the manuscript. (Researchers may wonder why some of the pages are imprinted with what looks like the footprints of a small and very cute mammal; in fact it is because my fingers are a little dirty from my recent encounter with the drain.) Holding on to the pages in the wind, I take out the sections in which the protagonist spends a year at a commune, is sexually abused by a stoned person, catches Hepatitis A and then is held responsible for accepting the court summons which spells the end of the commune, even though no one had told her *not* to accept packets from strangers who came knocking at the door and so how could she possibly have known? I screw up the pages and drop them on the ground, letting the wind shoot the paper ball across the patio like an air-hockey puck. After this deft excision, the narrative structure is, I think, much tighter and more focussed, and the other sections are allowed to shine like gems. Although slightly shorter, *The Ice Shelf* feels, in a strange way, *more* substantial. In any case, I still have screeds more crots to play around with. And of course I will be adding new material to the *roman* as I do field research in Antarctica, gathering the concrete significant details that will make the cold stuff seem new. I hope that not too much more of Antarctica will have melted by the time I get down there. I've read in the *Dominion Post* that a piece of ice shelf the size of New Zealand falls off the polar cap every day. I hope I won't have the misfortune of being on one of those pieces. I hope that coming from New Zealand does not increase the likelihood of being on a New Zealand-sized chunk falling off and in turn cooling the ocean. But, strangely, after living with that idea for a while the thought of floating away where there are no crots, no memories, no thank yous, and no little warmth becomes strangely exciting, like standing on a cliff and thinking you might jump, so you have to be very sure not to. I remember that when I first applied to go to Antarctica, I imagined myself quietly lying down on the ice and never waking up.

I suppress the idea of the little warmth that had become cold, which I have not thought about for quite a while.

Having improved *The Ice Shelf* with my edits once more, my fridge and I move through the glass doors to the foyer of the National Library, being careful not to make a grand entrance, as I despise that kind of attention-seeking. From the foyer, I can see through to the Kōwhai Reception Room where a collection of writers—at least I judge them to be that from their black clothes and uncertain expressions— are milling about with more worldly artists, all of them tipping drinks down their necks as if they've just crossed the Nullarbor Plain. I look for somewhere to stow my fridge before I join the fray.

After my sojourn at Hoki Aroha, I settled back into life in the city with Sorrell. I was lucky during the next period of my life to experience the input of a stepfather, Michael the First, and Mr Monkey, whom you will hear about in due course.

On arrival at the station in Wellington, I sat on my suitcase in the middle of the main causeway for a short while, no more than half an hour, and finally I saw Sorrell stomping towards me, a little wobbly, a little het up, but obviously it was a wonderful reunion. Sorrell pecked me on the cheek. I thought she might comment on how I'd grown in the last year, or how I looked well from the country air, or how I looked peaky after being ill, but I must've looked just the same, because in no time I was following her at almost a run along the causeway and out to the car. She had a new leather jacket and new tan tooled cowboy boots, which she kept glancing down at. I was hoping she'd call me Monster but she didn't.

'What do you think of the car?' asked Sorrell as we piled in.

'Nice,' I said, although I couldn't really tell. It was a step up from the old bomb she used to drive.

'It's a Porsche,' she said, smiling out the side of her mouth at me. I noticed she was very thin, scrawny almost.

'We're going to Michael's,' said Sorrell.

After a silence, I ventured hopefully, 'Not Poppy's?'

'Poppy!' exploded Sorrell. 'No fucking way.' And she rumbled about Poppy for a few kilometres.

'Um, who's Michael?' I asked, when there was a lull.

'A friend,' said Sorrell. After a moment she burst out laughing and added, 'Monster, just between you and me, I met him on a dating hotline!'

I laughed along with Sorrell. I didn't like to ask what a dating hotline was, especially when Sorrell yelled to the road ahead, 'He's the best thing that's ever happened to me!'

My hopes were high, then, as in the dusk we looped back and forth up the gorse-clad ranges above Upper Noa, leaving humanity behind on our way to Michael the First's house. Eventually we were bumping over a clayey moonscape towards a giant stucco house with a front door flanked by two massive pillars. Sorrell parked at a rakish angle on the expanse of dirt, and leapt out. 'Come on, Monster!' Thrilled, I retrieved my luggage from the boot and joined Sorrell under the portico which, to be honest, was quite forbidding. But Sorrell steered me into the vast entrance hall.

'Pretty good, eh?' she said.

I saw myself reflected, clutching my WWII suitcase, in the bottom corner of a gilt-framed mirror that took up most of one wall.

'It's amazing,' I murmured.

'Back in a sec,' said Sorrell. She clonked up the sweeping stairs two at a time.

I waited. A chandelier like a dandelion seed under a microscope hung from the ceiling which reached all the way to the top of the house. The vestibule floor was marble, and two vases the size of children flanked one of the doors. I realised it was cold, and there was the low hum of air-conditioning. Sorrell didn't come back, so I began to wander around the rooms on the ground floor. Oversized red table lamps, glowing in the dusk, led into enormous living rooms with white couches, red satin curtains and glass cabinets; a formal dining room with glossy, high-backed chairs; so many bathrooms I lost count, again with lamps burning just in case someone might want to be in there; a kitchen lined with expanses of brushed stainless steel reflecting the red of the sunset. At one point I wandered outside onto a terrace the size of skating rink that looked out over the gorse-permed valley. Darkness was coming on.

Eventually Sorrell came back downstairs and made me two-minute noodles. As I ate on a barstool at the kitchen island, she told me we were lucky to be here and not to forget that.

'Okay? No silly business.'

I nodded.

When I'd finished my noodles, Sorrell led me upstairs to a central landing that was bigger than any of the flats we'd lived in previously. Leading off it were bedrooms, bathrooms, dens, a jacuzzi room and a verandah, which looked out into nothingness. My room was big, pink and marvellously cushioned, and it had an ensuite.

After the commune, the luxury felt almost decadent—running water, a bed, food. The only problem was, it was cold all the time, but I wrapped myself in the copious blankets and throws that were dotted about. Michael the First's house was and remains the most comfortable house I've ever lived in. Good thing it didn't last too long, or I would've been ruined as a writer.

The next morning we had to be quiet because Michael the First was in bed and any sounds we made would echo up the marble stairs. Sorrell and I tiptoed out of the house, and she rolled the car then crash-started it a little way down the hill. She took me to Upper Noa Shoes to buy the most expensive pair of sneakers I'd ever owned before or since, and, by mid-morning, I was installed at Upper Noa Intermediate.

I met Michael the First that evening. He was cool in a swept-back Richard Branson way, and I liked him immediately. He presented me with a plastic handbag, and I was and am so grateful. I discovered that he ran a company importing handbags from China. Then, while Sorrell cooked, which I hadn't seen her do before but she seemed to have acquired a new skill of banging pots around in the kitchen and sighing loudly, Michael encouraged me to get into the jacuzzi. I didn't need to be asked twice. I went into my plush bedroom and changed into my togs, and a few minutes later I was in a glittery aqua-tiled room floating deliciously in warm, bubbling water.

Michael the First slid into the water, smiling, and said, 'It's like champagne, isn't it?' I hadn't expected to be joined by a hairy chest streaming with rivulets of water. Michael the First bobbed near me as the foam cascaded and the twilight encroached. He offered me a sip from his glass of bubbles. I took it to be polite.

'Nice, mm?' Michael the First smiled.

'Nice,' I said, trying to be as grateful as possible.

It could've been blissful, me floating warmly, my new stepfather with his head thrown back in a look of concentration. The only thing was, I didn't know Michael the First very well at this point, and I thought we should get a little bit more acquainted before sharing the jacuzzi—you know, play a game of Snakes and Ladders perhaps, watch a movie. I hoped that Sorrell would join us, but the pots and pans continued to ring out from the kitchen. Michael the First seemed to be enjoying the bubbles because he was jiggling along with them in a fun way. Presently, he sighed, a long, groaning kind of sigh. To tell the truth, I was a little alarmed at this sigh. It reminded me of certain sighs I'd heard at Hoki Aroha.

After his sigh, Michael the First turned to me. 'How are things, Princess?'

This question was on a par with 'How's tricks?', and in all honesty, I didn't know how to answer it. The root of the problem was not so much the 'things', although that is so vague as to be meaningless, but the difficulty of thinking of myself as 'Princess'. To be a princess was to feel like total shit.

We all had dinner together in the big formal dining room. The meal was okay, perhaps a little dry and burned, but after Hoki Aroha, it was a novelty to chew something, and I guess Sorrell was still on a learning curve. Michael the First didn't seem to appreciate the dinner as much as I did. He asked Sorrell what this shit was. She didn't reply. I felt a bit sorry for her, actually. I thought I saw her brush away a tear. There was something not quite right about how dinner progressed.

Tucked in my cushiony bed in my pink room, I leaned back and thanked my lucky stars. Here I was in a lovely big house with my own bathroom and a jacuzzi, plus I had a new pair of sneakers. Could life get any better?

Presently I noticed a puppet monkey poking around the side of the door and sliding up and down the jamb. It introduced itself as Mr Monkey in a cute monkey voice. To be polite, I giggled, though it wasn't very funny. I mean, I was thirteen. Mr Monkey was followed around the door by Michael the First. I felt kind of sorry for him that he'd so misjudged the level of my age. I tried to be as nice as possible to put him at his ease.

He brought Mr Monkey over to the bed and made him climb up my arm in a ticklish way. I laughed politely. Then Mr Monkey said in his funny voice that he wanted to get into bed with me. I didn't have the heart to say no, so I opened up the covers and let Mr Monkey hop in, which he did, with alacrity, laughing his funny monkey laugh and sort of joshing around. When Mr Monkey tried to go inside my pyjama pants, I suddenly realised—I'd been such a fool—that something was very wrong with Mr Monkey. I knew this, of course, from my Hoki Aroha days, where I'd got wise to the attentions of Mr Monkey-types. The truth is, I didn't care much for Mr Monkey, or his antics. There seemed nothing to be gained from putting up with it. There was a small risk that if I said anything no one would believe me and I'd be a pariah in my family for the rest of my life, but I decided to chance it. The best course of action seemed to be to yell like crazy, which I did. By the time Sorrell appeared, Mr Monkey had leapt out from under the covers and was dangling limply from the hand of Michael the First, who padded from one foot to the other beside my bed.

'What's going on?' asked Sorrell. Her eyes were darting around and somehow it looked as if she hoped she wouldn't find anything.

'Your daughter is having a tantrum,' said Michael the First.

'Monster,' sighed Sorrell, 'snap out of it, whatever it is.' She didn't like emotion in other people.

'He, he . . .' I couldn't get the words out.

Michael the First was hopping around as if he'd been burnt. 'This is just—' he was saying. 'This is just—'

Sorrell looked at Michael the First warily. 'What were you doing?' she asked in a little voice.

'Saying goodnight,' said Michael the First, wide-eyed. 'Is that a crime?' He backed out of the room waving his hands. 'If she doesn't want to say goodnight to her stepfather who gives her handbags and sneakers and lets her swim in a jacuzzi, that's fine. Not compulsory.'

When he was gone Sorrell put her head on one side and looked at me. 'Just keep out of his way,' she said tightly. 'We can't afford to leave.' She followed Michael the First back downstairs, where the muffled sound of TV news had taken up the airwaves.

I want to thank Sorrell sincerely for not taking me seriously in the face of pretty damning evidence. I'm certain that if I'd felt the least bit safe in my bed, if I'd been given the benefit of the doubt and had my feelings acknowledged and my reaction considered important, I might've grown up with a sense of unshakeable security, and as we all know, that is death to any writer.

But the events of that evening were not to pass unheralded. The next day when I arrived home from school, the Holden was parked haphazardly on the clay expanse, and I could just make out Sorrell's blond head sunk in the driver's seat. A puff of cigarette smoke drifted out the window like a speech bubble. I wondered what was wrong with the Porsche, which was sitting cutely in one half of the double garage, but, as I approached, I realised what was happening; our things were piled on the back seat of the Holden. My heart leapt with love for Sorrell—she'd got the message about Michael the First and had done the right thing. Feeling an exhilarating sense of validation, I broke into a run, schoolbag bouncing on my back, and in a couple of seconds I was at the car trying to wrench open the passenger door. It was locked. I peered through the open top of the window. Sorrel looked to be in one of her morose moods. She took her sweet time unlocking the door.

'He's kicked us out,' she croaked on the in-breath as I climbed in. Executing a 90-degree head swivel, she plumed smoke meaningfully into my face. 'Thanks to you.'

And thanks to you, too, Sorrell, for the colourful experiences, which is why I'm mentioning this episode in my Acknowledgements.

We roared through the flat, milk-lit Upper Noa Valley, between the scarred new-brick townhouses, the pristine footpaths that seemed to lead nowhere, and even though Sorrell being in a mood was a drag, I reflected that overall leaving Michael the First's mansion wasn't so terrible. I stayed quiet, biding my time until we got to Poppy's, where Sorrell would have a drink which would cheer her up for a good half hour.

Staying with Poppy wasn't as much fun as the previous time. During the rages, I cowered in the red room, which turned out to be a golden opportunity to write some of my early prose. But this pint-sized writer's retreat was not to last, and after a couple of weeks things reached such a pitch that we left in a night-time flurry and spent a night in the car. The next day, we moved into a room in Island Bay. This was the height of my *Annie and* period, living in a series of rented bedsits. Sometimes it was fun and we'd snuggle in bed together watching crappy TV, and Sorrell would hug me.

'All right, Monster?'

I'd nod.

But Sorrell was depressed most the time, and when she was depressed the Thing that Happened would come up. The Thing that Happened was Sorrell's grandfather had murdered her grandmother with a shovel out on the farm in 1923, and they hanged him. After that the kids all went pretty crazy, including Sorrell's mother, who was fostered on some awful dairy farm where she had to milk cows before school and the only way to keep her feet warm was so stand on a cowpat. The Thing that Happened caused a fissure that could never be repaired. When Sorrell was depressed and staring out the window she would say, 'We're fucked.' When things were really bad she'd lie in bed and lapse into Americanese. *'We're fuckin' fucked.'*

But reminiscing about the Thing that Happened and lamenting about being fuckin' fucked was better than living with Poppy or Michael the First and better than Hoki Aroha. So that winter and spring, when Sorrell stayed most of the day in bed and drank steadily from mid-afternoon, was actually one of the best periods of my life. I look back on it with fondness. I think I did a lot of growing up, learning to be in charge of making toast, our staple, and running to the corner shop to buy Big Ben pies. I also learned to take care of the rubbish.

Although we didn't have as big a carbon footprint as some people on account of not being able to afford to use the heater or the car sometimes, Sorrell did leave quite a trail of disposables in her path. I mastered the art of what to do when you forget to put the bin out on the street on a Tuesday night because you are too drunk to remember anything, and then another Tuesday night, and another and another. I became adept at assessing, by smell alone, when our rubbish had got to the point at which there would soon be a note in the letterbox signed by six or seven neighbours followed by a letter, more formal, from the City Council. I would decide that it was necessary to do something about it to avoid any shilly-shallying with the courts. Sorrell would try to avoid it by kissing me on the top of my head and calling me Monster, but it had to be done. I could judge the fullness of a public rubbish bin from a hundred paces, in order that a drop-off might be achieved in a nonchalant manner as one passed and looked up at the sky.

Sometimes it got really bad and then Sorrell and I would load seven or eight black plastic bags into the boot of the Holden late at night. They wouldn't quite fit, but the rubbish by this time was beginning to get a bit liquid anyway, so after some squashing the boot would almost close, and Sorrell would hurl herself behind the wheel, and together we'd take a meandering trip to a secluded part of Wellington like the lonely drag up the hill behind Newtown Park. I'd be on the look-out, scanning the horizon like Young Nick from the *Endeavour*, except not for land, for public rubbish bins. When I spied one, Sorrell would slam on the anchors and I'd jump out and madly jam a bag into it. Towards the end of the trip we'd get a bit sick of this routine and Sorrell would say wickedly, 'Let's dump them, Monster.' I'd laugh and remind her about the envelopes. I knew that if there was even a single piece of telltale mail with your address on it, you could get into a shitload of trouble. But Sorrell would say, 'Don't be a square, Monster, don't let the system turn you into a cog.' Looking back, this was one of the most bonding times between us, having a laugh about the rubbish. I'm so grateful to Sorrell, because I actually don't know many daughters who had this kind of intimacy with their mothers, where you could commit a little misdemeanour together and it was not just okay, it was hilarious. Giggling about our plan, Sorrell would veer to the side of the road and I'd leap out and lug the bags onto a grass verge. Usually by this time Sorrell would decide the location was so secluded she could risk stretching her legs and having a smoke. She'd get out of the car, and on the lonely hillside we'd look up at the sky. 'It's bloody beautiful, isn't it, Monster?' Sorrell would say. I got to know the Southern Cross like an intimate friend.

Reader, I haven't forgotten—don't worry—that I am recounting for you the illustrious night of the Antarctica Awards. Before my grand entrance to the Kōwhai Reception Room, I find myself needing to pop into the loo, so I park my fridge in a temporary position outside the Ladies. Inside, all is cool, white and tiled. Glancing at my reflection in the mirror, I note that my makeup has not been quite as fastidiously applied as I'd thought; my eyeliner has run and my face has the patina of a cracked Greek statue. Do I care? Not a bit. I tell myself, 'Janice, you have other fish to fry.' And for some reason, although a bathroom is abject, noa, a place of decomposition and endings, I am filled with a sense of possibility and growth among the whiteness, the primeval gourd shapes, the elemental drip of the tap. I haul my much-travelled manuscript out of my laptop bag once again. One day, no doubt, a researcher will enter through the doors of the Turnbull Library, engage in a whispered conversation with a librarian who will bring the original manuscript of *The Ice Shelf* ceremoniously from the stacks. The researcher (I imagine it will be a man, I don't know why, a little dishevelled but good-looking in a brainy, professorial way) will carry the folio to one of the glossy wooden tables and spend a morning, perhaps many mornings—perhaps he has secured a post-doctoral fellowship in order to study this text—turning the pages with white-gloved hands. He will wonder, no doubt, how the manuscript acquired its smudges, its coffee-rings, its rain-spatters. He might conclude that the blemishes speak of grit, of work, of real life, and ascertain that the novel represents an attempt to reverse societal destruction. I'm sure that the same goes for the papers of Hone Tuwhare—poems written on building sites, pages tattooed with the heat of a welding torch. (Not that I'm comparing myself with the great man, I hasten to add.) I'm happy to help out this hypothetical, unkempt researcher. I can report that on the evening of the Antarctica Awards, in the bathroom at the National Library, I feel the call of another edit.

I lick my finger and shuffle through the manuscript. In no time at all, I have cut out several sections in which the baby boomer S prostitutes herself to a white guy with a sense of entitlement the size of Belgium. I'm sorry to say, Reader, you will never get to read about the antics of Mr Monkey. Future Turnbull research fellows will cringe when they learn about this. I screw the rejects into the tiniest ball I can (thinking of landfill), which is actually not so tiny; about the size of a tennis ball. When I flush it down the toilet, the bowl makes heavy weather of it at first. I picture, rather cartoonishly, a bulge travelling the length of the disposal system, and I feel remorseful about the amount of water I'm using, but it is all for a good cause. After this, the most substantial of my edits so far, the manuscript feels much lighter and more pared-down. And so do I.

Back in the foyer, I decide my fridge is more or less okay where it is outside the bathroom. Bracing myself for the congratulations that are to ensue, I go in to the Awards.

In the jostle of the Kōwhai Reception Room, I literally rub shoulders with arts luminaries and rich corporate types as I secure a glass of fairly-disgusting-but-any-port-in-a-storm red. The literati are knocking back wine like there's no tomorrow, and an edge of hysteria comes off them like dry ice. I swallow as many vol-au-vents as I can while the tray passes, since I haven't eaten in a while, and begin to cruise among angular haircuts and commonplace objects pinned to lapels.

In my initial circumnavigation of the room, I spy quite a few people I know, not all of whom I want to talk to. Tree Murphy, for instance, sails unsteadily past pretending not to see me, but I have ignored her first. Her fiancé of the fluttering eyelashes trails in her phenomenal wake. I can tell he is tipsy by his brief beery glance. I have a big thank you apropos those two individuals later in these Acknowledgements. I also avoid Didi Musgrove like the plague, whose ministrations at Arts New Zealand I have already mentioned. I have to go past the drinks table again in my efforts (strenuous) to avoid the president of Feather, the professional writers' society that I am an Associate Member of. You'll note I said 'Associate Member', not 'Full Member', and there's quite a story attached to that, and this seems as good a time as any to offer my deepest thanks to Feather. I will divert from the Kōwhai Reception Room for a few moments.

*

146

The truth is that after my first book came out, Feather and I, despite my enormous admiration for the work they do, had a bit of a run-in. Feather maintained that because *Utter and Terrible Destruction* was under a certain number of pages, which we will say arbitrarily is fifty, and it *is* arbitrary, I couldn't become a Full Member of the society. (I have to add here that every time the term 'Full Member' was mentioned, I would visualise a huge, throbbing, veiny red cock. 'Associate Member' conjured something smaller and more rubbery. I suppose this is due to my creative nature, and I'm sorry if it is at all off-putting. I certainly don't intend it to be. I hope readers will, when they come across the terms 'Associate Member' and 'Full Member' in relation to Feather, be able to put these images right out of their minds.) To continue: because my book was under fifty pages, I must remain an Associate Member of Feather. Some people would be flattened by this summary denouncement, but not me. I'm made of sterner stuff. In fact, I'm all the stronger for the slight.

I would like to take the opportunity here to thank the person at Feather with whom I had a protracted email exchange after my book came out, a certain Don Willard whose own slim volumes of poetry you might've seen on the shelf in a bookshop, or if you blinked you might have missed them. There's a reason, of course, that Don Willard knows to insert lots of white space in his poems so that his books come out at fifty pages or more. As Membership Secretary of Feather, he is party to privileged information about the minimum-page rule and, as an insider-trader, he is the Martha Stewart of the literary world.

At this point I am having a little reverie that involves me going about discussing literature with people which goes something like: Have you read Such and Such? It's a brilliant book. / How long is it? / Well, it's forty-nine pages long. / Ah, it's not a book then, so no, I haven't read it. / What about this one? (I poke an apparently unidentifiable object under the other person's nose.) / What? / This. / *What?* / This, this book! / I can't see anything. / It's a book with forty-nine pages. / No, sorry, I can't see any book there.

In my emails to Mr Willard I pointed out that my prose pieces were tightly constructed; the lines went right to the other side of the page using all the white space apart from the margin; that is, they were justified. I argued that my crots contained more words that strings and strings of long poems did. I could've constructed my prose so it straggled down the page like McCahon waterfalls, like worms, like saliva, like a man peeing, and my book would've ended up with as many pages as *Remembrance of Things Past*. Mr Willard did not agree on any of the numbered points in my email and got quite defensive. In the end, Mr Willard—who signed himself Mr Willard all through, that's why I'm calling him that, and I think it reveals volumes, albeit slim ones, about his personality—had the last word which proves that for all their Up The Writer rhetoric, Feather are really fascists. I was economically disadvantaged by their hegemonic stance. Mr Willard should read *Animal Farm* and rethink Feather's 'fifty pages good, forty-nine pages bad' policy.

No sooner had I avoided Don Willard in the seething Kōwhai Reception Room than I had to hide again quickly at the drinks table because who should I almost bump into but Eve White, the administrator for the Authors' Fund. If I hadn't suffered enough in recollecting the forty-nine-page saga, another chapter of it was about to come rushing back, this time involving hard cash. The Authors' Fund is the body that collects monies for authors for library holdings in recompense for people who are too mingy to buy your book. There were fifty copies of my book in libraries throughout New Zealand—it's true I did donate a few of them—and, by rights, I should've had $119 per year for those fifty copies. The fact that my book doesn't have a spine has nothing to do with it. But oh no, because *Utter and Terrible Destruction* has only forty-nine pages, it wasn't eligible. I won't regale you with the months of haggling that went on, with threats of lawyers on both sides, although they actually had a lawyer. Anyway, it's not worth raking over the coals. Some things are just petty, and the Authors' Fund But Only Some Authors needs to learn that.

All the same, because I'm a glass-half-full kind of person (I might add, the glasses of wine they served at the awards ceremony were not anywhere near half full which is why I kept having to go back to the bar), I'm grateful for these spirited back-and-forth argle-bargles which served only to sharpen my resolve as a writer.

Who should I need to avoid next in the Kōwhai Room, but Dame Bev Hollis, who will be known to many, at least in New Zealand which narrows it down somewhat, and when we cut out the people who don't read novels and who don't read New Zealand novels, this is hardly someone you can buy a mask of and dress up as at Halloween. However, Dame Bev is a juggernaut in some quarters, and there could not be an awards ceremony without her. Here I need to reveal that I am actually a fond acquaintance of Dame Bev. In a small country like New Zealand, everyone knows everyone in the literary community; in fact you are probably related to them and, if not, you've probably been married to them at some point. The truth is that even if you have absolutely nothing in common with a person, even if they happen to be, say, old and stuck up and not very talented, just getting noticed by sitting on arts boards, you will know that person quite well.

I have a heartfelt thank you to make to Dame Bev and will break off from my account of the awards ceremony here to do just that. The reason for my thanks is that Dame Bev wrote a review of *Utter and Terrible Destruction*, even though it doesn't have a spine; this is the only review of my book to date and, as such, an important contribution to the culture surrounding the book. To be reviewed by Dame Bev is, on the surface, quite a coup. The review appeared on page 26 of the *Dominion Post* on 22 April 2010. Why a person already so successful as to have been awarded a dameship for services to literature would still write reviews for almost no money is curious. It may be because a dameship is actually not successful in monetary or global or real terms. But I'm fortunate that Dame Bev continues her hobby. If it hadn't been for her review, my writing life would've been entirely different. Not everyone gets advice from a master, but I was lucky enough to, and I quote: 'One wonders who Redmond thinks she is writing for—perhaps herself? In any case, the rather trashy and self-centred diatribe that is *Utter and Terrible Destruction* left this reader out in the cold.' I took Dame Bev's piece of searching critical analysis very seriously indeed. If not for the acutely observed insights, I might've gone on for years writing self-centred diatribes and not giving a toss whether people wanted to read them or not. Thank you so much, Dame Bev!

But I think where I most benefitted from Dame Bev's razor-sharp assessment was in the area of *trashy*. This is quite a laying down of the gauntlet. I'm completely in favour of reviewers who don't flinch, who engage in robust discourse rather than heaping praise about in a generalised and namby-pamby fashion. So I was only too pleased to be singled out by Dame Bev as deserving of the descriptor *trashy*. It has always been my policy to take criticism on the chin. I'm not one of these people who reacts to excoriation by making *ad hominem* attacks on their detractors. And so I pondered at length the nature of trash. Luckily, rubbish is a topic I am fairly familiar with, as you will have gathered in these Acknowledgements. Therefore I thought deeply about the implications of meta-sustainability for literature—where thinking becomes books, which become newspaper reviews, which break down and go into the atmosphere unseen like radio frequencies but there all the same to be picked up by writers with their antennae always on the alert. If not for Dame Bev's wise comments, I might never have done the critical thinking around a philosophy on rubbish as it pertains to writing; I might have continued to lure people to the misfortune of reading my work, a.k.a. rubbish, without the necessary new growth. My heartfelt thanks to Dame Bev. And now I'd like to share a colourful incident that occurred when I encountered her at a writers' festival at Borich Winery in the Wairarapa in June 2010.

Again, we are so fortunate in New Zealand that great writers—and I mean truly great, like Dame Bev—aren't too high and mighty to frequent insy writers' festivals such as the Borich. I'm sure Dame Bev could've been hobnobbing at Hay-on-Wye, the Edinburgh Festival or the Frankfurt Book Fair with other writers of her enormous stature, but no, she said a heartfelt Yes to the microscopic Borich Winery Readers and Writers Festival and appeared on several panels for a modest fee after throwing a tantrum (so the story goes) of only twice what the other panellists were paid.

The festival occurred close on the heels of the day the review of *Utter and Terrible Destruction* appeared in the *Dominion Post*, which was good timing. What are festivals for if not to facilitate vibrant discussion about our literature/s?

I was part of the Borich Winery Fringe Festival, and here, I must add my thanks to the organiser of the Borich, namely Nick Hope, for scheduling me to appear not in the festival proper but in the Fringe with a line-up of barely published, emerging and not the slightest bit emerged, indeed, submerged, writers. I have to say, when I heard I was to be a participant in the Fringe, I pictured myself as a ratty thread lying alongside other ratty threads at the edge of a beautiful, richly patterned Persian rug. Although this vision of myself may seem rather abject, I'm grateful for the insight it has brought me. If I'd been featured on a panel alongside writers of my true rank—that is, emerged, having had a book published by a publisher albeit without a spine—I would never have stood among grassroots writers who are of the people, at the coalface, and surely that's what writing is all about.

However, I have to confess that before I realised what a privilege it was to be fringe rather than rug, I was a little miffed. To get through the ordeal, I vacuumed up a quick line of coke in Mandy's bathroom (I was flatting with her during that period), and by the time I got off the bus at the winery, I was feeling much better.

The sky was purplish dark even though it was only four o'clock in the afternoon. From the festival noticeboard outside the long pink adobe-style buildings, I saw that the Fringe reading was to take place in the Summer Garden in the direction of the arrow. As I promenaded along the deep, elegantly pillared terrace, making for the outermost reaches of the winery, a crack of lightning rent the air and the patter of rain started up. I left the cover of the verandah and headed into the open to join the kick-ass crew in the garden, a grassy square dotted with pretty shrubs on the edge of the vineyard. It was indeed raining, rather heavily now, but we Fringe people didn't mind, and neither it seemed did the five or six audience members who'd had the foresight to bring golf umbrellas. From the makeshift podium we had a majestic view of the grapevines, glazed with rain, striping down into the misty valley. The organisers had got rid of the microphone because of the danger of death by electrocution, and with the size of the audience, it didn't matter, in fact it added to the intimacy. The natural tones of the human voice raised against a torrent is a truly wonderful sound.

Through the windows of the Pūkeko Ballroom we could make out, illuminated in the tinkling light of chandeliers, a sea of grey-coiffed people seated on plush chairs with gilt edges, an expanse of red carpet at their feet. They nursed glasses of wine and tittered occasionally in response to something one of the emerged writers said. From our position in the Summer Garden, it all looked very jolly. How glad I was that I was on the right side of the fence, ontologically, for a writer.

In the garden a poet with a grey ponytail and John Lennon glasses showed us his shaped poems which were getting rather pulpy in the rain. They were about the universe. Someone held a red-and-white golf umbrella over his head, and plaits of water cascaded about his feet. He ploughed on, and one had to admire his self-belief. I looked for his name on the chalkboard but it had washed off in a pretty trickle of pink and aqua. My own name had met with the same fate, but I didn't mind; in fact I found it fitting that 'Janice Redmond' had transubstantiated into a purple sludge that bulged slightly over the lower wooden edge of the blackboard.

Consider the opposite: to have one's name splashed across a shiny printed programme, clutched in the liver-spotted fist of a retired festival subscriber, is to live cuddled in the lap of the bourgeoisie. My sincere gratitude to Nick Hope for leaving me outside society, where one must reside if one is to be an artist.

After the grey-ponytailed poet, another submerged writer, this one wrapped in back from head to foot, explained how there was no meaning in poetry. I missed the last bit due to a sizzle of lightning and, three hippapotomi later (I counted), a rumble of thunder. Nevertheless, raindrops sprayed from the hands of six people clapping. The poet told us how her poems had come into being, why they looked the way they did on the page (or had, before the storm), and what they represented: the universe. I began to wonder if I'd missed some vital information about the theme of the event. My crots were not about the universe. As the woman in black began reading, I concocted a little speech in my head which would reframe my reading within the universe. By this time I was drenched and cold and I was thankful that the universe poems were short, such as 'I / de / con / struct / my / self'. They weren't the best poems I'd ever heard, but the audience clapped wetly, cheered, and even stamped their feet in the mud. I brushed the brown splatters off my calves in preparation for my turn on the stage.

When I began, it was starkly obvious that I should've been in the Pūkeko Ballroom performing for the people sitting in plush chairs under the sparkle of the chandeliers. But I didn't mind, I really didn't. The six people in the audience—four at this point because it was very wet and relatives tended to peel off once their loved ones had read—clapped appreciatively as I read several crots from *Utter and Terrible Destruction*.

As I've already discussed, art finds itself in extraordinary circumstances. I would like to thank the fringe-dwellers of the Borich Festival for the important lesson they taught me as I stood by and witnessed their tenacity, their good humour in the face of, well, being dreadful and as a result facing out-and-out rejection. The lesson is, keep going, even if you're absolutely hopeless. Never give up. How fortunate I was not to be with the chosen ones in the Pūkeko Ballroom, where I'm positive such a determined attitude would not have been possible. Thank you, Nick Hope, for relegating me to the Fringe; thank you, thank you.

When I finished, there was no one left in the garden. I'd been carried away with my crots but had noticed one or two audience members ducking inside during my performance. I don't blame them in the least—the rain was torrential. I'd probably walk away from hearing some interesting literature if I were being soaked to the skin. But I must admit, the Summer Garden seemed like a wasteland, and I felt the teensiest bit downhearted as I picked my way through the mud to the big Spanish terrace. As I was drying off in the foyer, who should I see coming out of the plush roomful of laughter and forgetting but Dame Bev of the review. A quick thumbnail description of Dame Bev, here: eyebrows raised in self-important expectation; earthy suits in coarse brown wool shot through with red flecks (as if Dame Bev is a fence and sheep have rubbed up against her, leaving tufts of wool marked with the bright dye of the breeder); shoes high and clompy (yes, a little hoof-like, a little sheepish, so I'm not sure if she is fence or sheep, but why not both?); the shoes causing her to tip forwards, which brings us back to the eyebrows because, as if they are her career, she throws *everything into them*.

When I told Dame Bev, there in the marble foyer, that it was very nice to see her, she pretended she didn't know who I was—the eyebrows airborne, the cheeks elongating like a nineteenth-century parson—a droll pantomime, in view of fact that my photo appears on several websites, and that she had reviewed my book, FFS. Never mind, I'm sure I have a few foibles too. I got the ball rolling (by this time I'd wrung most of the water out of my hair) by telling Dame Bev that actually I knew quite a bit about rubbish. Once again, she pretended to look lost, but I stuck to my guns. As it happens, I'm reasonably clued-up on the topic of composting—what can go in and what can't, the use of lime, the incredible stink—all information gathered during my time with Harry and Nico at the commune, although it never quite worked there. And, as you know, I also became well acquainted with the clandestine disposal of rubbish while living in town with Sorrell.

When Dame Bev chose to use the notion of rubbish as a literary conceit while reviewing my book in the *Dominion Post* in April 2010, she bit off a little more than she could chew. Yessiree, as they say in America, she picked the wrong person to mess with.

As we stood chatting beside the wine table at the Borich Festival, I said to Dame Bev that if you're going to use the word trash, you need to be able to define it, and could she? At first, she pretended to wave to someone else on the other side of the room, but I'd noticed a rubbish bin next to us, a large tub lined with a black plastic sack. As Dame Bev turned to leave, I tapped her on her woolly shoulder, snagging some fleece on my fingernail.

She turned, eyebrows first.

'I'm so sorry,' I said.

You might be wondering what kind of materials a writer tosses into a rubbish bin at a literary festival. Perhaps you're hoping that I can deliver an insider's view. I can do just that. Before I do, I should say there were probably two or three non-writers at the Borich Festival, i.e. the audience, or, in the terminology of the festival, readers. The sample of these readers would not have been big enough to enable any assertions to be made vis-à-vis rubbish, so I will call the group whose rubbish I am going to discuss writers, with a three percent plus or minus factor of error to allow for readers.

In my naïvety, I'd thought the rubbish of the writers would be of a high calibre. I was anticipating half-written poems on the backs of envelopes, quotes from presenters scribbled down during sessions but accidentally mislaid, tickets to hear celebrity writers—I expected this rubbish to be clean, dry and illuminating. Sadly this was not the case. I admit I was disappointed in the writers (plus or minus three percent readers) at the Borich Festival. This is the catalogue of their rubbish:

Coffee cups, coffee-cup lids, coffee-cup carriers, screwed-up Borich Festival programmes, serviettes made into paper planes, lolly wrappers, bookmarks advertising the Borich Festival, muesli-bar wrappers, aluminium cans, water bottles, half a mince and cheese pie, balled-up serviettes, paper bags from the Borich Festival books table, a black beret, pantyhose, a diaper, cigarette lighters, plastic cups with dregs of wine, a broken Rubik's Cube, plastic plates, plastic knives, forks and spoons, cigarette packets, ice-block sticks, a plush dog with the stuffing coming out, deconstructed sandwiches, polystyrene cups, used tissues, empty Panadol pouches, baby wipes, McDonald's wrappers, a worn toothbrush, *Poems of the Universe: An Anthology*, and all of the above mixed together like the maelstrom of debris that swirls in the middle of the Pacific Ocean.

Despite its poor quality, the rubbish served its purpose, maybe better than its refined cousin would have. In the end, I could just see Dame Bev's shiny black sheeplike shoes peeping out from the little mountain. The nineteenth-century parson look had returned to her face.

'Oops,' I said.

It was ten to two. In a few minutes I would be doing my second reading in the Side Tent at the Fringe Festival, but I was all of a flutter. It's not easy being an activist. People think it's a piece of cake to be brave and decisive, to know when enough crap is enough. In truth, it takes a lot out of you. I'd planned to read six pieces from *Utter and Terrible Destruction* and, seriously, I don't know if I would've done my usual good job on delivery—I am 'an amusing reader of [my] work', according to the blog *BookLovers*. Well, the Fringe audience never got the chance to find out for themselves, because I was escorted off the premises—not by security; what do you think this is, Jaipur?—by Nick Hope himself.

I'm getting ahead of myself. To return to the arty bustle of the awards ceremony: the Director of Arts New Zealand has embarked on a speech in which he raves about the talent of the Antarctica winners, which is, well, humbling. I would've tweeted about how humbled I was, but my phone was, remember, in a humbled position itself, embedded in a bag of rice in my hold-all. Then there was a bit of a diatribe about the history of the awards, building cultural capital and the importance of telling our stories. I find myself sliding down the wall in a bit of a trance and before long I am pulling out my manuscript and excising a section about several pretentious literary characters. Their presence in the text, I realise, was holding *The Ice Shelf* back. Just behind me is a big red Chinese vase like the one in *The Remains of the Day*. I ball the rejects and pop them in the vase. I notice a couple of people, Dame Bev and the head of the Authors' Fund, observing me with puzzled expressions. I zip up my laptop bag, straighten up and, feeling again a sense of levity, turn my attention properly to the speech. Unfortunately, it is still deathly. A cluster of young student types in black are hanging about, holding their chins and pretending to listen, and as I study them I remember with a pang my own youth, which is fading quickly. On that note I'd like to take the opportunity to make some very important acknowledgements from that time.

With the experience of Harry, Nico, Sorrell et al., behind me, I found myself, in the late nineties, on the cusp of adulthood, an excitingly sharp lip to teeter upon. I sashayed around Wellington, living in different flats, using the dole as a writer's grant until they found me a job, so I enrolled at Victoria University and spent several psychedelic years pursuing a Bachelor of Arts in a number of things. In the end I discovered I could educate myself better than any university could. During this period I also ran helter-skelter into the arms of a succession of lovers. I seemed to be rather popular, not to blow my own trumpet. Some of these liaisons, I have to say, were inappropriate. I'm thinking of a certain gang member, and the non-molestation order. But that's long past, and I am now able to go freely into the vicinity of Rintoul Street, Newtown, if I so choose. All in all, a somewhat tempestuous few years, but what can you expect when all through your childhood you saw a parade of vitriolic posturing and toxic entanglements?

However, I am ever thankful for my colourful background, otherwise I and my writing would be quite boring.

What I really wanted to mention here was my job at the Glass Menagerie, for two reasons: one, I have a hugely important thank you to make; and also because it was during this time that I acquired the fridge.

After dropping out of university, I was at a bit of loose end for a while—reversing night and day, probably drinking the teensiest bit too much, writing crots, having several intense friendships that foundered in the wee small hours because they were just too artistic, and if I remember rightly staying with Mandy on and off. Then I landed a job at a gift shop in Kelburn called the Glass Menagerie.

At that point my resumé wasn't in the best of health, to say the least. But I must've done something right in the interview, which was conducted by the manager Wendy in her poky but trying-hard office with its thick carpet and cartoonishly rounded armchairs. The interview started with Wendy peering over her filigreed bifocals at my outfit. I had on my usual big shirt and leggings, and understood pretty quickly that this was too boho for the position. Wendy tossed her pashmina with a sun-browned wrist that was bangled like the lid of a screw-top jar, and observed that I'd had a checkered career. I was halfway out of my chair, thinking it was all over, but Wendy gestured with her bangles that I should sit back down. There followed the single question of my interview, delivered with a slight toffee lisp: was I discreet?

I hesitated. I wasn't sure exactly what I was to be discreet *about*. All the same, I quickly gave Wendy my guarantee, in what I hoped was a not-too-shrieky tone, that I was the very soul of discretion. Wendy was probably about sixty, but her beauty treatments, her metallic hair and foundation, made her look older, and when she stood now, she had an elderly woman's authority, the kind of oomph that accompanies the knowledge that you're going to die soon so you may as well go for it. I staggered up too, then, and Wendy invited me onboard, welcoming me with open arms, literally, and a gust of Chanel No. 5.

'I have a feeling you and I are going to get along,' she said as we hugged.

The formal part of the interview seemed to be over, and I thought it was time to mention my conditions. We remained standing on the tussocky carpet. Wendy told me about her husband, Jan, spelt with a J but pronounced 'Yan'. 'He's from Holland.'

Wendy wanted to be friends with me, it seemed, telling me snippets about her life. She told me Jan didn't come in very often, but he was the mastermind behind the Glass Menagerie chain. I nodded and smiled as if this was the best thing I'd ever heard.

'I just fluff around,' said Wendy. 'I love the stock, you see. I'd give it away if I could. But my husband, Jan, spelt with a J, he has the business head.'

I was to start on the minimum wage. If it were up to Wendy I would've started on more, but she was quite silly about these things—there would *be* no shop, nor a job for me, if she were running things, because she was so sentimental. But there'd be ample opportunity for advancement. Wendy would've liked to have offered me several hours a day, at least six, on a fixed schedule, especially after meeting me and finding we got along so well. But it wasn't up to her, she was just a pretty face, ha ha—it was up to Jan.

'Unfortunately,' said Wendy, 'Jan says that just wouldn't work. For anybody.'

I asked, smiling, how it *would* work.

Wendy's teeth flashed—they were quite a pretty tortoiseshell. 'At least four hours a day. Once in a while, three. Sometimes two, if things are slow. There'll be the odd day, in the middle of July when the weather's terrible and no one's out shopping, when we won't need you at all, and you'll be able to have a lovely lie-in and catch up on all your important other things.'

The fact I wasn't too rapt about my zero-hours contract must've been written all over my face, because Wendy angled her head up under my nose in a reassuring way. 'I can imagine you ruining this place in the end. Can't you?'

I stepped back, puzzled. 'Ruining?'

'No, running! I said *running!*' We both had a good old laugh over that, and I followed Wendy's gaze out into the shop where the glass *objets* exploded with light. 'I'm sure Jan would agree,' said Wendy.

I was the teensiest bit disappointed, but nevertheless the job would fit nicely with my writing life for now, as long as I could afford to eat enough to stay alive. On my way out, Wendy gestured towards my body, indicating that I needed to do something about my clothes, so over the next twenty-four hours I bought two sixties jewel-coloured synthetic dresses with big geometric patterns (slightly tight on me) and a pair of black not-very-worn-out penny loafers, all from the op-shop, and two pairs of black tights from the supermarket. I didn't feel like me anymore, but I was willing to go with that.

Business was very friendly to start with, very chummy. On my first day Wendy brought in Neenish tarts for morning tea and we sat and had a really excellent rave in her office. She told me how she and her husband Jan, spelt with a J, who was from Holland, had grown the business from nothing and now it had franchises all over the country and Australia, too—which I knew anyway, there are Glass Menageries in all the shopping centres. When Wendy told me she and Jan owned a lifestyle block at Makara and bred horses, I started to respond in kind about Hoki Aroha but realised I should back off from telling her *too* many details. She might have read stuff in the paper anyway.

That first morning I was dispatched to the stock room, a dark, chilly, hangar-like space with avenues between staggering towers of cartons. Wendy instructed me in my task: I was to unpack boxes of glass *objets*—vases and platters, little glass animals with paws that tailed off as the knobbly end of the glass-blowing process—delving into a sea of polystyrene, and carefully disrobe them of their bubble wrap, then peel off the tiny Made in China stickers and replace them with bigger, green Proudly Made in NZ stickers from a gigantic roll. Wendy demonstrated on a big sea-glass coloured dolphin with her gold-lacquered nail, and I followed suit on a sleek red vase. She looked on as if I were a moron. 'Oh, well done, you,' she said when I'd completed my task. I surveyed my handiwork on the thick glass bottom. In truth, the red prototype did look as if it had come out of some hippy town in New Zealand, and even though it hadn't, I thought, What the fuck, life's too short! I replaced stickers all morning.

At lunch I found I was to take my breaks (apart from the introductory first morning tea) in the stock room on a little stool. A cold wind blew in the open door to the delivery bay. Wendy took her tea in the comfort of her office, not that I minded. I was happy to sit there shivering, eating my sandwiches in the half dark with a slight whiff of the toilet wending its way to me.

In the afternoon, Wendy tottered out of her office with a crisp new box and a smile on her face. This batch of labels were oval, white and edged with black, like stationery had been after the death of Queen Victoria, and they read 'Made by a member of the Ngāti Manu tribe'. Wendy showed me with her beetly nail where to apply the stickers on some carved tikis after I'd peeled off the Made in China stickers. I took a tiki in my hands and had a go.

'Um, Wendy?' I said.

She cocked her head patiently and I asked, feeling a bit *Cinema of Unease*-y, whether she could perhaps, you know, get into trouble for using these labels.

'Mmm,' said Wendy. Her skirt and pashmina framed by afternoon light gave her a draped dusty look, like a marble statue of a Greek goddess. 'Do you remember why you have this job?'

'Because I'm discreet?' I murmured.

'Exactly. If you don't want to work here . . .' Wendy gestured to the docking bay, and I followed her gaze through the open roller door. Rubbish blew about in the yard, illuminated in the sunlight. I thought of the beginning of *American Beauty*, with the plastic bag dancing about. I thought about how when Len Lye was four years old, he was kicking a tin can around outside and noticed the way the light bounced off it, and from that moment he was a kinetic sculptor. I spent the afternoon in the half-light replacing stickers.

On the way home after work I passed a secondhand shop on the edge of the shopping centre on leafy Upland Road, and noticed a stylish green fridge on display outside. Yes, this was my first sight of the very fridge you know so well.

The tough rays of the setting sun bounced off its corners, which were rounded and sleek like a horse's buttocks. I looked at it idly and reached for the price-tag fluttering from the clunky cream and gold handle: fifty dollars. But I didn't need a fridge. Mandy had a fridge.

The next morning, relabelling done for the time being, Wendy initiated me into the art of shopkeeping. The most important thing, she said, eyeing me over folds of a different but similar pashmina, was to smile. She showed her jewel-filled teeth to demonstrate.

'*You* create the climate in the shop,' said Wendy, 'you and only you.'

I was pleased to have been given such responsibility on my second day. Wendy's ringed fingers busied themselves with flaps of banknotes as she showed me how to use the till. She demonstrated with big, exaggerated movements how to wrap delicate *objets* in swathes of tissue paper, how to then slide them carefully into the thick paper carry-bags. And always, always, she said, be careful to take the price-tag off first because nothing was more vulgar than revealing the enormous price of a gift. Then, one must come out from behind the counter to hand over the carry-bag.

'Never, ever pass an item across the counter,' said Wendy. 'That is vulgar. Remember, you make the climate.'

We toured the shop together, inspecting the many glass shelves with their cargo of gleaming *objets*. Wendy instructed me on how to cajole but not annoy the customers. I was to hover discreetly like a waiter, not breathe down their necks. I was to answer any questions in a friendly manner but not initiate anything.

'Remember—the climate!' said Wendy.

'Yes, the climate,' I chimed.

To tell the truth, I was eager for Wendy to leave me to get on with it. I'd become excited at the prospect of being sole charge. Finally she swept back to her office and I was alone. I stalked around my domain, inspecting the stock. Wendy had a preference for reds and oranges. With the overhead fluorescent strobes bouncing off these colours, the shop was ablaze. Shelf after shelf reflected a network of gamma rays. The overall effect was of a fantastical world of heat and light.

Mid-morning, customers began to trickle in. It was as if Wendy had invited her friends to the shop, because they dressed like her and behaved like her too. They were always in pairs and they strode around looking at this item and that and exclaiming to one another, How darling! How adorable!

Listening to their conversation from behind the counter or roving with my feather duster, it was becoming clear to me that their visits to the shop weren't enjoyable; quite the reverse, they were agony. 'What to get Clarissa!' they would cry to their friend. After an interminable time of peering and touching, the friend would light on an *objet* and shriek, '*That* is the very thing for Clarissa! I can picture it in the beach house.' And, tipping the vase or jug or platter upside down to read the label, the friend would add, 'And look, Bobby. It's made in New Zealand.' And Bobby would reply, 'Yes, you're right, Pippa, I can absolutely imagine that in the beach house. The colours.' Pippa might add that the *objet* was rather pricey, but that didn't really matter because when one bought something made in New Zealand, one was supporting the locals. And the *objet* would be ferried with a fair amount of pomp and circumstance to the counter. I would swathe it in tissue paper while the women continued to circumnavigate the shop, and more often than not another *objet* would take their eye. 'Look, Pippa, I can picture this in Felicity's vestibule, can't you?' 'Why yes, I can. And look what it says on the bottom, it's made by a member of the Ngāti Manu tribe.' 'Who are they, Pippa?' 'Māoris, Bobby.'

I would *person* the counter, ringing up, wrapping, bagging, all the while smiling. The final bill would be rather large, with the customers seemingly unfazed by spending two or three times what I was to earn in the week. I'd feel like saying, why not give *me* the five hundred dollars, instead of spending it on another fucking vase for your friend to clutter up her Kelburn villa? But of course I didn't. I was responsible for the climate in the shop, so I maintained my customary poise and was friendly as hell. Wendy occasionally stretched her neck around the corner of her office, brushing Neenish tart crumbs from her lips and searching the shop with her hazel eye.

I enjoyed being front-of-house, watching the customers, admiring their generosity of spirit in the face of *what to buy*. I had time to reflect that giving is always a selfless act, even if it the gift is useless. Plus, the shop did a roaring trade in thank-you cards, which were white with embossed gold calligraphy. People were clearly very grateful to someone or other. I liked that. In a way, the very Acknowledgements you are perusing right now function as a series of thank-you cards in gold script, personally messaged and signed by yours truly.

At the end of my first week, I worked late, relabelling a new shipment that had arrived just on closing time. Wendy apologised that Jan couldn't run to overtime. If it had been up to her . . . But as we locked up the shop at ten o'clock she said, 'I'm so pleased you're on board, Janice. We're a team, you and me.' At that moment I felt like the stock on the shelves—valuable and precious.

One evening, after I'd been at the Glass Menagerie a few weeks, I was relabelling in the stock room when I saw, in one of the cartons of big red glass platters, an invoice. Up until then I had seen no paperwork. I was on my way to take the document to Wendy when something caught my eye. Checking that Wendy was in her office, because it did seem an illicit thing to do, I perused the bill. According to the tally, ten glass platters had cost twenty dollars. In the shop, the platters sold for one hundred and twenty dollars each. I glanced at Wendy through the titled blinds. She was on the phone, laughing and flinging her pashmina back, her gold bangles flashing. I continued with my peeling and stickering.

Things trundled on. Wendy was effusive in her praise of me, especially when I stayed late. 'What would we do without you, Janice?' she'd say, or 'You're a treasure, Janice.' I'd think, *pay rise!* seeing as she liked me so much.

One day, Wendy and I had our first little *contretemps*, not that it was much. I was flicking delicately over the shelves with my yellow feather duster like a cute little trained waxeye bird, when I accidentally knocked over a little red glass cat. As I bent to pick it up, I saw that its little ear was chipped off. I took the cat to Wendy and apologised. She tossed her pashmina, her gold jewellery rattling, and smiled.

'No matter,' she said. 'These things happen. And you're such a good worker, Janice.'

I felt warm inside.

'We won't tell Jan,' she said with a conspiratorial wink. 'The cat can come out of your wages. It's only twenty dollars.'

Now, I would've thought that working in a gift shop such as the Glass Menagerie, there would be a certain amount of breakage. In fact, I'd already seen stock arrive broken, and that didn't seem to cause much of a stir. Glass and breakage seemed to go together like a horse and carriage. It would take me two hours to earn twenty dollars, after tax. So I was a little miffed.

That afternoon when Wendy went out to do the banking, I sped into her office and riffled at lightning speed through the filing cabinet, looking for an invoice for the one-eared cat. I found it: one hundred cats @ twenty cents each.

When Wendy came back I was standing behind the counter staring into space.

'What's the matter?' she said.

'Nothing,' I said. But I was all a-jangle.

'Remember the climate of the shop,' she said as she disappeared into her office. I could see she had a Neenish tart in a paper bag which she was trying to hide under her pashmina.

The next day, I was apparently scowling as I did the dusting. When Wendy came through she said, 'Oh please, a little good humour. The climate of the shop!'

I made a lopsided smile, which vanished as soon as Wendy had passed by. I brooded all morning and sold a couple of vases and some curly gold thank-you cards. At lunchtime I sat on my stool and ate my sandwich from home and drank my drink. It was a cold day and I shivered as the Wellington wind whipped in through the delivery doors. The vodka and orange was just to get me through the afternoon. On my way back, Wendy stopped me and said, 'Janice, what *would* we do without you? You're a treasure,' and she asked me if I'd mind staying late to do a bit of labelling. I said I wouldn't mind. I think at this point it's safe to say that *Cinema of Unease* had set in. But I needed the job.

'That's my girl,' said Wendy.

It was probably about three o'clock, but it seemed later because the afternoon had clouded over and the light outside was the grey of an old gaberdine coat. The customers had been few and far between and I'd dashed out back to finish my drink, but I was, to be honest, bored, despite the magical atmosphere of the shop. I wandered around the shelves, inspecting the vases, the platters, the little cats with both their ears. They swam past me in a flicker of colour and shine that increased in speed, so that soon I felt like I was inside a car wash. As the colours torrented past me, I found myself caught in a heightened state of ecstasy and anxiety, lightness and heaviness, and suddenly I couldn't bear the confusion. To stem the flow of *objets*, I stopped in front of a display, a shelf laden with icy glitter. And I put out my hand and tipped the glass shelf vertical.

An array of vases, ornaments and plates cascaded to the floor, mostly red, like the gushing of veins. The noise was tremendous, and then the debris was beautiful.

From the corner of my vision I was aware of Wendy erupting from her office in a flash of turquoise. 'Oh my God, you stupid girl!' She stood in the jagged mess, gasping. In my distraction I had time to notice that one of her delicate veiny brown feet was bleeding through the bars of her gold sandal. 'I will call Jan,' she said.

I looked at her face again, its rictus, and in that moment I somehow understood from her shiftless expression that Jan did not exist. The timing of my realisation was unfortunate, because I stepped back in alarm and bumped something behind me, and a fresh cascade of glass plummeted to the floor. Wendy's shriek frightened me and made me turn to the left where I knocked down another shelf whose load shattered in a heap of shards. I turned to the right, and a further shelf toppled its cargo into the glittery heap that already covered the shop floor. At this point—quite distressed, as you can imagine—I literally saw red; I seemed to be in the *Inferno*. I began picking my way through the wreckage to my safe place, the counter. En route I knocked the last shelf. Oops. The remaining *objets* descended like a rain of blood.

At the counter, surveying the riotous shop and the backdrop of grey skies, I felt myself suddenly burst through my red haze, and I received from somewhere an enormous sense of power. I *was* the climate of the shop. I had risen up and exploded. Wendy limped towards me in her high-heeled sandals with her bleeding foot. The look on her face resembled the afternoon's clouds, but it was too late, it was done.

Suffice to say, I exited through the gift shop, picking my way in my penny loafers through the rapids of glass and out into the leaden air. On my way home, despite everything, I felt a little jolt as I passed the secondhand shop and saw the fridge, indoors now, standing like a Dalek among the steampunk jumble of bar-heaters and ironing boards. Somehow it looked sad, and I was sad. When I was back at Mandy's, I tore off my sixties dress and tights and climbed back into a big top and leggings.

After leaving the Glass Menagerie under a bit of a cloud, I was at a loose end. Of course I went to the union about my dismissal and they began a case for me, but I didn't feel very hopeful. Also—it never rains but it pours—I'd had a slight falling-out with Mandy over a power bill, which was unfair because the numbers on the On/Off knob on the stove had been worn away and it was impossible to tell which was which, and anyway it was all resolved later; but meantime I'd left Mandy's and moved into a bedsit in Hataitai at the top of a long zigzagging hill which lost the sun at two-fifteen in the afternoon even though it was summer. I felt that some areas of my life weren't going very well—especially work, money, accommodation, education, friends and family. If I was going to be the kind of person I wanted to be, a survivor, then I needed to get proactive. I decided to start with my love life, which had been languishing lately. I would find a nice boyfriend, or perhaps girlfriend, who knew? I wanted love. Doesn't everyone? Armed with sound advice handed down to me by Sorrell and Harry, from whom I learned the tenets of a good relationship by reverse psychology, I came up with a sterling plan that I thought would pretty much guarantee me partnered off in no time.

I asked every man I knew if he would have coffee with me, and a few of the women. If he or she agreed, and the coffee was had, I would ask him or her on a date. If he or she agreed, and the date was had, I would ask him or her if I could stay the night. If he or she agreed and I stayed the night, we would of course have sex, and I would be well on my way to finding a nice boyfriend or nice girlfriend. After several weeks of doing this, I found that several of my attempts to get a nice boyfriend or nice girlfriend had come to fruition, and I had five candidates. I must say, I hadn't anticipated such a rush, but it seemed a shame to get rid of any of them after all the hard work I'd put in, and at that point I didn't know if any of them would last, so I had coffee, dates and sex with all of them at breakneck speed over a two-week period.

The scheduling was a bit of a nightmare. Like a reporter, I had a little notebook that I'd been writing everything down in from the beginning of my campaign—who, when, where, what, how; it was crowded with incident. I was finding it difficult to make a decision about the lovers, in short. How to choose a nice boyfriend or nice girlfriend from the candidates? They all seemed nice in some ways and an incredible drag in others. None of them stood out as being *totally* nice, which would have made them resoundingly good boyfriend or girlfriend material, but none of them was terrible enough to strike off the agenda.

In between sleepovers, I'd go back to my flat, or bundle the lovers out the door if we were sleeping at my place, then I would compare the attributes of the candidates for the nice boyfriend or nice girlfriend on a flowchart in my notebook. To give you some idea of my process:

Pros	Cons
Good sex	Unfulfilling or no sex
Fun talk	Silent
Brainy	Stupid
Socially normal	*Cinema of Unease*
Good-looking	No oil painting
Financially stable	Insolvent
Nicely presented	Atrocious dresser
Abstemious	Addicted
Law-abiding	Convictions

The five candidates were Anton, Matiu, Eric, Miriam, and one whose identity I will save for later. You, Reader, can in a sense moderate my process. Here is a sample of best, middle, and worst.

Best: Eric. Excellent sex, fun talk, brainy, awkward socially, terrible clothes, heavy drinker, no convictions, financial prospects abysmal. A great fuck and fun to be with but nothing translates to outside the house, so basically he would be your stay-at-home pet.

Middle: Miriam. Fun talk, brainy, life of the party, good dresser, no addictions or convictions, good financial prospects. Good in every department except for sudden decision late at night that she doesn't like girls after all.

Worst: Anton. The only reason I didn't strike him off the list immediately was that he looked really cool in his clothes.

The trialling process was going extremely well, I thought, and I was certain that I would be able to choose quite soon, especially as I had a top candidate. I was slightly worried by the fact that I didn't want to be seen in public with him, but that seemed a minor inconvenience by comparison with some of the others. I kept trying out and sometimes I added or removed a tick from my grid, and I was working towards who would be the best statistically. But before that could happen, I struck a hiccup with my scheduling.

Late one afternoon at the end of my two weeks of dating, as the summer sun slanted into my flat, Matiu (good sex, fun talk, moderately brainy, bad T-shirts, zero financial prospects) encountered Anton in the doorway. Wellington is a small place. There was an incident involving a bed, a wardrobe, a locked door, yelling, some pounding upon the door, a window ledge, a broken door, screaming, police being called, police being cancelled, neighbours at the back door to see if everything is all right, and it is, it's fine. Everyone has gone, except me. And unfortunately, because Wellington is so small and everyone knows everyone, my efforts to find a nice boyfriend or nice girlfriend have gone the way of the Berlin wall in 1989 within the hour. By text, post and tweet. All in a sorry state. There is a souvenir I believe, my little notebook, with my papers in the sleepout at 56 Summer Street, Hataitai, for future reference.

Reader, something unusual has happened. I've slightly lost my thread. I can't remember who I set out to thank in relating this episode of my life. I know there must be someone, even multiple subjects of my gratitude. Was it the candidates for nice boyfriend/nice girlfriend who *came to the party*? Maybe. Was it Sorrell and Harry (see above)? Perhaps. Valour at Hoki Aroha, who destroyed any chance of my having a loving sexual relationship, which is a gift for a writer because how can you write when you are happy and settled? He is the closest, but somehow my lover experiment doesn't feel the right place to thank him. For once in these Acknowledgements, I am thankless. And, if truth be told, a little frightened, because without gratefulness there is destruction. I am worried that while I am down in Antarctica, an ice shelf the size of New Zealand will fall off, will float away and melt. I am worried that the people in my life will continue to float away. I am worried that I was not grateful enough for the little warmth while it was warm.

No matter. To finish the story of the five candidates—a development was about to occur.

I'd decided to call it a night after the double-booking fiasco and was just climbing into bed when I heard a tentative knocking. At first I thought it was some loose bit of board flapping in the gale, but it came again and again, and I realised someone was at the door. I went gingerly to investigate, opening the door a crack. Who should it be but the person with whom I was subsequently to spend nearly three years of my life only I didn't know it then? Yes, the timid knocker was none other than Miles, whom if you remember I'd first met at Meow Café and on that occasion had recognised as the quintessential Kiwi man. I may have been a bit harsh towards Miles earlier in these Acknowledgments, a bit hasty in my rush to damn him, perhaps spurred on by how things eventually unravelled. It wasn't always so grotesque.

We stood looking at each other in the doorway. Miles was so out of breath (the zigzag really was something) that his big square head was nodding like a horse. I was in my op-shop slip, vodka and orange in hand (as I write, I'm aware that this description might seem reminiscent of Poppy years earlier, but I am *not* like Poppy). At that point, of course, I thought he'd come to remonstrate about a certain Restoration comedy, and I was about to slam the door in his face. So not an altogether auspicious beginning. But no, he simply stood there looking hopeful, all set for our prearranged visit. It turned out this candidate for nice boyfriend/nice girlfriend wasn't friends or even friends-of-friends with any of the other candidates, and had failed to link with them on any form of cyber grapevine. I didn't say anything, just ushered him in, hurriedly swiping my nice boyfriend/nice girlfriend grid (which was in any case redundant) from the table as we passed it on the way to the couch. The rest, as they say, is history.

I suppose it might be true that we had an immediate rapport and found we laughed at the same jokes. I suppose it might be true that, when we kissed, my whole body and person thrilled to some new tune. I suppose it might be true that when he fucked me excuse my French I lost myself in him. I suppose it might be true that we spent hours whispering sweet nothings into each other's faces and I hadn't known that there was such a thing as sweet nothings. I suppose it might be true that he cared about what I thought. I suppose it might be true that we kept on having better and better sex and it never seemed to wane. I suppose it might be true that he tried to cater to my every need. I suppose it might be true

176

that he thought I was gorgeous and said so on a daily basis. I suppose it might be true that he wanted me to be happy. I suppose it might be true that I told him everything about my life (everything I've told you, Reader), and that he told me everything about his. I suppose it might be true that he wanted to be with me forever. I suppose it might be true that he said I'd made him the happiest man alive. I suppose it might be true that he loved me. I loved him too.

Nek minnit—it was quite whirlwind—we were moving into a fifties apartment with a view over the harbour; yes, the very apartment you know so well. Miles's parents had coughed up the deposit like a furball from a privileged Persian cat. I didn't like the politics of it, but in the end I didn't complain. I just went along with it. Rocking up to the building that first windy autumn day, it was exciting to get out of the car, to cling together in the courtyard and look up at the building that was to be our home. Miles leaned his big tufty head on top of mine and said, 'I think it's home sweet home, don't you?' I said I thought it might be. The building looked to me, on first glance, like an icetray tipped on its side, clean and white, with all its little square compartments. We lugged Miles's mattress from his old flat up all the steps—my first acquaintance with the jagged white Southeast Ridge—tossed it on the parquet floor and still had enough breath to leap upon it and have ferocious sex.

Over the next few days, in between sex and talk I wandered around the apartment marvelling at its bright northerly aspect, at the view of the sea endlessly delivering itself to the wharves, and at the notion that town was a hop, step and a jump away. I know this is all just material, so in essence not important, but still I thanked my lucky stars—

about everything, about Miles *and* the apartment. I was in love!

At that point the apartment was empty, but Miles's parents had spare furniture in their basement in Noa Valley (from a grandmother or something), and we could have it as soon as we organised a carrier. Of course, a house-lot of furniture! Middle-class people always have parents with spare house-lots of furniture. Miles liked that I found it funny. 'You're funny,' he said. And I was, all of a sudden. Miles thought it was fun roughing it for a while, and it was, plus it was summer. We slid around the bare parquet floors laughing, ate takeaways and drank red wine cross-legged on the mattress. We bought miniature cartons of milk which sometimes lasted until morning for a cup of tea, sometimes not. I hoped there'd be a fridge among Grandma's things, and Miles said there probably was, which meant certainly, because she had everything. But when I asked him to check, that was the one thing there wasn't. Still, it was ludicrous fun being in the empty apartment.

We lay on the mattress kanohi ki te kanohi (face to face, in this part of the world). Miles said he adored me. I said I adored him. I told Miles I'd never met anyone like him, I'd never felt this way before—which was all absolutely true; I'd gone bananas. Ditto, said Miles, and he gazed into my eyes. I fell into his deep brown endless pools and didn't come up for air for a long time. Miles told me about his childhood, which didn't take long because it'd been so happy. I told Miles about my childhood, obviously a bigger undertaking. I could keep Miles entertained for hours. Some of those stories I've unintentionally shared in these Acknowledgements. When Miles and I parted three years minus a day later, I hadn't even got to the end of all my stories. But I digress. During those first magical days and weeks in the apartment with only a mattress on the parquet floor, Miles told me he couldn't live without me, and I told Miles I couldn't live without him. This was *forever*.

We'd been there about five days when something else miraculous happened. On a breezy cloud-scudding afternoon, I was alone in the apartment (Miles was down at the gallery), and I decided I felt like a vodka and orange, just a passing fancy. I thought, Why not, Janice, why can't you give myself a treat once in a while? I went down Majoribanks to withdraw twenty dollars from a hole in the wall at Courtenay Place, and upon doing so I discovered that I had $10,020 in my account.

I would like to thank Wendy for handing me the opportunity to make a bit of cash. How curious that I was paid abysmally at the Glass Menagerie but that I ended up with this strange windfall—compensation for unfair dismissal and loss of wages. Despite Wendy maintaining to the Employment Relations Authority that I'd knocked over the shelves on purpose, it could never be proved. I was lucky that that afternoon there were no Bobbys, Clarissas or Felicitys in the shop. And, of course, I hadn't knocked them over on purpose! It was all an utter and terrible accident.

At the automatic teller that afternoon, I stood like a statue while the printout of my balance fluttered in my hand and my hair blew all over my face. A queue formed behind me, and I jumped aside, got out my phone and dispatched online payments to Mandy—with whom my line of credit was hefty in those days—my credit card, and a certain debt-collecting company with not very pleasant customer relations. I realised with delight that I still had enough to buy a certain object that I was quite fond of. I refer to none other than the handsome fridge I'd seen in the secondhand shop in Kelburn. It's true I had been starting to get on the verge of screamy at having a cup of tea in the morning with milk on the cusp of off. I headed straight up the hill on the cable car—no mucking about with steps.

As I approached the shop on genteel Upload Road, I was sure the fridge would've gone by now. Who *wouldn't* want it? Strangely—call me pathetic—my heart was pounding. But the second miracle of the day was that the fridge was still there, its glossy flank beaming from inside the depths of the shop. I stepped inside.

The air was cool. A mould and patchouli smell common to the secondhand trade permeated, with an overlay of furniture wax. I edged past shelves crammed with old souvenirs from Bali and Fiji, fringed table lamps, and big glass ashtrays with bubbles trapped inside. Although everything was moth-eaten, the shop reminded me of the Glass Menagerie with its surfeit of decoration, but did I feel the need to push one of the shelves over? Not a bit. (And not that I would ever consider doing that.) As my vision levelled out with the dimness, I noticed an old whiskery dude hunched behind the counter. I crabwised down an aisle created by chests of drawers, smiling like a New Zealander, and he reciprocated by glancing away in a *Cinema of Unease*-y manner.

The fridge was just as nice as I remembered it. Although the style was fifties, it was actually a replica, more like eighties (which is vintage, for a fridge). I had no interest in some new ultra-white thing with all the style of a dental implant. I liked this fridge. Without further ado, I went to the counter and handed over my fifty dollars. The whiskery man was small and yellowed from smoking, with not an ounce of body fat, as if all his reserves were poured into the shop. A silver thread of drool ran from his mouth as he rang up the purchase. He tipped himself off his stool, shuffled down the aisle and smeared a red SOLD sticker on the fridge door, reminding me of a photograph I saw once of the word 'Red' mown in green grass. I felt something warm up furiously inside my chest.

Back at the counter, the whiskery man gawped up at me, eyes yellow as banana lollies, ballpoint hovering over a fluffy invoice pad, and I gave him my address.

'Steps?' he croaked.

I described the Southeast Ridge to the best of my ability.

'And it'll be a hundred for delivery.'

My mouth must've fallen open.

'Dollars,' he added. And here the whiskery man adopted a folksy American tone which seemed to fit the occasion. 'And it ain't Monopoly money.' Clearly he had no interest in the climate of his shop.

I didn't *have* another hundred dollars. I told the whiskery man this, feeling, I have to say, a little ashamed. Money is like clothing. The whiskery man pulled a long, yellow-eyed face to indicate the sale was off, slapping his spongy invoice pad upside down for extra effect.

A pall of disappointment sank over me. I'd got used to the idea of fridge ownership and the loss of that, the loss of something which until just an hour before I hadn't thought I'd ever own, was a very great loss indeed. I was wondering what to do with this feeling when I noticed that the whiskery man wasn't opening the till to give me back my fifty. He was biding his time, and I knew the ball was in my court. This was a game. I realised then that the whiskery man wanted to sell the fridge as much as I wanted to buy it—maybe more. I called his bluff. I put out my hand to retrieve the fifty.

The whiskery man adjusted his position on his stool and looked out the window. As it happened, he said, he'd be driving over Mount Victoria way later. I tried not to seem too excited.

That very afternoon, the fridge was delivered to the apartment. The whiskery man grumbled in the courtyard, saying I'd kept the steps a secret—absolute lies—but he got on with it. I have to admit, the Southeast Ridge was pretty wicked, but finally the fridge was in the kitchen.

When Miles came home from the gallery, he did a double take.

'I got us a fridge,' I said.

'So I see,' he said.

We both looked at the fridge and walked around it, Miles in his loping, simian way.

'Nice,' said Miles. He asked if it was, you know, secondhand.

'Yeah,' I said, 'but good secondhand.'

Miles nodded. 'The thing about fridges is, sort of—'

'What?'

'Well, efficiency,' said Miles. 'Like, does the motor work, do the seals work, et cetera.'

We poked at the spongy rubber strip around the door, which was perhaps a little too spongy. It had never occurred to me it might not go.

'And the, you know, energy rating,' said Miles. He started fingering the fridge all over, mock frowning, but he could've been serious, it was hard to tell. '*Somewhere* there should be a sticker on it, with stars.'

I joined in, looking all over the beautiful green flank for stickers showing an energy rating.

'On a scale of, you know, one to five,' said Miles. 'Five is the best.'

'What does it mean when there are no stars?' I asked.

We laughed, and I poured vodka and oranges to celebrate the fact that we had a fridge, even though it had no stars.

'Cheers,' I said.

'Yeah, cheers,' said Miles.

But, despite the colour being as delicate as the underside of a leaf, the silver fittings like dew, I could tell he didn't like the fridge. Nevertheless, this was our fridge now. We walked it into the space where a fridge should be—hilarious, because we'd had a few celebratory drinks by now—and moved into it, transferring the few food items we had from the cupboard, to-ing and fro-ing flirtatiously like a rendition of the clean-up scene in *The Big Chill*, but of course we're much too young for that. We're not the generation that took all the money and stuffed up the planet. When we were done, Miles nodded his head in approval. It did look stylish, and if there's one thing Miles likes, it's style.

When we plugged it in, it went; it was a tenor. One minor spanner in the works, which I didn't mention to Miles—he was sort of passed out by then—was that the door didn't close properly. I tried and tried to make it fit tightly, to no avail. The squishy white seals pressed softly like the gloved hands of elderly cousins who don't quite like each other. Unfortunately, when it comes to fridges and doors, there's no halfway. I dashed down to the general store on Majoribanks Street (stopping at the liquor store on the way to visit my French New Wave cinema buddy, who I'd only just met at that point in time) and bought a stick-on kit with a hook, and while Miles snoozed, I fitted the little lock onto the side of the fridge. It wasn't too conspicuous, and it allowed the fridge to function, although it was quite loud, growling incessantly and, every hour or so, making an alarming noise like someone with sleep apnoea turning over in bed. The power bill from then on was always rather astronomical. But I still loved the fridge; I still got a kick out of having my very own fridge, or rather a shared fridge, because Miles and I shared everything in those days. On that night, when Miles had roused himself and come into the kitchen to make a pre-bed snack, he hesitated only briefly before unhooking the new lock and retrieving his special sandwich ingredients. I smiled from the kitchen doorway.

'Cheers,' I said.

Miles pursed his lips just a little. He really was the quintessential New Zealand man.

But a funny thing happened. As I lolled about in the kitchen, thinking idly about writing and things—because I've found that that is when the best ideas come, when one is thinking idly, and this to the tune of Miles's bumbling about—I began to feel not so good. I can't really explain it. I began to worry about Miles and me.

What say it wasn't true that we'd had an immediate rapport and laughed at the same jokes? What say it wasn't true that, when we kissed, my whole body and person thrilled to some new tune? What say when he fucked me I might not always lose myself in him? What say we stopped spending hours kanohi ki te kanohi whispering sweet nothings into each other's faces in a manner in which I hadn't known before? What say he didn't continue to care about what I thought? What say we stopped trying to make sure the other was happy? What say he stopped thinking I was pretty and stopped saying so on a daily basis? What say I stopped thinking that his simian body and big square head were sexy? What say I stopped telling him everything about my life, and he stopped telling me everything about his?

What say he didn't want to be with me forever? What say, if I got pregnant, he wasn't ecstatic and it didn't make him the happiest man alive? What say it wasn't true that he loved me?

I worried that it might not be true, and he might not be true and we might not be true. And then it looked like none of it was going to turn out to be true, as if I'd walked around us and looked at us from a different angle. Although Miles and I were compatible in every way, and especially in the way animals are compatible, and although Miles still managed to get up and go to work and I managed to progress with things, looking back, I guess things can't have been perfect between us. It didn't take long for little *contretemps* to erupt. Try five days after we'd moved into the apartment. Over trifles, I can't even remember what—a fridge. I do remember it was hard to discuss things productively with a character from *Cinema of Unease*. I admit I had the odd drink during this period. So did Miles. Although we fought a bit, overall it was good. No one is perfect. Miles is not perfect. I am certainly not perfect. At least we did manage to move all the furniture from Noa Valley into the apartment, which was a kerfuffle because of the Southeast Ridge and because furniture means things are serious and suddenly the fifties apartment was very full of big thirties mahogany and oak tables, chairs, bed, desk, swivel chair, couch, and easy chairs that were a bit formal with their curled arms and overstuffed damask cushions—not that I'm complaining, I hasten to add. There were good years, three, no two, well one, give or take a few months.

And then I find that I do love him and it is two years and a hundred-and-something days into the relationship. But it's too late. And as you know, Things Fell Apart. There was the little warmth that had become cold, and I was a murderer. And on Sago Pudding Night I ended up in the study,

185

perusing the Arts New Zealand website, my finger hovering over those magic words, How To Apply. I know that without the formative influences outlined above, I would not have had the oomph to hit that button. But I am getting ahead of myself.

In the Kōwhai Room, I whip from my manuscript a few pages in which the protagonist has a brief career in retail and falls head over heels in love. To be honest, I'm a bit rattled by the loss of this section, but I know it's for a good cause, that I'm practising restraint towards the overall economy of the text. In any case, as I screw up the ball of paper and add it to the others in the Chinese vase, someone pokes me and I realise my name is being called over the microphone. I shove the remains of my manuscript back into my laptop bag and trot up to the podium, where the CEO of Arts New Zealand pumps my arm and hands me a piece of cardboard which no doubt announces my Antarctica Residency. On the periphery of my hearing I'm aware of everyone clapping madly. Truth be told, I am a bit overwhelmed. I try to say thank you to the CEO, but no words come out.

Then it's over, and I feel myself spirited by the movement of the crowd from the Kōwhai Room to the woody landing. Chatter rises and falls around me like a didgeridoo and faces are chewing-gummy in the olive twilight, and I am still dazed, I think. That is, until I happen to glance over the balcony and am brought up short by the sight of three faces looking up at me with what seem like grotesque mock-smiles, but it must just be the stormy light falling on them through the tall glass doors. I remember with a jolt that the artists with whom I will go to Antarctica and I have arranged to go for a drink together. I give the threesome a queenly wave and scurry to collect my fridge from its parking space near the bathroom. As I sidle down the stairs trying not to squash people's toes, one of the Antarctica artists calls up to me, 'Where were you?' but it could be any or all of them because by their obviously established bonhomie they are already one. I arrive beside *them* in the foyer with my fridge, and feel my face emulating their three-headed leer. This is very promising.

Up close they separate into their entities—and of course I know them very well after our Antarctica training. Beatrice Grant, sporting a tonne of pancake makeup and wearing her signature long and only slightly pretentious eighteenth-century frock coat, looks me up and down and after a beat asks, with dancer-type eye-widening, what my fridge *is*. I laugh because the question is actually quite funny.

Tom Atutola is walking around the fridge with his arms folded, scrutinising it from somewhere deep, and after this assessment he eyeballs me and asks why do I *have* a fridge? The three of them stand in a crescent shape watching me. I explain, looking at each of them in turn, that I have a fridge because I like to keep food cold, and is that such a crime? This causes Clement de Saint-Antoine-Smith to roll his eyes just a little, but it doesn't escape me.

'I get that,' says Tom Atutola. 'I guess I meant'—he adopts an ironically pedantic purse-lipped smile—'why do you have a fridge on you *right now*?'

'About your person,' adds Beatrice Grant. Do I imagine her hands framing her face like Marcel Marceau?

At this moment we all move spontaneously through the glass doors and out into the musty twilight, collecting a blast of chilled wind on the parapet. As we trickle down the wide steps (like R.A.K. 'boldly bring I up the rear' Mason, with my fridge), I fill in the crew, at least their backs, briefly on the sorry tale of how I was evicted from my flat just this morning and I have nowhere to put my fridge. I'm hoping one of them will tell me they have a flat just over there and that they'll look after it.

'Fair enough,' says Tom from the street, 'but what will you do with it when we go to Antarctica tomorrow?'

'I don't think they'll let you on the plane with it,' says Beatrice Grant, and they all laugh, a bit unkindly, but I don't care, I'm made of tougher stuff. As I join them on the footpath, I tell them I'm hoping the evening will provide a solution. Clement de Saint-Antoine-Smith sweeps his hand out as if to indicate the sepia twilight city spread before us with all its possibilities. I decide to take this at face value and I nod, but no one offers anything.

We seethe down Molesworth Street like a silked Chinese dragon, the artists with whom I will go to Antarctica and me, plus my fridge. Although it's unseasonably gusty—our clothes are all abloom—the evening has a dirty beauty, a storminess seasoned with cold dots of rain. It's around seven thirty, still broad daylight. The air on Molesworth Street is hung with a green gauziness like the set for a production of *Swan Lake*, and it seems we are lost, the artists with whom I will go to Antarctica and I, in an endless moment and we go silent, not even a stray comment about my fridge as we ripple down the hill. Although the green air, the green street, the silence, are breathtaking, I'm scared, freaked like I was one time smoking strong hashish, when I'd thought I was receding from the world, never to return. That's what I'm thinking now, that we all might (or I might) never come back from this Limbo but will walk forever down Molesworth Street caught in green. Nek thing, it's over, the light has burst through its green phase to something with half-blue in it, and the chatter has started up again, the clever banter, and we are saved, the group of artists with whom I will go to Antarctica, and me, we are saved.

This may sound a little far-fetched, but I think it's appropriate here, having just described the dispersing of the literati on the evening of the state-funded awards, to thank New Zealand—yes, the whole lot of it. I wouldn't be the person I am today, the writer I am today, if I hadn't grown up in this amazing little country. For a start, we're clean and green. In New Zealand you can drive out into the countryside and there is only the odd hydro-electric dam to mar the view of rivers, lakes and mountains. Sheep and cows graze in the fields. Clouds scud merrily by. The sun shines brightly down, and if it happens to be through a hole in the ozone layer, that's not our fault; it's the fault of the rest of the world where there are too many people. We're fiercely proud of our little country, our do-it-yourself spirit, our social services, our human rights. You might've read news reports of people sleeping in cars, the pretty appalling infanticide stats. But we're a great little country, and our size is part of it, making us fiercely independent. We punch above our weight in our films, our wine, our dairy products. It's a good thing New Zealand isn't the size of, say, America, because if New Zealand had 300 million people, we'd have three billion sheep and 400 million cows. With that number of sheep and cows farting, the methane in the atmosphere might have already reached the level they say will make the stratosphere of the entire planet explode. If that happened, I wouldn't have written *The Ice Shelf*. I wouldn't be writing my thank yous to people who've helped me along the way.

You wouldn't be doing whatever it is you're doing. Even people out there with books of fifty pages or longer would be silenced. No one would be reading books. The few survivors would be thinking about things apart from literature such as scraping up the remains of their friends and families. It's a good thing that New Zealand is so small. Smallness is its virtue. Thank you, New Zealand, for being so small.

On that note, I have a very profound thank you to make, and that is to the earth, which may sound far-fetched too, but bear with me.

Those first months in the apartment, it seemed that Miles and I had an incredible power. Something had been unleashed—a kind of chemistry, a cellular smash-up, like we'd both been put into the Large Hadron Collider, but also metaphysical—I can't even describe it. I'm talking about sex and how it transformed everything phenomenally, indelibly. Sometimes it was as if we were one person joined into a two-headed beast, as if we were a new, monstrous species. It was both thrilling and terrifying. I suppose it was inevitable then that we started to bicker a bit, as I mentioned earlier, you might even call it fight. Yes, there were some fights. I found I was having to fall back on my calming method of count-to-twenty then pour a vodka and orange quite a bit, in fact, all through the day. Miles seemed to be using the calming method too. In fact, I was worried about Miles's alcohol consumption; whereas I could've stopped drinking at any time if I'd wanted to (but I didn't want to, and why should I?), I don't think he could've at that point in time. Often he'd pass out on the bed at night. I might've too, on one or two occasions.

One morning I found myself throwing up in the toilet, and when I went out to the liquor store to have a conversation about *À Bout de Souffle*, I noticed my breasts were aching in the cold wind. Although I didn't think this could possibly be necessary, I bought a pregnancy kit and took it back to the apartment. I stood in the courtyard summoning my strength to ascend the Southeast Ridge which somehow, that day, seemed fragile, impermanent, like a pretty, glinting stack of sugar cubes that might crumble in the next shower of rain and topple all over me.

Next morning, in the white tiled bathroom: the little pink plus-sign told me that a new thing was to be sprung from us. I called out, and there was Miles's black square head offset by the white rectangular doorway, both of us speechless and just making arghh sounds. It was so complicated, you couldn't fathom it. Meaning shuttled back and forth between a miracle and the most real, earthly thing you'd ever come across. The physical (action, chemistry) had made this mystical thing, this fate. Out of ferociousness, a delicate warm thing that hadn't been there before.

Miles and I were in agreement about getting rid of it.

The bar is crowded with civil servants sculling back their after-work suds and we're lucky to spy a table. As the artists with whom I will go to Antarctica make a beeline for it, I park my fridge in the corner and quickly join them under a huge papier-mâché caricature of a Member of Parliament, one of many that adorn the walls. You can't tell which Member is which because they're cartoonish, mostly lips. Incidentally, in this context I don't think of the word 'member' in the same way as I think of Full Member of Feather.

A narrow-hipped waiter with plus-sized ear gauges bounds over to our table and I order a vodka and orange, hoping there'll be a tab operating courtesy of someone, a filthy rich visual artist for instance, you never know. Turns out the waiter hasn't come to take our orders but to point at my fridge and to get, to be honest, ridiculously paranoid about it. He asks beadily around the table, 'Whose is it?' And the group of artists with whom I will go to Antarctica point to me in a not entirely friendly way, just saying. The waiter asks me what my fridge is. As I've already been through this with Tom Atutola et al. just a few minutes before, I'm all prepared with an answer. It's a *fridge*, I tell him. He says he can see that, and I ask him why he asked then, but he just says I can't have it in here. I ask why not and he says it's the bar policy. I ask how many people bring fridges into the bar; in other words, what kind of precedent there is for patrons bringing fridges in that need to be banned? The waiter pretends he doesn't hear my reasoning and tells me if I don't move my fridge, I'll have to leave. The manager is mentioned once or twice. 'Fine,' I say, 'we'll leave.' He says my leaving can't come too soon. I wait for the waiter to go away, but he doesn't. I scan the group of artists with whom I will go to Antarctica, as if to say, 'Let's get out of here, let's go to a bar with a less fascist policy on fridges.' As I gather my things, I notice Tom Atutola taking a breath and there is a strange moment of vacuum.

It's in this vacuum, a black hole where matter does not exist, that a certain *ennui* sets in. Because of my prior knowledge, my reading of novels and watching of films and not least my cohabitation with Miles for two years and 364 days, I have no trouble decoding the passive shoulder-hunching of the artists. Read: 'We couldn't give a flying fuck about your fridge.' But hey, what do I care? I'm not going to Antarctica to win friends and influence people, I'm going to find concrete significant detail for *The Ice Shelf*. I ask the group of artists to order me a vodka and orange while I'm sorting out about my fridge, and I leave them to their ontological New Zealand unease.

By moving my fridge out onto the street, I'm not giving up; I'm not complying with the management of the Backbencher. I am making a choice so that events can progress smoothly. There is a big difference between acting under pressure and making a strategic decision. As a writer, one makes decisions like this all day long; I'm well used to making policy decisions. So when I cock the fridge to 35 degrees and wheel it out the door of the Backbencher, I am not in the least defeated by the right-wing antics of the waiter, whom I can't blame personally as he is simply the stooge of management. Negotiating the door is a struggle, especially with the crush of people pouring in and out while looking at me askance, but I don't give a rat's arse and eventually, one of them, a young civil servant-type boy in a suit with fashionably short Pee-wee trousers, holds the door open for me. I park my fridge outside and sail on through.

I ask a party at the table in the window if they would kindly move so that I can keep an eye on my fridge, and I point outside. At first they pretend not to understand—they're shrieking twenty-year-old women, all off their faces. After a bit of shilly-shallying, they get the idea and totter off on their four-inch heels. I race over to our original table and tell the artists with whom I will go to Antarctica that we have a new pozzy in the window. Clement de Saint-Antoine-Smith asks who would steal a fridge. Then he asks it again, more emphatically: who the *fuck* would steal a fridge? I reply that I might, given the opportunity. They shamble to their feet, scraping chairs, sighing, gathering coats and bags and making all manner of commotion. Honestly, you'd think that they'd taken out a twenty-year lease on that particular table at the Backbencher. After what seems like an eternity, we move together like a massive crab to the table in the window.

But you know what? I am grateful for all the shoulder-hunching, the sighing and screeching, the wittering and whining, because when all is said and done, belonging to a community of artists is curtains for art. Read some Bourdieu and you'll see how being accepted into a comfy friendly lovely band of artists is so *so* bad for art that if we were all members (and I mean members in the rudest possible sense) of cosy little clubs of artists in which everyone pats all the other *members* on the back, there would be no art.

Finally we're settled with our drinks and a Mediterranean platter at the new table, from which I have a spectacular view of my fridge outside. We all start talking about our work, of course, and I listen while getting down on the bread and hummus. To be honest, I'd never heard of Beatrice Grant or Clement de Saint-Antoine-Smith until I met them at Antarctica prep a month earlier. I share a piece of friendly advice with Tom Atutola, whom I *had* heard of: tone down the glitter. People are just the teensiest bit sick of glitter, and he has so much else going for him. Tom gets the wrong end of the stick and I sense a garage door coming down between us, but I am not going to be affected by that. I continue chatting amiably with Beatrice Grant and Clement de Saint-Antoine-Smith, whom as I've mentioned I'd never heard of until recently, but I don't mind that they are so unsuccessful.

The subject of Art School comes up. The artists with whom I will go to Antarctica have all been to various prestigious establishments and, in between olives, they humblebrag like crazy about it. I certainly don't judge them for saying things like, 'I was hopeless at music school; it was my amazing fellow students who got me through.' The others chime in with, 'Oh Clement, you were the top student!' And, 'My show at Elam wasn't as good as I'd hoped, but I was blessed with the most stupendous luck.' 'Don't be silly, Tom, you were a star.' I'm not the least bit sickened by this show of false modesty, in fact, I find their fake self-effacement endearing. As our fourth round of drinks arrives and some bowls of kūmara chips because the hummus isn't filling the gap, the conversation sets me thinking about my own degree—my BA, which I'm taking a temporary break from—and I go into a bit of reverie.

Of course, I have massive thank yous to make vis-à-vis my studies. But before I tell that story, if you'll bear with me, I just want to quickly finish my enormous thank yous to Miles. After the discovery of the amazing situation, but before we'd had time to do the ethical thing (and who in their right mind would want to bring a poor little baby into the world when it's in such a sorry state), there was a development.

With the high-concept news, it wasn't surprising that Miles and I were fairly wound up the next night. We had a few drinks, which I suppose didn't help, and we ended up having a bit of an argument about whose fault this was and a few other things were, like the dishes and money and I think the subject of Dorothy might even have got mixed up in there. Yes, a bit crazy. Quite late, I decided to go and stay with Mandy for the night, and Miles agreed. ('Be my guest,' was what he actually said, 'and, you know what, um, probably don't come back,' but it was just in the heat of the moment.) I set off, it has to be said, at breakneck speed in the moonlight, and next thing I know, there I was toppling, toppling, down two flights of the South East Ridge.

There was a lot of pouring and plummeting and a lot of red, which continued in the ambulance and thence at the hospital where they sucked out everything that hadn't left of its own accord. It's strange; I can't remember the pain (they gave me drugs for it) in the same way that you can't remember summer when it's winter, and vice versa. You can't imagine what the world would be like if it was intensely hot all the time and there was no escape; you can't imagine permanent snow and ice.

Miles kindly came to pick me up from the hospital next morning. I travelled, a little wan, in the passenger seat, and I could tell from Miles's particular silence (different from his normal silence) that something was up. We pulled up in the courtyard of the apartment building and on getting out of the car and slamming the door and leaving me to trail after him, Miles said over his shoulder, 'You know what I think?'

I was gagging to know.

'I think you probably killed that baby.'

Following Miles's rectangular frame up the Southeast Ridge, I was, I have to say, quite shocked at this accusation. On the balcony I said, 'Probably?'

Miles turned in the doorway. 'Definitely,' he said. And he went inside and began to cook a special chicken dish for dinner.

After the chicken dinner, which I couldn't eat because I seemed to have a trapdoor in my throat, he announced that he was going down to Courtenay Place to meet Dorothy, and on the way out the door he said, without any qualifications, 'You're a murderer.'

At this moment I can't remember what I was going to thank Miles for when I began writing this part of the Acknowledgments, but I'm sure it will come to me, and when it does, I will thank him.

In the meantime, I will continue with my enormous thank you to a certain professor of English, a personage who had so much influence on my writing and whom I have already mentioned in relation to ENG 209: Theory of Creative Writing, without doubt the highlight of my BA so far. A part theory, part literature, part creative writing course, it was taught by none other than Big Julie the Pig—that was the affectionate moniker we gave Professor Julian Major. I've actually always had a soft spot for pigs, especially cute pink baby ones with curly tails and darling squeaks. This particular pig was a little bulkier, a little older, a little hairier and wrinklier, but still engaging, still adorable as he snuffled and snouted at the trough of male literature. Of course, Big Julie isn't really a pig, no more than certain of his favoured writers are pigswill. And by the way, I bear absolutely no grudge for being waitlisted for the course, as alluded to earlier. You hear these stories—J.K. Rowling rejected by eight publishers, the Beatles by Decca, John Kennedy Toole given the cold shoulder all his short life and winning the Pulitzer Prize posthumously. The list goes on. I wouldn't be surprised if there's a little person in the English Department still insisting that *Janice Redmond didn't present a good sample*. The sample I presented grew into the novel you are about to read, so I *think* I can rest my case in that regard. However, at about a minute to midnight on the 28th of February 2012, the day before the first day of term, I was accepted into the course. I never forgot that I hadn't made the first dewy cut, but thanks a bunch to all concerned. That knowledge only served to keep me on my creative toes throughout the semester.

There was an incident—really it was nothing, and the only reason I mention it is that I'm truly grateful to the Pig for his fleshed-out example of anthropomorphism. I learned a lot about pigs that year; I could write a novella about them, and one day I will. On the first day of class, I arrived on the Terrace, slightly breathless after trekking up Church Street Steps, but excited at the prospect of another class. The wind was skittish, the sunlight sharp. When autumn hits Wellington, it brings an electric quality to the air. The incident I am about to relate involves an essay by Ezra Pound. The essay was quite a good rave about *making it new*. I had no problem with that, or with the fat reading packet dispensed by the Pig. I sat on my cushion. The class, I should add here, was populated by students who were all a little younger than me and, I was to find out, a little richer and more self-satisfied, mostly from Noa Valley, but a nicer bunch of people you'd never meet. The afternoon progressed drowsily. A fly buzzed in a lazy figure-eight, and the Pig, draped on the floor like one of the scholars in *Déjeuner sur l'herbe*, his grey beard wobbling and gold-rimmed glasses slipping down his nose, read aloud from the canon. The Pig was always jolly and inclusive, especially going out of his way to be pleasant (and I *don't* mean condescending here) to the women and the person of colour in the class. He was a blast, often sharing his political views, which made us feel special to be so trusted not to report him to the university complaints authority. Besides, by the time they'd investigated, he'd be dead. There's a wonderful freedom comes with old age. If the world were going to end soon, for instance, old people wouldn't need to give a flying fuck.

But I digress. On this day, Big Julie the Pig read aloud sonorously from the coursebook. He had an amazing theatrical voice. For some reason I found his charisma a little bit threatening, and during the semester I would get into the habit, before I set off for class each Wednesday, of topping up a bottle of orange juice with the wee-est slug of vodka, just to help me relax through the session—something I'd normally never do, I hasten to add. As I listened to the Pig's fruity tones on the excellent notion of newness according to the antisemite, I browsed the coursebook and it occurred to me that this class did not encounter, nor did it seem it were ever going to, a single piece of writing by a woman, or person of colour for that matter, apart from the high colour that goes with a heart condition. So when the Pig's reading was finished and he was pacing the perimeter of the room while the class had silent pre-discussion time, scribbling ideas in our notebooks and glancing up to see how much everyone else was writing, I half put up my hand (raising my hand felt odd; this wasn't primary school, but neither were we quite grown-up here) and asked, 'Um, are we going to read anything by a woman in this course?'

The inward suck of breath from one or two of my fellow students was followed by a long silence disturbed only by the buzz of the fly. It seemed we'd be going home for semester break before any further developments occurred, but finally the Pig reared up on his trotters. '*What* do you suggest?' he asked in a round timbre.

When I peeked, he was eyeballing me, his brows a squiggle, the jolly manner gone entirely. A few names I'd stumbled across in SOC 113: Gender Studies flitted through my mind—Simone de Beauvoir, Hélène Cixous, bell hooks—but I hadn't actually read them (there was just too much to do), and I blushed.

The Pig was smiling again. 'Can I ask you, Miss—'

I supplied my surname and mumbled hopefully, 'You can call me Janice.'

Everyone laughed.

'Janice.' The Pig joined the tips of his fingers into a whare shape. 'Can I ask you a question, *Janice*?'

'Yes,' I said. This wasn't going so badly.

'Why don't *you* teach the class?'

More laughter erupted around the cushions. The room seemed to heat up astronomically and I worried briefly about global warming. It shouldn't be this hot in autumn. I mopped my upper lip. (Also, a few days before this there'd been the falling away I mentioned, and inside me was a strange cold space.)

'Now,' said the Pig, settling back on his cushion, 'unless anyone else has any complaints . . . ?' He flashed his gold-rimmed glasses and smiled, so it didn't feel aggressive. There were no takers. 'Then I suggest we get on with *making it new.*' He ended with a special, comical angling of the head at me, which sparked a fresh round of laughter, and I was grateful that *Cinema of Unease* was alive and well in the Theory of Creative Writing classroom.

But the Pig's wholesale disregard for feminist discourse or otherness of any kind is not why I want to thank him in these pages. No, I have a much bigger debt.

The purpose of the class, as outlined at the beginning of these Acknowledgments, was to ask—and perhaps answer; who knew?—the question *why write?* We tossed this question around the class, with robust input from the Noa Valley contingent (I didn't feel I could join in, due to insecurities packed down in childhood, for which I'm supremely grateful and without which I'd be a smug, self-satisfied Gen-X brat). The answer we came up with was *to make sense of things*. Who would've thought of that? I certainly *never* could've come up with such an insightful theory. If we didn't write, opined the Noa Valley peeps, we wouldn't understand what was going on; we couldn't unpack the complexities of our existence. Wow! I was just in awe of those guys. The Pig was getting really excited at the calibre of the answers and was up and pacing about on the balls of his feet, asking more questions in an Aristotle kind of way. But what if, but what if . . . ?

Quietly to myself, I wondered if it was in fact being brainy, which is why we're so industrially and technologically advanced, that has fucked us up the most. I didn't say it because then I'd have to blush to the roots of my hair again. So I simply pondered it, there on my cushion in the fly-zone, and I came up with this little equation, of which I'm quite proud, in answer to the question, 'Why write?'

I have no idea!

∴

I have no ideas.

I would like to extend my enormous thanks to Big Julie the Pig for offering me several invaluable experiences during my time in ENG 209. The first of course was my immersion in the literature of white men. If this hadn't happened at university, I have no idea where I would've encountered this particular group. I'd probably be entirely ignorant of the thoughts of white men. And I'm certain that having only male literary role models set me back, scarred me even, and was therefore hugely beneficial for me, as a writer. If I'd read the words of women in my chosen field, where would I be today? Likely I'd be strong and secure with an unshakeable sense of my own history and culture, but where would I *be*? I'd also like to thank the Pig for posing as a lefty feminist, when, in fact, he is a reactionary misogynist. The dramatic irony, the mask—what a gift for a writer! I cannot thank him enough. I also want to express my deep gratitude to the Pig for humiliating me in class on the 7th of May 2012.

The sense of shame I've carried with me has fed my writing and will continue to do so for many years to come.

But my biggest debt to the Pig is for helping me understand that there is no answer to the question *Why write?* This has left me deeply unsettled and worried for not only my own existence but the existence of humanity. Thank you, thank you, thank you muchly, Professor Big Julie the Pig.

Lastly, I am hugely indebted to my fourteen fellow students in ENG 209. We enrol in courses such as this because we're passionate about writing, but it turns out camaraderie is one of the best aspects of the whole exercise, a wonderful byproduct like casein. You get to know your peers very well indeed in the course of four and a half months, meeting every Wednesday morning as you do, for three long hours in a stuffy room. Perhaps too well. You might even catch something off some of them as they as they slobbered and spit their way through reading aloud their early drafts. Or from one of them in particular from whom you needed to protect yourself with an umbrella if you sat anywhere near her. A metaphorical umbrella of course, or raincoat, but I did not have any such techniques-of-fiction rainwear. I tried not to sit near this student, learning from experience early in the semester that one needed to hurry to class so one could choose a cushion far away from her. And most Wednesday mornings I was successful in this modest goal, running up Church Street Steps and arriving in somewhat of a lather, but it was certainly worth it, even if I were called upon to read early in the session and could barely get the words out. I simply mopped myself with tissues, took some deep breaths and rasped my way through whatever section of *The Ice Shelf* that I was workshopping.

In particular I want to thank one especially lovely peer, Emma Lloyd-Edwards. Emma hails from Noa Valley and no doubt grew up in a warm bungalow in a leafy street with two parents and a golden retriever and went to the same two or three lovely tight-knit schools and ∴ has *no fucking idea*, but that's splendid, that's all part of the rich mix of people who make up our marvellous world. The reason I single out Emma Lloyd-Edwards from among all the students of ENG 209 who are worthy of gratitude is a comment she made one day in her confident ringing voice. Emma Lloyd-Edwards' observation about a crot by yours truly was hugely instrumental in aiding my development as a writer.

We were workshopping two crots from *The Ice Shelf.* The Pig was going around the class one by one in an agonising way, letting *everyone speak*. Inevitably we came to the cushion of one Emma Lloyd-Edwards, who needed no invitation to speak but it is her comment I want to focus on here. And I quote: 'The second crot is self-absorbed; in fact both of them are, but the second one is worse. It's a question of authorial distance.' Having delivered her wisdom, Emma Lloyd-Edwards lolled back and played with her blond dreadlocks.

I looked up the term 'self-absorbed' on Merriam-Webster on my phone then and there. My studies at university trained me to take no prisoners when it comes to definitions. As I'd suspected: 'Self-absorbed: absorbed in one's own thoughts, activities and interests'.

I found the comment of Emma Lloyd-Edwards strange, I really did. Surely one needs to maintain a level of self-absorption in order to do anything, let alone create. Let's suppose Virginia Woolf had been enrolled in ENG 209 in 2012. Let's suppose she'd been in one of her good spells and had been writing *A Room of One's Own.* (Let's suppose that that was the project she'd pitched to get into the course, and let's suppose she'd got in straight away, rather than waitlisted and let in at the eleventh hour.) She arrives on a Wednesday morning with copies of the first section, which she hands out busily, and the class settles down on their tuffets to analyse it. First off is a long section about Virginia Woolf sitting on the grass outside Virginia Woolf's old college thinking Virginia Woolf's thoughts. Then a detailed description in Virginia Woolf-language about what Virginia Woolf imagines the men are having for lunch, followed by a detailed description of what Virginia Woolf and her fellow women scholars are going to have for lunch.

Excuse me, but isn't this a bit like posting a picture of your lunch on Instagram? And, not only that, the lunch you *imagine* the men are eating. Isn't that letting your own thoughts run a little riot? I can just hear Emma Lloyd-Edwards' contribution to the group about this work by Virginia Woolf: 'The second lunch is self-absorbed. In fact, both of them are, but the second one is worse. There's no authorial distance.' The rest of the class mumble assent because it's Emma Lloyd-Edwards after all.

Later on in the semester, Lloyd-Edwards goes to town similarly on Virginia Woolf's *room*, which is even more self-absorbed than the lunch.

I didn't write about what I was having for lunch, but perhaps I should have, and joined the excellent company of Virginia Woolf.

For the record, the self-same crot that Emma Lloyd-Edwards deemed 'self-absorbed' went on to be part of *The Ice Shelf*, which is the reason I'm going to Antarctica. I don't seem to remember seeing anything of that stature appearing from the pen or no-doubt parent-funded Apple MacBook Pro of one Emma Lloyd-Edwards. And I think *A Room of One's Own* got published too, despite its lunch. I rest my case.

I am, however, supremely grateful to Emma Lloyd-Edwards for pointing out to me my self-involvement in the area of the crot, and I suppose if I'd grown up in a bungalow in Noa Valley and spent my education at two private schools and had years of uninterruptedness in which to make friends and build my academic career, I'd be pointing the finger at others for their *differences* as well.

Until I met Emma Lloyd-Edwards and others like her in ENG 209, I wasn't aware how fortunate I am that I didn't grow up cushioned, cosseted and boring, with *no fucking idea*. So thank you, Emma Lloyd-Edwards, just for being there.

I must add that I did, in fact, revisit the crot because I took the comment about its self-absorption in the spirit in which it was given, not in spite or jealousy or plain stupidity; no, in the spirit of generosity of ideas, given freely towards a further draft. I actually would have changed this crot based on Emma Lloyd-Edwards' learned opinion gleaned from her vast knowledge and experience of writing, I really would. But as it happened, my editor looked at this crot too (Tree Murphy, who will be thanked later in these pages), and *she* didn't see anything about it that needed the least bit of changing, and so in the end I deferred to her professional advice. And if Emma Lloyd-Edwards ever has occasion to read *The Ice Shelf*, or, if she ever picks up the book in a bookshop by accident and put it down quickly, realising her terrible mistake, she might in a fleeting flick-through notice that the crot she so casually derided in a workshop in ENG 209 in 2012 is now printed on a page in a book in a bookshop.

I'd like to express my sincere thanks also to five students in ENG 209 who never talked to me, not once, during the whole four months, despite my saying 'Hi' multiple times on the way past in the corridor and again as we sat on our cushions, although by that time I must confess to being a little jaded from being cold-shouldered. Some people might regard their actions as rude or exclusive or snooty, but I saw it as enabling me to concentrate on my writing instead of taking part in wittering conversations about new flats and upcoming readings and literary magazines (I was only party to the Wednesday conversations, but I do have an imagination, and I did observe them trot off down Church Street Steps in a jostling bunch after class and it seemed they were going off to *not* write). The fact I was able to get on and complete my *Ice Shelf* without distraction means so much to me, and I'm truly grateful to these five students for allowing me many empty evenings. I'd thank them by name if I could remember them, but unfortunately they've sunk without trace as sometimes happens to people who've studied creative writing and achieved an A grade, whereas others who might've got a B, due to being indisposed at the time the Portfolio was due because a certain person showered them with droplets of infected saliva, go on to publish a book.

Getting to know my peers in ENG 209 made me realise just how lucky I'd been having Sorrell and Harry as parents. University didn't come cheap. You could see that as you glanced around at the sprawled bodies with their well-fed faces, fashionable clothes and $300 dreadlocks. They were being bankrolled by Mummy and Daddy. Most of these talented writers were younger than me by a good ten years and were still being spoonfed with never an inkling of what it's like to live in the real world apart from their fun little flirty waiting jobs which funded their Karen Walker jackets and ecstasy tablets. Mummy and Daddy forked out for every damn thing. To this day, I'm grateful that Sorrell's itinerant lifestyle and Harry's succession of marriages and left-behind progeny requiring child maintenance, not to mention his substantial weed habit, presented me with the opportunity to make my own way in the world. I wouldn't be the writer I am today if Sorrell and Harry had found it within themselves to fund one, just one measly qualification for me. Some people might think that having involved parents is to be enfranchised, but really, I'm the privileged one. It was a privilege to put the school fees on a credit card, the sort they banned in 2012. I can use the concrete significant detail. I know that plastic tastes like bile; I have the smell of debt in my hair, the grime of hard work under my fingernails. Those young writers whose parents have grubstaked them through writing school—what do they write *about*?

Lastly, I would like to thank all involved in the saga leading up to Portfolio Delivery Date.

On a cold June morning, I was waylaid going up Church Street Steps by a certain dog crap. The dog crap necessitated me rubbing my shoe against each and every clump of grass all the way up the hill, then visiting the toilets on campus, where I needed to practically empty the reservoir to clean my shoe and to cause a five-week power cut like the one in Auckland in 1998 because of my use of the hand dryer to dry said shoe. Only then could I show up at class. You can guess whom I ended up sitting next to. And no, I did not have the requisite Driza-Bone. And yes, I was then showered in minuscule globules of spittle, which were the fallout from a piece of fiction that seemed to have been written with this express purpose in mind; and yes, I caught a nasty flu bug. I would like to thank this precipitating student, whom I will not name, not because I am being coy but because my complaint to the University Council is still pending. But she knows who she is, and also knows I am so, *so* grateful to her that I was sick as a dog leading up to Portfolio Delivery Date. I applied to have my grade averaged from my performance during the rest of the year, which would've taken a lot of stress off my shoulders, but the university (meaning Big Julie the Pig) said *everything* rested on the portfolio being turned in. However, I prevailed, sitting up all night with a temperature of 39 degrees Celsius to finish my portfolio, and struggling up Church Street Steps in the morning to turn it in was one of the most formative experiences of my life so far. And of course, the portfolio was an early draft of *The Ice Shelf*, the very book you are reading. My sincerest thanks go out to the Typhoid Mary of ENG 209.

I notice that the artists with whom I will go to Antarctica are looking at me strangely. It seems the conversation has been bubbling on for some time without me amid the general pub din, but I don't care. I feel an edit coming on. In search of privacy, I get to my feet and wend my way through the crowded bar towards the bathrooms. But as I pass a coat rack thick with the suit jackets of public servants, it occurs to me that snuggling behind them would be as good a place as any. I push my way through the garments, and feeling I've entered Narnia, I crouch down on the floor where the flagstones are veined like leaves and cooler than expected under my fingertips, and in this shadowy place I tug out my manuscript. I find not just one part, but section after section which needs to be dispensed with. For the record, this is what goes west: the bit where the protagonist applies for Theory of Creative Writing and is, astonishingly, waitlisted, but gets in at the last minute when one of the chosen few is struck down with Mad Cow Disease. Unlike some of the other students who were chosen ahead of her, our heroine goes on to have the manuscript she began in the class published with a big fat spine that is very noticeable even when it has its toes to the wall in a bookshop. The upshot of this episode is that the protagonist comes face to face with her own creative survival—make that simply survival. The crisis is her moment of self-doubt, experienced when sitting cross-legged on a cushion in a big pale room daggered with Wellington light. The climax is her realisation that writing is the only lasting thing, then that it isn't, then that it is, then that it isn't.

Sitting under the coats, having finished my edit, it occurs to me—duh, hello!—that there will be WiFi in the pub. I haul out my laptop to take advantage (remember, my phone was in a bag of rice) and tweet quickly, Thanks muchly to the good folk at the Antarctica Awards of which I am a winner. So humbled!! Not bad going—two retweets and favourites immediately, and I reply, Thanks for the RT @heartwriter! Mwa mwa xxx, and Thanks for the RT @fringefestdweller! No retweet from Mandy, but I don't give a fuck.

Someone pokes their head into the shadows, and the late daylight winks through his earlobes. It's none other than our slim-hipped waiter. He asks, with enormous passive-aggression, working his lips, whether he can help me. I tell him I don't think so, unless he's a good line editor. He does the corkscrew gesture—the dickhead!—and retreats. Gathering my manuscript, I shuffle back through the fur lips into the real world.

What do I discover? Our table is now populated by young suits quaffing drinks and spraying food. The artists with whom I will go to Antarctica have disappeared. I check around the bar to make sure they haven't for some reason moved tables, but they are nowhere to be seen. When I pass our erstwhile table on the way out, one of the suits calls out to me cheerily, as if it's the best news he's had all day, 'You just missed them by a minute.' Thanks a bunch, I reply. Doubtless the artists have gone on ahead to the restaurant. I toddle outside and retrieve my fridge. The only problem is I don't know which restaurant we've chosen. I'm not sure what to do. It's eight-ish, and the thought that I don't know where I'm going to spend the night looms. But something will turn up. It always does. It won't be long till I've found the restaurant containing the artists with whom I will go to Antarctica in the vast metropolis of Wellington, and then the night will improve. Bolstered by that thought, I set off down Molesworth Street.

The weather has deteriorated, with squally gusts bringing rain. I'm a little cold in Mandy's light summer dress, especially with the hole in the side-seam, which is perhaps a little bit gaping now, and I'm regretting leaving my military jacket behind. I pause and unzip my hold-all, which is bursting at the seams. I'd had no idea what to pack, and Training Day hadn't helped. Would the interiors at Antarctica be air-conditioned like American houses, in which case I'd need only a summer dress and a few T-shirts and skirts, despite it being sub-zero outside? Or would it be like New Zealand houses, colder inside than out, in which case I'd need thermals, woolly jerseys, bed socks and a hot-water bottle? I've erred on the side of caution and packed a bit of everything.

I shelter in the entrance to the High Court and burrow down into my hold-all and find a singlet and a long-sleeved undershirt. At the same time, I come across my smartphone in its bed of rice, which I realise weighs a tonne, and I decide to give it all up as a bad job. I bin it—good shot!—in the receptacle on the street. It's amazing how material possessions fade into insignificance when one is going to Antarctica. Checking that there are no passersby, I quickly unzip the red dress and bung both singlet and shirt underneath. The dress splits on the other side when I elbow it back on, but I can't mind, there's too much going on. When I'm done, the black ribbed sleeves and high neck poke out, but I don't care. For good measure, I pull on a black fleece hoodie and zip it up to the neck.

I box on down Molesworth Street in the fierce wind and squalls of rain, shouldering my bag like a gym bunny without the adrenaline, tugging my fridge and managing the heels as best I can. I'm looking forward to getting to the bottom of the hill and under the verandahs of Lambton Quay. In the meantime, I happen to pass the very building where, not long ago, I consulted a lawyer about Miles and my separation, only to be confronted with bad news: the 364 days. Once upon a time, the very sight of this building and the memory of the tight chambers within would've been guaranteed to make me morose. But because of my new frame of mind, my decision to be thankful, I find my chest swelling with gratitude. I actually have a big thank you to make regarding the draconian statutes book of New Zealand, without which I'm sure I would never have written *The Ice Shelf*.

As I trot past, I remember the day I rocked up the lawyer's office, ready to sign on the dotted line. I confess that the phrase 'take him to the cleaners' was doing the rounds of my mind, but I didn't really mean it. A fair and equitable settlement, going halves on everything except the fridge, was what I was hoping for. That's the way it should work. But the Property (Relationships) Act 1976 had other ideas.

The truth is, on that afternoon in the lawyer's office, once my migraine medication had kicked in and begun to offset the headache brought on by the barrister's tie, I learned some very shocking news. I had left the apartment one day too early. Auē! Miles and I had been together for one day less than the legal definition of a civil union according to the Property (Relationships) Act 1976, that is one day less than three years (even though one of those years had been a leap year); ∴ we had never been a couple in the eyes of the law. This piece of legislation, no doubt rushed through Parliament in the dead of night by a clutch of Family First members, went like so: one day you wake up and you are entitled to half of a very nice modernist apartment in Mount Victoria with a view over the harbour; the building's stucco swirls are painted vanilla like Tip-Top ice cream, the neighbours have interesting jobs at Radio New Zealand and Deluxe Café and the Embassy Theatre, and the bars of Courtenay Place are only a hop, skip and jump away. Now backtrack to the night before and prepare yourself for a startlingly different scenario. You are standing out on the street in the wind under the whooping telephone lines. You wobble a little on the steep gradient and clutch your carpet bag, or its contemporary equivalent, the much less mythologised hold-all which contains all your worldly possessions. You own not so much as a teal-coloured kitchen tile of the fifties apartment. You have absolutely no idea where you will go.

Lambton Quay is strangely desolate tonight. The wind is something shocking, peppered with rain, and I cower-walk under the verandahs, trembling like a Tickle Me Elmo despite my layers of underwear beneath Mandy's thin red dress. It occurs to me that in the absence of another coat, I could put on my Antarctic jacket, so I pause in a shop doorway and haul the down jacket out of my bag. I'm soon enveloped in a fusty-smelling hothouse. While I'm figuring out the multiple zips, a middle-aged couple struggle by, the woman clinging to the man, and they look at me oddly, as if I might eat them. I am tempted to snarl, a strange reaction I know, and I can't fathom where it comes from, but I refrain and they move on. I give up on the zips and concentrate instead on doing up the copious domes on the jacket. It's while I am thus occupied that I realise I am right outside a restaurant— and that sitting at a table in the window are none other than the artists with whom I will go to Antarctica. I peer between the menus taped on the glass and as far as I can see the artists are laughing and carrying on and clinking beers. It looks like they're just settling in, so good timing. Without further ado I angle my fridge (and myself; now that I am bundled for Antarctica, I am not so portable) through the doors and find myself in a lovely Malaysian restaurant with pink tablecloths and delicious aromas.

But I have something to report that makes me rather glum. No sooner have I negotiated the doors than the artists with whom I will go to Antarctica rise up from their table and disappear at a run through some back exit. There in the middle of the restaurant, a bit hot from my Antarctic jacket, I slump next to my fridge. It hits me that it was not a misunderstanding that occasioned the artists with whom I will go to Antarctica to leave me in the Backbencher. And once again, they have indicated in no uncertain terms their preference for avoiding me.

Feeling the teensiest bit down, I continue along the graceful curve of Lambton Quay (curved because it was the beach before they tipped a hillside into the harbour to *re*claim land). All is desolate, it being the CBD, and people going home to their cosy beds. I begin to wonder if I might prevail on Mandy to let me stay one more night after all. In the foamy, wind-filled dark, I stop outside Parsons Bookshop. My feet are killing me—blistered heels, cramped toes—and I can't go a step further. Almost as if by poltergeist, my high heels somersault one after the other through the air and into the gutter. I must've kicked them off, but some vital interior life-force has propelled me and I'm not responsible anymore. It's the ache. With the same involuntary energy, I tear open my hold-all and pull out a pair of thick woollen socks and the snow boots. When I wriggle into them, they feel like milk by comparison with the heels. My audible sigh is taken by the wind. No doubt I look weird, in my dress, padded jacket and boots, but I don't care. There's no one around anyway. I'm reduced in some way, and boosted in another. Why do we do what we do? It all goes, in the end, anyway.

As I head off, I glance back at the shoes in the gutter. I can't take them to Antarctica with me. I can't take them back to Mandy's. They look lonely, and I feel sorry for them, but necessity rules. When everything is stripped away, that is all we will care about. In the end, I do what is easiest. I edit the shoes, leaving them by the side of the road.

At this juncture, I think it's appropriate to thank a *real* editor, someone who was instrumental in my securing the Antarctica Residency. I would never have been a contender for the Residency had it not been for the fact that the amazing Tree Murphy took a punt on my first little book. Under no circumstances do I take its coming into the world for granted—the doors it opened for me, the scores it settled with certain people. So, to Theresa 'Tree' Murphy, publisher of my first little effort, the *roman à clef* / autobiographical novella *Utter and Terrible Destruction* which appeared from Chook Books in 2009, albeit without a spine—thank you, from the very bottom of my heart. Even though my book doesn't have a spine, it has sold better than anyone could've imagined by the dismal publicity budget that was allocated to it.

Here I have a little story to share about the nature of my debt to Tree Murphy and Chook Books. The publisher–writer relationship really goes beyond the professional and becomes one of friendship, no matter how complex. Tree Murphy and Chook Books are the kind of outfit that great literature is built on. Risk-taking, flying in the face of convention. We're talking Shakespeare and Co., we're talking the Spiral Collective, who first published *the bone people*. Of course I don't rank myself in this league of heavyweights, I hasten to add, but I'm privileged to have had the fine support of Chook Books, no matter how small that support was compared with what they gave the other titles on their list—including the enormous flop of a poetry anthology which almost broke them and which I won't name here, because it wasn't anyone's fault except the publisher's and the editor's—and to have been part of this innovative and exciting venture.

After I'd sent my manuscript to Chook Books and Tree Murphy had grudgingly (although in retrospect that was all part of the gritty, back-and-forth, highfalutin, intellectual sparring that goes on between a writer and her publisher) accepted it for publication two years hence if she could get an Arts New Zealand grant, if not I would be shelling out, I burst on to a certain scene. I was, for instance, at the launch of Dean Cuntface's *then* new book at Blondini's. I can't remember the title, but I listened to some long speeches, drank some free wine and encountered a gathering of semi-interesting writer-publisher types. After the launch proper, the proceedings removed to the Matterhorn.

I found myself squeezed in at a table between two L=A=N=G=U=A=G=E poets, identifiable by, respectively, his black polo and her billowy silk top. The atmosphere was soft-lit and humming and the drinks were flying (there was a bar tab for an hour, which one needed to make sure one took advantage of) and so was the conversation, as you might imagine: a stimulating mix of off-the-cuff reviews of the latest poetry collections, novels and literary journals—the most cutting-edge one, according to all those present, seemed to be *Ika*—and insight into who was sleeping with whom in the literary community. I felt, as the writer of a book even though it didn't have a spine, absolutely in my element.

Across the table was a blond, long-fringed boy of about twenty-five who looked bashful but was nevertheless making eyes at me. I'm sure I wasn't misreading his fluttery attentions. I was wearing my black top with the stringy straps and the big floppy bow which drags the front downwards in a seemingly arbitrary way, but it is not arbitrary. (Some people's writings could be described thus, by the way.) Also, he was probably noticing the lively nature of the conversation in my little huddle. My neighbours either side obviously had not read Emily Post. They talked rather rudely across me, but I do have some manners, and I made it my business to engage fully in the banter. I mean, who hasn't read *Mythologies*? Who hasn't had a prickly one-night stand on Mount Victoria? I kept coming back, however, to the fizzingly electric eye contact with the long-fringed boy across the table. Eventually, when the two persons flanking me had relocated to the bar to continue their conversation, as if I could care less, the long-fringed boy walked around to my side of the table. For a literary person, he walked like a cowboy. It sent a shiver down my spine.

We talked and laughed. He was hilarious, and I was. Turned out he didn't actually write books, or write about them, or publish them, or promote them; he just read them. He would be one of the plus-or-minus three percent of readers at the Borich Festival. You do need people like that. He had a job in Government or something, I don't know what. And he was lovely. He had an agile face, an Adam's apple that travelled up and down his neck in a strangely alluring fashion which I couldn't keep my eyes off. He was a wee bit metrosexual, a type I don't usually go for, but at this point in my life I was over, well, not exactly *rough trade* but philandering bullies, as you will understand. I was drawn to the long-fringed boy's scooped-neck T-shirt, his soft leather jacket, his careful canvas shoes, his perfume. He was so funny and kind and huggable. Suffice to say, at the end of the night I found myself sitting on his couch drinking nightcaps, and then lying in his bed. If you understand the power of love and believe that it can come upon you suddenly, that it can hit you over the head from across a bar table, then you'll be able to imagine my feelings. At this point, I thought I was in love. I was imagining the life we would have together. We would have a measured, productive, deeply content existence in our happy home. I really needed this. I wanted it. It's true, I think, that you reach out for what you need, and I needed the levelling influence of the long-fringed boy. I'd reveal his name, but I consider it not politic.

I would like to thank the long-fringed boy for telling me that his two-year relationship with Tree Murphy of Chook Books was over. If I had known that they were engaged at that point, I would not have given way to my intense feelings and climbed into his bed in the rickety but charming Newtown flat and spent all night with the streetlight shining in on us. As it turned out, I have deep gratitude to Long Fringe for withholding this information, or should I say lying through his teeth, because nothing matches a complicated love life for giving grist to a writer's mill. There is nothing like heartache, remorse, regret and shame for adding zest to a writer's oeuvre. A little research ('The Horrifying Love Lives of Famous Authors' on flavorwire.com) will reveal that many of the world's great writers had adventurous sexual track records and bouts of unrequited romance. Not that I claim the status of greatness for myself, I hasten to add. No, I leave that to writers of enormous stature, such as Dame Bev Hollis. Who on second thoughts has a blameless history of monogamy. But a trawl through the lives of the greats— Shakespeare, Charles Dickens, Byron, D.H. Lawrence, Katherine Mansfield, T.S. Eliot, Edmund Wilson, need I go on?—will show that many of them were experimental, and many of them had the wool pulled over their eyes in the way that Long Fringe blinded me, having me wear a veritable scratchy balaclava of deceit.

The truth is, we didn't end up doing very much, Long Fringe and me. He wasn't really into sex in a big way. We groped each other and kissed a bit, although he had a funny taste which I kept puzzling over and that no doubt put me off my stride. He seemed to be off whatever stride he'd ever had. I might've almost come at one point, but I didn't, and he didn't. But still, I'd fallen for him and he'd tricked me, so that gave us a certain bond. It was enough to ruin a segment of my life, not so much leaving a hole in my heart or tears spilt— that would've been preferable—as leaving my book, *Utter and*

Terrible Destruction, which needed to be placed face-outwards on display tables because of its lack of spine, with its shoulder to the wall, as I later discovered on my tours of bookshops. Since, of course, it being Wellington, someone had spied me disappearing through the door of the Newton flat and had snitched to Tree and, being herself engaged to Long Fringe although I hadn't been made cognisant of this, she intimated that she was not pleased. Over the phone she wished aloud that she had never laid eyes on my manuscript let alone published it and vowed she would make it her business to ensure my book was as invisible as possible in any bookshop that had the misfortune to stock it, and subsequently she carried out this threat with a single-minded efficiency. Just like that, our writer–publisher relationship, with all its ups and downs, good and bad but nevertheless vibrant, was over.

So thanks *very* much to the long-fringed boy. Without his bare-faced lies, I would very probably have sold more books. I might've appeared on the Nielsen Bestsellers List for a week or two and got some traction from that— publicity, reviews, a writing grant, the opportunity to write more books, a contract with a proper publisher; in short, a life as a writer. By that stage, of course, I would've been in grave danger. My brow sweats even now as I recall what an extremely lucky escape I had from popularity, and I want to take the opportunity to extend my enormous thanks to Long Fringe for his far-reaching act of utter deceit, without which I would not be the writer I am today.

Walking much more easily now in my snow boots (perhaps a little heavy for Lambton Quay), I decide to look for an internet café where I can catch up on social media. I find a convenience store that advertises internet—although to get in I have to fight my way past a group of teenagers begging; from their preppy clothes and the mock-desperate way they're going about their panhandling, they seem like middle-class kids who need the train fare home to Noa Valley because they've spent all their money on weed. I brush past their jokey pleading and head through the bright café, which is set out in a utilitarian fashion, as if by kids playing shop. At the back is a red curtain with a homemade paper sign with a hollow red arrow pointing to 'the Internet'. In a brisk transaction, the young attendant, a boy with a buzzcut, very new jeans and a pink button-down shirt, accepts my four dollars for half an hour. He tries to stop me taking my fridge into the computer room, and we have a bit of a back-and-forth dialogue about it. In the end I agree to leave it outside the computer room as long as it's in eyeshot. The nice young man is just a little bit condescending in telling me that he doesn't think anyone is going to steal my fridge. I beg to differ, but oh well. I go behind the curtain.

In the semi-dark, ten or so teenagers also with buzzcuts and button-down shirts are seated at computer monitors bathed in red light. As I sit down at the one free monitor, my arms rub against my neighbour on each side, but neither of them looks up. I turn my head and see, up close, the ferocious computer-stare of my left-hand neighbour, and on the other side, the ferocious stare of my right-hand one. Their screens flutter with orange explosions as they shoot things. I get on with my task, which is of course to maintain my online presence in the absence of my phone and any decent free WiFi in the central city.

I tweet again about the Antarctica Awards and being humbled by meeting a group of spectacular artists. I feel sorry not to have a pic, but what can I do? Immediately my tweet is favourited by @fringefestdweller. I know Mandy isn't going to be favouriting anything of mine any time soon, but what the fuck? I'll return the favour. Then Linda Dent RTs me and replies, You rock @Janiceawriter! Yay!!! I reply, Thanks muchly for the RT @heartwriter, then attend to my housekeeping, retweeting people I think should be following me and unfollowing a couple of people who never like anything I tweet, plus retweeting announcements about people who've died and linking to a quite good article about how they're planning for when we hit 450ppm and it should be 550ppm but that's so frightening no one dares look at it and then everything stops because it's too late. Scary stuff.

And then, just when I'm wrapping things up, Twitter gives me a surprise. Right before my eyes, Linda Dent replies to the link I've tweeted earlier about Environmental Gratitude, thus: Brilliant article! Shame we middle class peeps keep mucking it up @Janiceawriter!!!!!

I sit back hard in my chair, feeling as if I've been socked in the gut. Is she accusing me of being a self-satisfied, middle-class, carbon-footprint-stomping brat? I read the tweet again to be sure, don't want to jump to conclusions, but yep, *we middle class peeps*, it says, clear as day. Breathing hard, I glance around me. My neighbours, with whom I am literally rubbing shoulders, must notice that their fellow internet user has just had a very nasty jolt. Surely they will break off from their gunning-down in order to offer me some solace. For all they know, I could've just found out about the death of a loved one, I could've got some test results confirming terminal illness. I'm sorry to report that my internet buddies keep their eyes trained on their screens, their fingers shimmying. So I set to dealing, on my own, with the shock of being accused of being a middle-class fossil fuels gourmand.

The confusing issue of my class is something I've had rubbed in my face many times over the years. I should be used to it. However, just because my parents went to university, it doesn't make me middle class. Middle-class children have walls that remain upright in their houses. Middle-class children have Christmas trees and get presents on Christmas morning. Middle-class children go to two schools, three at most, and have their tertiary educations funded by their parents. Middle-class children do not spend a year in filth and squalor in a commune and then find themselves expelled from it for accepting a summons no one told them *not* to accept. Middle-class children do not need to leave a stepfather at short notice because they have been accused of accusing him of sexual abuse. Middle-class children do not drive around in the dead of night looking for places to deposit stinking black rubbish bags. Middle-class children have fridges. I rest my case.

Aware that my half hour in the internet café is ticking by, I reply to Linda Dent (noticing Linda has changed her profile picture to a cabaret-ish one of her doing open mic): Speak for yourself @heartwriter! I am staunchly and proudly a member of the proletariat. Around me, the teenagers play on. There is an air of surreal intensity. For a moment, I almost forget where I am, what planet I am on, *who* I am. I forget that the room is pulsing with electricity and that as a result the world is warming up. I forget I am going to Antarctica in the morning.

Linda Dent replies, Sorry @Janiceawriter didn't mean to offend. Thought your parents were artists, yeah? I tap in quickly: Obviously you know nothing about art, class, or my childhood @heartwriter. Linda Dent replies: Never mind @Janiceawriter! Apologies! Onward. Mwa mwa <3 <3.

I summon every fibre of my being to explain to Linda Dent my state: @heartwriter you have no idea. Then I go over to Facebook, as is my wont. The link is there too, of course. I edit my replies, because I have room now, adding ABSOLUTELY FUCKING before no idea. Linda Dent replies to my reply, Sooo sorry, Janice! I'll delete my comment. Let's go back to how we were before xx. But it is too late. I don't care whether she deletes it or not. I go on to my friends list and unfriend Linda Dent with one sharp ping, feeling huge satisfaction when her smug, carbon-generating face melts from my page. I go back to Twitter and unfollow @heartwriter a.k.a. Linda Dent. Yuss!

Squeezing myself up from between my insensitive neighbours, I shoulder my way out from the curtained computer room. In the doorway, the attendant smilingly points me towards my fridge—as if I would forget. On the way out I dig for change and buy a pie from the warmer, which I eat in a few bites while storming up Lambton Quay, in a bit of a state, to tell the truth. But as I start to calm down a little, I decide that, when all is said and done, I should offer my deepest thanks to Linda Dent. Even though she is no doubt a blunt instrument when it comes to politics, I know that I am becoming all the stronger for having someone contest my socio-economic status in a public forum. Without that kind of unthinking dismissal of my identity, I would not be the writer I am today. My writing is born of the very need to assert my identity in the face of people like Linda Dent. So, thank you, Linda Dent, for all you've done for me. I really can't thank you enough.

I continue through town, towing my fridge and vaguely looking for the group of artists with whom I will go to Antarctica, although I'm not sure if I want to run into them under the circumstances. From the clock tower on a bank building, I see it is half past eight, and despite the wind mucking everything up, you can tell night is a hair's breadth away, and I am reminded of *L'Heure Bleue*, the first film in Rohmer's *4 aventures de Reinette et Mirabelle*, which I discussed with the attendant at the liquor store earlier in the day—the blue hour, the meeting place of day and night. At the end of Lambton Quay, I look back at the swoop; the light has gone a clear, glassy shade of blue-grey that delineates the edges of the buildings and curbs. The moment feels halfway between real and imaginary, distinct but heightened. When the moment passes—as it must, *l'heure bleue* is not really an hour but a second—it seems everything has been lifted, renewed, set going again. The future looks bright. I turn up Willis Street and into the full force of the wind.

As the evening begins its descent, I stop in the middle of the street and do a lightning quick operation on my manuscript. It does occur to me that I might be being too drastic with these cuts, but on second thoughts I still have my digital file, plus I can always write more. Down in Antarctica, I'll no doubt have an avalanche of ideas, so I go ahead and pluck out some crots about the protagonist losing her apartment in her separation and being vulnerable to the lying wiles of a long-fringed boy. I happen to be outside a sixties office block with a mustard-coloured tiled foyer which has seen better days—tiles missing and everything covered in a veneer of grime. I fire my edit into a similarly decrepit designer rubbish bin and continue on my way.

My time flatting with Mandy was a spectacular period for a host of reasons: Mandy and I got on like a house on fire (in fact at one point there was a small fire, but that was an accident), I was *fancy free*, I was practising my craft, and I was generally fulfilling my dreams in life. I didn't give a damn that I'd lost half the fifties apartment. I actually felt sorry for Miles, burdened as he was by possessions. After I'd set myself up at Mandy's, I wanted for nothing. When I offered rent, Mandy refused, saying that that would make the arrangement too formal—she really was a sweetie—so I truly was living a non-materialistic lifestyle. Of course, one of the really excellent things that happened during this time was joining Book Club. I have big thank yous to make to that happy crew.

It's worth giving a short history of Book Club here. A nicer group you'd never meet. Six wonderful women—oops, that's a little presumptuous—five wonderful woman plus yours truly, brought together by a shared love of literature or at least chick lit. It was absolutely brilliant, but slightly problematic for obvious reasons. I'd not been a member of Book Club before (apart from attending their Christmas bashes) because I had an inherently unfair advantage over the others, seeing as I actually write the things. It would be as if Serena Williams joined her local tennis club. Or, maybe not Serena, but a top-seeded player, certainly a pip. Mandy had always been totally upfront about the issue of me and Book Club. We're very honest with each other, no secrets. Book Club had put it to the vote more than once over its three-year run about whether or not I should be allowed to join. The members had collectively thought *not* because of my status. I completely understood. But that was then. Now, two things had changed: Mandy was the new convenor-slash-host, and I was living right smack in the heart of Book Club territory. As I explained to Mandy one evening during her BBC show, it'd be unfair for me to have to *go out* during the fortnightly meetings. Mandy murmured something about there being a bedroom, but when I pointed out how patently ridiculous it'd be for me to have to sit in my room during Book Club, she promised to see what she could do. I wasn't even sure if I wanted to *be* in Book Club at this point. But apparently a flurry of emails ensued, and Mandy reported back a few nights later that the members had voted yes. The process hadn't been plain sailing, though. Mandy stood on the rug with her arms folded threateningly, as much as anyone can be threatening in a dressing gown. There were conditions. Oh, here we go, I thought. I braced myself from the couch. But it turned out the conditions were nothing. My tenure with Book Club would last only for the duration of my residence at Mandy's. Fine. It's not as if there was an end date in sight. And there were three rules: 1. No alcohol at Book Club meetings. 2. Books to be decided by democratic vote and to be read by everyone. 3. No books written by members would be read by Book Club.

I chuckled, relieved, and realised I did want to belong to Book Club after all. 'What do you take me for!' I said. 'Of course, yes, to the conditions. Yes, yes, and yes.'

Mandy unfolded her arms and smiled in a rabbity way and I smiled back—as a fully signed up, bona fide Book Club Member. It was a blast flatting with Mandy.

Mandy pointed to a paperback on the coffee table. 'For tomorrow night.'

I probably looked sceptical at the idea of reading a whole novel at such short notice, because Mandy backtracked a bit. 'Well, if you can manage it. You don't have work, so . . .'

Don't have work?

'Mandy,' I said. 'I'm writing a novel.'

'Of course,' said Mandy. 'I just meant, if you decide to

read the book, you could. I mean, I have to be at the library at eight thirty for instance and—'

'Fine, fine.' I didn't want to make a big thing out of this.

'It's Rule Number Two, that's all,' said Mandy, and went to bed.

Rule Number Two. That's typical Mandy, I have to say. But, overall, she's a total sweetie.

As the night was young, I picked up the novel from the coffee table and inspected the cover image, a half-dressed woman viewed from behind. I read the blurb on the back. It was about a clothes mender who gets into a complicated situation fixing an Irish costume. I can't recall the title or the author now, but I remember thinking it sounded splendid. I have to confess, though, I didn't end up reading it. I was a bit stoned and I slept in quite late next day. Seeing as I'd only just joined Book Club, I thought they'd let me off Rule Number Two on this occasion.

I'm going to set out exactly what transpired at Book Club because I think it'll be of great interest and value to any persons who happen to go trawling through the Turnbull Library in the future with the aim of writing a literary biography of any of the members. You never know, maybe someone will write a biography of Charlene, Deb, Lydia, Liz or even Mandy. Perhaps I can provide some phenomenological material. But also, of course, I want to say a very big thank you in these pages to my outstanding Book Club pals. A nicer group of women you'd never meet. There did need to be some fairly instant changes made to procedure which I'll discuss in a moment, but first some character notes on the participants whom, as I say, I already knew from parties:

Charlene: late twenties, single, sporty-looking, Ngāi Tahu, went to Queen Vic before it closed down and has attendant big ego, librarian but not stereotypical mousy type which would've been preferable, thinks working in the fiction section of Central Library gives her greater knowledge of fiction than other people, wrote MA thesis on agency in *the bone people* which no one ever hears the end of, agency this, agency that, brings homemade banana cake to Book Club, capable of arguing until blue in the face about things like agency, pet word: agency.

Deb: thirties, married, one kid, NZ-Chinese, social worker, petite, talks about husband *ad nauseam*, Jack this, Jack that, texts Jack every five mins, reads books to relax (!) after stressful job removing children from their families, skites about winning English prize at Wellington Girls' College in the nineties, has absolutely no fucking idea about fiction, brings cheese board to Book Club and we're not talking Countdown, owns house with Jack, pet word: Jack.

Lydia: thirty, Pākehā, serial monogamist, trust lawyer, no kids, grey face, bony arse, knows absolutely zilch about fiction, doesn't even care about fiction, went to Queen Margaret College and has attendant big ego, lives in downstairs flat of parents' house and pays no rent, never brings food to Book Club, pet phrase: current boyfriend.

Liz: forty, Pākehā, married with two kids, built like a netballer, on maternity leave from job teaching high-school English, talks about baby Chloe *ad infinitum*, Chloe this, Chloe that, texts home *ad infinitum*, reads novels to relax, knows absolutely nothing about fiction, brings homemade quiche to Book Club, pet word: Chloe.

Mandy: Whom you already know, plus makes sushi for Book Club.

Me: Whom you already know! Brings wine to Book Club.

All in all, a vibrant, eclectic little outfit, as you can see.

I even noticed we were all different shapes and sizes so would be good cast together in a film, able to be distinguished at a glance. My first meeting began with hugs and shrieks as each member arrived at the top of the fire escape. They asked, one after the other like sheep, why there was a fridge in the corner of the living room, and we all had a laugh about that. At eight on the dot, we sat down on the L-shaped couch, at least Charlene, Deb, Lydia, Liz and Mandy did after a bit of musical chairs. I ended up sitting on a stool opposite. I didn't mind. The group launched into pre-book chitchat, a general lowdown on the fortnight just passed which mostly constituted discussion about husbands, babies and boyfriends. If you didn't have a husband, baby or boyfriend *currently*, there wasn't a lot you could contribute, not that I minded in the least. I did not mind. I realised, though, that the venue was good because at Mandy's there were no babies, Jacks, boyfriends, parents or MA theses which could be fetched and consulted at any moment. We started on the food which was pretty good, I have to say, and I was quite hungry, so I sat back and worked my way from the cheese board to the sushi while listening to the talk. A few tears were shed, something about a husband who sounded like an absolute prick, a kid who'd been bullied at school, a kid who *was* the bully at school but not the corresponding bully (that would've been awkward). All in all, with the food and the crying, I began to refer to Book Club in my mind as Cook Blub from here on in.

Although I had an unfair advantage, I was determined not to use it for my own gains, otherwise Cook Blub just wouldn't function. However, it was clear that some changes to policy were sorely needed, and as an outsider with a fresh perspective, I did seem to be the right person to implement them. The first and most obvious thing was to switch from herbal tea to wine. Whoever heard of a book club without wine? When I jokingly said wine was the whole point, the others tittered and I thought I'd won my case right away, but objections followed based on breastfeeding and having to go to work in the morning. Charlene even opined that a clear head was necessary to think deeply about a book. I didn't think a glass of Merlot was going to interfere with *agency* greatly. It looked like we were sticking with tea, but after I'd cracked open a bottle I'd purchased earlier at the liquor store (where I'd had a conversation with the shop assistant about *La Règle du Jeu*, during which it had occurred to me that even if the characters in French New Wave cinema were sometimes uneasy it was on no account a *cinéma malaise*, rather their unease was confident and cool, and French people had no trouble with the suspension of disbelief, whereas in New Zealand cinema there was always a feeling of, *This is us in a film, don't we look funny?*). I digress. I noticed the members of Cook Blub seemed to have no trouble getting down a sip or two of the wine purchased from the lover of French New Wave cinema. Within ten minutes the bottle was empty and things were a lot more fun than they'd been at the beginning of the sesh. With some ethanol in everyone's system, I moved that Cook Blub officially adopt wine rather than cranberry tea as its drink of choice. Deb, who seemed to be the cheapest drunk and that was saying something, seconded the motion, and there were ragged but unanimous ayes. Thus wine was instituted as a Cook Blub routine. I was pleased because I didn't want to be the sole provider of beverages, especially seeing as the others were clearly better off financially than me with their professional jobs, their houses, husbands and parents. If I'd been able to bludge off anyone, perhaps I would've thought differently, and maybe I too would've been able to read novels to relax.

Finally we got to the book, and I'm pleased to say, took it in turns to speak—no one dominated, it was all very civilised as you might expect from such a nice group of women. They mostly talked about whether they believed or didn't believe the events of the book (whose title I can't remember and whose author I can't remember). Lydia said she believed it when the protagonist hid the man. Deb said she didn't believe it when the protagonist hid the man. Charlene said she believed it when the protagonist ripped the costume she'd previously mended; it showed agency. Liz said she didn't believe it when the protagonist ripped the costume. (Mandy was in the kitchen making tea, the wine being long gone.) The discussion was vibrant, with agreement and disagreement, with furrowing of brows and laughter. When they laughed, their combined teeth all in a row looked like someone's collection of crockery. This was Cook Blub heaven.

I felt at a slight disadvantage not having read the book; alienated is probably too strong a word, but I did get the teensiest bit sick of what was believable and what wasn't believable, so I went out onto the fire escape to have a smoke and check my messages. I tweeted, Thanks Book Club, you gals are kick-ass! #ilovebookbuddies #bookclubrocks. @fringefestdweller retweeted my tweet, and also @heartwriter (this was before the big debacle). I replied, Thanks for the RTs @fringefestdweller & @heartwriter. I knew they'd be jealous as hell. I looked out at the city. To the west, the sky had a streak of red through it. The air was still, which is eerie for Wellington. I hoped this unusually clement weather wasn't signalling some kind of catastrophe. As I rolled my joint, I ruminated on the discussion about the novel, and it occurred to me that we all want to believe in something at all costs, even if it isn't true. I looked out again at the sky and the red streak had gone, died—night had come on.

When I got back inside everyone was hoeing into the banana cake and gearing up for a democratic vote on what we'd read next. Now here's something interesting. I thought the others would vote for some chick-lit novel with a picture of a half-dressed woman who'd got into a lot of romantic bother walking away from the camera; or even chick-with-dick lit, something by Nick Hornby or Jonathan Franzen. I was prepared for this, even looking forward to it. Lo and behold, Liz reminded everyone that the next Cook Blub meeting was Classics Night. The only question was 'Which classic?' and this was causing a Mexican wave to ripple through the kink in the L-shaped couch.

I was pleased, because I personally had a few classic novels up my sleeve that I'd never got around to reading (or, in one case, rereading). I recited this list to Cook Blub: *War and Peace, Anna Karenina, Crime and Punishment, The Brothers Karamazov, The Idiot, Moby Dick, Clarissa, Jane Eyre, Wuthering Heights, Remembrance of Things Past, The Scarlet Letter, The Scarlet Pimpernel, The Red and the Black, Silas Marner, Great Expectations, Oliver Twist, David Copperfield, A Tale of Two Cities, The Iliad, The Odyssey, Ulysses, A Portrait of the Artist as a Young Man, The Strange Case of Dr Jekyll and Mr Hyde, The Glass Bead Game, The Tin Drum, Les Misérables, Tess of the d'Urbervilles, Far from the Madding Crowd, The Mayor of Casterbridge, Jude the Obscure, The Ice Shelf, Nausea, The Grapes of Wrath, East of Eden, The Pearl, Of Mice and Men, One Hundred Years of Solitude, Midnight's Children, Leaves of the Banyan Tree, A Passage to India, A Room with a View, Howard's End, Animal Farm, Nineteen Eighty-Four, Brave*

New World, Madame Bovary, Tristram Shandy, Don Quixote, Sense and Sensibility, Pride and Prejudice, Mansfield Park, Emma, Catch 22, The Trial, The Metamorphosis, The Castle, Wide Sargasso Sea, Heart of Darkness, Mrs Dalloway, To the Lighthouse, The Invisible Man, The Bell Jar, Lady Chatterley's Lover, The Great Gatsby, Tender is the Night, Tom Jones, The Moonstone, The Lord of the Flies, Middlemarch, The Sound and the Fury, As I Lay Dying, Beloved, The Canterbury Tales, Candide, The Portrait of a Lady, Lolita, The Magic Mountain, To Kill a Mockingbird, Vanity Fair, Barry Lyndon, Robinson Crusoe, Dead Souls, and a few others.

I posited each one in turn, but it gives me no pleasure to report that Cook Blub greeted each suggestion with a 'No', which was at first a murmur but got exponentially louder with each iteration, thus: (x = [classic novel], y = No).[2] Repeated many times, it sounded like a list poem I'd once read in a verse novel about a young woman giant, which went, '[Classic book ending in 'o']? No.' And by the end the 'Nos' were very loud indeed.

As nobody had yet suggested another classic novel, I began to think the members of Cook Blub didn't know of any. But then there was a development. Liz, brushing cake crumbs from her fingers, announced—duh duh dah— *Frankenstein.* It seemed that this particular classic novel was vastly superior to the classic novels I'd been putting forward, because it got an immediate and heartfelt 'Yes' from the Cook Blub members, a 'Yes' that could've been heard, like a rugby try, all over the neighbourhood of Mount Victoria. Feeling pleased with themselves, the Cook Blub members once again revealed their respective sets of teeth. I could only attribute the enthusiastic response to *Frankenstein*—the *only* classic novel *not* on my list—to the fact it'd been chosen prior to my arrival at Cook Blub. Which turned out to be the case.

There's worse. A brief discussion ensued in which I couldn't possibly take part because it was about *Frankenstein*, and here's the really interesting thing. It became apparent that the other members of Cook Blub—a nicer group of women you'd never meet—had not only chosen *Frankenstein* earlier, they'd already read it. Lydia even happened to have a copy handy, pulling it from her red leather tote, which might tell you something about the premeditation that went into choosing Cook Blub books (and her handbag budget). I now suspected that the book about the clothes mender had been pre-read, and it dawned on me crushingly that *all* the books chosen for Cook Blub had been read by the members, perhaps recently, perhaps years before, I don't know; thus they were relieved of the chore of reading a new book in the next two weeks and were free to get on with Jack, Chloe, the current boyfriend, their jobs, and being on maternity leave from teaching high-school English. I, it seemed, was the only member of Cook Blub who had not read *Frankenstein*, which I thought grossly unfair.

However, I am not one to rock the boat, so I accepted the decision in good grace. And as the members dribbled down the fire escape, I chalked up to experience my first Cook Blub meeting.

The next day I was lolling on the couch—to be honest, there wasn't a heck of a lot to *do* at Mandy's. My natural habitat is a big house full of interesting people whom you have raves with at the kitchen table. Not Mandy's scene, so yeah, on this long day, one of many long days, for want of anything better, I picked up Mandy's copy of *Frankenstein* and applied myself to the blurb on the back. I'm sorry to say, apart from being the teensiest bit annoyed that I'd had no say in the choosing of this book and that the others had already read it, my abhorrence was immediate and physical. Shudders ran up and down my spine at the notion of a monstrous creature who lumbers about decrying his existence and destroying things and people. When I opened the book, it was even worse: the sight of the letters with their baggage of serifs, all in creepy black-and-white and bearing the lode of the monster, was too much for me at this point. I returned the book to the coffee table.

As the fortnight limped along (Mandy in her dressing gown by eight each night) and I still couldn't find it in myself to approach *Frankenstein*, I decided the best course of action was to read one of the classic novels on my own list. And yes, I was fully aware of Rule Number Two, but I was confident I'd be able to do something about changing it in my capacity as newest Cook Blub member. Having overturned Rule Number 1, I seemed to be the new broom. I perused my list, summoning my existing knowledge. Like knowledge of the Kardashians, it's hard to avoid at least a cursory acquaintance with the plotlines of classic novels. But here, unfortunately, was where I came unstuck. With mounting horror, I read that monsters in some shape or form populated many of the novels on my list, whether it was Moby Dick, Mr Hyde, Casaubon, Blanche Ingram, Bill Sikes, Uriah Heep, Alec d'Urberville, O'Brien, Milo Minderbinder, Inspector Javert, Robert Lovelace, Mr Kurtz, and so on and so on. Monstrous villains abounded. I began crossing off all the novels stalked by monsters, and my list shrank with each departing creature. Finally, as I struck a line through *The Grapes of Wrath* (the evil dustbowl was unthinkable), and with Classics Night looming, I had only one book, or at least a draft of a book, left.

*

When Cook Blub reconvened we sat companionably once again on the L-shaped couch (I didn't mind my little stool), drinking wine, eating salmon canapés (Deb) and guacamole (Liz), which were very nice, and after an interminable time of small talk, we prepared to unveil *Frankenstein*. I wasn't looking forward to this, but there would be other Cook Blub nights.

Charlene began by saying that she believed it when Frankenstein-the-scientist created Frankenstein-the-monster (like a peasant he took his master's name), and she liked his agency. Oh yes, said the others, they believed it utterly. Deb said she believed that Frankenstein-the-monster was capable of horrific deeds, and the others all chimed Yes, they believed it, too. It was very believable. Lydia asked if everyone believed it when he murdered Frankenstein-the-scientist's younger brother William? They did, they all believed it. Did they believe it when Poor Justine Moritz, the maid, was wrongly accused of the murder, a set-up by Frankenstein-the-monster, and condemned to death? Yes, they did, they all believed it. Did they believe it when Justine didn't even seem to mind that she was falsely condemned to death but saw it as part of her duties as a maid? They did, they believed it, even though 'on Wednesday I am to be hanged' was not very *Bridget Jones Diary*. Did they believe it when Frankenstein-the-monster demanded a girlfriend because he was so lonely? They did, they did. Did they believe it when Frankenstein-the-scientist refused to provide this because otherwise there would be no end to monsters? They did. Did they believe it when Frankenstein-the-monster escaped over the ice with Frankenstein-the-scientist in hot pursuit because he was worried about the damage Frankenstein-the-monster would do? Yes, yes, they did believe this. Did they believe it when Frankenstein-the-scientist died and Frankenstein-the-monster blubbed over his death? They did believe it. They believed every word.

Mandy reappeared from the kitchen—where she always seemed to hang out—and hovered uncertainly with a tray of tea. 'I believed it when he lies down and seeks shelter, however miserable, from the inclemency of the season.' Here she blinked and turned her head as if listening to some mysterious source, and finished, 'But, moreso, from the barbarity of man.' There was a silence while Mandy put down the tea, then the others rushed to congratulate her on her phenomenal memory.

I must've looked blank because Liz said, in a school-marmish tone to tell the truth, 'It's a quote from the book.' Mandy half smiled at her own cleverness, which was just a little sickening.

'Woohoo,' I said.

Eight eyes on the L-shaped couch—a nicer group of women you'd never meet—trained on me. Mandy said diffidently, 'Um, you did agree to read the book, Janice, remember?' Charlene and Deb made room for her and she sat down quickly, almost disappearing into the join of the couch. I felt *slightly* as if they were all in a row facing me.

I think it was Charlene who asked in a big voice, 'Janice, did you read *Frankenstein*?' Charlene would not get a role in *In My Father's Den*.

Lydia commented, 'It looks like Janice has broken Rule Number Two.' Someone thanked Lydia for hitting the nail on the head.

There was a bit of a clamour, the gist of it about my membership of Cook Blub, but also Mandy had just made the tea and someone had got milk out of the fridge and poured it into all the cups, but it was from my fridge and it had been put there by someone at the last Cook Blub meeting two weeks earlier, and now there was the foulest smell of rotten dairy and everyone was covering their noses and running about the room trying to escape the smell and someone opened the fire-escape door and Mandy ferried the cups to the kitchen to tip them out but tripped with her tray and grey spoilt milk flew all over the floor and the couch and there was a great argy-bargy.

When things had quietened, and everyone was sitting down again although parts of the couch were unavailable, I explained how I had not been able to bring myself to read *Frankenstein*. I told them how keenly I was affected by the idea of the creator, the monster, the monster's destruction and his loneliness. It all seemed so abjectly awful. By this time I was pouring out my heart. I told everyone that I had reread *The Ice Shelf* (draft) instead. I expected this news to be greeted with congratulations (after all, I had not wasted my fortnight's reading), and I gave a synopsis of the book.

The row on the couch were silent, none of their teeth visible.

Finally, Deb furrowed her brow and said, 'It seems that the protagonist of this book—'

'*The Ice Shelf*,' I furnished.

'Whatever,' said Deb. 'It seems like *she* is a monster.'

The other agreed raggedly. Yes, I believe that, I believe that, I believe that, they said one after the other. Something travelled slowly down inside my chest, like the New Year ball drop in Times Square.

Then it was all over and they began to clunk down the fire escape. Mandy appeared from the kitchen looking forlorn and desperate at the sight of the departing backs, and she called out urgently, 'We forgot to choose a book for next time!' Which halted them in their tracks, because this authoritative tone was unlike Mandy, and they poked their heads back in the glass doors like a nodding bunch of roses.

'Please don't go before we choose a book,' said Mandy, pink and weak now she had their attention.

It was then that I made my last serious challenge to the policies of Cook Blub, to Rule Number Three. I suggested we read *Utter and Terrible Destruction*. (The forty-nine-page problem seemed obsolete now.) I handed copies through the door to the assembled.

Charlene's drawn breath could be felt rather than heard. 'There is a policy,' she said in her librarian voice, 'that Book Club does not read books by its members.'

They meant me, because who else in Cook Blub had written a book?

Then they all got going with their opinions, with their different shapes and sizes clustering in the doorway. Deb was strident on policy, Lydia on precedent, and Liz said Chloe was so cute the other day. I admired their passion, but the fact remained, I was in Cook Blub, now, and Cook Blub had changed. Mandy said it looked like there was not actually going to be a book chosen this time, which would be a big shame. No one listened to her, and I felt the teensiest bit sorry about that. They all left quickly, clattering down the fire escape. During this stampede (I was reminded of the getaways in the Book of Exodus and *The Grapes of Wrath*), a copy of *Frankenstein* came sailing through the doorway and hit Mandy on the head. I'd never seen her so enraged. She cried out, 'Was that necessary?'

From down below Deb could be heard saying, 'I'm texting

Jack,' and Liz replying, 'So fucking what?' and Charlene saying, 'We're sick to the back teeth of fucking Jack.'

Mandy stood on the pink rug holding her head. I moved to the couch now I had the opportunity, collecting the thrown copy of *Frankenstein* on the way. We looked at each other and listened to the women argue into the night. I must say, even though Cook Blub was quite marvellous, I was feeling a little bit off them, and I planned to talk to Mandy about us starting our own group, just us, which we could have 24/7.

However, things were soon to be taken out of my hands. One night during the week, Mandy came into my bedroom in her dressing gown and milled about. Finally she said, twisting her face, 'Janice, I have something to tell you. I hope you won't be upset.' I said of course I wouldn't. Mandy said, 'No really, not fly off the handle or anything,' and I said, 'Mandy, have you ever known me to do that, just spit it out.'

Mandy told me the news: Cook Blub had voted to get rid of me. Of course, that wasn't the term she used. It was more of a *not a good fit, discontinue my membership* sort of thing. She meant I could go get fucked.

'I'm really really sorry, Janice,' she said. 'It wasn't me, it was the others.'

I said fine, whatever. I didn't mind, really I didn't. In fact, I'd never really wanted to belong to Cook Blub in the first place. Ah well, it was an experiment that didn't work out. I bear absolutely no malice to the members of Cook Blub, a nicer group of women you'd never meet, and in fact I want to thank each and every one of them—Charlene, Deb, Lydia, Liz, and yes, Mandy—for their candour. It wasn't working, me being a writer and them not, them being middle class and me not, and they said so. It was a brave and strong thing to do. Also, if I hadn't had the experience of being shunned by a group of very nice women, I wouldn't have built up the sense of isolation necessary to be a writer. Thank you, Cook Blub, very very much indeed.

I should add, to show there were absolutely no hard feelings, that the very next day the latest *Landfall* arrived in the mail and Mandy had a poem in it. She opened it right in front of me in the living room where I was sitting with my laptop trying to write, and I didn't mind the interruption. I congratulated her mightily, because I'm full of admiration for Mandy. I tweeted straight away: Woot woot! Congrats to my dear friend @mandycoot <3 <3 <3 and added the link, and a few minutes later, when Mandy was sitting on the couch hunched over her phone, she replied, Thanks @Janiceawriter xxxx. We looked at each other across the pink rug.

As it turned out, none of this Cook Blub drama mattered an iota, because one day soon afterwards, I got an email from Arts New Zealand informing me that a place had become available for me on the Antarctica Residency. Waitlisting and eventual success was becoming a pattern, and I wasn't complaining. I remember sitting in Mandy's living room with my laptop on my knees, reading the email and thinking that being kicked out of Cook Blub, evicted from the fifties apartment, none of it needed to feature on my radar. I had bigger and more important fish to fry, for five days in December.

I tweeted my good news. Chuffed to be awarded the prestigious Antarctica Residency esp along with other brilliant recipients. Humbled. Thanks @ArtNZ! There was an instant barrage of activity, including from @ArtNZ, who followed me (yeah, finally), and a retweet from one of my followers in the UK, a sailor/poet/mother/activist. I replied, Thanks so much for the RT @wavemaker! And they replied, Don't mention it @Janiceawriter, and I replied, I hope you are having a lovely day @wavemaker. They replied, I am thanks @Janiceawriter. Later in the day, @heartwriter and @fringefestdweller and of course @mandycoot favourited it. I took all this as a very good sign.

A few weeks later, I attended the four-hour prep session for those travelling to Antarctica to help ensure 'personal and environmental safety on the ice'. An afternoon might seem a short time to cover such a big topic, and in fact it did turn out to be lovely and low-key, I'm guessing due to the no-blame policy of the Accident Compensation Commission; that is, the government will fork out for your injuries, and no one will be held accountable. It's a good system, it's worked for years, and it suits the New Zealand she'll-be-right philosophy. In some ways it could be equated with *Cinema of Unease*. If any of us—me, or any of the group of artists with whom I would go to Antarctica—were to slip on the ice and break our neck due to lack of training, Scott Base would say, sorry about that, yeah nah, there's free surgery available and a few months' convalescence, have a nice life. Oh, and a fifty-dollar voucher towards your next trip to Antarctica, which is fully transferable so your relatives can redeem it if you find you never walk again, or if you die.

I turned up at the training facility in Ghuznee Street, up some dingy stairs in a long, dark room that looked as if someone might be organising a last supper there. As my eyes grew accustomed, I saw an expanse of bare floorboards and, at the back of the room, a knot of people in arty black coats. I guessed correctly that they were the very artists with whom I would go to Antarctica and whom of course I hadn't met yet. They looked stunningly cool and I greeted them warmly—Beatrice Grant, Tom Atutola, and Clement de Saint-Antoine-Smith, whom I've already introduced in these Acknowledgments. They nodded tightly, redolent of *Cinema of Unease*. It occurred to me that hell might freeze over before you could get a smile out of this crew. I wasn't bothered. We were busy. There were forms to fill in, equipment to organise, instructions to take on board, fire safety to be learned. It seemed that the greatest possible danger that awaited us on the ice was the threat of fire, even though Antarctica is mostly water. I guess it would take a lot of energy and, crucially, a lot of time to heat up enough water to put out a fire. I'm reminded of the performative doing of the dishes at Hoki Aroha—the cauldron, the blazing logs. Also: 'Water, water everywhere, and not a drop to put out a fire.' Isn't life ironic? Isn't the planet ironic!

Before I go further, let me introduce you to our tutor, Kevin, whom I want to thank mightily in these pages. Kevin was small and wiry and wore a shiny green paramedic outfit. He never laughed but spoke like a broadcaster delivering extremely bad news.

Kevin taught us basic first aid. Slings, splints, eye-bathing, vomit-inducing, when not to vomit-induce, recovery position, and CPR. The artists with whom I would go to Antarctica and I joshed our way though, striking poses with the slings and things. It was all a bit of a laugh and a good bonding experience, although it seemed the other three had bonded previously. I didn't mind. Plus, I felt a bit sorry for Serious Kevin. It was especially funny to be crouched over the half-manikins on the floor and engaged in an activity involving rubber, lips, puffing and suchlike. I was fairly dizzy at the end of it. The artists with whom I would go to Antarctica and I all gained a Certificate in Basic First Aid, awarded to us in a makeshift ceremony in which we trooped up to Kevin and received our certificates still warm from the photocopier. I'm proud to say that in the event of an emergency I'd be a useful person to have around. Next time I'm at a reading, say, and someone collapses on stage and they call out, 'Is there a doctor in the house?', if there is no answer and if there is also a resounding silence in response to the next question, 'Is there a nurse in the house?', and no answer to the next question, 'Is there an enrolled nurse in the house?', when they get to the *next* question, that is, 'Is there someone with an Two-hour Certificate in Basic First Aid in the house?', then I will not hesitate to volunteer my services.

The next stage of the course was Preliminary Environmental Evaluation. Full marks to Kevin for being able to say the acronym PEE with a straight face. I'm afraid I and the other artists didn't have such self-control, I suppose because we are artists. We all got the giggles. The other three in particular seemed to be having an hilarious time. I did too, and I didn't mind that they seemed to shun me. Kevin told us what to expect of the environment when we arrived at McMurdo Sound. First off, it seemed that flying to the polar ice cap was no different from arriving in a provincial New Zealand town.

'If no one is there to meet you at the airport,' said Kevin, 'wave down the shuttle.' There was a shuttle, and apparently a bus stop, which I hoped would not be situated in blizzard conditions, and the shuttle that picked us up from there would then transport us to Scott Base. I knew all about not being met at a remote station. I would be absolutely fine thanks to my solo trip to Hoki Aroha at the age of eight when I was not met at the Taihape Train Station; thanks very much,

Sorrell and Harry, I always knew that that experience would come in handy.

Kevin instructed us to respect the ice, not to leave any litter, not to pour any beverages onto the ice, not to walk on soft ice. I went into a bit of trance listening to him—his newscaster tone was strangely calming—and as I was thinking my own thoughts, I assumed Kevin was advising us to *not*, on any account, make snow angels, because transferring your body heat to the ice would make that piece of ice warm up; your body would then go numb and the warmed piece of ice would break off and float away and finally, when it had got so small as to not be visible anymore, it would melt altogether, it would be gone, it would be *sea*, and the sea level would rise on some distant piece of real estate.

As I came out of my reverie, Kevin was explaining how to escape from a burning building because, as outlined above, fire is the biggest danger on the ice. If the building caught fire, there would be no water to put it out on account of the water being otherwise engaged, that is, frozen, not yet subject to global warming, apart from the New Zealand-sized chunks that had already fallen into the sea. In the event of a fire, there was nothing to be done apart from running out onto the ice. Kevin instructed us in this practice: if you should hear the fire alarm in the middle of the night, on no account remain lying in your bed. Instead, run out of the building by the nearest exit. If you should hear the fire alarm in the middle of the day, on no account keep eating your lunch in the communal dining room. Instead, run out of the building by the nearest exit. If you should hear the fire alarm while you are in the bathroom, on no account continue sitting on the toilet. Instead run out of the building by the nearest exit.

Towards the end of the afternoon, Kevin brought out a box of gear: sturdy boots, big brown padded jackets, gloves and beanies. We tried them on for size, chucking boots at each other and having fits of laughter, at least the other three did. I got on my boots and my jacket. The jacket had a tight-fitting hood, multiple zips including one right up to the chin, elasticated bands around the wrists, and a toggle to draw tight around the thighs so that not even the smallest zephyr of icy air would chance an assault on the body. The padding had accumulated in clumps and it smelt of rodents. I stood there in the upper room in my jacket and, for some reason, it hit me—I was going to Antarctica! It occurred to me that I wasn't quite sure what I was going to do when I got there. I hoped I wouldn't do that weird thing where people are drawn to the edges of cliffs and jump off. I hoped I wouldn't go out and lie down on the ice just because it was there, and I was there too, and I had a corresponding cold space inside me that longed to be part of, to lose itself in, a frozen world.

Loaded up with our big brown jackets, our boots and our first-aid certificates, the artists and I tumbled down the steps into the late afternoon sun. The other three were doing renditions of Serious Kevin and generally having a really excellent time. On Ghuznee Street they milled about for a minute or two, doing Kevin, until all that was left of him was a few high bleats of laughter, then someone suggested the pub and they set off jauntily towards the Mall. About half a block away, one of them, I think it was Beatrice Grant, looked back at me and waved madly. I waved back, grasped my Antarctica gear tightly and ambled across town to Mandy's.

When I began writing this section, I was going to thank Kevin, but now I can't remember what I was going to thank him for. It may well occur to me in due course.

*

My fridge and I, still slightly at a loose end, have progressed as far as Cuba Mall. The dusk is well and truly underway now and the mall is criss-crossed with the gluey light of convenience stores and the infraredness of bars. Every so often an angry patron, cheeks ablaze, erupts from the doors of one of the latter establishments and staggers into the night. Judging by the leathery sound of thuds, somewhere in the distance a fist fight is happening. I mosey up the mall, weathering the doleful stares and random shouts of lost souls in pursuit of pleasure. As I approach the bucket fountain, I press myself against shop windows to avoid being drenched when the contents of the big dipper are inevitably hurled sideways by the wind. As a result of previous dumpings, the pavement runs like a small river. I skirt around a busker with a big beard and a creased face who is trying to sing but has no voice. Well-oiled revellers boo him as they pass. Further up, a bronze-painted man posing as a statue shivers muddily under a neon sign.

I don't know where to go or what to do. I wish I had enough money to park myself in a nice warm bar to pass the time. With the wind howling and the mall ever more gloomy, it occurs to me—why not just rock up to the Matterhorn and see what eventuates? Why fucking not, Janice? I wheel along a hushed, red-lit passage which opens onto a frowsty lounge with a shiny bar and coin-like tables. I stash my fridge in a dark corner, so dark I don't expect to be harassed about it, and I sashay between the patrons. Things are busy but orderly with an overlay of hysteria. This is a different rung from the mall. As there are no empty tables inside, I end up in the little garden out back where the smokers congregate in their cultural Siberia. In fact it's kind of cute out there, with the raised shrubberies tangled in fairy lights and the arty-looking people knotted around tables. I perch at the free end of a long table with a group at it. When the party gets up to leave, I notice some of them have left tides in the bottom of their glasses, so I scoot along and combine them into a single glass and soon have the best part of a drink. I'm not usually given to this kind of behaviour, but I figure the alcohol kills any germs. Don't they use alcohol for cleaning stuff at the hospital? And Christians seem to think they won't die from sharing the blood of Christ. Armed with my drink, I look around for diversion. My fridge is within sight, so I'm not worried anyone will take it.

At the table behind me sits a weedy-looking couple, dressed for a revolution in berets and thick, army-style jackets with epaulettes. They are having a game, it seems, with a slim volume. They are shuttling the volume back and forth between them quickly, as if playing ping-pong. Each time the woman has the book, she flicks through it ferociously looking for a particular bit, but she's never fast enough and the guy snatches it back and goes straight to a page and reads aloud. I hear snippets of important-sounding words like 'mendacious' and 'deliquesce' before the woman takes possession again. After a while they notice me and look a bit self-conscious, but we exchange friendly nods. I sip my wine/spirits/beer, which actually isn't too bad. I decide I may as well turn around properly and say hello. I open with, 'I couldn't help overhearing . . .', indicate the book and mention that I happen to be a writer.

They try to hide their interest, in an endearing, quintessentially New Zealand way. We chat and what I find out is that the man is a writer too. Not only that, he is the writer of the book that is being manhandled. It has just come out from a little local press, and the couple is out celebrating his good fortune. They tell me their names, Simon and Sarah, and I tell them mine. It is then that Simon looks interested. He puts his bereted head on one side. Sarah follows suit.

'Are you the author of *Utter and Terrible Destruction*?' asks Simon.

I confess that I am, and I feel myself go strangely shy under their gaze.

'I've read it!' says Simon.

'Really?' I feel a jumble of emotions at this development—glee, nervousness, dismissal; it's hard to explain. I consider admitting that my little volume is really quite modest with its forty-nine pages and no spine, but Simon continues: 'Yes, I keep up with all the small presses. Don't we, Sarah?'

Suddenly we are all great friends. We shake hands solemnly, clink glasses and take celebratory sucks of our drinks. If the world were to end right at this moment, the planet struck by a meteor, a tsunami wiping out Wellington, we'd cling to each other under the table in the Matterhorn and feel fully connected as humans who happened to exist at the same time. I almost wish an earthquake, the Big One perhaps, *would* come now so that Simon, Sarah and I could die together wrapped in each other's arms. But it doesn't come, and I ask if I could have a squiz at the book. Sarah and Simon trip over themselves to say yes, and the volume is more or less shoved into my hands.

I begin to flick through the book. After a few moments, I look up at Simon, at his innocent, wide-eyed face in direct contrast with his revolutionary garb, and consider whether I should break the bad news to him.

This is what I have found: the *book*, so-called, may be very handsome with its lovely cover, and it even has a spine. But, unfortunately, this publication has only forty-nine pages.

Quite quickly, I work out that telling Simon is the only humane thing to do. What if he were to go out into the world thinking that his publication was a book, only to find out in a much more public arena than our table at the Matterhorn (I am thinking Borich Festival) that it is no such thing? I figure that having me tell him right here and now, with just three of us and in the half dark, is the kinder act.

'This is not a book,' I say, in the very nicest way I can.

'Pardon?' he says, his eyes popping a bit. Sarah's eyes pop too, underneath her beret.

I explain to them the definition of a book according to the Society of Authors and the Authors' Fund. I relate how this little publication will not make its author (i.e. Simon) any more than an Associate Member of the Society of Authors, nor, even if it is to be circulated in public libraries by the tens of thousands, will it make him a single cent in revenue from the Authors' Fund.

Simon blinks. No doubt this is tough to hear, but all in a good cause.

Suddenly, Simon and Sarah, as if by some prearranged pact, scrape back their chairs and get up from the table. They leave the Matterhorn quickly, their berets bobbing through the crowd. This is slightly confronting, but they leave half a glass of wine each. Every cloud has a silver lining.

It's true that I feel a bit bereft and self-conscious, abandoned at the table like that, especially surrounded by vibrant groups having a wonderful time. I consider uplifting my fridge and leaving the Matterhorn myself. But then: who should come in but one of the five men from my dating grid? I'm not kidding. Eric. Not only was Eric *on* my list, he was top of it at one point. Wellington is a small place, so I suppose these coincidences are not surprising.

I recognise him instantly even in the fairy-lit dimness of the garden by his big hair, beard and broad, olivey face; he's a dead ringer for Karl Marx. Eric takes a seat along the bench from me. Like the last time we met, I notice everything about his presence immediately, his washing powder and tobacco smell, the way he spills out of his clothes on the edge of overweight. For some reason, I find this lush quality sexy, enough for now, anyway. What's more, he seems to be alone. I scoot a little way along the bench, nothing major, and a rise of the eyebrows tells me he recognises me too. I remember that with Eric there's rarely eye contact. We clink glasses and start to make convo. I expect he'll want to talk about the evils of Capitalism, and he does quote an article from the *Guardian* about fracking in the North Sea, but it's mostly DJs, and before long we're deeply engrossed.

'May I recommend Flippinhell and Pocket Lipps?' Eric asks the table.

'You may,' I say.

'And the scene at the Fat Angel. It's a thinking crowd,' he says, drawing fondly on his cigarette.

It's all about thinking, I say.

'The intersection of acoustic and digital is actually the jumping-off point.' He's quite drunk.

I remember he works in a bookshop (that's why he scored low for financial prospects—it's all coming back to me), and I inquire after business. Apparently it's going well.

'What do you do again?' Eric asks

I quickly get to the main point: I am Antarctica-bound. 'Like, tomorrow,' I say.

'Tomorrow!' He squints into the middle distance and his eyes are deep and wrinkled like his trousers. I tell him about *The Ice Shelf*, its history, the economy measures I've applied to it this evening, and the concrete sensory details I will acquire on the ice.

After some more thoughtful drags on his cigarette, he revs up his eyebrows and asks my ear, 'What's on for tonight?'

'Nothing,' I say. 'So far.'

At last, somewhere to spend the night.

Before we leave the Matterhorn, however, I feel the familiar tingle of an edit coming on. I tell Eric to wait a mo and he chain-lights a cigarette and gazes up at the sky while I open my laptop bag and thumb through my printout until I come to the section in which the protagonist falls in love but realises quickly that it isn't the real thing; in fact, it is a disappointment, it is absolute shit, and the love interest is a monster and probably she is a monster also and the two of them reside in a kind of hell. *The Ice Shelf* is much more riveting without it. For the second time, I pause for a moment, wondering if I am being too extravagant with my shedding. But I do have my digital file, and I also remember that I'd never had any trouble with ideas; of ideas, I am a renewable resource. I ball my edits. Eric follows as I uplift my fridge and we head out of the Matterhorn.

Outside in the mall, the weather is even worse—colder and windier. I stuff the culled pages into the closest rubbish bin and zip up my jacket.

Eric indicates my fridge. 'Is that in case you want a drink of milk?' He snorts, and as we meander he gives a quick, freefall homily about the dairy industry, farting cows, methane and fertilisers. He sounds as authoritative as if he had half a science degree, but I know it's all just from the *Dominion Post*. Seeing as we are on the subject, I think I may as well ask directly, more or less, if he would babysit the fridge for a week or two.

'Yeah, nah,' he says.

I breathe a sigh of relief.

He tells me he lives up 246 steps, not counting Church Street Steps. We laugh. I remember I like him.

Going up Church Street Steps with the fridge is a bit of toil. We probably should've gone down to Lambton Quay and taken one of the lifts to the Terrace, but after a few drinks, I guess our judgement is somewhat impaired but in a really excellent way. Halfway up Church Street Steps we sit down for a rest, breathing hard. The city twinkles below us like a virus. Eric laughs into his beard. I laugh. It is pretty hilarious. We kiss. His mouth, when I can get at it through the beard, has taken on the cold of the air, which makes the tobacco taste woody. He has to keep turning away to catch his breath. I'm not getting a whole lot out of the kiss, but I have bigger intentions.

When we get to the top of the steps, I'm tired, but Eric is wheezing like he's on life support. He leans against the tall wooden fence of one of the big villas on the Terrace and manages to rasp out, 'Why don't you ditch. The fridge?'

I tell him I can't possibly do that, and anyway, isn't he going to look after it? He squeaks, 'I was. I am.' But he doesn't sound convincing and I'm already beginning to wonder if Eric is the right person to look after my fridge.

We continue up the Terrace and turn into the first loop of Salamanca Road. Eric stops again. 'Why don't you leave it behind there?' I follow his gaze to a bus shelter cobbled to the hillside. He manages to add, 'Who's going to take it? At this hour of the night?'

I have to concede, probably no one—except me, of course, and I laugh and Eric coughs. I am reluctant to kiss goodbye to my fridge, even temporarily, but can see the impossibility of lugging it up 246 steps without Eric needing triage. He manages to help me stow it behind the shelter and to break small branches from trees on the bank as cover. These slide off the fridge in a trice, but using gobs of Eric's quickly-chewed gum, we assemble, hilariously, a military-style camouflage.

Without the fridge, huffs Eric, we could cut through the cemetery. Do I mind a few dead bodies? His beard wobbles; he is quite a laugh. To be honest, I do mind, but it is ten o'clock-ish, the weather is awful, Eric is near death, and I am worried he'll change his mind about our date night, so to speak. We double back across the road and start up the steepest bit of Mount Street. As we flatten off into Wai-te-ata Road, I look back and can just make out under the streetlight the leafy smudge that is my fridge. I feel a pang. But I am aware that I *can* leave it there. I *can* actually walk away.

The cemetery is just a pocket and will take only a few minutes to get through. We climb the almost-vertical steps that soar up into the grave area. Eric seems to have recovered somewhat, and I'm experiencing that feeling you have if you push your arms hard against a door jamb then step outside the frame and your arms float up of their own accord, as if there's no gravity. That's how I feel *not* towing my fridge. Whether this is a letting go or a loss, I can't tell. Something else has taken over.

Further up into the cemetery are big gnarly pōhutukawa, so it suddenly goes darker and we are showered randomly in fists of water shaken off the trees in the gale. Eric squelches ahead on the muddy path, and I bring up the rear, grazing my fingers on the rough headstones. As my eyes become accustomed to the light, I see that we are surrounded by chipped Victorian graves and weedy patches mosaicked together. I'm the teensiest bit nervous. At one point I think

I see a ghost rising up from a grave, but I soon realise it is a couple fucking against a tombstone, fused together like flies. Their doleful moans mix with the sighing of the trees. Further on, a little cluster of Goth-looking types have lit a bonfire on a grave and are roasting sausages. Against the fire, their gesticulating limbs are like Kali, and as we pass I see their tongues glow red in the firelight as they talk about their Film Festival picks. But actually, the Mount Street Cemetery isn't too bad, for a cemetery, and before long the wan light of the exit appears at the top of the hill.

We are nearly there when a voice screeches Eric's name. 'E-ric! *E-e-ric*!' A dreadlocked woman with a lanky frame emerges from the gloom.

Eric looks around. 'Oh, it's you.'

'What's *happening*?' yells the woman. Up close she has wide, mad eyes. Her dreads are straw-coloured and a lattice of complicated black bra-straps pokes out the top of her tattered op-shop dress.

'Well, Holly,' says Eric with a tired, ironic air, 'we're just on our way home.'

Holly looks from Eric to me and back again and her face scrunches questioningly.

'This is Janice,' says Eric.

'Hi,' I say.

Holly's face scrunches tighter. 'Why?'

'Because.' Eric looks up mock-soulfully at the sky as if pleading for mercy.

Holly falls into step behind Eric, and I follow them both up the muddy last few metres to the road. The notion of sex is fading fast, but I am still hoping I can stay the night.

'Are you a student?' I ask Holly's back, to make conversation.

'Yeah!' says Holly to Eric in a tone that indicates she isn't ever likely to be.

The entrance to the flat is via a thicket of wet foliage which Eric fights his way through, seemingly letting each frond slap in Holly's face because periodically she says, 'Ouch! Thanks a lot. Ow! Thanks again.' I guess Eric is too out of breath to care. When we finally reach his rotten back verandah, we have to wait for Eric to negotiate the door and I hope we don't fall through the splintery gaps into another world.

Inside, the place smells acridly of borer bomb. The kitchen is dark and slopes downhill. The flat has all the known tropes of the urban scavenger, such as the milk crate over the light and the stolen traffic sign. As we traipse down, a woman sitting at the table gets up and follows us as if she'd been waiting for us to collect her. 'Rose,' calls Eric over his shoulder, by way of introduction. Rose is skinny and twitchy like a fox. She mumbles something and even in the dark her teeth look bad for a twenty-something. We troop down the steep passage and upset a curtain of beads as we go through into the bedroom.

Rose and Holly fling themselves on a couch in the bay window, and Eric disappears out another door to a sort of sunroom. I perch on the huge rolled arm of the couch and take in the vast, purplish room, the open suitcases that seem to serve as drawers, the lamp with a cloth over it. On the floor is an amalgam of several mattresses heaped with blankets. A head pokes up from among them.

'Is it night-time?' comes a blurry voice.

'No,' says Holly. 'It's the crack of fucking dawn.'

'Don't be a witch,' says Rose, then adds kindly to the person in bed, 'It's fucking night-time.'

The person staggers up from the bed clutching a blanket

around her, hurtles over and flings herself onto the couch. Holly pulls in her feet as if they've been splashed by the juice of a recycling bin and looks reproachful. We all look out the window at the wild trees.

'That's Phlox,' says Holly.

'Janice,' I supply, but Phlox seems none the wiser.

'I know!' says Rose. She kneels up on the couch and furrows down behind it, messing with the thick curtains. She holds up a bottle of vodka like a trophy. 'Let's make cocktails!' Rose and Holly touch knuckles and even Phlox raises a smile. I'm not complaining either.

We all slog back uphill to the kitchen.

Rose flicks on the light and screws herself into a low cupboard. When she reappears, her blond dreads are cobwebby, like a cat that's been under the house, and she's holding a blender. Its crazed plastic jug twinkles beautifully. Holly, Phlox and I stand about with our arms folded while Rose rampages through the top cupboards and assembles a forest of bottles and old fruit and things in packets. While she opens and bangs cupboards, Holly tells the complicated story of her evening before she encountered Eric and *her* (jerking her head at me and soliciting looks from the other two) in the cemetery, which includes a series of drunken encounters with people she half knew. I can't keep track, but the story causes Rose to abandon her cocktail-making at one point and explode, and she and Holly have a brief, vicious spat, but it seems to blow over. Periodically, Rose tells Holly to shut the fuck up, and Phlox agrees.

Eric appears again, very stoned, and is informed of the cocktail decision. Without hesitation but with a fair bit of grunting he hefts himself up on the bench. The countertop creaks as he wobbles along it, strangely light on his feet,

257

opening all the high cupboards, saying, 'This could go in a cocktail, now this could definitely go in a cocktail.' He tells everyone to watch out, and we stand aside respectfully as cans rain down and make gouges in the floor.

I think I should probably leave, but I need a place to sleep. I think about my fridge, on its own down behind the bus shelter, and I hope it's okay. I've worked out that there's no way Eric will be taking it on board.

It seems Eric might fall from the bench, and because of his hefty frame, a tumble probably won't do him any good, not to mention the floorboards. I start to bleat at him, 'Be careful, Eric, don't fall.' Rose and Holly join in, and we all chorus, 'Be careful, Eric, don't fall, Eric!' I'm bonding with Rose and Holly over jointly entreating Eric not to fall. Phlox draws intensely on a cigarette and says, 'I don't give a fuck, let him fall if he wants to.'

'Be careful, Eric, don't fall, Eric!' Rose and Holly and I chant, laughing our heads off together. But after we've done this a few times, I catch both Rose and Holly exchanging rolling glances, as if they've just that moment *seen* something in me. My last 'Don't fall, Eric!' is solo, and Rose follows up with a blatantly mocking, 'Ooh, don't fall Eric!' It seems that our friendship, which had blossomed to something lovely in a minute or so, has now dwindled, like a flower unfolding and dying on time-lapse photography.

Eric jumps down from the bench with a few bottles under his arms. The bottles have dregs in them, vodka and tequila and such, and Rose and Holly poke out their necks accusingly. 'How long have those been up there?' Eric doesn't even bother shrugging. Somehow his body weight makes up for everything. They plough on with the cocktails, Rose stations herself at the bench to cram bananas, raisins, crackers and a can of peaches into the blender. Boxes of allspice are passed round and sniffed like a drug. The first sounds from the blender are a shocking gravelly rattle. Rose cuts the power and snatches up the jug to inspect it. And suddenly she screams. '*The lid! The middle of the lid!*' The lid is apparently in the blender, shredded to a pulp. The girls scream. 'Rose, you fucking *idiot*!' And from somewhere in Eric's belly comes the rumbling edge of hysteria.

Not to waste the alcohol already in the blender (I suppose), Rose adds more to the cocktail from the assortment of ingredients. A thick grey concoction materialises within. Soon we are sipping the porridgey findings from old Marmite jars. It isn't too bad. 'Cheers,' we all say, 'cheers.' Rose and Holly both curl their lips when they clink my jar. Phlox sits on the bench next to the kitchen window, looking out on the desolate night and swallowing.

For the next batch, Holly has a go on the blender, and we all encourage her like soccer hooligans, even me—'*Go* Hol-ly! *Go* Hol-ly!' Holly reaches willy-nilly for bottles and packets, and pours them all into the blender. When she turns it on, there is an almighty eruption and grey matter sprays powerfully all over the kitchen.

After the shrieking and cowering, Holly dangles the power plug in her hand and informs us in careful drunk-talk that this is the consequence of having no lid on the blender. Her observation is greeted with silence and then more hysterics. It is Phlox's idea that we waste not want not, and she leans over and attaches her mouth to the window.

Eric says, to all and sundry, 'Would you care to join me for a cocktail?'

The girls yahoo.

'Who am I quoting?' asks Eric.

'Don't give a fuck,' says Rose.

'No, go on, who am I quoting? "Would you care to join me for a cocktail?"'

Eric eyes me while licking his coat sleeve in an intimate way, for some reason. I know sex is off the menu, but I don't give a fuck.

We all proceed to lick the mixture from the table, the chairs, the floor. Eric climbs back up onto the bench and licks the ceiling, saying periodically, 'Can I interest you in a cocktail?' I feel myself getting fairly drunk as my tongue rasps over rough surfaces. Eventually we've finished the kitchen and are drinking cocktails from our Marmite jars again, and I knock back a couple partly because they are quite substantial with their bananas and canned beans, and I am hungry.

Rose and Holly have embarked on an argument, something about a boy they've both had sex with, comparing their orgasms, of which Rose had six, but Holly says they would've been small ones. Rose says no, big, enormous ones. Holly says she is a liar. Rose says Holly is a liar. Their yelling escalates until I can't get the gist of it anymore. They tug almost playfully at each other's clothes and hair, but soon this turns less friendly.

Phlox unfolds herself from the window and stands over them. 'Hey!' They follow each other round the kitchen, skidding a bit, screaming invective, their gums peeled back redly like burst cheerios, but breaking off to lick up the odd forgotten dollop of mixture when they encounter it. For quite a while they scream and cry uncontrollably. I don't really know what to do. Eric watches passively from a kitchen chair, blinking and turning his thumbs like rotisserie chickens. I look up at the lightshade. After what seems like a long time, the girls start to gulp and calm down, their faces pulsing like shellfish each time they sniff. Finally, Eric says to all and sundry, 'Let's go to bed.'

Like the end of the visit to Uncle Albert in *Mary Poppins*, when they have to stop laughing and come down from the ceiling, nothing is funny anymore. The kitchen, trashed from the cocktails, feels suddenly sober, and sober now seems terrible because everything was hysterical before. It makes you wonder whether it's worth being happy.

Eric has left the kitchen. I go into the bedroom and there he is, lying in the middle of the mattresses. He cranes up, pats beside him. A puff of dust rises up as he sinks back. I lie down gingerly in my clothes. The bed is a bit smelly, but it is a bed. Eric is snoring at the ceiling before I've even pulled up a blanket. A few moments later Rose appears naked, walking through the room as if it were water. She clambers on top of Eric momentarily, but he calls out something from his sleep and shrugs her off like an earthquake. I can hear Rose saying, 'Fuck you then, fuck you,' into the blankets. I touch Eric's face for some reason; it's dry and leathery, and I smoosh his cheek up and down. In his sleep, Eric turns away to spoon Rose, the action causing his snoring to skip a beat and then recover itself shudderingly. In the dark, Holly gets in next to Rose. A while later, Phlox gets in next to me. She is all cold and poky, and falls asleep in seconds.

I stare up at the streetlight flickering on the ceiling as the trees gesticulate in the gale. Squashed between Eric and Phlox, I am strangely comfortable. I feel I know these people really well, like I've spent weeks with them, or at least several intense days, like the days I am to spend with the artists with whom I will go to Antarctica. We've shared something—the sloping flat, the cocktails, the laughing and, what's more, the laughing's aftermath, the loss. I think, if the world is going to end now, we would hold hands, all five of us, and it would feel right, almost as right as being with people you were related to, had grown up with, had spent years of your life with. We would build on our forged bond and slip from this world together, feeling comforted by our association as humans.

I listen to Eric, Rose, Holly and Phlox snoring like a small orchestra tuning up, then I make another attempt to wake Eric, turning to pinch his earlobe, I don't know why. I suppose I want someone to talk to. As I do, something quite major gives way on the red dress in the vicinity of the waist. Eric stirs but bats me away and returns to his woodwind instrument. I could just sleep here, but suddenly I can't bear the thought of my fridge on its own down behind the bus shelter. And also I am getting unbearably hot, despite the cold night. I get up and collect my stuff. I have to say, I feel like shit as I plough up the wooden hill of the passage to the back door, let myself out and descend the 246 steps onto Kelburn Parade, and the cold wind. As I go, I remember that it was Holden Caulfield—the 'would you care to join me for a cocktail' quote.

I would like to take the opportunity here to thank Eric for leading me up the garden path (literally), and my thanks also go out to Holly, Rose and Phlox for pretending to be friendly and suddenly withdrawing it all with no warning, because without these clobberings to the ego, what does a writer have to go on? 'Adversity reveals genius, prosperity conceals it' (Horace). Not that I think of myself a genius, I hasten to add, but I've had a lot of help from people. I thank every last one of them from the bottom of my heart.

*

Reader, I have something to tell which is not really a thank you, but I would nevertheless like to relate it in these Acknowledgements. As I've mentioned, Mandy put me up from the day in late February when I arrived under unfortunate circumstances, right through until the very night of the Antarctica Awards ceremony (thank you, Mandy). All in all, staying with Mandy was excellent, and I was very lucky (thank you, Mandy).

But one afternoon in July, I was mooching about with, truth be told, nothing much to do. Hail was pelting against the French doors in a grotesque display, even by Wellington standards. Earlier, I'd ducked down to the liquor store and had a pretty riveting convo with the assistant about *Hiroshima Mon Amour*, but had luckily got home before the downpour. I was just settling down on the couch with a vodka and orange—a bit premature, but the dark clouds made it seem later—when I noticed, still on the coffee table, the copy of *Frankenstein*. I hesitated, then picked it up.

I'm quite thick-skinned, as you've no doubt ascertained, Reader, but I have to confess, when Cook Blub came up with the general consensus that I'd invented some kind of monster in *The Ice Shelf*, I was shocked. I know it's pathetic, especially as the Cook Blub members don't know crap about fiction, as outlined above, but all the same, even after several months, I couldn't get the notion out of my head. Indeed, the idea had festered (perhaps like its own monster, but not really!). On that stormy winter's day, something drew me to a certain brink and I looked over into what might be, but probably wasn't, an abyss.

I began to flick through the fat, fluffy-edged edition of *Frankenstein*. You know, it wasn't so bad. There was Victor Frankenstein, clearly a brainy young man with high aspirations, pursuing his studies in science. He had a story to tell, but who doesn't? So far so good. I fixed myself another vodka and curled up on the couch.

I read that Frankenstein's monster complained of being lonely and wanted another monster to be his friend. Trying to be obliging even though the monster had wreaked a fair bit of havoc (including committing the murder for which Justine Moritz was hanged, which I remembered from the discussion at Cook Blub), Frankenstein-the-scientist started creating a fresh monster—a monstress, to be precise, as if from the rib of the first monster. But as tales of the original monster's antics reached Frankenstein-the-scientist, he realised that if there was a monster and a monstress and they became friends, in fact grew to love each other, or even if they didn't love each other but liked each other in that way, or even if they didn't like each other much but they both just happened to be there, that would mean little monsters, and the little monsters would have monsters, and in the end the monsters, because there were so many of them and they were well, monstrous, would ruin everything. Faced with this realisation, Frankenstein-the-scientist reneges on the deal, refusing to create a monstress, and Frankenstein-the-monster is so upset he retaliates by killing Frankenstein-the-scientist's bride, Elizabeth, on their wedding night.

I was starting to find all this a little shocking, it's true. My instinct to avoid *Frankenstein* had probably been right. But it was too late now; I was embroiled. I pressed on— skim-reading because it was so appalling, so I might've missed a few bits. But I didn't miss the episode about how Frankenstein-the-monster, angry at being denied his monstress, treks over the ice to flee Frankenstein-the-scientist, and how Frankenstein-the-scientist chases him, down the nights and down the days, because even without little monsters, even with just one monster, he is worried about the damage he could do. But although he searches and searches, Frankenstein-the-scientist cannot find Frankenstein-the-monster on the white expanse, and he despairs. It seems his very knowledge of science, his inquiry—in essence, his great brain—was responsible for unleashing the monster, like a genie let out of a bottle, a black widow spider released from a box of Australian grapes into New Zealand, like ice sheets melting into the sea. As he traipses over the ice, Frankenstein-the-scientist knows he has sealed his fate; he has created his own destiny.

Breathing hard, doing my count-to-twenty routine then fixing another drink, I gave myself a break from the relentless story and flicked back through the book. I was doing okay. *What abyss, Janice?* I said to myself. Then I noticed something shocking, something which even to recall makes me break into a cold sweat. At the end of Chapter II, I tripped over the following words: 'Destiny was too potent, and her immutable laws had decreed by utter and terrible destruction.'

Although I was lying on the couch, I nearly fell off it, such was my state of stupefaction and confusion. Yes, *utter and terrible destruction*, the very title of my *roman à clef.*

It had been lurking there all the time, but I hadn't known.

Perhaps I did know. Perhaps I had ignored evidence.

Unable to go any further, I threw *Frankenstein* across the room. It landed wedged in behind the fridge, its fat grey pages open like a miniature, ever-silent accordion. To calm my nerves, I found a novel on Mandy's bookshelf whose title I can't remember by someone I can't remember about a female character I can't remember except that she goes to Italy and buys a pink villa, plants herbs, cooks excellent pasta dishes, meets some very nice villagers and eventually a nice man and lives happily ever after. I read it and was temporarily soothed.

To return to the evening of the Antarctica Awards—this already hectic night seems to grow more hectic by the hour. Leaving Eric's, I decide I am not going to tough out the Mount Street Cemetery again, so I take the long way down; I stomp along beside the solid pale bungalow-style houses whose leadlights twinkle under the streetlights and exude an air of people who pay for their grown-up children to get an education instead of making them work in the Glass Menagerie. I hate them.

From some way away I see my fridge poking its smooth flank cutely out from behind the bus shelter where I stowed it. As I get closer, I experience a fast-forward of memories— my days as the solitary 'Annie' figure of *Annie and Moon*, the exciting afternoon I bought the fridge with my compensation money from the Glass Menagerie, the evening Mandy and I uplifted said fridge from the apartment in an hilarious sequence of events. Spurred on by this jumble of virtual *memento mori*, I hurry towards the shelter and am soon reunited with my special appliance. I reach up to brush leaves tenderly from its satin top.

We're on the road again, my fridge and I, heading instinctively downtown like a couple of penguins towards the ocean. I'm sure I even waddle a bit, such is the weight of my dear fridge on its cart, my Antarctic hold-all, and the not inconsiderable weight of my laptop bag. At six in the morning I need to be at the airport to catch my domestic flight to Christchurch, so it makes sense to head east. Whichever route I take, we face quite a hike, and my cart arm *is* sore.

When I happen to see people running towards the yawning entrance to the cable car as if this is their last transport out of hell, I hurry too, joggling along with my bags and my green charge.

I'd thought it would be too late for the cable car to be running, public transport in Wellington usually favouring an early night, but they seem to have put on an extra service for some kind of Christmas do that has just wrapped up in the Botanical Garden. Merry people, half seas over and wearing Santa hats, are pouring out of the garden gates and onto the eyrie-like cable car platform. Snippets of drunken Jingle Bells float on the night air. I join the melee, although I suppose it's to be expected that there is the teensy problem of how to get my fridge onto the cable car. Sure enough, I see the driver in his black coat with a red paperback tucked under his arm, eyeing me suspiciously as he scurries along the platform like a KGB agent. I slow my gait and pretend to be interested only in the panoramic view over Wellington city rather than appearing to have any ambition vis-à-vis boarding the wine-dark cable car. Once the driver is secured in his little driving cubicle—his head bent over what I imagine is a Steven King novel, *Misery* perhaps—I push through the crowd and mind the gap, wrangling my trolley over it. In a trice I have my fridge positioned in the space just inside the carriage doors. I congratulate myself on my success in boarding at all, which seems to signal a pleasant change. I'd been starting to get a phobia about just missing out on things at the eleventh hour—dinner with the artists with whom I would go to Antarctica, and of course the prime example, the apartment. Indeed, as I see from someone's wrist-watch that is jammed up next to my face, it is one minute to midnight.

The carriage is a bit of a squash, if truth be told—standing room only—and rather Gothic. I am held in place by the merrymakers, who now swing from overhead straps as if dead. No hope of venturing further inside and perching on one of the oxblood seats. An initial jolt like an electric shock and the hoot of a whistle indicates our journey has begun. As we sway downhill, sharp objects in people's pockets spike me, and the smell of sweat, beer and farting is ubiquitous. I weather the frowns of my fellow passengers; in a paramount example of *Cinema of Unease*, no one voices their opinion about me and my fridge verbally, only via dark looks. No matter. As we cruise sedately down the incline, I am lulled by the motion of the carriage and the comforting thought of the long trek I am being saved in riding the cable car. My breathing is slow and deep, going right to the bottom of my lungs, as if I'm stepping out of the sea. I feel serene, not trussed by anxious thoughts of my fridge or the night ahead or what I will do when I get back from Antarctica. As we emerge from the first tunnel, I smile, gaze out over the slatted buildings and noirish folds of the city and find myself, despite the adverse conditions in the carriage, mulling over *The Ice Shelf*. An edit rears its head. I feel compelled to execute it then and there, lest I forget.

I manage to remove my manuscript from my laptop bag without bending my elbows, quite a feat, but holding the pages down low, jammed against my body and with fellow commuters pushing and shoving, I can see just enough to remove a piece of the text in which the protagonist begins to feel that life is, in a way, futile, that she has just been created randomly by some kink in the universe and perhaps even just for the universe to get a kick out of her. At the same time, she has a job replacing stickers on objects, basically lying, and that is what she feels about her whole life; that it's a lie. I screw this section up and have no choice but to let it drop on to the cable car floor. The novel is immediately lighter, better.

In fact, it is very light indeed. To my enormous surprise, I realise that I am clutching in my fist the very last page of *The Ice Shelf.*

But I have no time to contemplate the thoroughness of my edit. Perhaps I have my guard down due to my unaccustomed calm, I don't know, but I am not prepared for what happens when the cable car steampunks into the first stop at Salamanca Road. As I am mashed against the doors, hold-all over one shoulder, laptop bag over the other, fridge wedged against the wall, the cable car doors suddenly open, noisily and speedily like a nuclear fission. I'm hurled out onto the platform and as I fly, my laptop bag is flung off my shoulder. I hardly know what's happening, it's all so fast, but once I have steadied myself, there's nothing I can do but watch my bag spin across the tiles, sail out into the air and twist and turn in a graceful slow-motion somersault, down, down into the darkness.

I stand numbly on the platform, contemplating this terrible development. The doors to the cable car hiss closed, then, and the carriage continues its Thunderbirds-speed descent with my fridge still inside.

This critical juncture seems as good a place as any to pause to consider, once again, the notion of thankfulness. At this point I have to report a small dent in my optimism. The thing is, it makes no sense to be optimistic *or* pessimistic because we don't know the outcome of anything. Earlier tonight, this long night of the awards, I had no idea how my evening was going to unfold. I didn't know whether things would get better or worse. But because I'm human and, I'm the first to admit, not mindful enough, I feel a little puncture in my heart.

And as I write these Acknowledgments, I'm aware of a wound in the fabric of my gratefulness which I hope will not transfer itself or in any way dampen the genuineness of my thanks to you all. Because, as I've already said, I could not have written what's left of this manuscript without you, and I am humbled by that thought.

As the tail light of the cable car disappears into the next tunnel on the incline, I feel the teensiest bit downhearted contemplating my options. My laptop and bag have been taken by the night in the most chilling way, and I'm facing the fact I will never see them again. On the other hand, my fridge will still be in one piece. The cable car people will likely not be very pleased to discover it at the final stop, but it is just a matter of me collecting it from the terminal. The journey down to Lambton Quay is a winding loop through the city. There's a reason Wellington has a cable car—the hills are so steep that many of them cannot be scaled on foot. But I'm buoyed by my own stoicism. After stuffing the last page of my manuscript—and I have been quite a ruthless editor—into my Antarctica hold-all, I set off down the dark, pitching zigzag that leads to Salamanca Road. Imagine my surprise when, on the first zig, I spy, poking out from the cable car tracks that soar just over my head, the black rectangle that is my laptop bag!

I race back up to the platform, praying—well, as I don't believe in God I content myself with hoping like hell—that my laptop has not suffered too much of a knock. The fact it has only fallen a short way seems like the most incredible, serendipitous stroke of luck. All I need to do is crawl a little way out onto the cable car flyover, being careful not to touch the tracks, which are electrified, then scoop up my bag and retreat. It doesn't seem like a Herculean task.

From the platform, I peer down the slope. Compared with the station, the incline falls away into darkness. I must confess to being nervous as I feel my way into nothingness, shuffling like an opium addict. But soon my eyes grow accustomed to the light and I see, in the low, ambient city light, that I've reached the place where the flyover leaps out from the hillside and down to the next contour, where a station is wedged among a jumble of steps. I devolve and begin to crawl out onto the suspension. The ground is rather shingly, the carriageway not as wide as it seemed when I surveyed it from the zigzag below. There is just a little wriggle room either side of the track. I wriggle along. Fortunately the last cable car trip of the night has already happened—I was on it!—so I won't have to contend with any oncoming carriages. Thank goodness for small mercies. But then I look down. The flyover is the height of, say, a fifteen-storey building. Way below, the motorway is strobey with late-night traffic. A mouthful of bile shoots up from my stomach.

Clinging to the verge, I tell myself, Janice, you can do it, in the same tone I summoned when I applied for the Antarctica Residency. Why Fucking Not, Janice? I inch forward. My mantra is not having the effect I hoped for, not on the scale of an arts council application. To be honest, for all my personal pep-talk, I am beginning to wish I'd never set out on this journey. My hands are sweating, my knees are scraped, I can barely see, and I swoon dizzily every time I so much as peek down at the surging motorway. I keep going only because *not keeping going* means facing the prospect of turning around and going back, and I don't know how I am going to do that. Also, my laptop bag is no more than two metres away, very close to the edge. Janice, I say, somewhat weakly now, keep going, Janice! Thank your lucky stars! I feel the uncertain shroud of *Cinema of Unease* settle over me.

At this point, I take a breather and *do* happen to glance up at the stars. The night is now clear and a pointillist scatter of the stronger heavenly bodies, those that can assert themselves over the city lights, twinkle. They are beautiful. With my head thrown back, I remember looking at the stars with Sorrell on nights when we delivered rubbish bags to obscure points of the city, often on high, winding roads which engendered a sense of vertigo, both real and metaphorical. There on the flyover, teetering above the motorway, probably not the best position I've ever been in in my life, I thank Sorrell. I thank her then, and I thank her now in these Acknowledgements, for bequeathing me the 'Risk, risk anything' attitude. I recognise that not many other people I've encountered in my life would have the gall, the balls (if I may be so boy-centric) to go after their recalcitrant laptop like a shepherd goes after her (his) lost sheep.

The realisation of how lucky I've been with my role models empowers me, and I surge forward the last couple of metres, caring nothing for my knees, my hands, for the fifty-metre drop to the motorway. With cars streaking like neon fish below, feeling dizzy as hell, I army-crawl the last metre to where my laptop in its bag rests on the edge of the flyover. I sigh with relief that I'll be reunited with the digital iterations of my novel, not to mention my hardware. I reach out and the tips of my fingers make contact with the cool vinyl of the bag—my beloved concertina, my personal Limbo—and I just about have it in my grasp. But at that moment, a huge gust of wind spirals up from the foment of air between the flyover and the motorway. I feel the vinyl recede from my fingers and my laptop bag is flipped over the edge.

For a moment I lie still, my head on the gravel, abject, like a priest giving himself over to a life of paedophilia. I don't want to, but I drag myself forward and peer over the edge of the flyover. I look down and see that the laptop and the bag have parted company. The bag is still zeroing down on the wind. And on the slick motorway, bits of metal spray out like sparks from under the wheels of speeding cars. That was my laptop.

I have to say, a tiny hopeful thought, even then, goes through my mind that this is not the end, that I could scoop up the pieces, dodging cars, and that a computer geek with a beard and baggy jeans working out of a prefab on a disused site might reassemble those pieces lovingly. But it's just a thought.

I shuffle back from the ledge and look out at the panorama of Wellington, trying to stay calm. Then I feel a vibration on the flyover and hear a buzz coming from below. A carriage is travelling up the incline. Clearly, there is one last journey of the night. If I was worried about how I am to turn around on the narrow verge and make my way back up the flyover to the platform, I need not have concerned myself. I don't know how I do it, but I somehow do. I have a memory of grazes, cold air, heartbeat, my life flashing before my eyes. I recall the taste of milk about to go off, a night of black plastic rubbish bags, and how it felt to become a woman. Before long I'm back on the zigzag, treading my way down the winding road to town. As I go, I think about how, in Antarctica, I will lie down on the ice, and the small coldness inside me will feel at home. I hope there will be enough ice for me to lie down in. I hope that my lying down in the ice will not cause a new piece the size of New Zealand to fall off; I hope I will not warm Antarctica with my grief.

*

The northerly comes in ferocious fits and starts, and I shrug my Antarctic jacket closer around me. My arms feel strangely light, not weighed down as they have been for the last few hours by my fridge and my laptop bag. But this lightness gives me no pleasure. I am like a rudderless vessel bobbing through the night. I notice a backache that had not presented itself when I was in the process of acquiring it, that is, dragging my fridge and shouldering my computer. The roar of the motorway reminds me that I'm approaching the neighbourhood where my laptop met with its demise; I try not to dwell on it but to concentrate on the present, and on thankfulness.

At a crossroads, where Salamanca Road turns into the more citified Bolton Street, I happen to glance left up Wesley Road and am aware that just over the darkly wooded brow of the hill lies the Lady Norwood Rose Garden. Not that I am going to make a detour at this time of night, of course, but I am reminded of a certain wedding I attended in the gardens back in February. Now it's all water under the bridge, and as you know, I'm not one to bear a grudge; the happy couple was none other than Miles and Dorothy. I will take this opportunity to make some overdue thank yous re that auspicious event.

It was a beautiful wedding, all pink but not the least bit kitsch and, as I say, it was held in the manicured but dangerous regimen of the Lady Norwood Rose Garden. On the late afternoon of the wedding, I approached through the south beds, which turned out to be tricky—an unfortunate time of year in some respects; late summer, so the roses were resplendent in their second bloom and their massive prickles. Thanks are due to the wonderful staff at the Emergency Room of Wellington Hospital who so tenderly tweezered the thorns, and to the lovely house surgeon who, on learning that I have a low pain threshold, prescribed a nice long course of Celebrex, plus some Amoxil in case infection reared its ugly had. I was able to return to the champagne table just a little bit bandaged and to join in the wedding festivities, which featured dancing into the night.

The night was once again unseasonably warm and still, of the kind that makes Wellingtonians worry the world is coming to an end. (The opposite, I might add, to the inclemency of the weather on Antarctica Awards night, also in summer.) The air was tepid, perfume drifted from the rose beds, cicadas scutched. And so to the wedding. As I say, it was a beautiful occasion. Some of my former friends—who'd pretended to be chummy but had gone the same way as the apartment, and it's true that I *had* only known them for two years and 364 days—shot me thunderous looks every time they whirled past me on the lawn. I'm incredibly grateful that I was subjected to this poisonous eyeballing because it gave me a chance to dig deep into myself for the wisdom to rise above such pathetic display of small-minded posturing. My deepest thanks are due to Tricia, Jeff, Melanie, Sue, Carmel, Dean, Paul R, Paul M., Liz and Bronwyn, oh, and Dan, not to mention my former de facto in-laws, whom I thank sincerely for not ever becoming related to me in any way, shape or form. I needn't worry that any offspring of mine will carry the square-head gene, the low-to-the-ground simian build. The truth is, I didn't care about attempts to turn me into a social pariah. I was having an excellent time, and I know that underneath, Miles was pleased I was there. I know Miles very well, and I know what that stony expression means perhaps better than anyone, and certainly more than Dorothy.

It was only at the very end of the evening, late-late, as I sat at one of the trestle tables in the summer house (which was just slightly *ersatz* Versailles) eating pavlova—reminded a little of *Howards End* and feeling very sorry for poor Jacky—that I sat back and contemplated how the night would proceed for Miles and Dorothy from here on in, compared with how it would go for me. Mandy had gone on one of her hysterical throwing-me-out jags, so I didn't know where I was going to spend the night—reminiscent of the very night on which I am writing this down, the night on the eve of flying out to Antarctica. Despite my efforts, I didn't seem to be able to get the attention of the nice waiter who had been topping up my glass. I could see Miles and Dorothy dancing on the moonlit lawn, kissing and pawing each other like bears. Once again I was struck by how unattractive she was, and I experienced another ontological hiccup in relation to myself. With my pavlova-laden spoon halfway to my face, I glanced up at the stage and noticed that the microphones (there were two) were unattended. The podium had recently been the site of some speeches, not the least bit sick-making.

I've always been rather good at limericks, though I say it myself. I was famous for them as a teenager. I hope I'm not blowing my own trumpet when I say that I showed signs of writing promise even then. An hilarious limerick about a teacher with a pole up her arse that I etched with a safety pin on the toilet wall got me expelled from Wellington East, which I've always regarded as a feather in my creative cap. I can't think of anyone interesting who wasn't expelled from school. Not that I'm claiming the label 'interesting' for myself, I hasten to add. I got up from the trestle table, wiped pavlova from my front, and tried to get up to the podium. The flimsy steps were uneven and I missed my footing for a moment but soon recovered and picked myself up off the wet grass. I might've lost a shoe, but I still made it to the microphones. While I'd been dilly-dallying over my pav, I'd composed a limerick that I knew would have Miles in stitches.

There was a young bridey called Dot
whose face was wet, hairy and hot.
In order to wed
the groom stood on his head
and said 'Dotty, I do' to her—

At that point in my recital, several of the 'friends' jumped up onto the stage and carried me down to the lawn. I must say I felt a bit like Lady Gaga after her Monster Ball concert at the Vector Arena. As for my own performance, in retrospect I'm grateful that the final line of the limerick was left dangling and for this I thank my former buddies. For me it turned out far better not to iterate the last word. I picture the word slaloming downwards and coming to rest on the dewy grass of the rose garden, from where it might flutter off to kingdom come, or be danced, bit by bit, into the plush grass, blueish in the moonlight. All things must pass.

I found myself being pushed rather roughly into the back seat of a car and driven, a little nauseously, down the winding road away from the Botanical Garden. Thanks to the 'friends' for the ride, and for not filling up the airwaves with idle chatter. They would've been absolutely at home in *In My Father's Den*. I lay quietly on the back seat and almost managed to hold on to the pav until Tinakori Road, but not quite. Sorry about the upholstery of someone's only slightly ostentatious Citroën.

Tinakori Road is unlit and empty at that hour of the

morning. As I set off to find the footpath in the dark, a little lopsided from my lost shoe, I thought back to the moonlit lawn. I was sure I'd seen the happy couple look up from their ungainly groping and smile at my limerick. I am lucky to be able to count both Miles and Dorothy amongst my closest friends.

Having been deposited by the cable car at an inopportune stop after the demise of my laptop, I am trundling back down past the university, that collection of Victorian and modernist buildings all mucking in together. No one is about and I feel tall in the dark. My footsteps answer me on the other side of the road. My first task is, of course, to collect my fridge from the cable car, the next to find a place to spend the night and hopefully someone more reliable than Eric who will look after said fridge while I'm in Antarctica. Something will turn up. The Terrace, when I turn into it, is like a wind tunnel. I battle the gusts and cling to everything: my hold-all, my jacket which balloons out so strongly I think I might lift off the ground. Caught in this fury with not much sense of where I am apart from in weather, I feel welling up in my diaphragm a strong urge to edit. I want to prune the section of my novel in which a wedding is called off at the last minute because the groom finds out a whole lot of terrible stuff about the bride—that she's not who she says she is, she's a confidence trickster like Amy Bock who pretends to love people in order to swindle them. It's probably the soapiest bit of the novel, so it really does need to go.

Unfortunately, it has already gone.

I scale down some wet, dirty, Dickensian steps which lead darkly from the Terrace to Lambton Quay. After one block of the Quay, I turn into the lane that leads up to the cable car terminal. The alley feels synthetically claustrophobic; you'd expect filthy fake grass. Once past the news agents and the tea shops, I stand in the yawning industrial-revolution mouth of the cable car tunnel which seems sooty despite the line being electrified, and I peer past the ticket booth to the waiting area. A security guard dressed like a character from *Grease* is pirouetting into the corners with a flashlight. Instinctively I hang back, but I've already spied my fridge stationed in the middle of the scene as if performing to the bleachers. The security guard is having a called-out conversation with someone, and I see the bobbing grey head of a woman in the ticket booth. A frozen feeling creeps over me. I get the gist he's talking about my fridge. I think I hear the word *gash* repeated several times amid the tinkling sound of cashing up. He and the woman are like smugglers from *Famous Five*, and I half smile at that. But I'm perturbed, too, and can't decide whether I'd rather have a gash in my fridge, which would destroy its insulation, or in the carriage, which might get me into some kind of trouble.

There's worse to come. The security guard, now swallowed by the yawning mouth of the tunnel, turns and calls clearly, 'Geez she was lucky, poor old biddy!' A gate clangs somewhere. I am, of course, mortified, imagining an old woman with a big purse lying kersplat in the carriage, knocked over by my rogue fridge. I press myself flat against the darkened window of a tobacconist's. The right thing to do would be to present myself to the security guard from *Grease* and the grey-haired ticketseller. But as I stand intimately close to the items of death, the cigarettes and cigars, the tobacco pipes, I wonder—what good would it do for me to talk to the cable car people now? The damage is done. It is done, and nothing can change it.

I wait, plastered against the cold glass, wondering what to do. I cannot abandon my fridge to these people; it is unthinkable. On the other hand, I'm pretty sure they won't just hand it over to me. If there is a gash in the carriage, if someone was knocked over, there might even be police involved. To be honest, I'm scared.

As I'm trembling and considering my options, the grey-haired woman comes out of her little cubicle and disappears around the back. I hear voices receding and when I poke my head out experimentally, I see that indeed both she and the security guard have gone, at least temporarily. I don't need a second opportunity. I rush up the last few metres of the lane into the waiting area, grab the handle of the trolley, and jolt my fridge into motion.

We have bounced back, my fridge and I. We are on our way back down the lane to Lambton Quay by the time I hear the angry bellow of the security guard. To the sound of footsteps thwacking, I duck into an arcade and snuggle my fridge and myself into an empty wedge under a massive flight of stairs. There we wait until the security guard's footsteps have calmed and the curses have waned.

I pat my fridge all over, like a farmer a cow at the stock market, inspecting it for damage. A couple of scuffs on the nether regions; nothing serious. I hope that the dark smudge I wipe off on my sleeve isn't blood. I'm feeling a bit rattled, to be honest. My options—which just a few hours ago were wide open, and the summer evening full of hope—seem to have narrowed. Despair, both for myself and for my fridge, begins to creep over me. But I'm made of tougher stuff, I really am. And it is then that I remember Linda Dent.

I palm my forehead in a gesture even I recognise (in a moment of selfie-like analysis) as simultaneous castigation/

congratulations: *Idiot/Of course!* If there's one person I'm sure will put me up for the night, and likely look after my fridge for the duration, plus can probably be prevailed upon to drive me to the airport first thing, it's Linda Dent. *Linda Dent!* It's not that I haven't thought of her earlier in the evening; indeed, on the way to the awards ceremony I had her in the back of mind. The only problem is, I'm not sure how to get in touch with her now. I'm sort of wishing that I hadn't unfriended her, even though she was outrageously insensitive to me on social media. But Linda, she's not so bad. We always had a good talk when we ran into each other at book launches. In fact, the last time I saw her at the Borich Festival, we had a really excellent rave, her with her little face and latest iteration of giant glasses. She's actually kick-ass. If I know Linda, she will have got over our little *contretemps* and anyway, it's just Facebook, it's not real.

With a renewed sense of purpose I hurry one block back along Lambton Quay—the wind is nuts, going inhale-for-four-exhale-for-seven, like some kind of anti-anxiety exercise—and I pop into the selfsame internet café as before, do the whole beyond-the-curtain-at-the-back-of-the-shop thing all over again. The attendant and I do a shorthand negotiation about my fridge this time (? / No / Fine then), and I nestle in next to the teenage gamers and send Linda a fresh friendship request. I sit back and await her reply. Linda is one of those people who sits hunched over their social media waiting for the next red dot, replying within a second.

While I'm waiting, I look around at the gamers stoking their red flickering screens in the half dark like so many devils with pitchforks. After a minute, Linda still hasn't accepted my friendship, so I decide I may as well attend to my other social media, as I've paid for the minimum half hour anyway. I tweet, Countdown to Antarctica, still pinching myself! Kudos to @ArtsNZ! A moment later, @fringefestdweller retweets me and replies, Good going @janiceawriter! Big hugs <3 It'll be the middle of the afternoon in the UK. I wonder if @fringefestdweller is hitting on me from afar, with the hugs, seeing I've never met him, and I begin to wonder if he's a bit of a creep. But I don't have time to go into it because the night is wearing on. I check the *Guardian* quickly to see if any famous writers have died and Bookman Beattie to see if anyone I know has published a book with a spine. No, on both counts. And no acceptance from Linda Dent. I'm getting a bit worried that she's signed off for the night; even Linda has to go to bed at some point. Luckily, I've been to her house, to a launch party she had one time for a book she'd self-published. It's in Island Bay. I look up the exact address on the old Facebook event. Trent Street. I remember it, a beautiful summer afternoon with the smell of the sea coming in the open windows, and the speeches fuelled nicely by boxed pink wine. There was a lovely warm atmosphere and the crowd, Linda's friends, were enthusiastic about Linda's book. To tell the truth, I was the teeniest bit jealous, but I later managed to plough that feeling into my work in a productive way.

In the internet café, I finish with a final tweet. Edits going swimmingly #ilovemylife, which @nighthowler likes immediately and at the same time he also retweets my last tweet. I'm in the middle of thanking him for the RT when my screen dies, with no preamble. I'm disappointed that that has happened before I've heard back from Linda Dent a.k.a. @heartwriter, which means she is probably off the agenda, but such is life.

*

I'm cower-walking again, up Willis Street in the gale which seems to have had a personality switch, is a demon now; it blasts and twists around me from every angle, including underneath, making my heavy jacket flaunt itself like a mainsail. Unearthly bongs and rattles emanate from security doors and rubbish bins, sounds you hear only when there's no one around, as if some presence has been lurking all along, waiting for you to be alone on Willis Street in the small hours of a Wednesday in early December. I don't know where to go, I don't know what to do, but it seems this state of emptiness—and perhaps the lonely state I find myself in, from which position I hope I don't have to face the end of the human race—allows a thought to sprout.

I wonder tentatively whether it has been long enough, that is, whether there's been enough water under the bridge, for me to turn up at the fifties apartment with the view of the harbour and ask to stay for one lousy night. I walk along Manners Mall, thinking the notion through in more detail. The air suddenly smells briny even though the harbour is a kilometre away, and I realise what's happened: the wind has swung around to the south. That's what all that play-acting was about; it was a northerly trying to be a southerly. Plus, I'm starving hungry. I have no choice but to buy a burger from the twenty-four-hour McDonald's, even though it's like eating silage, and I wolf it down in the green-lit tiled expanse, watching over my fridge, which I've left outside. While I'm in McD's, a teenager in sweats comes and squats down next to the fridge, looking it up and down as if it's a person. Binning my burger wrapper, I hurry back outside.

The boy is hugging himself against the cold, and as I approach he begins begging hopelessly, holding out his wizened hand and pleading from his deep purple eyesockets.

I'm his only customer. I hitch up my fridge and take off. Further along Manners Street, I look back at the boy and we share a brief, terrified stare. There's no one else to make eye contact with.

I'm tired but I have to keep going, I have no choice. I put one foot in front of the other and soon I'm in Courtenay Place, which happens to be in the general direction of the apartment. The nightclubs are still reasonably busy. I pause outside one bar to rest for a moment. A knot of intensely angular people look at me through the gold lettering on the window, and I consider going in on the off-chance that someone will buy me a drink, or even that there's some antipasti or equivalent left unattended. But the thought of it depresses me, and I continue along the now slightly rubbishy street. An electric stream of people—black clothes, fluorescent teeth, bright blue hair and some red—parts around me like a school of tropical fish. The atmosphere is crazed, hilarious, a little dangerous. Breathing hard, I move inshore, away from the main flow towards the doorways of bars, bumping into knots of people spilling out to smoke on the street. A face or two, three, looms momentarily in mock puzzlement at my fridge. And another and another, and people arch out of the way of me coming through with my fridge on its cart.

In fact, they're laughing, and I realise they are laughing with me. This cheers me up. I smile back at all the people. I start to feel a connection with them, with the Courtenay Place crowd. It occurs to me that, in general, people are great, aren't they? Give people an unusual situation and they'll come to the party. Unless they're a psychopath, or perhaps a sociopath. If there was a catastrophe right at this moment, an earthquake perhaps, or if the methane from the ocean rose up and devoured us, I would join hands with these people, the revellers, and we would look at each other, really look, and talk, and although we'd only just met, we would go down together feeling a sense of commonality. Something expands in my chest at this realisation. I'm thankful to belong to the human race, even to be living on this knife-edge. One day we'll all go, one day it will be over; but we will have been together, which will make meaning of the end. And I think of all the endings I've had, leaving houses, schools, people—and how, no matter how emotion flowers up, there is always a moment when it's all over. It's the thought that we will die and will leave everyone we know behind that makes us care passionately about the moment and care nothing for the future. And, in those minutes, moving along Courtenay Place, I understand what it is to not give a fuck.

At the Taj Mahal (once a public toilet on a traffic island, now a bar) I pause and look up the long scoop of Majoribanks Street that hazes into the distance. Away from the clubs, the people and the smoke, the fresh air has cleared my head. I turn my attention to where I'm going to spend the night. There is a certain fifties apartment that should be half mine, or at least it should be a quarter mine, or one bedroom should be mine, or the space where the couch is in the living room should be mine, or one night on the couch should be mine, and would be but for one lousy day, one arbitrary day in the scheme of the universe.

I set off up the hill, tugging my fridge. Having had no luck finding anyone to look after the appliance in question, I'm thinking I'll let Miles and Dorothy have it back temporarily until I'm settled again after my trip to Antarctica, seeing as Dorothy wanted it so much in the first place. Well, let her have it. And the whole fucking apartment. Let craziness rule. It *does* seem quite surreal. The villas either side of

Majoribanks Street look all cardboardy, like a stage set, as if they're about to fall on me. As I trudge, I recall the trip I first made up this street with the fridge, the night Mandy and I moved it from the apartment to the safety of her flat, and I chuckle at the thought of the rescue—how we go out on a limb to preserve what's ours, to hold tight before it's too late.

I arrive at the apartments and park my fridge in the courtyard next to the garages. On second thoughts, worried someone might steal it, I grab the cart and begin my bumping assent of the Southeast Ridge, eight flights of steps. This takes a huge effort and I stop frequently to rest. Finally, I'm on the landing, breathing hard, the cold air scorching my nostrils. I summon my energy and begin skimming along the balcony, trying not to knock over peg baskets and potplants this time, but I do upset a few. The night is dark, the lights dim, and despite knowing this like the back of my hand I lose count of the doors. When I hear a certain clunk and look down at a familiar cactus rolling like a grenade, I know I'm at the right apartment.

I knock on the door. After a litany of unbolting, Dorothy opens up. She's in her dressing gown, hair askew, skin sallowly makeupless—looking, in a nutshell, dreadful. She seems a little shocked to see me and the fridge. Her neck twitches like that of a sparrow. I explain right away that I just need to stay for the one night. I hasten to add that they—she and her hubby, who happens to be my ex-partner-in-crime, Miles—can have the fridge back, for a while.

I don't think this account behoves Dorothy particularly well, and I've wrestled with my conscience about telling it, but in the end I think it's important for posterity to set this down. Dorothy turns into a screaming banshee. You'd think she *wasn't* now married to my former partner; you'd think she *wasn't* currently clocking up points, only a matter of time, towards part-ownership of the fifties apartment (which even matches her outfits) under the terms of the Property (Relationships) Act 1976. In between all the yelling and screaming, I get the impression that my request to stay the night has been turned down. I start to beg, and I hear little whimpers of my pleading whenever Dorothy draws breath between screams. She is staunch—gosh, she is so un-*Cinema of Unease*. She slams the door in my face and my vision is filled with the moonlit blue.

I stand on the doorstep of the apartment where I lived for two years and 364 days. The thought of taking my fridge back down eight flights of steps right now is too much, and although I know I have to do it at some point, I decide I'll have a little rest before contemplating my next move. I'm exhausted, no doubt from my long evening of editing, walking and thinking, not to mention attending the awards ceremony. And, really, in the scheme of things, there's no hurry. Did you know, Reader, that despite global warming, the universe is actually slowly cooling, the sun dying out after its Big Bang quite some time ago? Eventually, nothing will matter. In the end, we'll all be gone and all creation will be gone. I sink down on the balcony, just for a few minutes. Curled up against the cold, the thought crosses my mind that I'll just spend the night here. Although the concrete is rough and damp, there are worse things. I rock back and forth to soothe myself. From down below comes the sound of a cat yowling, and there's the subtle tick and crack of the building existing. I could almost drop off to sleep.

And here I've remembered what I was going to thank Miles for, so if you'll bear with me. It's an important thank you, a big debt, so I must rectify that now, although I probably don't need to go into too much detail. It's to do with things falling apart, which they can do in life, inevitably. And I will say that the atmosphere had become tense. The apartment, which had been an awesome place up until a certain point, felt cold. I remember times of wandering around town feeling that I didn't want to go home. That is not a nice feeling. It means you have no home. Also, I'm not proud to say that I was drinking quite a bit. Miles had stopped, which I found insufferable. There's nothing worse than a reformed anything. Of course, I don't blame Miles. He had that terrible, uptight, Noa Valley upbringing, which was behind a lot of this—even the things in the apartment seemed part of it. His grandmother's furniture, his father's chairman-of-the-board desk—all were tainted.

The fight that happened the night before Sago Pudding Night involved all of the furniture in the apartment and all the things in the apartment. Somehow the things were all involved. They watched, they jeered. They were not innocent; they were hateful. The heavy, leather-topped desk in the study was especially hateful. Everything we'd thought would make us comfortable had ruined us. The fact is, Miles suddenly went grotesque. The things I'd liked about him before—his big square head, his close-to-the-ground strength—now seemed ugly and despicable. And everything I liked about me—my comfortable plumpness—felt gory and disgusting. Even the wind seemed malevolent; not as strong as usual (we were in that strange subtropical phase) but whirling occasionally, out of the blue, against the windows. And the lines we said—Miles with his string of qualifiers which he couldn't put aside, and I couldn't bear, and I don't know what my words were, but his words and mine fit together like wrestlers, locked and destructive.

He did manage to say, without any qualification, 'You are a murderer.'

And I argued ferociously, because it was true.

We raged, red and scary. I was even scared of myself. He was the monster, and I was the monstress. Sex released this in us, and now it had taken over, taken over sex, talk, our minutes day to day, everything.

The things that could create life destroyed us. And the wanting to be comfortable ruined us. It is all a horrible paradox.

And at the end we used up our love. It plumed into the air like smoke and disappeared, and now it's gone.

I want to thank Miles from the bottom of my heart, but I find I still can't remember for what.

I realise I've drifted off a bit, lying here on the balcony of the apartment building, and I'm brought around by the furious pop of the little kitchen window being forced outwards. Dorothy's voice edges through. She yells that she'll call the police. I open one eye like a dog. I'm getting used to Dorothy.

I half sit up, pricking the palm of one hand on a cactus, and when I recover from that, I murmur once again that they can have the fridge. And I mean it. They can keep it, for all I care. Dorothy's visage fills the window like a mask. She gestures at her phone, rather threateningly in my opinion. I don't need to be told four times. I gather my things and begin the long, bumpy, dangerous descent of the Southeast Ridge to the street, sucking from my hand the elemental taste of blood.

In the courtyard, I'm beginning to crumble from exhaustion. My muscles are trembling and my feet feel like lead. There's no one about. In the shelter of the garages,

I hunker down on the concrete tiles, which are gritty as a foreshore from windborne dirt. My teeth are chattering. I turn my jacket collar (and it's quite a collar) up against the wind; it's summer, but this is Wellington. Not knowing what else to do, I lay my fridge down on its side with the door open on the ground like a patio. I slide out the wire shelves and stack them on top of the fridge—actually the *side* of the fridge; the world has gone topsy-turvy, and nothing means what it used to mean. Maybe it never did. Thus arranged, the fridge is like a little bach, a summer house. I climb inside and coil inwards like a foetus. Sheltered from the wind, I'm immediately warmer. I yank up the door. The few stars I can see over the top of the apartment building disappear as the seal hisses shut, and I am plunged into darkness. Inside the cocoon of the fridge—which should be cold but is tepid, which should be white but in the darkness is pitch black—I am soothed. I decide to lie for a while in this haven, to recover from my eventful evening, to warm up, to rest a little, and then I will continue on my journey. When I get up, I'll decide what to do my fridge. Something will materialise, I have no doubt. There will be a solution. But in the meantime, I put that thought on a train on my distant horizon.

The warm dark becomes more and more pleasant. I breathe deeply and feel the tension in my muscles flee like so many lemmings. It's strange to be lying there, because this was the strange thought that had entered my head about Antarctica, that I would lie in the cold and make it warm. As I remember this, I unwind even more. The idea of getting up is becoming more and more remote. I could stay here all night. It's probably very late—I'm losing track of time. I'm lightheaded, but mostly incredibly relaxed and floppy. For the first time since I set off from Mandy's at five thirty the previous evening, I feel no urgency. In fact, it's the first time since I left the apartment on the 29th of February that I've felt so calm. No, for the first time since I passed Theory of Creative Writing, for the first time since I was dismissed from the Glass Menagerie, for the first time since I moved into the apartment, since I met Miles, since I left Hoki Aroha, since I stood on the hill at night with Sorrell looking at the Southern Cross. I've never felt so relaxed in all my life.

I begin to drift off, properly this time—I really am exhausted—and to enter the tag-end of a dream that began before I was aware I was dreaming. Perhaps the dream started hours ago, I don't know, I don't know how long I've been sitting on a vast frozen steppe in my lumpy padded jacket, and in my mittened fists I'm holding, as best I can, big wooden knitting needles and from one of the needles hangs a long piece of shiny, rumpled, scarf-shaped snow, but I realise I'm not knitting anymore, the snow has slid off the needles and I'm pulling it undone in enormous yardarms of coldness; I'm undoing it. I'm undoing snow. At the same time, I know I'm not really on the steppe, I'm koru-ed up in a little knot inside the dark fridge, and when I get out of the dream it occurs to me I should open the fridge door to get some air because it's quite stuffy. I try to push the door open, but as I do, I hear the makeshift lock that I attached so many months ago click home. I push again, but my arms are pathetically boneless, like flippers against the weight, and the door stays solidly shut. There's a sense of impossibility, of being pitted against an inanimate object that is bigger than me, that outsmarts me. I make one almighty attempt at hurling myself, half rolling, against it, but it's useless. I don't have the strength. I sink back and lie in a huddle for a moment. And I find it doesn't matter anyway, because I prefer to go back to my knitting or my unknitting. I leave my struggle behind and I sink deeper and deeper into the warming, unravelling cold.

A gash of blinding light opens up before me; surely the sun is coming up on another day. I shade my eyes from the glare, and when I get used to it I realise what has happened. A vast piece of ice has cracked off from the main ice shelf and has floated away. I think I see a polar bear cub, the cutest creature on Earth, tumble from the shelf into the gap with a splash. The furry bundle bobs desperately in the water and for a moment it seems it will succeed in hauling itself back onto the shelf, but it doesn't, it sinks back down into the water and disappears and that is the last I see of it.

A face is peering at me. It takes me an indeterminate period, perhaps a few minutes, or a long time, to register that this is not the hairy, snout-nosed face of a polar bear, I'm in the wrong hemisphere, and maybe in the wrong dream. This is a human face, a male face, cheekboned, pale, messy, intense like an Egon Schiele drawing. He's saying something but I can't make it out because of the roar of something in the background, like stage effects and which I figure out is the wind. I'm coming to. I remember first that I'm me, I'm Janice and I live on Earth. I remember that I'm curled in my fridge and that the fridge, if I could see its colour clearly under the blanding streetlight, is green. When the man speaks again, I feel a gust of his breath, foul as compost. He's spitting, 'Here you are, here you are,' over and over, and I realise he's crazy. I struggle out of the fridge and sit in a bundle, the wind slamming me. The man crouches in a theatrical gesture of concern. His clothes are so dirty they've gone to oilcloth, and for some reason I would like to mend the L-shaped rips in his gunmetal coat. He's reciting, 'I saved you, I saved you,' over and over.

Right then, on the concrete, under siege from the saviour, I remember my lost manuscript, and I'm seized with panic. I knew this before, of course, but the realisation grips me now like delayed shock: *The Ice Shelf* has gone. My economical, edited version, with all of the bad bits cut out like overripe fruit—it's gone; my full digital version is gone. Tears spring into my eyes. I shrug off, violently like an earthquake, the man's smelly tender finger from my cheek.

It's gone. It's all gone.

One thing you might have discovered about me as you've read these Acknowledgements is that I'm quite tough. It goes with the territory of being thankful. I'm a glass-half-full kind of person, I know that appreciating what one has gives one resilience. Sitting there beside my green-on-the-outside-white-on-the-inside bach, it occurs to me that the edits I so casually discarded might not be gone forever. My thoughts scramble back to the various points in the evening when I tossed away bits of the story, here, there and everywhere— in a drain, in a toilet, in a vase. What was I thinking?! And although these were the parts that, in my wisdom, I'd decided at the time were better expunged, they are still *story*, and I realise now that they were precious. With my heart clobbering my ribs as if to be let out, I struggle up from my *ersatz* holiday home and fight my way past the smell and aura of the man, who leaps aside, a bit crestfallen to tell the truth, but I simply have no time for thanks. There's nothing for it. I resolve to retrace my steps and try to find the pages I have abandoned in the course of the evening.

Of course, there's the risk I'll run myself late for the plane (I estimate it's around two o'clock) and will end up having to make a mad, stressful dash for the airport, maybe even having to hitchhike. (No money for a taxi, alas.) But, on weighing it up, I think the risk of cutting it fine is worth it. What am I even *going* to Antarctica for, if it isn't to write this damn book? If I find my edits, then I'll have something; I'll have a version of the story, the bits I'd thought excess but now that I have nothing else, will be everything, will mean everything.

Like a polar bear falling off a melting ice floe (and I don't think, under the circumstances, I'm being too fanciful here), I leave the fifties apartment for the very last time.

With my fridge in tow and my hold-all shouldered, I jog all the way back down town, waggling like a fish. By Courtney Place I'm already saw-breathed with tiredness. I slow to a walk as I pass soporific bars (the patrons have thinned dramatically) and further on to the apocalyptic mouths of empty shopping arcades. Rather than retracing my steps, I plan to search in geographical order all the places I did an edit. That will be much more economical—and I allow myself a snigger at this irony. Of course I know there's not a lot of hope in finding my discarded edits, but surely there's a sliver of a chance, and I have to give it a try. I have nothing else.

The dark, heavy-framed windows of the Backbencher blink square-eyed like a nerd as I approach. The establishment is closed, as predicted. Beside the heavy door layered with generations of tacky paint, I angle my fridge so it won't careen down the hill and visor my hands on the glass just in case there's anyone in there, kitchen staff tidying up, a cleaner; you never know. Not a sausage. In the frosted reddish light seen through my palm-viewer, the grotesque papier-mâché caricatures on the walls leer down with their shadowy eyesockets. I can make out the coat rack at the entrance to Narnia, except it's not Narnia anymore, all the coats have gone but for one forgotten jacket swinging limply in some kind of breeze offered up by the space. The moony flagstones beneath have been swept bare. I peer some more, trying to will my edit to materialise where I dropped it under the rack, but it's not going to happen and I sigh and accept the fact that I'll never remember what the protagonist went through in the Theory of Creative Writing class she was let into at one minute to midnight.

Ah well, it was always a long shot. I have many more opportunities to retrieve my edits, so I remain in reasonably good spirits as I head up Bowen Street. The four-lane slope, usually jam-packed and barping with horns, is ghostly; supermarket bags tumble like the seeds of a swan plant. I plough on up the hill in the gale, my clothes horizontal *à la* Petit Prince. The National Library will be closed, but I can't let it rest; I'm on a mission. Anything is worth a try, isn't it?

On the broad steps of the library (having parked my fridge on the street where I figure it'll be safe for a minute or two), I recall how I blithely screwed up, like there was no tomorrow, a key moment from *The Ice Shelf* to do with the young protagonist's adventures at a commune. It breaks my heart somewhat to visualise the ball of paper, intricate like a skull, tumbling downwards as if in a certain Eisenstein film, and I know it's hopeless, and indeed the Odessa-looking landscape is spectacularly empty of paper balls. There goes the section in which the protagonist is sexually abused by a stoned person in a commune, catches Hepatitis A and is held responsible for accepting the court summons which spells the end of the commune, even though no one told her not to accept any packets from strangers who come knocking at the door.

But, lo and behold, as I emerge near the scary glass doors (they somehow make you aware of the damage they could do), I almost bump into a security guard rattling an orchestra of keys. He's mostly stomach, his polyester orb set like a giant black pearl between the wings of a bomber jacket. I'm pleased to see him. As I stumble through my story, his face takes on a series of sceptical maroon-coloured twists, but I keep going and somewhere along the line he seems to take pity on me; I find myself talking to his back as he manipulates the keys, escorts me inside and tells me over his shoulder in a strangely fluting voice that this needs to be snappy.

We cross the huge, empty polished wood floor. Trotting behind the guard's squeaking clodhoppers, I tell him I need to check the bathroom and we divert upstairs immediately. In the doorway to the Ladies, the guard turns his purple face away decently from the newly flickering strobe and chinks his keys, which I interpret as some kind of stopwatch. I'm quick. I dash in and am reunited with the tiles, the sealed quality, the subliminal drip going on somewhere. I know there's no future in the cubicle where I flushed and flushed, but I check anyway, peering into the bowel of toilet number three, hoping for an episode about the protagonist's sojourn with a stepfather and a puppet, but there's just the faint stench of urine and mould.

On the landing, I tell the security guard about the Chinese vase, not feeling hopeful, but his cheeks spring up like frog's legs and he's smirking; it seems he's beginning to think this is a lark. Puffing and farting, he leads me up the stairs. I don't need any more encouragement. I follow close on his heels. When I spy the red vase standing like a little saint in the far corner of the Kōwhai Reception Room, my heart leaps. Surely my edit will be inside. I skate across the hardwood floor and squint into the china throat as if with a monocle. Yes! At the bottom, my screwed-up edit is nestled like a carved ivory ball. I feed my arm into the vessel, but although I'm plunged right up to the shoulder, my fingertips wriggle into nothingness.

The guard is yapping into his phone now, tromping back and forth across the doorway as if he's in an art-house film. I don't wait for another invitation. I lay the vase down gingerly on its side—it crunches on the floor very slightly—and peer inside. The paper seems stuck on the bottom; I suspect chewing gum. I roll the vase back and forth and look inside again, but *no change* (like the *I Ching*). I'm determined I'm going to retrieve the edit, which if I remember rightly concerns love.

The guard continues to cross the doorway and talk into his phone, his voice travelling up the register. It seems there's a drama going on. While he's otherwise engaged, I brace myself and wrap my arms around the vase—the crazed surface is rough and slippery, and when I try to heft it, it's as heavy as an eight-year-old. I upend it gingerly, its bottom near my face, and give it a tentative shake. Craning around the vase's horizon, I see that nothing has come out. I shake it again and again, and I create an imaginary place mid-air where each convulsion stops because there's nothing else but make-believe to rail against. Six or seven almighty shakes, but on the last one (it would be), the vase slips from my grasp and wallops the floor. I glance at the guard, but he's on a roll. The vase lies on the hardwood, split in two neat yin-and-yang shapes.

My heart thumps madly, and I've almost forgotten why I'm here. I grab my poor screwed-up paper ball from one side of the vase. My assessment was right—it was stuck to the bottom with chewing gum. I unfold it feverishly to see which bit I'd thought so little of to edit out during the awards speeches. But this paper is not about love.

It is some kind of schedule—oh, the irony—it's a programme for the Prime Minister's Awards for the Arts. The list of recipients, literary stars, success stories with happy childhoods behind them—this alone makes me depressed, but more so, I'm gutted that this is not my text.

I'm quite distressed and my hands are shaking, but I know I have to get out of here in short order. I skid out onto the landing where I almost bump into the guard as he pockets his phone and hurries past me into the reception room. My last sight of him is his purple face turning in slow motion towards me. I tumble down the stairs as fast as I can with my hold-all, press the green release button on the doors, and I'm outside in the wind again.

The permanent loss of my National Library edits, not to mention the Backbencher edits, are all quite disappointing. But I keep buoyant. There are still the grounds of Parliament.

I enter through the upper gate, wind down the snaking path to the flat expanse outside the Beehive and trudge across the springy, close-shaved lawn towards the drain where I tossed my edit all those hours ago. The rusty grille has accumulated more leaf matter and rubbish, no doubt the result of an evening of wind. I kneel down to stare into the dungeony chute and a smell of acrid damp rises up to greet me. The black oozing sides of the drain catch what little light comes from a lamp nearby, but it's a long way down and all I can see at the bottom is the odd glint when a droplet lands, from the echoey sound of it, in a shallow, confined pool. No hope of finding the edit I so casually discarded, the tale of the protagonist's crazy baby-boomer mother and her sociopathic but thankfully briefly starred girlfriend, which has been relegated to the city's waterways.

Getting up rather wretchedly, I catch sight of a figure tipping down the steps of Parliament towards me. As he gains the lawn, I recognise the same strutting security guard from earlier in the evening. What a long shift he's doing. The labour laws in New Zealand really are shit. I grip my trolley and make for the iron gates that exit to the cenotaph and the tomb of the unknown soldier.

I try to keep my spirits up—all is not lost; I still have the chance of finding at least two of my edits. Back down on Lambton Quay I pass homeless people lying along the footpath. A poor old dude in a foetal position outside upmarket Kirks follows my progress with one eye, like a dog, and I smile, feeling like a complete arsehole and forgetting momentarily about my edits. I wonder what we'd do, this old guy and me, if the world were to end just now as I was walking ahead of him, if millions of tonnes of seafloor methane rose up and suffocated us and every last living creature, and these were our last moments on earth. Would I hold my nose and sit with him, or just not notice the smell, and hold hands as we burned up? Would we feel a connection with each other, happening to be on Lambton Quay together at the end of the world? I leave him behind and things go on as they always have, and I start to think about my edits again.

This is my second visit to the cable car depot tonight, so I'm beginning to feel as if I live here—and my fridge is likewise well-acquainted—as I make my way up the covered lane to the ticket box. The place is deserted, lit by a single naked spotlight which is impossible to look at. The ticket person has gone, the security guard has gone. A clock on the wall, I notice, says it's almost three. A pigeon awake at this hour pecks at secret things on the concrete floor under the bleachers. I stand in the cool spotlit shadows and peer through the gates, which are now firmly shut. The cable car is parked at the bottom of the incline. I know there is the slimmest of possibilities that lying on the floor in that carriage is an edit in which the protagonist feels acutely the futility of existence. I can't believe I tossed it away, just like that.

I grip the cold rough iron bars of the gate and shake them. Then something incredible happens. The gates swing outwards in my hands, clanging slightly, and I find myself with my arms flung open and tipped forward with the heaviness of the ironmongery. My involuntary laugh echoes eerily around the depot. So apparently the security guard was too busy behaving like John Travolta to lock up properly! I'm not going to look a gift-horse in the mouth. Leaving my fridge beside the ticket booth, I tiptoe through the yawning gates.

The carriage is nestled nose-down, as if it came to a sticky end and embedded itself in the level platform. As I step close to its retro, Wild West flank, I feel a chill emanating from it. I try the clunky silver handle and step back in surprise as the door swings out, almost collecting me. As I step inside, the carriage sways with its own private Richter scale. In the vinyl-and-oil smelling interior, my eyes pull all the available light from the splashy dark and I take in the boxy, utilitarian surfaces inside the car, the vibrating wires that soar overhead and out of sight like the flightpaths of crows, the black curve of the Victorian tunnel walls. I am swallowed by the insistent chaotic lines of industry and, standing there, tears come; it's pathetic. Nothing works, and nothing will ever work again because there are no people here, only me.

I remember my edit, and look at the floor. Swept clean. What I did here, what I undid here, it's gone.

*

On Willis, I make for the spot where I left my edit in which the protagonist loses, in a spectacular miscarriage of justice, her share of a fifties apartment in Mount Victoria. I reach yuckily into the designer rubbish bin outside the has-been sixties office block. Again, the missing tiles, the scratched-up shine, the embedded filth—it makes your heart sink that once upon a time everyone would've been congratulating themselves on modernity. No luck; the cleaner has visited.

Cuba Street is all but deserted, the bars closed. I slug up towards the bucket fountain, nodding like a donkey with tiredness. A couple of people are sleeping in doorways, rugged up, and a suspicious-looking man is loping down the street. I haven't got time to be scared. I'm on a mission. I arrive at the rubbish bin outside the Matterhorn. It's full, and I rush towards it. In there somewhere is a section about lost love, about loss negating love in equal portion so there could be no headway, and as time goes on, loss beginning to accelerate, $\therefore$ as fast as love starts to grow, something bats it down, uses it all up, so in the end, there is only loss.

Biting the bullet, I begin to go through the bin. I take every piece of rubbish out one by one and drop it on the ground. I don't need to tell you that it's pretty disgusting, this detritus of fast food and alcohol—even worse than the waste produced by the writers plus-or-minus-three-percent-readers at the Borich Festival. But I keep going. Out of the corner of my eye, I see a small cart arriving at the top of the mall. A rubbish man is working his way down the street, emptying every bin, and I thank my lucky stars that I got to this bin before he did.

I get to the bottom. There is no edit.

Then I realise: I have been looking in the wrong fucking bin! A few metres away is another bin, the bin in which I deposited my edit. The rubbish man in his small cart has arrived at this bin; he wrangles the black plastic bag out of its cage, tosses it onto his cart and drives away. I run after him, calling, but he does not look back as he continues on down Cuba Street.

I try not to be downhearted. I shoulder my hold-all and grasp my cart. Though all seems hopeless, I must go on.

I head along to Courtenay Place and eventually I am toiling up Majoribanks Street. I park my fridge at the bottom of the fire escape and scale the steps. The glass doors are locked, but it doesn't take much to shake them open. I step onto the pink rug. This is the exact place where I spread out my manuscript and made the decision to be economical. The curtains billow out from the open French door. I hear faint snores coming from the bedroom; Mandy was always a deep sleeper.

I tiptoe to the kitchen and work the pedal on the bin in which I deposited my first edit all those hours ago, before setting off to the awards ceremony. I remember tucking the pages right at the bottom, under the other refuse, the bit where the protagonist is kind of sick of her boyfriend and is confident there will be many other people she feels this way about. Love will be a renewable resource.

The bin is empty. Mandy has put the rubbish out.

I am devastated.

Surely Mandy will let me curl up and grab an hour's sleep and leave my fridge here while I am in Antarctica. I fold myself onto the L-shaped couch, the place where Cook Blub once sat all in a row, spouting their opinions about agency and belief. I'm drifting off when I am disturbed by a scream. It's Mandy standing in the living-room doorway. She's wearing her dressing gown, her hair is wild, and she looks like a harridan. When I reveal my face from the under the throw, she sinks her shoulders.

'Oh, it's you,' she says thickly. She glances about. 'Where's the fridge?'

'Downstairs,' I say.

'It's not coming in here.'

'I know,' I say, as if that is completely obvious, but I'm disappointed.

Now that I am discovered, I know I have to go. I sit up and make a bit of a thing of getting up, putting my head in my hands. I look sideways. The paperback about the monster is still mashed against the wall, open, as if weeping.

'Can I have a cup of tea?' I ask.

Mandy has her arms folded and her head sunk in the fluffy folds of her dressing gown. She shakes her head tightly. I put on my boots and Antarctic jacket, watched, I am aware, by Mandy from under her eyebrows.

'You're wearing my dress,' she says. 'And it's ripped!'

I look down, and it's true; it is quite ragged. 'Do you want it back?' I ask Mandy, in good faith.

'No,' she says. There's something new in Mandy, a new decisiveness. No trace of *Cinema of Unease*. I'm actually impressed.

The wind buffets me dangerously on my descent. The yard at this hour is dark and creepy, the one pathetic tree in the middle of concrete fighting the gale. I shiver. To the right against the corrugated-iron fence is a line of four red-topped wheelie bins which constitute the rubbish collection for the whole villa. I consider opening each one to see if I can find the bag that Mandy has tossed. When I open the first one, the smell of rotting food makes me gag. The bin is full to the top with stuffed plastic bags, many of them splitting, their skins glinting under the streetlight. I reach out and touch one, feeling the strange warmth brewing within. I cannot do it. I cannot put my hands down into the rubbish.

My edits have all gone. They have gone.

I'm outside the Taj again, on the traffic island that is the confluence of Courtenay Place, Mount Victoria and the boulevard that leads to the southern suburbs. There's nobody about, and the atmosphere is desolate. I am due at the airport at six. I'm at a low ebb, almost collapsing, if truth be told, from tiredness. My back is aching. I still don't know what to do with my fridge. My options are narrowing to a sharp point, and frankly time is running out. Plus it's cold and I need to keep walking. I decide that although I don't know if Linda Dent has re-accepted my friendship, I have no choice but to front up at her place and ask her to look after my fridge and to put me up for the rest of the night, which I'm sure she won't mind. I set off for Island Bay: along Kent Terrace, past the bronze statue of Queen Victoria with her sharp nose in the air as if she can't stand the verdigris, around the Basin Reserve where the classically round walls are under permanent renovation. Machines sleep like dinosaurs among the rubble.

I pass the wide steps of the hospital which, oddly, beckon; I imagine myself briefly on a trolley squealing along a lino corridor, paramedics fussing over me while I ask them if my fridge is all right. But my reverie is short-lived. I must plough on towards the tumbledown, verandahed shops of Newtown, which from a distance seem glumly denuded of their fruit displays and plastic leis.

I'm heading away from the shops and up the hill which forks off towards Island Bay when I notice two things. One, there's a lot of junk piled up on the sides of the road, creating surreal gutterscapes in the half dark; it must be inorganic collection time. Plus I realise I'm across the road from the complex where Clancy lives. No sooner have I had this thought than I hear a loud shout. 'Suga!'

Across the street, I can just see Clancy's topknot poking up above the tall mesh fence on the perimeter of the complex. I duck around broken furniture and paint cans and tow my fridge across the road. 'Suga!' she's saying. Juggling her cigarette, she drops a bag of rubbish into a wheelie bin, darts outside the fence and hugs me.

'What are you *doing*?' she asks. She's wearing winceyette pyjamas.

'Going to Antarctica,' I say. 'What are you doing?' Because it's, like, the middle of the night.

'Oh, I just woke up and remembered—' she gestures dismissively at the bin. 'But wait, wait, you're going to Antarctica? Yuss!' Clancy punches the air. 'Why didn't you *tell* me?'

I mumble something. I'm actually shy, despite everything.

'Then they worked!' says Clancy.

'What?' I ask.

'The tactics! You reviewed the book by Roderick the Dick?'

I tell Clancy yes, and she squirms with delight.

'And you went to Dean Cuntface's book launch?'

I nod.

'You retweeted all their, you know, tweets?' Clancy takes a celebratory drag on her cigarette. 'Good for you, girl! So what else has been going on? Did you put a deposit on an apartment?'

'Not quite yet.' I don't have the heart to tell Clancy about the 364 days.

'Never mind, Suga,' says Clancy. 'Keep going. That's all you can do.'

We stand quietly for a moment in the greyness. Then a strange look comes over Clancy's face. She has noticed my hand resting on the bar of the cart.

'Wait, is that yours?' she asks, pointing to my fridge.

I tell her, briefly, the whole story.

'Suga,' she says. Then, 'Suga,' a few times. She finishes her cigarette. 'What you should do,' says Clancy, kicking out lightly in the direction of my fridge, 'is leave the fucking thing here. You wouldn't read about it, but hello! It's the inorganic collection.' And she flaps at the jumble of all the stuff people have thrown out, the broken custom-wood furniture, the deflated air-mattresses and old vacuum cleaners.

'And stay the night,' says Clancy, 'what's left of it. I've got the kids so it's just the couch, but you're welcome to it. I'll drive you to the airport in the morning.'

The thought of a hot cup of tea and a place to curl up in the warm flat tempts me. And maybe I should leave my fridge with the inorganic collection. It would be the most sensible thing, at this point in time. I consider it, while Clancy tells me about her new project, a community poem thing on a blackboard at the library where everyone writes their stuff but they've had a bit of trouble with people writing obscenities, plus she's got a great new class, they totally rock. She interrupts herself to ask, 'So, what about your manuscript? How'd the edits go?'

I hesitate, and Clancy gets it. 'Come on, come inside.'

I feel a small coldness deep in my body. What should be warm is cold. I have to go. I knew it all along, of course. I can't leave my fridge, not after all we've been though. I can't stay at Clancy's. I'm going to Linda Dent's because Linda will be the one person who will look after my fridge.

'If you're sure,' says Clancy.

'I'm sure,' I say, and I smile even though I don't really feel like it.

'Take care of yourself,' says Clancy, and we hug and she clanks back inside the gate.

I'm about to head off to Island Bay when something occurs to me. I haven't said thank you.

'Clancy!' I call.

She looks around, her hand already on her door handle. 'What?' There's a frisson of annoyance on her face. I can see it, even in the dark.

'Nothing,' I say.

'Take care, Suga,' she says, and goes inside.

Then I continue up the hill—quite a climb, but I make it, and soon I'm dropping away down past the football fields towards Island Bay. When the clouds part briefly I catch a glimpse of the cup of sea that is Island Bay nestled between its hills in the distance at the bottom of the valley. The wind catches me and it's a struggle burrowing into it with my fridge. The southerly is cold and howling now, and I try to keep my teeth from chattering with thoughts of the cup of tea (hopefully with something in it) that Linda will offer me and the cosiness of her couch and the nice big woolly blanket that I will snuggle into for two or three hours before I have to head to the airport.

As I get nearer the beach, the odour of salt and fish takes me back to my childhood stint at Island Bay School and the little bedsit that Sorrell and I lived in without a fridge. I'm near Linda's in Trent Street, a short, low-lying street that hunkers down just lower than the Esplanade. You wouldn't want to be here in a tsunami.

I open the latch on Linda's little gate and trundle up the narrow path past the shrub-studded pocket-garden, *Lost in Space*-like in the darkness. The front door is inset shyly on the side of the house—recalling the era of the bungalow, surely the architectural equivalent of *Cinema of Unease*. But I have concerns other than cultural comparisons as I knock on the bobbly glass, smiling inwardly at my own stupidity. What a mug! Why I didn't come here earlier in the evening, instead of setting out disastrously with the artists with whom I will go to Antarctica, I'll never know—and then getting waylaid by the likes of Eric? If I'd come straight here, I'd still have my laptop, I wouldn't have had to chase my edits all over town, and I'd be tucked up in bed right now snoozing before the alarm, a cup of tea, and my ride to the airport. But I decide not to follow that train of thought which could have the capacity to make me the teensiest bit downhearted. I shiver and knock again on Linda's chattering door.

It takes me another ten minutes of vigorous knocking to realise there isn't going to be an answer. Maybe Linda is an especially deep sleeper. Maybe Linda is on drugs! Joking. She could be away. If so, I wonder if there's a chance I could let myself in. I'm sure Linda wouldn't mind. We go way back.

I edge into the little weedy concrete yard at the back, and immediately my heart leaps. In the conglomeration of out-buildings (washhouse/toilet/shed) is an empty carport—suggesting that Linda is in fact away on holiday, or something. Things are looking up. I'm positive that if Linda knew of my plight, she'd let me leave my fridge here until I'm settled again. I wheel under the corrugated iron roof, feeling immense relief. As I do, a big cold drip, no doubt an offcut of the rain earlier, plummets down the back of my neck. I shudder violently, outraged, then laugh at myself for attributing some malevolent intent or at least trickery to the weather. Avoiding the oily, furry patch in the middle of the parking space, I stop and take in the vibe; boxes, tools and plastic chairs are arranged around the perimeter like an audience to a stage. Yep, this is it. Without further ado, I nestle my fridge in the least-cluttered corner between a scarred wooden bench and a bike. Finally, a temporary home of sorts!

I feel as if I've had a load lifted off my shoulders and I stand, just being, listening to the wind whistling and rumbling. All will be well. It's then that I notice a power socket on the one solid wall of the carport. It's set on an exposed beam, makeshift-looking, but it is a socket, and it seems to beg me to plug in my fridge, especially because as I look at it, I hark back to last night when the weird thing happened at Mandy's, to do with her dodgy power box and me being blamed. I decide to put my mind at rest.

The shower of yellow sparks that erupts from the back of the fridge followed quickly by a sizzling sound and an acrid, fishy burning smell makes me jump. It's too dark in the carport to inspect the damage with any reliability, but when I peer around the flank it does seem that the area where the power cord strikes out on its own with umbilical independence has been scarred black.

It's been a very long night. I pace around the yard, distraught, I have to say. I find myself wringing my hands. The concrete tiles, the opportunistic dandelions growing up between, the shambly outhouses, ripped sky above—all has taken on a kind of personhood, as if they're watching me in my distress, in a detached kind of way, but watching nevertheless. I shake my fist at them, at the chairs and boxes in the carport, and pace some more. Even though the yard is sheltered, it's still cold and the gale, without a clean run, draws upwards. My Antarctic jacket balloons like a fifties dress, and I fancy for a moment that I might be sucked aloft like Dorothy. But I simmer down enough to remember that I could still, hopefully, stay the rest of the night at Linda Dent's. Dear Linda Dent! Even in my stressed-out fug, it occurs to me she might have a key somewhere, under the mat or tucked in some cobwebby crevice around the back door.

I visor through the dusty window and see plastic toys and tiny shoes and socks scattered all over the kitchen floor. The fridge is covered with wild, crayoned drawings and the bench is a godawful mess. It's as if a family got up and left, just like that, abandoned everything suddenly for some strange and terrible reason. A clock on the wall says 4:40. The scene is desolate, and I am desolate. *J'en suis désolée,* I remember from French class. Linda has no children. She is a neat freak.

I come to the unfortunate conclusion that Linda doesn't live here anymore.

I'm tarrying on the footpath across the road from the foreshore, wondering what to do. The massive concrete seawall—I take in the full panorama to right and to left—is smashed to pieces. Last time I was here, on a beautiful summer's day a year or so ago on the occasion of Linda Dent's launch party, children ran along the wide concrete parapet as if it were the Great Wall of China and groups of Italian fishermen leaned in against the scooped-out wall lip and smoked and talked, the emphatic softness of their conversation bouncing out over the water to the scraggy little island fifty or so metres offshore (the island of Island Bay). I remember now, in the news, the big storm, the like of which no one had ever seen before. The wall lies in tonne-sized concrete curls on The

Esplanade, as if a stone giant has gone to the hairdresser and said, *Take it all off!* Now, with no barrier, no line in the sand, Cook Strait powers up and over the high point of the beach and froths across the road with a fuck-you attitude. After all, it's the sea. The tide seems to be going out, and as each wave dribbles back home, more and more of the Esplanade, once the site of Sunday drives, is revealed. It is textured with a kind of oily sand-art. Some boundary between function and freedom has been broken; antidisestablishmentarianism of beach and asphalt. I look down at my feet. My boots and the wheels of my cart are sodden and foamy from the dregs of a wavelet. We walk.

Seeing it's five-ish in the morning now and I have to be at the airport by six, I need to make a move. With no bus, no taxi, no phone, and no money, the quickest route is around the coast. To the casual observer (but of course there is no observer at this hour) I must look like the Ministry of Silly Walks or an Olympic walker as I rock along the Esplanade, northwards from the beachfront, away from the chunks of wall which, when I glance back, look like the Elgin Marbles. To my right, the sea is angsting itself again and again on the rocks below; the backdrop of sky is shingled and opalescent like a pink pāua. On my left, hills climb; I'm moving outside of the bones of the valley. A light goes on in one of the cottages nestled in at the bottom of the cliffs, and the first bird, a bellbird I think but I don't really know, tolls somewhere in the scrunched bush above. I notice that the wind has dropped quite dramatically and that the air is much warmer. I'm suddenly steaming underneath the weight of my Antarctic jacket, and I stop to tear it off and stuff it into my hold-all. The red dress, held together now only by my hoodie, flutters in the odd, light gust and I feel relief, coolness.

I'm following the coast road as it swoops out to the first rocky outcrop after the shelter of the bay. The neat row of cottages, snuggled up in a united front against the sea, is thinning. The darkness is falling away, and as I reach the point from which I can see more bays scalloping around to the flat, hazy airport in the distance, I notice that the air has gone blue. The tight, shrubby perm on the hills isn't black anymore but a bluey-green like the Blue Mountains; the waves are a luminous, rippling, metallic blue like a teenage girl's smartphone; the sky has gone from pink to a soft, cotton baby-blue. Everything is still; the air, the light, me. I stop in my tracks with my fridge. I know what this is. It is *l'heure bleue*.

I think back to the last blue hour, eight or nine hours earlier, twilight on Lambton Quay. At that point, everything seemed robust and possible, the tissue of the blue impregnable, and everything was still to come. When it passed, there seemed no doubt there would be another and another blue hour, so the change was festive, interesting. But this moment, *this* blue hour, feels fragile, as if it has no substance, as if night and day hang at a terrible crossroads; when it passes, something will be smashed. And it does pass, in my next breath, and the scrub on the hills is now a dull green, the sea navy, and the air has no colour at all. I am suddenly afraid.

I'm still sweating. I take off my hoodie and stow that away too and sit heavily on my hold-all in order to get the zip done up. I have the impulse to put all this, all that I'm experiencing, into words, to write it down, to make sense of it, but it seems too late. I trudge on in the lightening air with the crash of the sea on one side, the bush livening with birds on the other.

A few metres past the point, I do something that I know is very wrong, and I feel the teensiest bit ashamed to even relate it here, but I have no choice—to do it or to tell it; it must be told, otherwise what's the point of these Acknowledgements, or even of writing *per se*? In short *Why write?* (I have no idea! ∴ I have no ideas.) So on this occasion, walking around the coast to the airport to connect with my flight to Antarctica, I have absolutely no choice in doing what I am about to describe: I wheel my fridge onto the strip of gravel, the ledge between the footpath and the rocks two or three metres below where the harbour continually breaks itself. I lever the fridge off its cart, and I leave it there on the verge and walk away quickly with just my hold-all. If only I'd foreseen what would happen! If only I'd had a better plan of action earlier in the night, last night; or if I'd plotted days ago, weeks ago, what to do. If I hadn't stored the fridge in Mandy's living room for ten months, if I hadn't taken the fridge from the apartment; if I hadn't bought it from the secondhand dealer in the first place, I would not be in the position of having to dispose of it.

I tell myself not to look back. There are worse things, people do a lot worse. I won't look back, I will look ahead, to the airport which is coming into focus in the new bright day. I stop to hastily unzip Mandy's dress, what's left of it, and to peel off the undershirt, stuff it (with difficulty) into my hold-all, and quickly zip the dress back up.

Walking again, I feel ludicrously light, as if I might float away. This is right but it is wrong, and a few tears come and I say under my breath, but it stays with me because the wind has gone, Janice, don't be ridiculous! As I begin the next indent of the coast, I can't help myself: I look back to the rocky point, and am just in time to see my fridge topple silently down onto the rocks. On impulse I launch back, to save it, my fridge—no, to save the rocks. But there's nothing I can do. What would I do?

I have my flight to catch. I need to hurry.

I toil on around the coast, and as I pass the next rocky point, the sun throws a sliver of radiant light over the horizon which spills across Cook Strait. I stop, blinded. This is the real dawn. Now I realise that the blue hour was just a passing moment. I'm tired, and even though I should hurry to make the airport in time, I figure having a short rest makes good sense, it will allow me to keep going in the long run. So, at Moa Point, where the coast has straightened out, in fact has become quite desolate, utilitarian, scattered with odd, unnatural-looking rocks, I sink down onto the walkway. At six o'clock (I'm guessing) the first plane roars up from the airport and whines out over the hills. I am bathed in the smell of diesel. There's another plane, and another.

As I sit on the rocky shore at Moa Point, I start thinking about *The Ice Shelf*. I haven't given much consideration to it for what seems like days but in reality is several hours. All of a sudden, with the sun getting me right between the eyes, it hits me that there is one section left. I don't know why I've forgotten it—I suppose the stress of the evening, my sense of homelessness, my loneliness, my terrible childhood; there is a host of reasons why I might not have my wits about me. Reader, do *you* recall the piece of writing I stuffed into my hold-all all those hours ago above the motorway, after the demise of my laptop? Well, no doubt you have had an easier life than me. If nothing else, I'm a survivor, a glass-half-full kind of person, and even though the last section is not half a glass, not even a quarter of a glass, is more like the milky ring at the bottom which has gone smelly, I plunge my hands between the cold zippy teeth of my hold-all and my fingers close around the crisp page of the very last extant section of *The Ice Shelf.* Shading my eyes from the bounce of sunlight across the harbour, I scrutinise the text. I see, on skimming through, that it concerns the falling of red matter. I am sure that if you've been following these Acknowledgements, you will have guessed what is contained in the last edit.

The last edit concerns, of course, the baby. It all takes place at one moment and that moment is the point of no return. Warnings have become meaningless, denying has become obsolete. There is no more holding on, there is no more explaining, there is no more making sense of things. This is what happens: the redness which although it might not look exactly human, is human, is ejected from what might have been thought its home. If it could think, it might even call this place 'home'. Vacating home, the baby tumbles down a long avenue in a maelstrom of blood. It erupts into oblivion, which is a blessing. Nothingness is preferable to agony.

Our flesh will be singed red and begin to bubble. The pain will be excruciating and we will scream, but no one will help us because everyone else will be screaming in agony, writhing and twisting, their eyes rolling back in their head. The hair on the heads of multitudes will be alight like halos but burning out quickly and leaving prickles like the gumfields and scarred scalps. There will be the smell of flesh cooking, and the screaming will go on and on, relentless, until it does relent. And then there will be silence. At that point, everything will have turned to ash, quite quickly because of the extreme heat—the skin of the people, the houses, the cars and trains and planes, the forests, the mountains; the lakes, the rivers, the sea will have been sucked up as steam. If anyone were watching, they might liken it to an experiment they conducted in science class at school, where elements were combined and left overnight and, upon the student's return to the sulphur-smelling lab in the morning, crystals would have formed.

But nobody will be watching. Nobody will be recording, no recording angel.

And then the ice will begin to develop, slowly at first, surprisingly, although it will have been known that something would happen, something would develop. It was known, but it was gone ahead with as an experiment, to see what happened. But now the notion of experiment has been dispensed with because the experiment seems to have taken charge. The experiment has decided that this is not an experiment; it is real, it is real life.

This is what all the experiments were leading to.

This is the final chapter.

But as the cold deepens, there will be no one to take notes on it, to observe its sensory details, to photograph it, to make sense of it. Even without this documentation, this contemplation which formerly may have seemed necessary, the phenomenon will still occur. The phenomenon will be its own artform. Ice will come over everything at an accelerating rate, as if there's no tomorrow. It might say, about itself:

like there's no tomorrow
∴ there will be no tomorrow

At Moa Point, I shed some tears. I know it's pathetic, but I can't help it. I let the last page of *The Ice Shelf* be taken by the breeze. At first the page tumbles over the gravel, desultory, aimless. Then it pitches suddenly over the drop and lands on the rocks below. I think it's going to get sodden and break down in a rock pool, and that would be a fitting end. But there's a gust. The wind isn't strong now, it's light, but there are stray puffs coming at odd angles and one of these, a small blast from below, whisks the page up and up. And after a couple of dips back down to the rocks, to the water, it lifts up like a kite and climbs higher and higher. It's airborne, it's given itself to the weight of air, to the superior air, and it sails up and out over the sea to join the lonely gulls and the clouds.

It must be seven, by the light. A little jet wobbles up into the high wind above the straits, the plane to Christchurch, the plane to Antarctica.

It is the end of thankfulness. It is the end of love. The page is now a dot high in the sky, among birds. The page and the birds cascade further up and out, and I watch them until they are gone and it is the end of creation.

Links

Blog: janonice.com

Twitter: @janiceawriter

Friend me on Facebook: facebook.com/janiceawriter

Acknowledgements

I am immensely grateful to the people who saw this book along its path. Thank you to the wonderful team at Victoria University Press—Fergus Barrowman for shelf life, Ashleigh Young for deep-thinking and pitch-perfect editing, Kirsten McDougall for her 'Get in behind'; to my colleague Ant Sang for bringing Janice and her fridge to life; to all at the International Institute of Modern Letters—Clare Moleta, Chris Price, Damien Wilkins, Emily Perkins, Katie Hardwick-Smith and Ken Duncum—for a marvellous year and an unexpected final draft; to the University of Auckland and the Michael King Centre, especially the tireless Karren Beanland and Tania Stewart for fellowshipping quite a chunk of this book; to Creative New Zealand for part-financing these two fellowships; to my agent Lyn Tranter who went to great and insightful lengths; to Bill Manhire for advice about clothes and flights; to my colleagues and students at Manukau Institute of Technology who inspire me every day; to Deborah Ross of my Honolulu book group who laughed at the early days of Janice; to John Newton for advice and encouragement; to my beloved children, Temuera Sullivan and Eileen Kennedy, for being there, and being hilarious. To John Kennedy Toole for writing a novel about a lost soul with a hotdog cart; to Mary Shelley, of course, for making the Frankensteins; finally, this book is dedicated to Kathy Phillips of Honolulu.